Allon

Book 6

Dilemma

Shawn Lamb

Allon Books

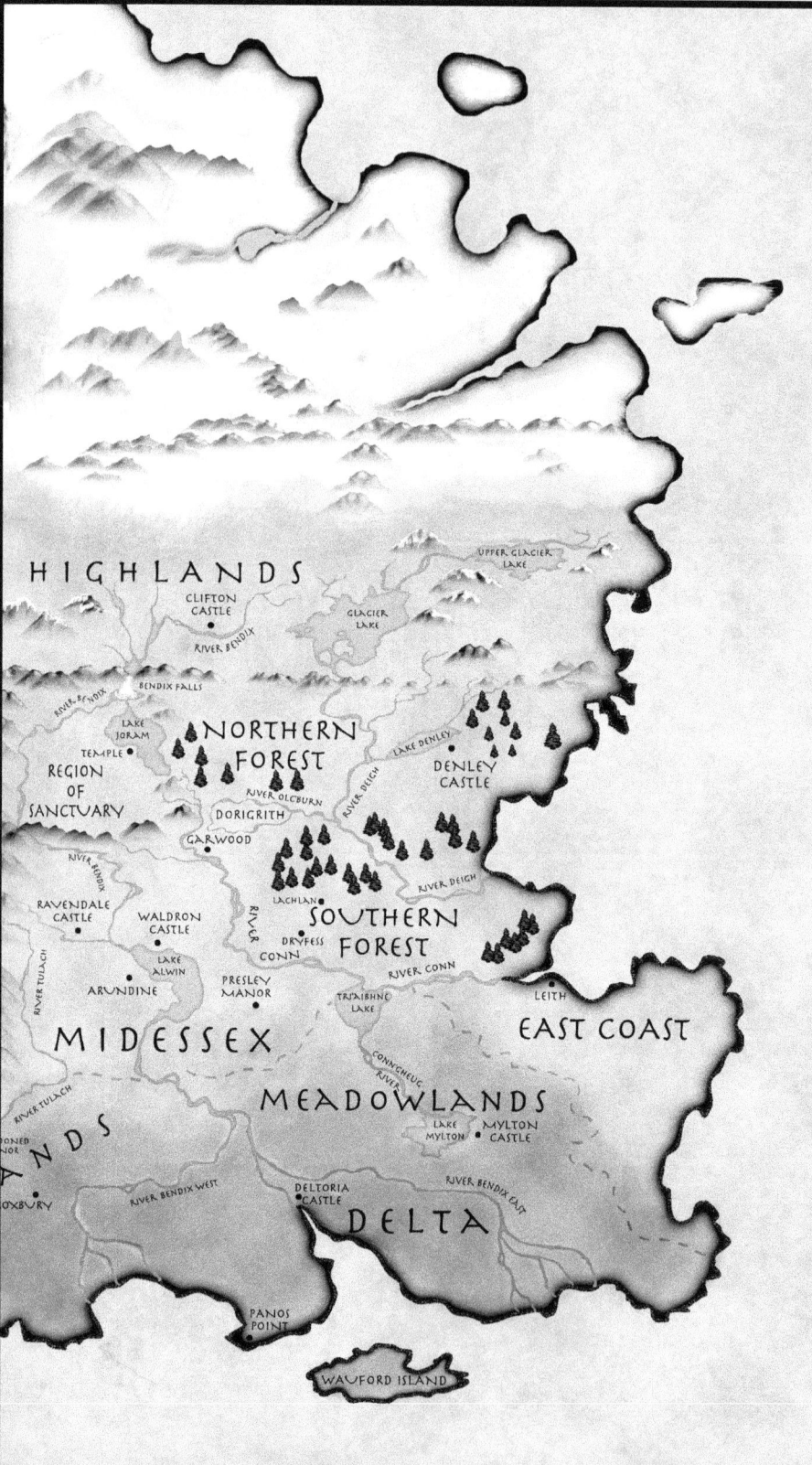

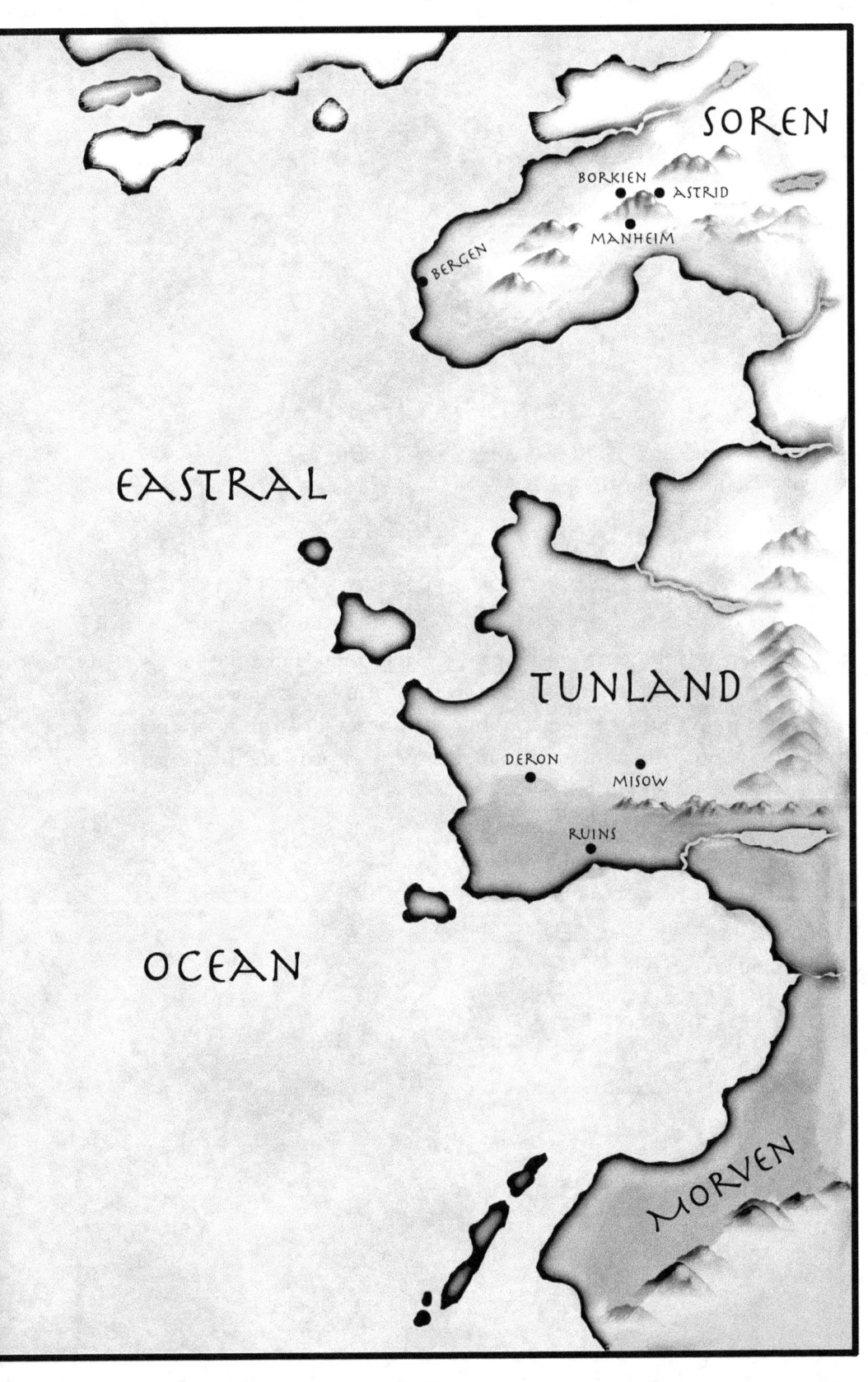

ALLON ~ BOOK 6 ~ DILEMMA by Shawn Lamb
Published by Allon Books
209 Hickory Way Court
Antioch, Tennessee 37013
www.allonbooks.com

Cover design by Robert Lamb

Library of Congress Control Number: 2012913768

International Standard Book Number: 978-0-9829204-7-3

Other Books by Shawn Lamb

ALLON ~ BOOK 1
Published by Creation House, a division of Charisma Media

Published by Allon Books

ALLON ~ BOOK 2 ~ INSURRECTION
ALLON ~ BOOK 3 ~ HEIR APPARENT
ALLON ~ BOOK 4 ~ A QUESTION OF SOVEREIGNTY
ALLON ~ BOOK 5 ~ GAUNTLET
PARENT STUDY GUIDE FOR ALLON ~ BOOKS 1-4

Historical Fiction
THE HUGUENOT SWORD

Coming from Allon Books
Young Adult Fantasy Fiction
ALLON ~ BOOK 7 ~ DANGEROUS DECEPTION

Historical Fiction
GLENCOE

MORTALS

ALLONIANS

King Tyrone – age 33   Queen Tristine – age 26
Prince Nigel – age 29
Princess Necie, wife of Lord Angus – age 23
Lady Mirit, daughter of Baron Mathias – age 26
Chad, squire to Prince Nigel – age 17

COUNCIL OF TWELVE

Vicar Uriah – age 57   Region of Sanctuary
Lord Angus, Duke of Allon – age 24   Southern Forest
Baron Erasmus – age 55   Delta
Baron Mathias – age late 60s   West Coast
Baron Hollis – age 55   East Coast
Sir Hayden – age 30s   Lowlands
Sir Gareth – age 67   South Plains
Lord Malcolm – age 52   North Plains
Baron Ned – age 48   Northern Forest
Lord Fagan – age 46   Highlands
Lord Allard – age 63   Meadowlands
Lord Bosley – age 43   Midessex

SORENS

Alaric, a middle-aged farmer
Leif, twin brother of Alaric
Magda, a Sigvard
Adelaid, a Sigvard
Elfrida, a Sigvard
Grissel, a Sigvard leader
Ulrika, Supreme Commander of the Sigvard
Perti, second-in-command to Ulrika
Ludmilla, high priestess to the Valkerish
Iryn, an elder priestess
Bergeta, a novice priestess

IMMORTALS

GUARDIANS

Captain Kell – Commander of the Guardians of Jor'el
1st Lieutenant Armus – Guardian Advisor to the King and Queen
2nd Lieutenant Avatar
Mahon
Egan – Overseer of Prince Titus
Vidar
Gulliver
Eldric – Guardian Prime Physician

TRIO LEADERS

Gresham	Midessex
Priscilla	East Coast
Chase	West Coast
Callie	Northern Forest
Wren	Southern Forest
Alrick	Delta
Zadok	Region of Sanctuary
Nixie	Meadowlands
Barnum	Highlands
Derwin	Lowlands
Mona	North Plains
Auriel	South Plains

SOREN

Freja, High Valkerish
Wilda, a Valkerish
Karah, a Valkerish
Skule, Lord of the Tavar
Breck, a Tavar
Lokien, a Tavar
Virgil

Chapter 1

PANOS POINT WAS THE MOST SOUTHERN PORT CITY in the Delta Region of Allon. Even in winter, the region's climate remained mild and tepid. As a result, the city became a hive of activity this time of year since most of the northern ports experienced winter gales or blizzards.

In the afternoon sun, buildings near the wharf cast long shadows over the dock. Before the bow and aft lines of the arriving ship were secured, Mirit appeared on deck. Her turquoise eyes scanned the mass of people on the dock. She was a comely woman of twenty-six, and after seven months in Tunlund, her auburn hair had grown passed her shoulders. For years she kept it short to accommodate her occupation as a sword-wielding entertainer traveling the back roads and highways of Tunlund with a tribe of gypsies. Since learning her true identity as the daughter of an Allonian nobleman kidnapped years earlier by pirates, she no longer needed to maintain her manly appearance for showmanship's sake. She still wore breeches, doublet and sword. Only her attire changed from gypsy clothes to representing the royal family of Allon, in royal blue and silver suit.

Prince Nigel joined her near the rail. Three years older, he stood a head taller with golden brown hair and blue eyes set in a pleasant clean-shaven face. He fastened the matching cloak over his blue and silver Jor'ellian Knight uniform.

"I'm certain he's here. He wouldn't miss your homecoming," he teased.

"Lady Mirit, you forgot your cloak," said Chad, Nigel's seventeen-year-old squire. His red hair shimmered in the late afternoon sun. Mirit didn't respond, still looking at the crowd when he placed the cloak over her shoulders.

"There!" she cheered, seeing a waving hand. "Papa!"

"The gangplank is in place, my lady," said Avatar, the bronze-haired and goateed Guardian warrior with silver eyes. At seven-and-a-half feet tall, he towered over the mortals. He smiled and stepped aside to let her hurry pass.

She raced down the gangplank to greet her father, Baron Mathias, Lord of the West Coast and a member of the Council of Twelve. Even in his late sixties, he remained a dashing man with a full head of graying brown hair, neatly trimmed salt and pepper beard, and deep green eyes. He engulfed her in a bear hug.

"You look well. The crossing was easy?"

"No, but I couldn't wait to get home." She hugged him again.

"Baron," said Nigel.

"Highness. Welcome home. I hope your mission was successful."

"We left a very happy Uriah establishing Fortresses and schools all across Tunlund."

"Excellent. The king will be pleased."

"Speaking of, is all well at Waldron?"

Mathias smiled. "You are once again an uncle. Only this time of a girl, Mikaela."

"A girl? Not a fourth son?"

"Ay. Tristine and Tyrone were surprised, but very happy."

Avatar boomed with laughter. "Phoebe was wrong!" he said of the assistant Guardian physician. "It will take her centuries to live this one down."

"You warriors will see to that," said Chad, snickering.

"Armus probably already started."

"Come. Let us toast Mikaela's arrival. We'll start for Waldron in the morning," said Nigel.

From the long shadows of a nearby alleyway, two men emerged, both middle-aged, fair of features with shoulder length blond hair. The only difference in appearance is one wore a scruffy blond beard and the other clean-shaven. Their clothes were heavier homespun garments in contrast to the bright style of the folk at Panos Point. Both were armed with short swords, but they didn't act like soldiers being cautious and fretful in watching Nigel and his group pass.

"When do we approach her?" asked the scruffy one.

The other considered for a moment before answering. "Tomorrow, away from town."

<hr />

Shortly after breakfast, Mathias, Nigel, Mirit, Chad and Avatar left the city riding north. Guardians easily outpaced horses, so a mount wasn't necessary, but in the company of mortals, Avatar chose to ride. Finding an animal capable of handling his size proved tricky, thus a hardy draft horse was selected being bred for strength and not speed.

Normally the journey from Panos Point to Waldron Castle took eight days, six days if the journey proved pressing. However, with the chill of winter and being pelted by cold annoying rain, Nigel reckoned the journey could take nine to ten days. Not that matters were urgent, he simply wanted to be home and see his new niece.

Going to Tunlund wasn't something he particularly wanted to do, but necessary. His clandestine role of a gypsy sword-handler helped to facilitate his mission to recover his kidnapped seven-year-old nephew Titus. The Tunlundian King Dante planned to use Titus to start a war with Allon. Nigel's role brought him in contact with many interesting and mysterious individuals, Mirit being one of them. She was irritating and irreverent at their first meeting, challenging him to duel. Him! A Jor'ellian Knight and the King's Champion challenged by a woman. He only meant to placate her, but he soon discovered her expertise in handling a sword.

Even though their constant bickering grew contentious, he sensed some secret confounding her behavior. This became manifested when she surprised Nigel, Chad, Avatar and herself by speaking Allonian without thought. He knew of her rescue from a shipwreck a decade earlier but she couldn't remember anything about her past or how she spoke Allonian. Her confusion made Nigel look beyond her cynical nature and the façade of swaggering confidence to see a woman battling to reconcile her past to the present.

Unfortunately, just as their relationship took a friendly turn, he learned of her involvement with Titus' kidnapping; an act of betrayal for which he never thought he could forgive her. That was until he saw her killed in an attempt to save Titus from being sacrificed to a false god. Jor'el used her unselfish death to perform a miracle to restore her life. The Tunlundians witnessing the event, turned from their false god to worship the Almighty Jor'el. Their journey back to Tunlund was for Mirit to help the new government in establishing civil order by touring the country and retelling her story. Uriah, Vicar of Allon, also helped by established places of worship where they were welcomed. Some towns and villages resisted the change and rejected the new religion. Usually they withdrew peacefully, not wanting to force people into believing, but in a few places the people grew violent, forcing Avatar and a handful of Jor'ellian Knights to fight and bring them to safety. Overall, the journey to Tunlund went well.

Being home, perhaps he and Mirit could come to terms with what happened and their feelings for each other. Well, at least he could deal with his love for Mirit, still uncertain of how she felt. In Tunlund, they were whisked from one end of the country to another having only enough time to sleep, eat and take care of personal necessities before

11

moving on to a new village or town. Now, as they leisurely made their way to Waldron, he enjoyed the sights and smells of Allon.

He glanced to his right. She rode beside him. "You're quiet."

"So are you."

"I'm enjoying being home."

"I didn't see much of Allon last time," she said, looking at the countryside bathed in winter's bleak gray and brown hues. The cold rain began to increase.

"The Delta, Lowlands and Midessex are flatter and more open than Tunlund. The upper regions are where you'll find the woodlands, foothills and mountains."

"I prefer the forests of Allon. Tunlund seemed dirty and overgrown," groused Chad.

"Trees are trees," said Avatar with disinterest. "The spirit of forest gives the sense of being."

"I'm sure Wren and other forest Guardians will appreciate your sentiment," quipped Nigel.

"If you tell them, I'll deny it."

"Spoken with true warrior arrogance."

"You would know," said Mirit with a teasing smile at Nigel.

Mathias laughed. He gathered his cloak in an attempt to ward off the rain. "At this pace we won't make the inn before nightfall."

"Sorry. We're so used to the outdoors we didn't consider your comfort." Nigel kicked his horse into a canter, as did the others.

Avatar's horse lagged behind so he had to shout. "It won't do any good! I sense the rain will soon turn to ice."

"An ice storm in the Delta?" asked Chad, checking his mount to speak over his shoulder.

"It has happened in the past."

"Naturally or by Guardian making?"

"Both."

"Avatar's right," said Mathias, now yelling since the wind howled. "Four inches of snow covered the ground when I left Waldron and more on the way according to Barnum. The Highland valleys are two feet deep. We should find a place to pass the night."

"Nigel!" called Avatar.

He checked his horse to let the Guardian catch up. Avatar leapt from the saddle before the horse stopped and handed the reins to Nigel.

"Take the beast. I'll find a place faster on foot."

He ran northwest toward a grove of trees two miles away and covered the distance quickly. Aside from matted wet hair and damp clothes, he did not suffer the effects of weather. Although by the look of his white breath, the temperature grew colder.

Entering the grove, he discovered a good-sized ravine ran through the length of the grove with a creek at the bottom. Used correctly, the ravine would provide shelter from the impending ice storm. Avatar emerged from the trees about a quarter mile north of where he entered. Nigel moved the group closer to the grove so he waved them over.

"A ravine will serve for the night. Not completely dry, but it will shield us from the storm."

In the deepest part of the ravine, they tethered the horses and erected makeshift lean-tos. Since the weather didn't trouble Avatar, Chad and Nigel shared one lean-to; Mathias and Mirit shared the other. Between them, Avatar tended the fire. He snared and cooked two rabbits during the time they built the shelters.

"I hope we don't have to do this all the way to Waldron," complained Mathias. He squirmed to get comfortable so he could eat without getting pelted by the occasional ice penetrating the shelter.

"We won't. Since my mount is slowing the pace, we'll leave the beast at the first inn we find and I'll proceed on foot. We'll make better time." Suddenly Avatar stood, hand on his sword.

"What is it?" asked Nigel.

Avatar put up a hand for silence. Barely a second later something flew from behind and over his left shoulder, just past his face. He drew his sword in reaction. The others jumped in anticipation, but relaxed at seeing a crow land on a nearby tree branch.

Chad laughed. "I think his experience in Tunlund is getting the better of his Guardian senses. He draws upon crows."

Avatar slammed the sword back in the scabbard and sat by the fire.

Mirit laughed, stood and brushed off her hands from eating.

"Where are you going?" asked Nigel.

"Some place a girl can have privacy. Don't worry, I'll avoid killer crows." She tossed a wink at Avatar before moving off into the trees.

She followed the ravine just past a bend, close enough for security, but far enough for privacy. *Rustle, rustle!* Her ears perked up, but she wasn't too concerned. *More crows.* Something was thrown over her head and a hand covered her mouth to stifle any outcry. More than one set of hands pinned her arms to her sides. She struggled to free herself. They began dragging backward. In the blindness of the sack she couldn't tell how many while the thickness prevented her from biting through to the hand pressing the smothering cloth against her nose and mouth. They didn't drag her far, perhaps because her struggling proved bothersome.

"We don't want to hurt you, only speak to you," a male whispered in her left ear. "Please! We need your help."

She ceased at hearing the unusual request. However, at first opportunity she would make her displeasure known.

"I'm going to let go. Please, don't scream."

True to his word, he removed his hand, but the sack remained in place, as did the hands holding her arms. "Why are you doing this? Who are you? One scream and—"

The hand clapped down over her mouth. "No! Please! We are desperate, and you are the only one who can help us."

The sack moved when she nodded and he let go of her mouth. "Why take me by force? Why not simply ask for my help?"

"You are a great warrior and command the giant. We feared you would set him upon us if we displeased you."

"Giant? You mean Avatar?"

"*Ja!* We fear him and the others with you."

"Chad's only a squire. But you have nothing to fear from them. At least you didn't. Me like this is a different story. Release me."

"Will you give us your word not to call your *varingi?*"

"I promise I won't call for help." The sack was ripped off her head and the hold on her released. She blinked to adjust her eyes to sudden light. Two men of middle-aged with similar fair features, yellow hair and dressed in rough homespun clothes knelt beside her. The only difference was facial hair. "Who are you? You don't sound or look like Allonians."

"I am Alaric," said the clean-shaven man. "This is my twin brother Leif. We are from Soren."

"It is to the far north of Tunlund," added Leif.

Her glance shifted between the brothers. "I know where it is. I did business with the border clans. What are you doing in Allon?"

"We came to take you back to help us," said Leif.

"All the way from Soren?"

"Ja, but we went to Tunlund first and learned you sailed for Allon. We raced to catch you, but did not arrive in time. We waited two days to take the next ship," replied Alaric.

"You left after me, yet arrived before? How?"

Leif smiled, large and proud. "Sorens are sea people. We helped the captain avoid the gale your ship must have sailed through."

Their answers actually proved more confusing than clarifying. "That doesn't tell me why you traveled all this way and how I can help you."

"Mirit?" called Nigel from somewhere nearby.

Alaric clapped a hand over her mouth to stop a reply. "You speak and they come and kill us."

"Mirit?" shouted Mathias.

She ripped Alaric's hand from her mouth. "Papa!"

Alaric wrestled Mirit, trying to silence her yet ended up crying out in surprise when lifted into the air.

"Don't hurt him, Avatar!" She scrambled to her feet.

Nigel, Chad and Mathias rushed from various directions, all with their swords drawn.

15

"No!" she said. "I'm fine. They came from Soren needing help."

"Help?" said Avatar, skeptically regarding Alaric, who didn't like being suspended in mid-air. "This one appeared to be hurting you."

"He feared being killed if I called out. He's scared. Look at him."

"It's true. We mean no harm. We need her help," pleaded Alaric.

"Put him down," said Nigel.

Avatar dropped Alaric. The latter scrambled to rise and stand next to Leif. Both stared in worry at Avatar, eying his height, sword and dagger.

"You said you needed help, why?" asked Mirit.

They remained anxious of the others, but especially Avatar.

"I told you, they won't hurt you." She waved to Nigel, Chad and Mathias, who took her cue and sheathed their swords.

"You will not be displeased by our answer?" asked Alaric.

"How can I be if you are the ones in trouble?"

"She is not displeased by what we did and is not angry at our presence," said Leif to Alaric.

Nigel folded his arms across his chest. "There is nothing to fear, so speak freely."

Alaric and Leif regarded Nigel in wonderment then turned to Mirit. "This is the second time he has spoken. You permit this?"

She couldn't help but laugh. "I couldn't keep him from speaking if I tried." She grew curious at their disturbance. "Do you have a problem with him speaking?"

"In Soren, it is not permitted for a man to speak in the presence of his *lafdi*," replied Alaric.

She heard Nigel's annoyed grunt and spoke to the brothers. "But you are speaking to me."

"And tremble at the thought of doing so," said Leif.

"Enough!" snapped Nigel. "Explain yourselves."

Alaric and Leif looked in fear between Nigel to Mirit.

"Highness, I believe I understand," said Mathias. "I heard stories of Soren, but questioned the credibility since it seems so different from what we know. Their actions show the stories are true. Their society is the reverse of ours. Women rule and men are subservient."

"Highness?" Alaric questioned Mirit.

"He is Prince Nigel, brother of Allon's Queen Tristine."

"Ah! We have heard of her. Perhaps we should speak to her."

"You won't speak to my sister unless I say so! And I have yet to hear why I would even consider the possibility. You accost Lady Mirit but claim it is because you are in trouble, then balk at the idea of speaking to me. Differences aside, I should box your ears for such insolence."

"Peace, my prince," began Avatar. "I sense no falsehood or duplicity rather they are deeply troubled and traveled a great distance."

"The giant speaks truth," urged Alaric.

"I am a Guardian, not a giant."

Alaric's still appeared unconvinced, but continued. "We are humble farmers. We seek help before Soren is torn apart by the *Valkerish*."

"Ja," agreed Leif. "If the evil Valkerish win, they will send the *Sigvard* to slay us and send us all to *sheolde*."

Avatar straightened and squared his shoulders, features turning fierce. "I have heard of the evil Valkerish. They are called—"

"No!" exclaimed Alaric. "To say their name is forbidden. They will strike us dead where we stand."

"Truly, they are afraid," said Chad.

"Ay," agreed Nigel. "Give up your weapons and you may come with us and I will tell my sister of your fears." He motioned to Chad, who stepped forward to receive the swords.

Alaric and Leif willingly submitted.

Chapter 2

BARNUM'S PREDICTION OF SNOW PROVED CORRECT. Six more inches blanketed Midessex, making travel slow and frustrating, as the depth of snow reached ten inches. Avatar remained mounted. This helped keep Alaric and Leif in check. Although impressive on foot, being mounted on the large black horse made the Guardian appear even more imposing and intimidating.

Nine days later, the last rays of twilight faded and light from the oil lampstands lining the last mile to Waldron illuminated their way. Workers kept the castle road clear of snow. Sitting in the midst of a rising plain, the massive size, strength and attention to detail of Waldron stunned Alaric and Leif. Two gatehouses flanked an elaborate oak and wrought iron gate. From the gatehouses stretched fifteen-foot-high walls, ending in massive square corner turrets at each intersection.

In awed silence, the brothers rode into the Grand Courtyard of white marble cobblestone with a fountain in the center. Being winter, water only trickled in the fountain to prevent the mechanism from freezing. Across the Grand Courtyard stood the Great Hall, a carved stone structure of grand proportion to impress the visitor with the strength of

Allon's King. To the right of the fountain was the Castle Chapel honoring Jor'el and more elaborate in carving, stained glass and awe-inspiring architecture than the Hall.

A less ornate gate stretched diagonally from the Great Hall to the Chapel and separated the armory, stables, carriage house, soldier's barracks and servant's quarters from the Grand Courtyard. Another smaller wrought iron fence and gate ran between the Chapel and the right gatehouse. This area housed the Jor'ellian priest's quarters and the Chapel gardens. Accessible to the Chapel, yet outside the main walls, was the family cemetery and royal crypt.

A two-story enclosure ran from the left front side of the Great Hall leading to building on the west wall. This corridor served to divide the Guest Quarters from the Family's Private Quarters on the west and south walls. The lower level served as a galley way, while the second story housed Waldron's offices, the King's study, Captain of the Guard's office, and the private quarter's of the King's Champion. The galleyway served as the final section enclosing the Family's Courtyard and Garden.

Grooms met the arrivals, respectful of Nigel, Mirit and Mathias.

"Well, well," began Wess, general of the King's army, and a man in peak physical condition even at age forty-five. "Highness. Enjoying the weather of home?" he teased.

Nigel laughed. "After seven months in Tunlund, this is pleasant. Where are Tyrone and Tristine?"

"The nursery, I believe." He noticed Alaric and Leif. "Who are these?"

"Visitors. See they are cared for until I send for them."

Wess skeptically eyed their rough appearance. "As guests?"

"The barracks."

"Ay, Highness. Gentlemen." The brothers left with Wess while Nigel and the other proceeded inside the main building.

In the nursery, Tyrone sat on the floor playing with his younger sons, five-year-old Fraser, and three-year-old Eli. Tristine stood beside a cradle.

Two high-ranking maidservants waited with their backs to the door watching the wrestling match. Over the noise of giggling boys, most didn't notice Nigel and the others enter. Armus noticed since he stood in his customary place beside the door. He equaled Avatar in height only brawny in arms and broad in the chest and shoulders. He had brown hair and bright chestnut eyes. Around his neck he wore the silver Temple medallion signifying his rank of Lieutenant of the Guardians. Serving as Guardian advisor to the king, he wore the formal white and gold uniform, the tunic barely covered his bulk. A large leather and gold belt held a handsome scabbard sword and dagger. He smiled when Nigel put a silencing finger to his lips then approached Tristine.

"I hear I have a niece."

"Nigel." She hugged her brother. In height they stood nearly equal, she at six-feet-tall to his six-feet-two. At age twenty-six her youthful features matured into an attractive woman with long golden hair and crisp hazel eyes while her charming smile held an impish edge.

"Uncle!" cheered Fraser. He and Eli ran to Nigel, who bent a knee to greet them.

The moment Nigel stood again, Tyrone grabbed him in a bear hug. A strong, intelligent thirty-three-year-old being of half-mortal, half-Guardian descent, his mortal side kept him from reaching the average Guardian height of seven feet but still tall at six feet eight inches. Contrasted to his black hair, his eyes were a striking cool grey, bold evidence of his heavenly half. An intense look from him made one aware he possessed a perception beyond mortal comprehension. At this moment the eyes shined with delight and he steered Nigel to the crib where the infant slept.

"Greet your niece. Mikaela, named after my mother."

"She looks smaller than her brothers," whispered Nigel in an effort not to disturb her.

"But just as strong."

Nigel smiled. Tristine appeared tired; her eyes dull and face pale. "Are you well?"

She just nodded.

"Congratulations, Sire," said Avatar.

"Thank you, and welcome home. I'm sure the journey was difficult in this weather. You must all be hungry and tired."

"Nothing being home won't cure," said Mathias, his arm about Mirit's shoulders.

"Still, go rest. We will feast and talk this evening. Armus."

The Guardian lieutenant escorted the others from the nursery.

Nigel remained and made closer inspection of Tristine's unusual quietness and fatigue. "Was labor hard?"

"Winie, Reva," said Tyrone to the maidservants and ushered the boys to their nurses. He and Tristine then drew Nigel from the room.

In curious concern, Nigel stopped in the hall. "Is there something you're not telling me?"

"Privately, brother," said Tyrone. Tristine remained quiet.

He accompanied them to the royal apartment. Once there, Tristine went from looking tired to fighting back tears. The change in her demeanor heightened his concern. "What's wrong?" he asked her but Tyrone answered.

"Two months ago Tristine and Arista were returning from Garwood. The weather was foul, resulting in a carriage accident. The impact and injury began a premature labor. Armus brought Tristine back to Waldron. She was in danger of bleeding to death, so Eldric had to take Mikaela by way of surgery. It is a miracle both survived."

He went rigid at the explanation. "You should have sent for me."

Tyrone took no offense at the rebuke. "It happened so fast, there was nothing you could have done to help either Tristine or … Arista," he said the name soberly.

"Meaning?"

"She died in the accident."

Stunned mute, pain and grief crisscrossed his face at hearing of the death of a beloved aunt.

Tristine took hold of his hand. "There was no easy way to tell you."

"What of Angus? Necie?" he asked in a thick, choked voice concerning Arista's son and his youngest sister.

"Shocked. But Necie is doing very well, taking charge at Garwood."

Tyrone kindly smiled. "She said as wife of the duke and sister of the queen, she must show as much courage as her sister did during the Tunlundian crisis."

Nigel didn't respond rather stared at the floor, jowls flexing between anger and grief.

"I am sorry we didn't wait for you to take off your cloak, but if not now, you would have heard from someone else."

"Excuse me while I wash off the muck of travel." Nigel didn't look at either of them and left.

Tyrone winced in regret. "Maybe I was wrong not to send for him."

"You know whenever Nigel is hurt or angry he tends to speak thoughtlessly. We had time to grieve, but he has not. Give him that time," she said.

Reaching his quarters, Nigel dismissed his valet, Chad and Avatar, who waited to tend him. He wanted solitary time to think and come to terms with Arista's death. Like her late husband, Darius, she bore no blood relation, but dearly loved. Darius was his father's foster-brother and most loyal supporter. He became Duke of Allon when Ellis assumed the throne. Arista, along with Wess, Bosley and Avatar, helped Shannan flee with the infant Nigel during an insurrection to oust Ellis and kill the newborn prince. Shortly thereafter 'Uncle' Darius married 'Aunt' Arista. They named their only son, Angus, after Darius' father and the man who raised Ellis. Angus was eleven when they believed Nigel killed in a hunting accident. However, the accident proved to be an assassination attempt by the Guardian Morrell.

Nigel survived with the entire left side of his face and body crushed, leaving him crippled. Consumed by self-pity he allowed his family to believe reports of his death and wandered Allon as a crippled beggar. Not until those who tried to assassinate him launched a coup against his father did he abandon his wandering to try and save his family. Alas, Darius and Nigel's mother, Shannan, died; neither knowing he lived. Thus being reunited with his family proved bittersweet.

To help cope with the loss, Arista turned her attention to the children, especially Nigel, helping him to readjust to his family. She filled the void left by Shannan's death and wept tears of joy and pronounced blessings upon him when Jor'el healed him, a miracle sought by his loyal childhood Guardian, Avatar. Hearing of her death was hard. In recalling her care and concern for him and his sisters, he came to understand Tyrone's first concern was for Tristine and Mikaela's survival, than comforting the bereaved.

Besides, he didn't know my whereabouts. I don't even know for certain where I was when it happened, only somewhere on the back roads of Tunlund in an obscure town or village. Two months. It could have taken that long to find me and travel back. Poor Arista. He smiled at thought of her. *You died doing what you loved, helping us. You were present when the other children were born. No doubt you wanted to be with Tristine for Mikaela's birth. Rest in Jor'el peace, dear aunt.*

All this he thought while bathing and getting dressed. He stood before a mirror completing his suit. He wore his Champion's uniform for most of the seven months, so tonight he chose princely attire of royal blue and black velvet doublet and breeches with brocade trimming in silver braiding.

The opening of the door came with hardy shout. "Uncle!"

Titus rushed in, Avatar behind him. Now eight years old, Titus looked more like Tyrone with dark brown hair and mortal color blue eyes. The boy had grown in a few short months so when Nigel bent down to greet Titus he pretended to be unable to lift him.

"I think you're too big for me lift anymore."

Titus laughed and hugged Nigel. In that moment of embrace every event in Tunlund flashed across Nigel's mind. The thought of anyone using the boy to start a war enraged him. Nothing short of finding Titus alive and whole would satisfy. Mirit told him how during their time of capture by Hueil, Titus remained strong in his faith in Jor'el and unwavering belief Nigel would find them and Tyrone defeat the enemy.

"I saw Mirit. She's letting her hair grow. Mama gave her one of her gowns for the feast." He pursed his lips in recollection. "Mirit said she didn't remember ever wearing a gown. But she's Baron Mathias' daughter, so she must've at some time. I told her Dame Matilda looks like a stuffed peacock."

Nigel laughed.

"What's so funny, Uncle?"

"Nothing. I'm just glad to see you."

"I wish I could attend the feast."

"You know the rule, not until you are thirteen."

Titus pouted.

"The same rule applied to your mother, Necie and I."

"Can I at least walk with you to stairs?"

"Ay. When all is ready."

"All is ready," said Avatar. "I came to fetch you when I met the young prince in the hall."

Elaborate arches lined the Great Hall. Magnificent wrought iron torch holders were built into each column. Three massive oil chandeliers hung from the white, gold and blue mosaic ceiling. Highly polished marble inlayed tiles depicted the royal seal in the floor. At either end of the Hall were two huge oval stained glass windows. Through the front window, outside moonlight cascaded onto the floor. The Council Chamber lay behind the Hall and shared the rear window. Below the rear window, the thrones were situated on a raised platform. The large gold and mahogany chair was for the king, the smaller throne for the queen. The platform was large enough for converting into a high table for feasting. Other tables filled the Hall, all lavishly decorated for the occasion.

This night, Mirit and Chad occupied places of honor at high table with the royal family. To accommodate Chad for this evening's feast, he was given a regal suit of green and gold rather than his squire's uniform. At normal functions, he stood behind high table to wait upon Nigel. Tonight, he sat two chairs down from the King!

Tristine sent her personal maid to tend Mirit along with a beautiful white and blue gown with silver accents. Mirit became pampered from head to toe, a jeweled silver headdress adorning her curled hair. She just sat when Nigel and Avatar entered. She flushed, her heart fluttering at the sight of him handsomely dressed in princely attire. Caught by surprise at the warm sensation, she was grateful when Armus asked if she needed anything, diverting her attention from Nigel.

"No, thank you," she replied. In that brief moment she regained her composure. Or so she thought. Once Armus stepped back she tried to act casual, but her attempt rendered useless when Nigel caught her eye and smiled. He held her eyes until he stopped and bowed.

"You look stunning, my Lady Mirit."

She wore a nervous smile. "Thank you, Highness. Though I confess, I haven't worn such finery in many years."

"It suits you."

Her blush deepened.

Armus watched the exchange. "Highness. You are seated on the other side of the king."

"Really? Who is to sit here?"

"The duke."

"Angus?" snorted Nigel with a laugh. "Tell him to sit on the other side of Tyrone."

"Tell me yourself." Angus arrived with Necie.

At ages twenty-four and twenty-three respectively, they made a striking couple. Angus stood tall and broad shouldered with the dark hair and eye coloring of Darius; Necie slender and graceful with brown hair and beautiful doe eyes. After hugging and kissing Necie's cheek, Nigel greeted Angus; his hand remaining on Angus' shoulder and steadily regarded his younger brother-in-law.

"How are you doing?" he asked.

"We are well."

"Really? You're not just saying that to keep from spoiling my homecoming, are you?"

"No," said Angus, a friendly smile appearing.

"What of you? Tristine said you are angry with Tyrone. You shouldn't be. Angus stopped him from sending for you," said Necie.

"You did? He didn't tell me."

Angus frowned at the answer. "Tyrone often takes responsibility for the actions of others when he shouldn't. Mother knew the importance your mission to Tunlund and prayed for you daily. She wouldn't have wanted you to cut it short. To honor her, I thought best to let you complete your mission."

Nigel nodded, his expression growing misty.

At his discomposure, Mirit spoke. "Your consideration is admirable, Your Grace. Indeed our mission was successful."

"I'm glad to hear it. My dear, this is Mirit."

"I'm happy to finally meet you. I'm sorry for being unable to thank you before now for saving Titus."

Mirit graciously smiled. "You were occupied at the time."

"Ay. Daria's birth and Titus' return on the same night was an unexpected surprise."

"Your Grace, Duchess," said Armus, motioning toward their seats.

"I'm sure we'll speak more this evening," said Angus to Mirit before he and Necie left.

Nigel sat beside Mirit. He caught Chad's eye. The lad smiled, proud and excited. "Is the view different from the table?"

"Indeed! I only hope the excitement doesn't affect my appetite."

"I doubt anything could do that."

Trumpets sounded, announcing the King and Queen's arrival. All rose and paid their respects, the men bowed and ladies curtsied. Three members of the Council of Twelve beside Mathias were at Waldron. Lord Fagan of the Highlands brought his family south to escape the harsh northern winter for the more modest climate of Midessex. Baron

Hollis, of the East Coast, was mild-mannered man of cheery disposition. He arrived at Waldron to give his annual shipping report. As brother of General Wess, Sir Bosley of Midessex proved a frequent visitor.

Tyrone cut a regal figure with his black hair, light gray eyes, and a gold coronet. To match her gown, a tiara of diamonds and peacock blue stones adored Tristine's pampered golden hair.

"Mirit, you look beautiful. The gown becomes you," said Tristine upon arriving at high table.

"Thank you, Majesty."

"Don't you agree, Nigel?"

He widely smiled, eyes admiring of Mirit. "Most definitely."

Mirit blushed and smiled.

Tyrone indicated for everyone to sit but remained standing to greet the guests. "Friends, we gather to welcome home Prince Nigel, Lady Mirit, Chad and Avatar. From what I've been told, the journey proved successful. Hearing Lady Mirit's story, the people of Tunlund have embraced Jor'el. Vicar Uriah is well on his way to establishing five Fortresses and ten schools of learning."

A rousing pounding on the tables and chorus of "Here! Here!"

Nigel took Mirit's hand in support when she shied at the attention.

Tyrone made motion for quiet. "After Grand Master Hampton says the blessing, eat and enjoy. Later we shall hear from Prince Nigel and Lady Mirit."

Grand Master Hampton took his position on the floor to say the blessing. When Vicar Uriah was not in attendance of the royal family, spiritual responsibilities fell to his assistant. When he finished, servants brought in platters of food to feed the royal family and their guests. Soothing melodies from the royal musicians accompanied the conversation and laughter of the guests.

Although hungry, excitement curbed her appetite and Mirit ate lightly. Nigel's gallant and polite conduct was so very different from when they first met. She thought him arrogant and condescending when he ridiculed her manner of dress and swordsmanship. Even after her miraculous reviving and confessing his feelings for her, he remained careful in speech and action during their return journey.

Careful? I rebuffed him, claiming I needed time to readjust to a life I barely remember. And now? She watched him speak to Wess, who sat on the other side of him. *He's pleasant, charming, completely relaxed. He's home. Home.* The thought struck her and she looked to her father. *After all these years, I have yet to go home to be with him.* Mathias smiled and raised his tankard in salute. She returned his smile. *After the feast.*

A half-hour later Armus approached Tyrone and whispered.

"Really? I don't think I've ever heard of Dresden."

"What is Dresden?" asked Tristine.

"Apparently a kingdom that has sent an ambassador."

"He comes bearing gifts," said Armus aloud.

Tyrone considered for moment then said, "Well, I suppose he's hungry. Send him in."

Armus left the Hall and returned shortly with two other Guardian warriors, Ewert and Bailey, all escorting a middle-aged man with pale blonde hair and a great beard. His clothes were plain and for traveling but made from good homespun wool. He carried a metal cap under one arm and a sword at his hip. He appeared more the warrior than ambassador. Beside him walked a tall ample woman about twenty years of age. She was not heavy, rather robust, and pretty with two long golden braids hanging over her shoulders, rosy features, and blue eyes. She too wore good quality traveling clothes. They stopped before the high table.

Upon sight of the strangers, conversation halted and the musicians ceased playing when signaled by Tyrone to do so.

"Sire, Ambassador Ivor of Dresden." Armus stepped aside but Ewert and Bailey remained behind the strangers.

"Sire," said Ivor, bowing. The woman curtsied.

"Welcome, Ambassador. What brings you to Allon?"

"I come with gifts in honor of Your Majesty, and with the hope of forming an alliance between our kingdoms." Ivor spoke in a heavily accented Allonian, but he could be understood.

"You speak our language fairly well, Ambassador."

"I could say the same of Your Majesty about Dresden. Though our accents are different and phrases of which I am not accustomed to hearing."

"Interesting. I wasn't aware of a shared language."

"There are many things Dresden and Allon have in common, Sire. And the reason we hope for an alliance."

"In time perhaps. First we should become acquainted. Please, you and Lady—?"

"Lady Gilda, Sire."

"You and Lady Gilda join us."

"Forgive me, Sire, but custom requires I present the gifts before sitting to break bread." Ivor pulled a parchment from his belt. "This is an accounting of the gifts. Two chests of silver coins, fifty yards of Dresden wool, ten horses, twenty casks of our finest ale, twenty tanned hides of leather, and Lady Gilda to grace your court."

"Lady Gilda?" asked Tyrone in surprise, staring at Gilda.

In a discreet motion, Tristine slapped his arm when he stared too long.

He turned from Gilda to Ivor. "Does this complete your custom?"

"It does, Sire."

"Then please, join us. Over there, by Baron Mathias."

Mathias stood when Tyrone gestured to him. Ivor bowed and Gilda curtsied before joining Mathias.

"Odd. Whoever heard of giving people as a gift?" said Mirit.

Nigel's eyes narrowed in displeasure. "The Morvenians presented a royal princess to our father as an offering for divine appeasement."

"Ay," chided Tristine in agreement, her harsh glare on Gilda.

"Which I'm certain Ellis refused," said Tyrone.

"Ay," said Nigel.

"But you didn't," she chided.

"What was I to say?" he began in discreet dispute. "Refusal may cause trouble, and until I know more about Dresden it is best to be agreeable."

"To what extent?"

He leaned closer to whisper in her ear. "Only to the extent of courtesy, my love."

Mirit watched Ivor and Gilda. "They remind me of people from the northern tribes."

"You know of Dresden?" asked Tyrone.

"No, Sire. Medgard, Lendar and Soren," she spoke with prompting glance to Nigel. He took his cue.

"We met two farmers from Soren, who claim to need help. They tried to kidnap Mirit to force that help."

Surprised, Tyrone leaned forward in his seat. "When was this?"

"Our first night outside Panos Point. Apparently, they were waiting for her and followed us. Something about women ruling their society and she is the only one who can help."

"Why should they think so?"

Nigel's reference to *women* irked Mirit but she answered Tyrone. "They said they heard what happened to me in Tunlund and believed it a sign that I am the one to help. They haven't said much else. They are afraid of Avatar and believe I control him." She chuckled and looked behind her chair to Avatar, who stood in this customary place with Armus and Mahon. The Guardian flashed a wry smile.

"Where are these farmers now?"

"Here," said Nigel. "I decided it would be best until we ascertain the trouble. They seem genuine in their appeal and very frightened."

"I'll speak to them tomorrow. For now, tell us of Tunlund."

For the next hour, Nigel, Mirit and Chad recounted their travels in Tunlund. Several times during the retelling, Nigel noticed Lady Gilda lean close to speak to Ivor, who nodded, but he never spoke in return. She motioned to high table, glaring at Tyrone and Tristine in an unfriendly manner. Discreetly, Nigel motioned Armus to him.

"What do you know of Dresden?"

"Nothing. Then again, mortals are always fighting and creating new kingdoms to dominate."

Nigel pursed his lips in brief thought. "Learn what you can. Some thing is odd about them and I'll sleep better knowing what." At Armus' departure, Nigel caught Tyrone's curious regard. "Later in the study," he mouthed the words and Tyrone nodded his understanding.

While the royal family and guests feasted in the Great Hall, Leif and Alaric were well fed in the servant's hall, a large room off the kitchen. Around ten-thirty at night they left to return to the barracks for the night under the watchful eye of two royal guards. At an intersection, where one hall led to the main corridor and the Great Hall and the other to the rear entrance, guests were seen leaving, retiring for the evening, but two people in particular caught the brothers' attention.

Alaric seized Leif. "Look!"

Leif paled in fear. "You don't think she knows we're here?"

"What are you two talking about?" demanded a guard.

"We must speak to Lady Mirit. It's a matter of great urgency." Alaric began to move down the main corridor when the guards stopped them.

"The likes of you will not disturb the king and his guests." The guards pulled Alaric and Leif from the main corridor to the back hall.

"Please! We must speak with her," shouted Alaric, struggling against the manhandling.

"What's going on?" asked Wren, the tall, beautiful, green-eyed Guardian huntress. Unlike the warriors, she wore dressed in forester brown and green and carried a dagger, crossbow and quiver.

Alaric and Leif became mute with terror and fell prostrate at her feet, faces to the floor.

The reaction briefly stunned Wren. "What are you doing? Get up."

Alaric glanced up then quickly lowered his head.

"On your feet. You don't bow to me," she insisted. When Alaric and Leif remained prostrate, she motioned the guards to help them stand.

"Please, Great One, if we have found favor with you we need to speak to Lady Mirit," said Alaric.

"That's not up to me."

"Avatar. He at least tolerates us," said Leif.

"She tells him too," said Alaric.

Wren stared at them during the exchange. "I'll speak to Avatar. In the meantime go back to the barracks." She watched them leave with the guards until all were out of sight then headed toward the Great Hall.

Meanwhile Tristine left Tyrone, Nigel and Armus in the study, being told of matters to discuss before Tyrone joined her for the night. Although tired, it was good to have Nigel home.

Two royal guards stood at the entrance to the family quarters and bade her goodnight. At either end of the hall two more guards stood watch to ensure the security and privacy of the royal family. The royal apartment was the middle door of the corridor and to the left. Upon entering, Tristine found Lady Gilda sitting in a chair before the hearth.

"What are you doing here?"

"Waiting for the king."

"In our chamber?"

"Naturally. Since he retires here, where else should I be?"

"In the guest quarters."

Gilda's face screwed up in displeasure. "That is unsuitable under the circumstance."

"What? You are a guest, it perfectly suitable," refuted Tristine, her temper flaring at the woman's arrogant attitude.

Gilda remained in her seat, stubborn and fixed. "He accepted the gifts and appeared pleased to do so. I am entitled to be here."

Fire rose in Tristine's eyes. "You are entitled to nothing but our hospitality!"

Gilda stood to confront Tristine. "By his act of acceptance, I am now his *wife* also. When he comes he shall choose between us."

Tristine balled her fists to keep from striking Gilda. "Guards!"

Four soldiers quickly arrived.

"Take Lady Gilda to the guest quarters and see she remains there."

"Ay, Majesty."

With spite, Gilda snarled at Tristine when escorted from the room.

Tristine could not calm down. Though outrageous, Gilda's words struck a nerve because of the way Tyrone looked at her earlier. *He wouldn't. He couldn't. But the gifts? Did you know?*

In hurried, determined steps she left the chamber. Anger, frustration and hurt grew at the thought he knew what he was doing. *'Refusal could cause trouble', he said! Ha! Your acceptance has caused trouble.*

By the time she reached the study, fury filled her face. Her blustery entrance and slamming the door startled Tyrone, Armus and Nigel.

"Tristine, what's wrong?" asked Tyrone.

She ignored him to order Nigel and Armus. "Leave! I will speak to my husband alone."

The harsh unusual dismissal caught Nigel off-guard. "Tristine—"

"Out!"

Although curious, Armus guided a perturbed Nigel toward the door. "Peace," he said, only Nigel wasn't about to leave. Tristine turned her focus to Tyrone so Nigel stopped, motioning Armus to remain silent.

"Tristine. What is wrong?" Tyrone repeated his question.

"Don't *Tristine* me. How dare you!"

"How dare I what?"

"Don't play ignorant. It is bad enough she was in our bedchamber because of you!"

Her accusation stymied and confused him. "Who was in our bedchamber?"

"Lady Gilda! The gifts you accepted were her dowry! She said you would choose between us since she is now also your wife."

Dumbstruck, Tyrone stared at her. Nigel and Armus moved from the door, both looking as shocked as Tyrone.

"Dowry?" echoed Nigel.

"Ay! And why are you still here?"

"Because I've never seen you so upset with Tyrone, and to hear you accuse him of infidelity is astonishing."

"I haven't done anything!" said Tyrone in defense. "Tristine," he took her hand. "I am sorry she upset you, but it's not true. You are my wife. The mother of my children and the only woman I have ever loved."

Her anger began to subside, but not completely. "What about the way you stared at her?" Pain crept into her voice.

His shook his head in befuddlement. "More curiosity than admiration or desire. Mirit said it, who gives a person as gift?"

"I couldn't believe her nerve. How did she get into our chamber?"

"I intend to find out."

"At once, Sire." Armus left.

"Where is she now?" asked Nigel.

"In the guest quarters under guard," she said.

Tyrone rolled his eyes, flaring her anger again.

"What did you expect me to do? Allow her to remain in our chamber?"

"No, of course not. But your action may be considered a insult."

"Was I not insulted?"

"You had every right to take action. I only wish you spoke to me first."

"Peace!" snapped Nigel. "Being angry at each other won't solve anything. Tristine, how could you even think Tyrone capable of such a thing? He's as much a victim as you because her actions now cast doubt upon his character and fidelity.

She fought back tears. "I didn't want to believe it at first."

"What changed your belief?"

She became frustrated. "I don't know! The more I thought, the more … I don't know. I'm sorry," she wept.

Tyrone held her. "So am I. I never thought accepting an act of homage would cause such trouble." He turned her face to him and spoke in all tender sincerity. "Truly, I have not looked at another woman nor do I desire to do so. I am proud, pleased and content to have you as my wife for now and however long Jor'el gives me breath."

She clung to him, fighting back more tears.

At a knock at the door, Tyrone nodded for Nigel to answer. Mirit, Armus, Wren and Avatar arrived.

"Now is not a good time," said Nigel.

"The king will want to hear this," said Armus with conviction.

Nigel stepped aside to allow entrance. Tristine separated from Tyrone and wiped her eyes.

Mirit spoke in sympathy to Tristine. "If I knew sooner, things might have been avoided."

"How do you know? Does everyone know?"

"No! Armus told Avatar and me when we came to tell the king what we learned concerning Ivor and Gilda."

"What?" asked Tyrone.

"They are not who they pretend. There is no such kingdom as Dresden. They are really from Soren."

"How did you learn this?"

"Alaric and Leif are the two farmers we told you about. They recognized Ivor and Gilda and sought me out to tell me about them."

"*Sought* is a relative word, my lady. They prostrated themselves at my feet," said Wren with discomposure.

"What?" said Tyrone, trying not to laugh.

"I heard a commotion in the back hall and went to determine the cause. Upon sight of me they fell to their knees, faces to the floor."

Avatar smiled. "They reacted similarly to me only I wasn't worshipped," he said, and received a jab in the ribs from Wren.

"The behavior is odd," said Tyrone.

"It gets odder," began Mirit. "They said Ivor is not an ambassador but Gilda's manservant. She is a member of the Sigvard, those who serve the Valkerish, Soren's goddesses. It is from the wrath of these goddesses they came seeking my help."

"A unique tale, but why come to Allon in the guise of an ambassador and proceed to upset the royal house?"

She shrugged. "They didn't know. They're worried their journey had been discovered."

"I believe I should speak to these farmers."

Armus said, "I sent for them after speaking to Lady Mirit and Avatar. They are in the hallway awaiting your pleasure." To Tyrone's nod, he fetched Alaric and Leif.

Wary of the Guardians, Alaric and Leif moved cautiously.

"Have no fear. Lady Mirit says you have a story to tell."

Alaric turned from Tyrone to Tristine, his face and voice shaky. "You are Queen Tristine?"

"I am."

"Will you listen to our tale?"

"My husband, the king, has granted an audience. Speak and we will listen."

Alaric's gaze shifted between Tyrone and Tristine. "Your manner of life is so different. We will try to do as you ask, Majesty."

"Why did you come seeking Lady Mirit's help?" asked Tyrone.

Alaric looked with uncertainty from Tyrone to Tristine. "Answer him," she said.

"There is a dangerous rift in the Valkerish threatening to destroy Soren. The evil Valkerish, whose name we cannot utter, killed several of the good Valkerish and forced some Sigvard and the priestesses to begin human sacrifices."

"The shift in the balance of power threatens the stability of Soren! For a thousand years there have been Valkerish and then the evil ones came," said Leif to Tristine.

"You fear to speak their name, why?" asked Tyrone.

Again Alaric looked to Tristine. "I told you to speak freely," she said.

Alaric turned back to Tyrone. "To speak their name means certain death. We would be struck down where we stand."

Tyrone cocked a confident grin. "I doubt your evil Valkerish have power here. Jor'el and his Guardians will outmatch them."

Alaric and Leif were cautious in regard of Armus, Avatar and Wren. "They may balance out the evil," said Leif to Alaric.

"You consider good and evil in balance to one another?" asked Nigel.

This time the brothers looked to Mirit, who nodded, and Leif replied to Nigel. "Ja. Is that not how it is in Allon?"

"No, Jor'el, the Almighty, is a benevolent god. He created the Guardians to aid mortals and to ensure justice."

"We heard you have only one god. The one who brought Lady Mirit back to life. Because of that we believe she can help restore the balance, Majesty," said Alaric to Tristine.

"What does this have to do with Ivor and Gilda?" asked Tyrone.

For a fourth time, Alaric glanced to Tristine and she grew firm in feature and speech. "You don't need my permission to answer the king!"

Alaric nodded, though his face showed conflict. "Whatever brought Gilda here, is not good. Being of the Sigvard, the evil ones control her."

"How?"

This time Alaric tried not to look at Tristine before answering Tyrone. "They are goddesses and can do anything! They took my only daughter." He voice cracked.

Leif pleaded to Tristine. "Forgive Alaric, Majesty. He is a desperate father. We are uncertain if the evil ones plan to sacrifice her or force her to become a priestess."

"I understand a father's desperation. Unfortunately, I'm not certain of what we can do to help, or even if we should," said Tyrone, his tone growing agitated by their behavior.

"You must! Gilda's presence is a bad omen for Allon. The evil ones' mark is upon your kingdom!" exclaimed Alaric in desperation to Tristine.

Tyrone squared his shoulders. "Do not presume upon my good graces to make threats against my kingdom."

"No, Majesty," pleaded Alaric to Tristine.

"You will speak to me, Master Alaric!"

"Sire." Armus came alongside Tyrone and calmly said, "I sense they mean no harm or disrespect, but are correct about their countrymen."

Tyrone took a moment to calm down. "We will consider all you have said. Master Alaric, you have my sympathy in regards to your daughter."

Armus took the cue and escorted the brothers from the study.

"Infuriating to be ignored isn't it?" Nigel asked Tyrone.

"I don't know. They obviously elevate women to a place of high esteem. Worship even," said Mirit, fighting a smile to Tristine.

"I often heard mortal men say they worship the ground some women walk on. Until today I didn't understand what they meant," said Wren.

At Nigel and Tyrone's chagrin and Avatar's frown, Tristine and Mirit attempted to curb laughing.

"Goddess worship aside, I must decide what to do about Ivor and Gilda," said Tyrone.

"Worship appears to be the core of the problem," said Avatar.

"Ay. But how to ferret it out is the question?"

"Confront them."

"Naturally. But in private or in public?"

"The gifts were given and accepted in public making our guests unknowing witnesses to your supposed marriage vows," chided Tristine, her earlier anger returning.

"The queen is correct, Sire," began Avatar. "Word will spread, casting further doubt upon your character, which could be advantageous to those less inclined to your reign at home and abroad. Besides, I have heard of the Valkerish. They act in tandem and have characteristics similar to a Trio."

"Could they be Shadow Warriors?" asked Nigel.

"No. I heard of them before the Great Battle which is when Shadow Warriors first appeared."

"How is that possible?" asked Tristine.

Avatar shrugged. "I don't know. Armus might, since he is from the beginning. Kell most definitely."

Tyrone nodded. "Get word to all the guests I require their presence in the Great Hall at nine o'clock tomorrow morning."

Avatar and Wren saluted and withdrew.

"Sire, what should I do about Alaric and Leif? They came a long way to find me," said Mirit.

"That is a matter for prayer. Whereas I sympathize with Alaric as a father, I don't know if it would be wise as a king to intervene. Perhaps the confrontation will provide the answer."

"I hope so, otherwise I don't know if I can make such a choice. After everything else, all I want to do is find some peaceful solitude."

Nigel made Mirit face him. "You won't be alone."

"I know. Only you tell my father about me leaving Allon again."

"I think I'll leave weathering that storm to the king."

Tyrone frowned. He wasn't in a humorous mood.

Tristine took Tyrone's arm. "The hour is late and I am tired."

"Ay. We bid you both goodnight," Tyrone said to Mirit and Nigel and left with Tristine.

Chapter 3

THE Great Hall was clear of tables and chairs and only the thrones remained. By eight thirty in the morning, guests began assembling. Avatar and Mahon flanked the thrones. Two royal guards stood at the bottom of the platform with two more at each door for a total of six. Royal pages waited at their posts. Being a formal gathering, the room buzzed with questions but no answers to the summons since the guards wouldn't speak and the Guardians polite in deferring to the king.

Shortly before nine o'clock, Chad appeared in his squire's uniform escorting Mirit, who wore a dark blue velvet day gown. He brought her to a place of honor to the left of the platform then exited the Hall.

A moment later, trumpets sounded and those gathered in the Hall became still and quiet. Armus marched to his place on the platform and announced: "Lords and ladies, King Tyrone and Queen Tristine. His Royal Highness Prince Nigel."

Regally dressed to hold court, Tyrone and Tristine entered, followed by Nigel in his King's Champion uniform, Chad behind Nigel. Everyone bowed to the royals. Nigel took his customary place at the base of the platform near Mirit, Chad flanking him. Tyrone and Tristine mounted the steps. Tristine sat but Tyrone remained standing to address the gathering.

"Lords and ladies, I called this audience for one purpose: to confront a public deception of our royal person to which you were all witnesses. The deception distressed your queen and cast aspersions upon your king. To this confrontation I call you to give your prompt and full attention." He sat and signaled to Armus, who in turn gave the order.

"Bring forth the accused!"

From the back of the hall, Ivor and Gilda appeared with their hands bound and escorted by Ewert and Bailey. Sight of the ambassador and his companion as prisoners caused murmuring among those assembled. The Guardians halted the mortals at the base of the platform.

"Before we begin, Grand Master Hampton will offer a prayer for wisdom and truth," said Tyrone.

Hampton stepped forward from his place at the right of the platform. "Let us pray." He waited only briefly as everyone, except Ivor and Gilda, bowed their heads. "Almighty Jor'el, we come seeking your wisdom and discernment for our king, Tyrone, whom you have appointed to rule over Allon. In your name he protects us and levies justice. May all here feel your presence as our king seeks to determine the cause for this deception, and may you be honored by the outcome. *Tangiel.*"

"*Tangiel,*" everyone echoed, except Ivor and Gilda.

For a long silent moment, Tyrone regarded the pair before him. Ivor appeared apprehensive but Gilda rigid, features fixed and eyes leveled at him, showing no fear. He returned her stare, ready for confrontation, and not the way he looked at her last night. Tristine tried to keep a smile from her face when he spoke his great displeasure.

"Since you chose to make your display public last evening, you have this one opportunity to redress yourselves in public. I suggest you make the best use of it. Ambassador?" The light grey eyes were icy and challenging of Ivor.

Sweat formed on his face. "Sire, I ..." He glanced to Gilda.

"You seek Lady Gilda's permission to answer me?"

41

Gilda made a slight nod toward Tyrone, to which Ivor quickly spoke. "Of course not, Sire. What was the question?"

"You are stalling, Ambassador. Speak plainly or I will speak for you."

The struggle on Ivor's face came out in his nervous reply. "S-s-sire, if I—I speak as you want, I risk everything."

"If you don't, you risk everything. What is your choice, *Ambassador?* Or should I say, servant?"

Ivor fell to his knees. "Sire, I beg for mercy! I was forced to act."

"Coward! Speak not to the infidel," spat Gilda.

The reaction from the crowd to her insult came loud and measurable. Nigel stepped forward, clasping the hilt of his sword.

"Curb your tongue, woman!"

She snarled at him. "If I were not bound, I would kill you where you stand, *hund das cniht.*"

"Enough!" snapped Tyrone. "You compound your deception with insults."

In scorn and purposeful slight, Gilda turned away.

Ewert forced her to face Tyrone. "You will submit, woman."

To the Guardian's action, she showed the most concern.

"I see we now have your attention," said Tyrone.

"Your giant may force me to look upon you, but it will not loosen my tongue. The Sigvard answer only to the *Tavar!*" She lifted her eyes. "May the mighty Tavar hear my plea—!"

Deafening thunder roared and shook the chandeliers. Bright light filled the room, making everyone fearful and shielding their eyes. The force knocked Gilda to her knees. Ewert and Bailey reached for their swords. Nigel and Chad hurried to stand in front of the platform, swords drawn; Armus, Avatar and Mahon at their backs, also armed. Tyrone stood to shield Tristine.

From the fading light, a tall powerful Guardian appeared, his sword leveled at Gilda.

"Speak not that name in this place!" he commanded, golden eyes flashing fire. Set in flawless features and heightened by black hair, the intimidating and deadly look made Gilda pale in fright.

"Kell!" said Tyrone in relief.

"Sire." The renowned Captain of the Guardians arrived in his full glorious battle uniform, a gold cuirass emblazoned with the ancient symbol of Jor'el covering his chest. From the shoulder clasps of the cuirass hung a short purple cloak. Instead of a belt, a purple sash held his magnificently crafted scabbard and dagger.

Armus came alongside Kell and with a brief nod, acknowledged his captain. Nigel flashed a small grin of relief and signaled Chad to put up his sword. Avatar and Mahon didn't sheath their weapons and stood at the ready, flanking Kell and Armus.

The crowd remained agitated, curious, and apprehensive, so Tyrone said, "Be at ease. All of you know Kell." He sat. "Captain, I take your appearance to mean Jor'el is not pleased by such blasphemy."

"Indeed not," said Kell, loud so all could hear. "This creature prays to a power, that before Dagar, sought to usurp Jor'el. For their betrayal they were banished from Allon and forbidden from ever returning, they or their descendants."

Hearing the name of Allon's most feared adversary brought murmurs from among the crowd.

"So this Tavar is made up of mortals?"

"Ay, Sire."

"No! The Tavar are immortal and powerful. You will all cringe before them," said Gilda indignantly.

Kell reached down to seize Gilda. "You dispute me?"

"Stay, Captain! I want to hear what she has to say. Perhaps she will answer why they have come to Allon."

"As you wish, Sire." Kell waved the other Guardians to stand aside before he jerked Gilda to her feet and to face Tyrone. "Tell the king what you know."

Gilda remained stubbornly silent.

"I'll tell you since she'd rather die than betray the Tavar," said Ivor.

"Double coward!" she cursed Ivor.

"Ewert, Bailey, take her to the dungeon," ordered Tyrone.

After Gilda left the Hall, Kell waved for Ivor to stand. "Well?"

"Gilda, my mistress, is of the Sigvard, those serving the Tavar, the evil half of the Valkerish. At this moment, war rages between the good Valkerish and the Tavar for control of Soren. Alas, the Valkerish are losing and if destroyed, Soren will be vulnerable to the wrath of the Tavar. Even now they employ many Sigvard to wreak havoc upon the people. They have even begun human sacrifices! My own sister was among the first victims, which is why I am here," said Ivor in a thick hoarse voice.

"Blackmail? But you said Gilda is your mistress," said Tyrone.

"She is, Sire. My sister was sacrificed as an example of what would happen to the rest of my family if we failed to destroy you and weaken the royal house of Allon."

"How?"

Fear etched on Ivor's face and he shrugged. "Gilda was sent to create discord and division to minimize resistance and ensure victory, for once the Tavar have conquered Soren, they plan to invade Allon."

"Sire!" Mathias stepped forward. "Say the word and the fleet will go on full alert."

"Ay!" said Baron Hollis, second-in-command of the navy to Mathias.

"The army stands ready, Sire," said Wes.

"Indeed. One question remains before I issue the order. Why do the Tavar want to invade Allon?"

"I don't know exactly, Sire. I only know they despise Allon's god and seek revenge."

Tyrone stood. "Gentlemen, secure Allon!"

Immediately Mathias, Hollis, Wes and others in positions of authority left the Hall.

"Sire!" Ivor fell to his knees. "Please, grant me protection. Gilda will kill me for betraying her."

Tyrone's deliberate look at Ivor was brief before he spoke. "Mahon, take him to Grand Master Hampton's quarters and stay with him until he is assured of safety."

Mahon saluted then he, Hampton and Ivor left.

Tyrone extended his arm to Tristine for departure. "Captain, accompany us to the study."

Kell sheathed his sword to comply.

Nigel began to leave when Mirit's hand thrust forward to stop him. Her expression fretful and she drew close to speak. "Do you think Alaric and Leif sought me to stop a war?"

He squeezed her hand and grinned with reassurance. "I'll find out. But whatever the answer, we will face it together." He kissed her cheek, to which she threw her arms about his neck. For a moment he held her. "Chad, take Lady Mirit to the private salon and remain with her. Avatar," he said over his shoulder before leaving the Hall with Avatar.

Tristine, Angus, Armus and Kell were with Tyrone when Nigel and Avatar arrived.

"Word must be sent to the Council," said Angus.

"Ay. Tell them to come to Waldron at all speed," said Tyrone.

Angus withdrew.

"What about Alaric and Leif?" asked Nigel.

"You think they knew about this plot?"

"Doubtful, although it validates their story. The question is what to do now."

"Who are Alaric and Leif?" asked Kell.

"Two farmers from Soren, who came seeking Mirit's help in dealing with the Valkerish," replied Nigel.

"Why Lady Mirit?"

"Because of Tunlund."

"Interesting," mused Kell.

"They are frightened of the Tavar and believe they will be instantly killed if they speak the name. And have a healthy fear of Guardians."

Tyrone chuckled. "I'd hardy call prostrating themselves at Wren's feet healthy."

"What?" asked Kell in astonishment.

"They cowered in fear of me at the first meeting," said Avatar with a wry grin.

"They believe Mirit controls you," began Nigel. "And begged her for mercy from the giant," he said to Kell, jerking a thumb at Avatar upon the word *giant*.

Kell's curious and pondering glance shifted between them.

"Females rule their society, Captain," began Tristine. "During an audience Alaric and Leif kept looking to Mirit and I for permission to reply to any questions put to them by Nigel and Tyrone. Apparently those of the Valkerish are believed to be goddesses."

"The men are fearful of women, while the women scorn men. Before you arrived, Gilda called me an infidel and refused to answer me."

Kell shook his head in confusion. "This is odd. Those banished were mortal males."

"Avatar said it happened before the Great Battle."

"Obviously, much has changed since she spoke of the Tavar as powerful immortals," said Nigel.

"That's how Ram and Razi were viewed," began Armus, speaking of Dagar's unnatural half-mortal, half-Guardian offspring. "Perhaps by some twist of fate the Tavar—"

"No!" refuted Kell, fierceness rising in his features.

"Appear to be immortal like Ram and Razi," continued Armus, unfazed by Kell's outburst.

"And the females descendants of those banished," added Avatar.

"Makes sense," said Tyrone.

"Ay," the captain reluctantly agreed. "Yet it would be best to know the enemy Allon will face." He looked squarely at Nigel. "Would Lady Mirit be willing?"

"Willing isn't the word I'd use, but if it is required, ay. Along with Chad, Avatar and I."

"Not good enough," said Tyrone in dispute. "The Valkerish are believed to be goddesses and the Sigvard ruthless females. The make-up of the group must reflect their perception of reality if it is to succeed."

"They worshipped Wren," said Avatar, wryly.

"Auriel," said Kell, ignoring Avatar's wit. "Three Guardians and three mortals. Three males, three females."

"Agreed," began Tyrone. "Unlike Tunlund, I want this mission on a time schedule. Two weeks from when you land, you're to rendezvous back with Gulliver, regardless of what you have or haven't learned."

"I hope it will be enough time," said Nigel.

"It must be. I don't want a repeat of wondering and worrying about your safety. Speak to Mirit, but I want everyone ready by morning."

Nigel nodded and slightly frowned. "What about Mathias?"

Tyrone cast a side-glance to Kell. "I'll leave that task to the captain."

The family salon was a warm intimate room of cherry wood with special mementos and miniatures of various family members at different ages. The most endearing was a painting of Ellis and Shannan together. Vicar Archimedes commissioned it immediately after the coronation to save for history the likeness of the Son of Tristan and the Daughter of Allon at the moment of their victory. Ellis was nineteen and Shannan, eighteen. Both dressed as common foresters from their days hiding in Dorigrith until the appointed time in Prophecy. Ellis' golden hair was longer and a bit unkempt. His sword was not the weapon of a King or Jor'ellian knight. He stood stalwartly straight, hands resting on the pommel as the sword stood point down before him. Shannan stood to his, her brown hair loose with the sides pulled back. In her right hand she held her bow, and upon her left arm sat Kato, the majestic eagle. Torin, a large magnificent wolf, sat in front of Shannan and Ellis. Together, they toppled the worst evil Allon had seen since Dagar's Great Rebellion.

Archimedes meant well, but the memories and feelings the painting invoked for Ellis and Shannan were too personal to share, and they chose to keep it private. Once both passed to the heavenlies, and if their children agreed, the painting could be viewed publicly. But it never left the salon, Tristine, Nigel and Necie wanting to hold onto some personal memories of their beloved parents.

Mirit stared at the painting. Chad moved alongside her.

"I remember the day the last vestiges of Dagar were defeated. Alas, Queen Shannan died. It greatly affected Nigel that she didn't know he was alive."

"I can see why. He looks like her in hair coloring and shape of his face. But I also see his father in his eyes and expression." Her gaze lowered from the painting and her voice grew melancholy. "I don't remember my mother. My father and I haven't had much time to become reacquainted, too much time gone. Now, I may be needed to stop a war." His touch on her arm made her look at him.

"If that happens, you wouldn't be going alone."

"Indeed not," said Nigel. He and Avatar arrived unnoticed.

"Not going or not going alone?" she asked with skepticism.

"Not going alone."

She lowered her head and sighed.

Nigel joined her and Chad stepped back. "Mirit, this goes beyond Alaric and Leif. The true identity of the Valkerish and Tavar are in question. Kell doesn't know who they are. Considering the threat of invasion there is an urgent need to learn the enemy's identity."

"So we go to Soren," her voice barely above a whisper.

"Wren and Auriel will join us."

To this, she looked up, curious. "Who is Auriel, another Guardian?"

Avatar answered, "Ay, a female warrior. According to the king we must appear to embrace their perception of the Valkerish and Sigvard."

Mirit snickered, her composure renewed. "Meaning you, Chad and Nigel will be subordinate to Wren, Auriel and I."

"I've been subordinate to mortals before," said Avatar dryly.

"I'm a squire," added Chad, tossing a wink at Avatar.

Mirit flashed a challenging smile at Nigel. "Wren and Auriel are Guardians, so that leaves one person unaccustomed to following orders.

And if you act contrary like you did on summer circuit the ruse will fail, *Your Highness.*"

His shoulders sagged. "Just call me *hund das cniht*. Whatever that means?"

"Dog of a knight, roughly translated," said Avatar, making a growling '*r*' sound.

Mirit suppressed her laughter. "Most of Soren speech is similar to Allonian. Come to think of it, that might be part of the reason I recognized your speech. Stamos traded with the border clans."

"Then language won't be a problem," said Chad.

"Not for normal communication. Still, there may be times to speak privately," said Nigel.

"We all speak the Ancient."

"I'm still learning," refuted Mirit.

"You know enough for our purposes," said Nigel. "Now we must prepare. Tyrone wants us to leave by morning."

"What about telling my father?"

Nigel grinned. "Tyrone gave that assignment to Kell."

Chapter 4

ALARIC AND LEIF WERE OVERJOYED at their plea for help being heard and volunteered to act as guides. To facilitate the mission, all donned homespun wool clothes similar to the Soren brothers. Being from a more southern climate, waterproof sealskin and fur lining were added to the outer coats, gloves, and boots for Nigel, Chad and Mirit. With sealskin being a rarity in Allon, Gulliver, the renowned sea-Guardian, managed to procure some elsewhere. It took more time for preparation than originally estimated, thus they would not be ready to leave Waldron until two days later.

In the pretense of warrior women, Wren, Auriel and Mirit wore metal caps, fashioned like the one Ivor wore. Sealskin lined the cap for Mirit to ward off the chill of the metal. Nigel, Chad and Avatar wore woolen cowls and cloaks against the elements. For Avatar these were more for a show of commonality and not necessity.

Alaric and Leif told of the need for *snawe-scoh,* snowshoes; leather straps strung across a wooden frame that tied to their feet to evenly spread body weight over the snow and prevent sinking. When not needed the shoes were slung across the back.

From Waldron they journeyed to Leith, the main port on the East Coast. Gulliver charted a course to sail as far north along the Soren coast as the weather permitted to allow them to disembark before traveling inland on foot. To sail around the most northern fjord into the Sea of Bejorn to Soren's chief port would be too difficult considering the time of year. The infamous icepacks of Bejorn would impede the journey and perhaps prove fatal. Although known for his navigational prowess, Gulliver was not reckless, thus they would head for Bergen.

The Sea Guardian manned the helm of a frigate, a ship sturdy of sail with a rowing pit on either side of the main deck. The breeze ruffled his silver hair as sea-green eyes studied the horizon. Mahon stood beside him. Ewert and Bailey sat on deck with their backs against the main mast, waiting for when their brawn would be needed. Nigel, Mirit, Chad, Avatar, Wren and Auriel gathered below deck to plot the route overland.

Priscilla, Guardian of the Fair Winds, manned the crow's nest. Gulliver's instinct of the sea combined with her command of the winds, gave hope for a relatively smooth journey. In marked contrast to her fellow Guardians, pale yellow hair reached past her waist with part of it braided and coiled on her head like a crown. Sky blue eyes held a mischievous glint while the rich pink lips smiled. She wore a dress of light and dark green reaching her ankles and gathered about the waist by a gold belt fastened with a shell buckle. She closed her eyes to sense the wind. She flinched and her eyes snapped open. Dark gray and ominous clouds lined the horizon.

"Storm on the horizon!" she called down to Gulliver.

"I see it! Can you lessen its impact?"

"I tried!"

"Try again!"

She closed her eyes and concentrated. After a moment she hung her head with a painful grunt from the effort. In a flash, she appeared on the quarterdeck beside Gulliver. "No good. It's more than the wind. The temperature is dropping. It could erupt into a blizzard, and that would take you, Barnum and me to combat together."

Gulliver scowled and stared at the approaching blizzard. "Bergen is still two hours away. Tell Nigel and the others to prepare to be tossed around. Mahon, stow the sails. All right, you lazy warriors, time to earn your keep. Into the pit," he called to Ewert and Bailey.

"Why does Kell stick us with *him* every time *he* needs strong backs?" complained Ewert.

"To teach you patience," said Bailey. They took their place in the pit, Bailey on the right oar and Ewert on the left oar.

Priscilla entered the wardroom. "Highness, there's a blizzard ahead. The sea will get rough."

"A natural storm?"

"Ay, but too large for Gulliver and I to deal with alone. We need Barnum."

"Can we avoid it?"

"No. We must sail through to reach Bergen."

"Very well. Do your best."

Priscilla left. Leif and Alaric didn't look so certain.

"Don't worry. Gulliver will get us there safely," said Auriel, the Trio Leader of the South Plains. Strawberry blonde hair complemented her vibrant jade eyes. Whereas Alaric and Leif acted fearful of Wren, sheer terror filled their faces about Auriel. Comparatively, Wren appeared less fearsome with her dagger, bow and quiver, than Auriel with the large lethal sword across her back, dagger at her right hip, and a chakram on her left hip.

The brothers gave reluctant nods.

"Then are we all agreed on the route?" asked Nigel.

"Ja," said Alaric.

"Good. Now, about our assignments: Wren and Auriel will be seen as Valkerish with Mirit a Sigvard. However, there are only six remaining Valkerish, three good and three evil."

"Sounds like a Trio," said Auriel.

"Easily explained since they were originally banished from Allon and would be familiar with the form and function of a Trio."

"You think the Valkerish came from Allon? Like these?" asked Alaric about the Guardians.

"Not Guardians, mortals. Banished by Jor'el for their blasphemy and insurrection. They and their descendants."

"That is why Captain Kell appeared when Gilda spoke blasphemy," said Avatar.

"If all Sorens are their descendants, why were we not confronted by Jor'el?" asked Leif.

"You came seeking help, Ivor and Gilda came to cause harm. The Almighty is merciful and understood your hearts."

Leif seized Alaric's arm. "*Bruder*, do you think it is possible about the prophecy?"

"Ja."

"What prophecy?" asked Nigel.

"There is an old prophecy many have forgotten because the balance has remained for a thousand years. I did not think it of myself until hearing about this banishment. It says that before the end, mighty ones will come from the place of beginning," replied Leif.

"We only thought to bring Lady Mirit back because of Tunlund. She is blessed and can help us restore balance. But what you tell us goes beyond what we thought," added Alaric.

"Indeed," said Nigel. He gazed at his companions. Mirit's face was set but past the fixed expression lay disturbance. To the world she presented a self-assured façade, but he learned to read those eyes. Preventing war from coming to Allon weighed heavy on her, but the possibility of fulfilling foreign prophecy added an unforeseen burden.

"Should we mention Allon?" she asked.

"No, *from the place of beginning* will suffice. What they think is of their own imagination," said Avatar.

"The rest of us need to determine our status," said Nigel.

"Alaric and I are your guides," said Leif.

"Leaving Your Highness, Chad, and the giant as varlets," said Alaric.

"I'm not a giant," insisted Avatar.

"To Sorens you are a giant since there were only a few male Valkerish. They were believed to be relatives, but are gone now. They had no authority and were treated no better than varlets."

Wren exchanged private smiles with Auriel. "Will you claim him as kin, or should I?"

"Oh, I will," snickered Auriel.

Nigel, Chad and Mirit tried not to laugh too loud. "Do you think you can handle the demotion?" Nigel teased Avatar.

"It will be a difficult," he said more serious than expected, making Nigel curious.

"Why?"

"Because I'm female," chided Auriel.

"Gender has nothing to do with it," rebuffed Avatar.

Wren laid a hand on Avatar's arm to intervene and explain to Nigel. "Avatar is older and higher in rank than Auriel, whereas he and I are equal in age and station."

"So this is a true role reversal?"

"According to our hierarchy, ay."

"Sounds like someone else has difficulty submitting to subordinates," said Mirit to Nigel.

"Any mistake can be hazardous," said Auriel directly to Avatar.

He drew to his full height, stung by her statement. "I do not back down from a challenge."

"We both need to keep our wits, Avatar," said Nigel. "Chad, you'll be with Wren, and I'll be with Mirit." The ship violently heaved. "Providing we get there in one piece." Mirit slapped his arm, motioning to Alaric and Leif. "Sorry, bad joke. Gulliver will get us to Bergen."

Mahon came to fetch Avatar to help Ewert and Bailey keep the ship on course. Though the blinding snow and howling wind, Gulliver wrestled with the helm and the warriors rowed. After an hour the snow and winds began to abate. Whether Priscilla managed to calm the wind or the storm blew itself out, didn't matter. The worst was over.

The last rays of twilight broke through the gray clouds at Bergen. To avoid curiosity of the natives to the uniqueness of too many Guardians, Nigel instructed Gulliver to anchor the frigate in the harbor. They would use a rowboat to get to the dock. The story of Avatar being Auriel's brother proved plausible considering their similarity in size, manner, and dress. Being a warrior, Auriel might be considered the group's leader, thus she would initiate contact.

Chad climbed out and secured the boat to the dock. Once on the wharf, people tossed them guarded looks of fear and curiosity. Wren, Mirit and Auriel took the lead with Alaric and Leif. Avatar, Nigel and Chad followed.

Alaric drew alongside Auriel. "Great One, there is an inn down the next street to the left."

Those at the inn recoiled when Auriel, Wren and Mirit entered. A portly woman nudged a burly, pot-bellied man. He hurried to greet them, timid and bowing.

"Great Ones! It's been years since the Valkerish so honored me. And the Sigvard," he said of Mirit, a tremor of fear in his voice. "Please, whatever you desire is yours."

"We will test your hospitality. Food and rooms," said Auriel.

He caught sight Nigel, Chad, Alaric, Leif and Avatar. His eyes grew wide, lingering on Avatar. "How many rooms, Great One?"

"Three naturally. You don't expect us to share, do you?"

"Of course not. Your varlets can sleep in the stables."

"They will tend us and sleep outside our doors."

"As you wish. Follow me to your table." He led them to his best table. His wife hastened to brush off crumbs and another woman set down tankards and a large pitcher of ale. Auriel, Wren and Mirit sat. "The food will be only a moment." They scurried off.

Nigel and Chad began to sit when Alaric and Leif stopped them and shook their heads. They took up position near the wall. Mirit watched, biting her lower lip to keep from smiling. Keen to her attempt to curb amusement, Wren poured the ale and pushed a tankard toward Mirit. The latter took a drink to recover her role-playing.

"Our arrival caused quite a stir," said Auriel, half into her tankard, which she used for observation of the other patrons.

"Let's hope Alaric and Leif are correct and Valkerish do eat and drink," said Wren.

"I know Sigvard do," said Mirit with a teasing smile.

Auriel emptied the tankard and soundly set it on the table, a sly grin at Mirit, but Wren hesitated. "If he's offering us food and drink, then we accept."

"As a test or for real?"

"Hardly a test for so timid and unsettled a greeting."

The innkeeper, his wife and two other women placed the food on the table: bowls of stew, roast pork, bread, cheese, cabbage and potatoes.

"I hope the food meets were your approval, Great Ones," he said.

Auriel waved for them to leave. Wren stared at the food. Again Auriel spoke. "You're a goddess, remember. You would hardly pray to yourself for a blessing." She tore off a piece of bread and ate.

A hand touched Wren's shoulder from behind. Avatar took the pitcher to refill her tankard.

"*Fois agus ith*. Peace and eat," he whispered in the Ancient and poured ale into her cup. She began to eat the stew and he stepped back.

Leif whispered in Chad's ear before he and Nigel waited upon Mirit and Auriel.

Chad quietly relayed the message to Auriel as he fixed her plate of pork and potatoes. "Leif says we're not to eat until you are done."

She nodded and pushed aside the empty bowl to take the plate.

A few minutes later the innkeeper approached. "Is food to your liking, Great Ones?"

"It is adequate," said Auriel.

He smiled in pleased relief. "Anything else? Sweetmeats, strudel?"

"No. Leave the ale and feed our varlets."

"At once." He signaled to the others, who rushed to help. He led them to the back corner and gave them the food.

Mirit smiled as Nigel sat in a dim corner eating. What a change from last week's feast. He caught her eye and she turned aside pretending to wipe a sleeve across her mouth to cover her amusement.

"Try not to enjoy it too much," said Wren.

"You won't enjoy ordering Avatar around?"

Wren wryly smiled. "I always enjoy getting back at warriors. Present company excluded," she said to Auriel.

"I may be a warrior, but I'm only a female to Avatar." She cast a snickering side-glance to their companions in the corner. "Still, they say sibling rivalry can be fun."

"Great Ones, I have prepared the best rooms. For when you are ready to retire, of course," said the innkeeper.

"See the rooms are acceptable," Auriel instructed Mirit.

Mirit knew Auriel sent her to do reconnaissance, just like a Valkerish would use a Sigvard. Alaric and Leif told them varlets were for menial work with Sigvards used for more important duties. Despite her smaller size, Mirit suited the role of Sigvard, being very skilled in armed combat.

The innkeeper led her down a first floor hallway to the back of the inn. There was a door at the end of the hall with a lock and bar, presumably an exterior door. He went to a door on the right wall.

"Here is the first room."

The large room held a large bed, chest of drawers, a small table with two chairs, a window, and a door at the back of the room. A fire in the small hearth warmed the room. Personal items decorated the room.

"Does someone live here?" asked Mirit.

"Mine and my wife's room, but it is the best."

Mirit stepped into the room and checked the window for ease of opening. Outside was a small enclosed courtyard. She reckoned the other door lead to an anteroom since it didn't have a bar like the other. She tried the handled, locked. "This can't be an outside door, so open it."

He reached under his apron for a ring of keys attached to his belt and unlocked the door. She pushed past him and into the other room, which was slightly smaller with a narrower bed, window, nightstand, and door that led out to the courtyard. Instead of a fireplace, a small stove stood in one corner, its pipe ventilating through the ceiling.

"This belongs to someone as well?"

"Our daughter. The third room is across the hall, Sigvard."

The third room appeared identical to the second room with no exterior door. Pleased, Mirit returned to the table and reported her findings to Auriel and Wren.

"Do we retire this early or not?" she asked.

"Retire. The less contact the better," replied Auriel.

When they rose, the innkeeper scrambled to accompany them.

"Your attendance is not necessary," said Auriel. She signaled to the corner for the *varlets*. All entered the first and largest room. "So far so good?" she asked Leif and Alaric.

"Ja. It is best to rest. The journey to Manheim is long."

"Mirit can have this room, I'll take the second, Wren across the hall. You two stay with Avatar," she said to Leif and Alaric.

"Ja, Great One," they said in unison and Avatar ushered them away.

After Wren and Chad left, Mirit took the snowshoes off her back. Nigel looked down the hall. The innkeeper's wife watched them. He shut the door.

"You sleep on the bed, I'll take the first watch." He moved toward the hearth and pulled the snowshoes over his head.

"I wouldn't take your cloak off. You'll need it in the hall." She smiled and tossed him a blanket. "To keep up appearances," she added.

In the hall, Leif and Alaric sat flanking Auriel's door both using blankets for warmth. Chad sat beside the door to Wren's room wrapped in a blanket. Avatar sat by the exterior door at the end of the hall. He didn't need a blanket. Guardian sleep was in reality a meditative state, but to the casual observer it appeared no different than mortal sleep.

Chad grinned at Avatar when Nigel appeared. "We wondered how long it would take before she threw you out."

"Ha, ha." Nigel wrapped the blanket around his shoulders and took a seat beside the door.

Just before dawn, Avatar, Auriel and Wren roused the mortals. Nigel stretched, stiff from the cold. Chad was not much better, while Alaric and Leif suffered no ill effect from sleeping on the floor in the cold hall. Mirit appeared rested, smiling mischievously at Nigel as they walked to the main room.

After a breakfast of fresh cinnamon bread, eggs, sausage, cheese, and warm chocolate, they packed provisions for the journey and left the inn. Being a coastal town, the road inland from Bergen climbed for several miles before reaching a snowy plateau. The road closest to town was kept relatively clear for traffic, but once on the plateau the snow grew deeper making road maintenance more difficult, though the depth of snow did not warrant snowshoes. The plateau was flat with sporadic groves of bare trees and tall pines dotting the bleak white landscape; good open pastureland in the summer.

By midday they only travelled eight miles, a slow pace, but given the snow and cold temperature, an adequate distance. They encountered no other travelers.

"You said Manheim is four days from Bergen. Are the roads all this difficult?" asked Nigel when they paused in a small grove to eat and rest.

"Some, those not near villages or towns. At this pace it may take six days," replied Alaric.

"Once there, how will we get the attention of the Valkerish?"

Alaric and Leif exchanged smiling glances. "They will know before we reach Manheim. The appearance of two unknown Valkerish and a Sigvard in Bergen will spread quickly," said Leif.

"And a giant," said Chad, tossing a smile at Avatar.

"I'll make certain *my brother* is known," teased Auriel.

Nigel clapped Avatar's arm, a gleam of teasing on his face. "Remember, I try to tell you what it's like to have sisters."

Avatar said nothing; his thinly veiled expression of tolerance at the humor was enough.

Alaric finished his portion of the bread and took a swig of ale before speaking. "There is a small settlement six miles from here, on the other side of the plateau. We can stay there tonight."

Due to the restraints of travel, conversation was minimal. Alaric and Leif accompanied Auriel in the lead, followed by Wren, Mirit, Nigel, and Chad with Avatar keeping rear guard. The plateau grew narrow and winding.

Auriel hung back to join Wren at sight of a lone, large white wolf with overly developed haunches. It walked parallel to them, using the trees for a screen. "It's been following us for an hour now."

"So has the other." Wren pointed to the right yet kept walking normally. This one was larger and darker than the other.

"Biggest wolves I've ever seen."

"They're not completely natural. Too big in the haunches, the eyes too yellow and the teeth—"

They reached the trailhead where the path started down. Alaric spoke in harsh warning. "Great Ones! The *ulf* have found us."

"They serve the Tavar," added Leif.

"We see them." Auriel then asked Wren, "Can you communicate with them?"

"I won't know until I try, but now is not the time and place. We're going to descend, and the pass looks too narrow for confrontation."

"They will kill us, or worse, take us to the Tavar," insisted Alaric.

"Stay calm. Your excitement could agitate them. The best defense is to continue as if you're not frightened. Go with Auriel; I'll wait for the others."

Auriel took the brothers to begin the trek down.

Wren eyed the wolves and when the others joined her, whispered a warning. "Beware of the wolves."

"I think there's more to fear from the climb down," said Chad concerning the narrow rocky pass. A drastic slope to a deep ravine lay on one side and a sharp fifty-foot drop to a frozen river on the other side.

"I'll take the lead so hold on to me," said Avatar in his dry humor.

"What about taking us down the Guardian way?"

"Not with the wolves around. Something's not right, and dimension travel will leave us vulnerable when reappearing," said Wren.

Avatar shrugged and smirked at Chad. "You heard her. Hold on."

Nigel chuckled when Chad followed Avatar, not holding onto the Guardian. Mirit followed Chad. Nigel walked behind Mirit.

Wren kept an eye on the wolves. The beasts came together and stopped short of the trailhead, both eyeing her, bare fangs dripping with saliva. Indeed, these were unnaturally large and ominous. "Come no further," she commanded.

The white one began to back away when the other snarled and snapped, halting its retreat. She watched the wolves communicate to each other in snarls and grunts. This time when white one turned to leave, the darker one followed. Whether the wolves were withdrawing for good or only making a temporary retreat was hard to tell, but perhaps they could reach the bottom safely. Wren followed the others.

The mortals concentrated on the climb down the slippery, hazardous slope. Wren glanced back to the trailhead and didn't see the wolves. Suddenly from the less steep side of the ravine, the wolves attacked.

Avatar pulled Chad out of the way before the darker wolf could take him down. Auriel's sword cleaved the wolf in half. Wren was unable to reach Nigel in time when the white wolf leapt at him, taking him over the side toward the river.

"Nigel!" cried Mirit, taking an impulsive step to catch him, but Alaric and Leif seized her to keep her from slipping over the edge. Nigel and the white wolf crashed through the thin ice into the partly frozen river.

In a flash, Avatar disappeared from the trail and reappeared at the water's edge, pausing to locate Nigel. Ten yards from shore the white wolf emerged first and lunged at something in the water. Nigel's head broke the surface just when the wolf attacked, taking him back underwater. Avatar rushed into the river. Nigel again broke the surface now only twenty feet away and desperately fighting to breathe and get away from the wolf. Again the wolf pulled him under.

Avatar dove at the spot where they went down. He dragged the wolf to the surface, one arm wrapped around its neck and both hands on its jaws. The strong beast tried to throw him off and they fell back into the water but did not completely submerge.

"Avatar! Hold its head up!" shouted Wren.

It took effort, but the instant Avatar raised the wolf's head out of the water, Wren's shaft struck deep into the base of its skull, killing it. He released the beast to float away on the current.

"Where's Nigel?" called Mirit.

Avatar spotted Nigel, still underwater and not moving. He dove and discovered Nigel's cloak caught on a submerged log. He broke the clasp holding the cloak and brought Nigel to the surface.

The others anxiously watched him carry Nigel out of the river and lay him on the ground. Fearful, Mirit bit her lip at seeing Nigel pale and unconscious with claw marks across his neck and chest where the wolf tore through his clothes.

"He's not breathing," said Avatar. "Take my breath and live," he spoke in the Ancient and blew air into Nigel's mouth. Nothing. He repeated the phrase and again blew into Nigel's mouth.

Terrified, Mirit watched him administer the Breath of Life, the same method Vicar Uriah used to restore her life.

Avatar tried a third time to revive Nigel. A great gasp and Nigel began to choke. Avatar turned him on his side and slapped him between the shoulder blades. Nigel retched and some water came out of his mouth, his breathing labored, but he was alive.

"*Furasda, daor te,*" said Avatar, a hand on Nigel's forehead. He grew calm but trembled uncontrollably. "We must get him warm."

Wren anticipated the situation and assembled wood for a fire. "*Teine,*" she said, flicking her fingers at the wood. A roaring fire appeared.

Avatar placed Nigel on a log nearest the fire. Chad wrapped his dry cloak around Nigel then removed his cowl. Mirit sat beside Nigel, took the cowl from Chad, and placed it over Nigel's head. She opened her cloak, threw her arm about his shoulders with the cloak and closed the cloak about both of them.

Avatar moved to the fire, opened the nap-sack and withdrew several items, including a packet and a cup. He spoke the Ancient and liquid appeared in the cup then he emptied some mixture from the packet into the cup and swirled the contents over the flames to warm it. He knelt in front of Nigel and placed the cup to Nigel's lips.

"Drink." Due to shivering, he held Nigel's head steady.

Nigel finished drinking, laid his head on Mirit's shoulder and closed his eyes.

Leif and Alaric watched in amazement. "What did you give him?" asked Leif.

"Wine with trefoil and borage, for strength and to prevent a chill."

"And his wounds?"

"They're not life threatening, but a chill could be."

"He disappears and reappears in a flash of light. She speaks and fire appears. And what is that strange language?" said Alaric.

"The Ancient language of the Guardians," said Auriel.

Both Alaric and Leif regarded Auriel, Wren and Avatar in awe then Alaric said, "Indeed, Guardians are wondrous beings. No Soren sailor could have made the crossing from Allon to Bergen in three days. It takes at least a week. Then this."

"They are as powerful as the Valkerish," said Leif to his brother.

"That's what we're here to find out," said Avatar in stern warning.

"By those beasts I'd say they possess some power," said Auriel.

"The first priority is to get Nigel to a dry warm place for the night," said Mirit then asked Alaric, "How far is the settlement?"

"Another three miles down the road. But if he is incapable of traveling—"

"I'll … manage," stammered Nigel, eyes still closed.

"No, you won't. I'll take you," refuted Avatar.

"What about the others?" Nigel asked with difficulty.

"We can walk. You must get warm and dry," said Mirit. When he looked at her, she smiled. Once again he rested against her shoulder.

"I'll go on ahead. Otherwise they won't know you," said Leif.

"We can all go," said Avatar.

"How?" asked Leif.

"Trust us." Auriel stepped between Leif and Alaric, taking both by the shoulder.

Avatar took Nigel from Mirit, carrying him rather than letting him stand. Mirit stood beside Wren. Chad joined them. In a flash, all disappeared, reappearing fifty yards from the settlement. Alaric and Leif fainted. Wren held onto Mirit and Chad until the swooning sensation passed. Nigel was again unconscious. Auriel roused Leif and Alaric.

"What happened?" asked Alaric, disoriented.

"You fainted. All mortals do when they dimension travel."

Leif gaped in surprise. "The settlement."

The settlement was two houses with several outbuildings, a stable, and corral. No one worked outside and smoke rose from the chimneys. Near the buildings, two dogs started barking. Wren took the lead when one dog grew aggressive and moved to confront them.

"*Fois, mo beag caraid,*" she said. The dog became docile, wagging its tail to greet her. The other dog also approached to be petted.

"How did you do that? Yoki does not like strangers," said a man from the threshold.

"I have a way with animals," said Wren.

She stood and his eyes widened at her height. "Valkerish!" The others approached, deepening his apprehension.

"Have no fear. We come in peace. One of our varlets is injured and we seek shelter for him."

"Ja. Come inside," he stammered, still wary.

Inside, a woman and three small children gathered at the table eating. When Avatar entered carrying Nigel, one of the small girls screamed and ran to hide behind her mother.

The man moved to calm his anxious wife and children. "They come in peace. He is injured and needs care."

"We won't hurt you, little one," said Avatar, kindly smiling at the girl.

"My brother speaks true," said Auriel.

"They have come from the place of beginning," said Alaric.

"Place of beginning?" questioned the man.

"Ja. They are good and kind."

The man warily regarded the Guardians before pointing to a door at the back of the house. "You can put him in that room."

"He'll need clothes until his are dry," said Mirit.

"Ja, Sigvard. I have some he can use. In the room."

Chad followed the man.

"Do you have any soup? He will need nourishment once he is dry and warm," said Wren.

The wife appeared nervous then took a bowl from her eldest son and pushed it toward Wren. "Take this."

"We won't take food from a child."

"It is all we have!"

In a casual manner, Auriel crossed to the hearth where an empty pot sat on a slab. Wren and Mirit spoke to the wife, so Auriel placed the lid on the pot, put her hand on the lid, closed her eyes, and offered a silent prayer, lips moving but no sound. Smiling, she lifted the lid.

"You are mistaken. The pot is full," she said.

"No, it is empty," said the wife, cautious in her approach. She marveled at a full pot of steaming hot stew. "Merciful Great One!" She fell to her knees and kissed Auriel's hand. "Thank you. Our provisions are all gone. I thought we'd starve." She wept.

Auriel was slightly taken back by the wife's vivid display of gratitude. "You won't starve."

Again Alaric and Leif watched in wonder.

Chad and the man emerged from the room with Nigel's wet clothes.

"Erik, look! The Great One gave us food," she said eagerly, drawing her husband to the pot.

"This a blessed day! We were going to let the children eat their last meal—" Overcome, he knelt before Auriel. "Thank you, Great One."

Auriel accepted his display of gratitude with a small uncertain smile.

"I told you they were from the place of beginning," said Alaric.

"Here," said the wife. "Hang the clothes before the fire. I'll fetch stew for the varlet."

Chad noticed Mirit concerned and Wren displeased. When Eric took the clothes, Chad moved to stand by Wren and Mirit. "What happened?" he asked in a low, curious voice.

"Auriel filled the empty pot with stew so they wouldn't starve," said Wren.

No further words were exchanged when the wife approached with a bowl of stew. Mirit took the bowl and spoon and went to the room. Nigel lay on the bed bare-chested with Avatar cleansing his wounds.

"Close the door," she whispered to Avatar.

He did so then returned to the bed.

She sat on the edge of the bed. "The wounds don't look too serious."

"Thankfully, no, but I am very sore."

"The medicine I'm using will prevent scarring. What happened in other room?" Avatar resumed tending to Nigel.

"When we asked for food for Nigel, the wife took it from the eldest boy claiming it was all they had—"

"I won't accept it," said Nigel.

She shook her head. "This isn't it. While Wren and I spoke to her, Auriel made stew appear in the empty pot. Overcome she fell to her knees thanking Auriel because she believed they would starve to death.

The husband did the same and proclaimed this a blessed day. Alaric and Leif agreed."

Nigel flinched, though Avatar tried to be careful in his administration. "Seems you Guardians are making acolytes everywhere."

"We are doing what we were created to do. I wasn't about to let you die, while Auriel provided for a poor family we imposed upon."

"And the wolves? What power controlled them?" asked Mirit.

"Hard to say, but until we learn more about these Valkerish we must tread carefully." Avatar wiped his hands on a towel after he finished salving Nigel's wounds.

"I think the wolves were a sign we have caught the attention of the Valkerish," groused Nigel, who squirmed to get comfortable.

"How? We've only been here a short time. Could they have known we were coming because of Ivor and Gilda?" said Mirit.

He shook his head with a low groan and rotated his neck and shoulders.

"Enough discussion. You need to eat and rest so we can continue our mission and discover the answers," said Avatar.

Nigel nodded, and accepted Mirit feeding him.

Chapter 5

FTER A NIGHT OF REST, Nigel's headache was gone. Fortunately, the claw marks were superficial and not debilitating, though he complained of soreness and moved sluggishly upon rising and changing into his clothes. Once he was ready, Auriel told the couple they would leave without troubling the family about breakfast. The couple tried to convince Auriel otherwise with a stream of praise for upon waking they discovered their store of barley, oats and molasses had been replenished. However, Wren insisted on the need to depart.

Standing in the threshold to bid their guests farewell, Erik asked, "What is your name, Great One?"

"Auriel."

He smiled. "*Aurieldeag*. The day of your coming shall always be remembered by our family, Great One."

Avatar frowned in disapproval but his objection became pre-empted by Wren. "Time to go."

Once again, Wren and Auriel led the way with Alaric and Leif. Mirit kept pace with Nigel while Avatar and Chad brought up the rear.

"I'm not certain what to make of that," said Nigel over his shoulder to Avatar.

"I will speak to Auriel this evening."

"You both act like she did something wrong. I thought Guardians helped mortals," said Chad.

"We do. It's not helping that causes concern, rather the response."

"They seemed grateful. Moreso than many in Allon."

"That's the problem, Chad," said Nigel.

"Why? I thank Avatar and other Guardians for their service. Why should the Sorens be any different when they are miraculously fed?"

"It is the way in which gratitude is expressed and received. I appreciate Avatar more than I can say. In fact, I love him like a member of my family, but I don't worship him."

The sentiment visibly touched Avatar. "I could not ask for, nor hope to receive greater appreciation. However, Guardians who do not serve mortals on a daily or intimate basis tend to forget that appreciation isn't always expressed. Auriel is a capable warrior, but new to her position in a Trio. As such, she needs to learn how to deal with mortals on a continuous basis. But no, she did nothing wrong in creating the stew."

"Or the other provisions," said Mirit.

He smiled and shook his head. "I did so before everyone woke."

Nigel laughed, a quick look ahead to the others. "Does Auriel know? I mean they will celebrating *Aurieldeag*, not *Avatardeag*."

"I'm sure she suspects it was either Wren or myself."

Wren glanced back at hearing laughter. Due to Nigel's impeded pace, the gap widened between groups. "Scout ahead," she told Alaric and Leif. "What was that all about?" she asked Auriel in the Ancient when Alaric and Leif were out of earshot.

"What? I just gave them food."

"Not the food. *Aurieldeag*, the Day of Auriel."

"Can I help it if the mortals of Sorens are more grateful than the mortals of Allon?"

"Hush!" she said, a cautious glance to the lagging group. "Don't let Avatar hear you."

Auriel scoffed. "He of the tremendous ego. Mighty in arrogance."

"What do you mean?"

She glared crossly at Wren and huffed. "Ay. You wouldn't know. You are the famed huntress and have not felt his stinging abuse."

"Abuse?" echoed Wren in surprise. "I've never seen Avatar abuse you, or any Guardian."

"His clever tongue is well known."

"Ay, he teases, and I felt his *clever tongue*, but that's not abuse."

Auriel scowled. "As I said, you are a huntress, Vidar's equal, and he treats you as such. Not Avatar, and I am every inch the warrior he is."

"Your words are spiteful. Avatar is older, wiser, and higher rank than you and deserves respect."

"I mean no disrespect. I would simply like to be appreciated."

Piqued, Wren stopped Auriel. "That is the exact attitude which festered in Dagar and led to the Great Battle."

Angered by the rebuke, Auriel jerked away. "I'm not Dagar!"

"Is there a problem?" called Avatar.

"No problem." Auriel moved on before the others reached them.

Wren visibly debated what to say, but when Avatar went to pursue Auriel, she stopped him. "You will only make it worse."

"How?"

"Trust me. If I need help, I'll let you know."

In a brief consideration, he looked ahead to Auriel. "Very well."

"What about the wolves? Do you think we'll encounter any more, or something like them?" asked Mirit, catching them off guard by her change of subject.

"I don't know. I couldn't get past the sense of the unnatural to the core of what or who controlled them," replied Wren.

"Did it feel anything like the Dark Way?" asked Nigel.

She cocked her head in thought. "No. The Dark Way holds full control over a creature. These argued about whether to attack us or not."

"Argued?" echoed Chad.

"Argued," she said emphatically. "The white one hesitated, but the darker one inched closer even when I commanded them to stop. I thought the white one convinced the other to leave. Rather, I hoped, because I didn't think they would attack on such dangerous terrain."

"We should continue, Alaric and Leif are signaling," said Avatar.

The rest of the morning passed without much conversation as they climbed out of the glen to another plateau where the snow was deeper.

Avatar helped Nigel finish the climb. Evidence of exertion and pain showed on Nigel's face when he bent over to catch his breath. "We should rest," said Avatar.

"No. It's a hard climb. I'll be fine in a moment."

"We will need the snowshoes until we can reach the wood." Alaric pointed two miles ahead.

Nigel took the shoes from off his back and plopped onto the snow with a loud exhale.

Mirit sat beside him, her snowshoes in hand. "It's more than the climb."

He said nothing, strapping the snowshoes onto his boots.

Avatar rummaged through his knapsack until he found what he was looking for. "Give me your flask," he said to Nigel. He put some herbs into the water, corked it, shook the contents and gave the flask back to Nigel. "Take a good long drink now, then a swallow every ten minutes."

"This is the second concoction you've fixed. Since when did you become a healer?"

"Since being charged with your care. I can't recall a mortal lad suffering as many, cuts, scrapes and all manner of injury as you."

"I wasn't that bad," snickered Nigel in dispute before taking a drink.

"I can well imagine you as Avatar says," said Mirit, smiling.

"Don't let Avatar fool you, Mirit. Eldric and the king gave him instructions before we left," said Chad.

After ten minutes Nigel felt sufficiently rested to continue. The snowshoes served well in crossing the plateau. Once again Nigel lagged behind, so Alaric and Leif reached the wood before the others. The brothers had their heads together, arguing when the rest arrived. Nigel breathed more heavily and appeared pale.

"Is there a problem?" asked Wren.

"Ja, Great One—" said Alaric.

"Stop calling me that! My name is Wren."

Auriel frowned at the rebuke but spoke to Alaric. "What's the problem?"

"This is *Sigwald*. Where the Sigvard live. It is haunted. Only the brave dare enter."

"Haunted by what?"

"Ulf, trolls, monsters. The Sigvard are left in peace since they serve the Valkerish. That is why we avoided it last time."

"Is there other way?"

"The road circles south and will add three days to the journey."

"No," began Nigel. "We don't have the time to spare." He put up a hand to stop Alaric's protest. "We came to make reconnaissance and learn about the Sigvard and Valkerish. Lead on."

The brothers hesitated.

"Don't worry, we're here to protect you," said Auriel.

Alaric gave stout nod. "We will not need the shoes under the trees."

Once they removed their shoes and fitted them in place on their backs, Alaric and Leif took the lead. Mirit kept a keen eye on Nigel while Chad and Avatar stayed within arms reach.

"You three don't need to hover, I'll be fine," said Nigel.

"You're being stubborn. We should have stayed another night," said Mirit.

"Another night may have helped Nigel, but not our group," said Avatar.

"Meaning their response to Auriel?"

"Ja," he groused.

"I still say she didn't do anything wrong and you're making a fuss over nothing," said Chad.

Nigel heavily sighed and shook his head, fatigue evident on his face and in his gait.

For an hour they walked deeper into Sigwald, but by the fading light couldn't travel much further before finding a place for the night.

"There's a small clearing up head," said Auriel.

In a tight group of trees and several fallen logs, they made camp. Auriel and Wren went in search of game. Chad, Alaric and Leif fetched wood for a fire. Nigel tightly wrapped his cloak close and sat on the ground, his back against a log, his face paler and sweaty.

Mirit felt his forehead. "You have a fever."

"I'd hoped the borage and trefoil would prevent a one. I'll make it stronger." Avatar made another remedy.

"It's been a long time since I felt this ill," grumbled Nigel.

"Being attacked by a wolf and falling into a frozen river will do that." Avatar held the cup to Nigel's lips and spoke a blessing in the Ancient. "*Jor'el beannaich seo an iocshlaint.*"

Nigel grimaced at the initial taste, but finished the remedy.

"I told you I was going make it stronger." He placed his hand on Nigel's head and spoke again in the Ancient, "Rest in the knowledge Jor'el hears and answers prayer."

"*Tangiel,*" said Mirit. Nigel just grunted.

Wren and Auriel returned carrying a slain boar. The female Guardians prepared and roasted the boar. Within an hour, they feasted.

"I've never known boar to taste so good. What did you say when you placed it on the fire?" Leif asked Wren.

"I said a blessing."

Nigel fell asleep after the remedy, so Mirit roused him to eat. He wasn't hungry, but she insisted. After a few moments, he refused to eat any more and went back to sleep.

When the mortals settled down for the night, Avatar approached Auriel, who sat on the other side of the fire. "Quite a sight to have someone fall at your feet, isn't it? I thought they'd faint at the sight of me." He motioned to Alaric and Leif sleeping side-by-side.

Auriel used a stick to poke the fire. "Wren said you replenished their supplies. Why? To show me up?"

He grew stiff at the accusation. "I claimed no responsibility even when they assumed it was you, so why question me?" She continued to poke the fire and he grabbed the stick to get her attention. "We are here to protect the mortals of Allon, not impress the mortals of Soren."

"I know. Remember, I am a warrior, and aware of my duty."

From her post at a nearby tree, Wren watched the terse exchange between her fellow Guardians. Suddenly she whipped out her bow, and she turned in anticipation of an intruder. Avatar and Auriel rose, armed and taking up position in a triangle to shield the mortals.

At a loud, growling war cry ten human-like creatures, large and burly, rushed the camp. They were wild and barbaric looking, having overly exaggerated facial features, fierce teeth and stood as tall as Avatar. They wielded clubs, swords, and axes. The Guardians reacted instantly to the attack. Wren's first shaft caught one of the creatures in the throat. Auriel's sword deflected an axe, making the creature stumble at the force of her parry. Avatar intercepted two of the creatures armed with swords.

Mirit and Chad were on their feet and armed. When a groggy Nigel tried to rise, Chad stopped him.

"Stay down!" He and Mirit took up a defensive position around Nigel, watching the Guardians engage the unknown enemy.

Wren managed to get off three shots before the creatures were re-enforced. She used her crossbow to deflect a club aimed at her head. The move brought her to her knees.

Auriel sliced off the arm of her attacker. Seeing Wren on her knees, Auriel snatched her chakram and flung it at beast. The weapon sliced through the back of its thick neck, nearly severing its head before flying back to her hand. Avatar pulled Wren to her feet a second before two more creatures rushed them.

"Trolls!" exclaimed Alaric. He and Leif urged Mirit and Chad toward the dying fire, but Mirit shook off Alaric to stay with Nigel. "Light is the only thing that will stop them."

Mirit and Chad each took Nigel by the arm, and practically dead lifted him to bring him closer to the fire. "Avatar! Light repels them!" she called. A roar from behind alerted her to an approaching troll but she was knocked aside in an awkward attempt to dodge the swinging club.

Chad's sword caught the offending troll in the shoulder, slicing its hide. A backhand from the troll sent him off his feet.

Avatar shoved the last of his attackers aside and made his way to join Auriel. "Light!" Both warriors took their swords by the hilt, pointed them downward and stabbed them into the ground with the command, "*A'lasadh!*"

The entire camp filled with blinding white light. Unearthly yowls and cries came from the trolls. Those on the fringe of camp, fled into the woods. The ones engaged in battle turned to stone. Those wounded or dead first turned to stone then crumbled into pieces.

The light faded. Avatar and Auriel pulled their swords from the ground. He tapped on one of the standing stone trolls and it crumbled. "Interesting."

"Anyone hurt?" asked Auriel.

"A little sore from being swatted aside like a fly," groused Chad. He helped Mirit stand. "You?"

"I'm in one piece."

Avatar knelt beside Nigel and felt his forehead. "This didn't help your fever."

An arrow flew between he and Nigel, landing beside the fire. Avatar bolted up to shield Nigel the same time Wren loosed a shaft in the direction the arrow came from. They heard a thud, followed by a surprised, painful groan, indicating a hit.

"Put up your weapons or we shoot to kill!" called a female voice from the darkness.

"It is you who will die if you don't show yourselves," said Auriel. At hearing another arrow let loose from behind, she whirled around and snatched the arrow in mid-air before it could strike her.

A shorter sword-swinging figure charged Avatar. He easily turned aside the attack, shoving the person in the back. She fell face first into the dirt next to the fire. Mirit's foot came crashing down on the attacker's shoulder blades, her sword leveled at the head.

"Move and you die," she warned.

"Enough!" shouted the same female voice. "Who are you and what are doing in Sigwald?"

"We seek the Sigvard," replied Auriel.

"Who would be so bold as to seek the Sigvard?"

"I, Auriel, a Valkerish from the place of beginning."

A moment of silence followed the reply then a shadowy figure appeared between the trees. "How can we be sure you are who you claim?"

"Come and see," said Auriel, but the figure didn't move. "Unless you are afraid."

"I fear nothing." She stepped into the firelight, and tossed off the hood of her cloak. Judging by her size she was mortal but appeared strong and formidable in her leather breastplate over a woolen tunic. Light brown hair hung in a long thick braid down her back. Her expression turned to surprise upon seeing Auriel. "You have the appearance of a Valkerish."

"I am, as is Wren. This is my brother, our Sigvard, and our varlets."

She looked at each in turn, paying particular attention to Avatar, disapproval on her face. "You allow your brother to travel with you? Do you not fear treachery?"

"What better way to prevent treachery than to keep him close?"

She snarled at Avatar, but the expression changed to placid toward Auriel. "I am Magda, second-in-command to Grissel of the Sigvard."

"Why did you fire upon us rather than make your presence known?"

"We didn't know who you were or what you wanted, so we tested you. Unfortunately, you mistook our warning shot for an attack and killed one of our sisters."

"What were we supposed to think? An unknown shot fired in the dark requires a response," rebuffed Wren. Upon her approach, Magda looked up. She might have been shorter than Auriel and Avatar, but she stood seven feet tall.

A hint of nervousness passed over Magda's face. "Indeed, Great One." She tried to recover her composure by taking a step back from Wren. "Now we know who you are, and offer the hospitality of our outpost. If you will have your Sigvard release our sister Adelaid, you can follow us."

Mirit waited until Auriel nodded before removing her foot and sword from the fallen Sigvard. Adelaid scrambled to her feet, sneering.

Chad aided Nigel to stand but Nigel stumbled and fell against Chad.

"One of your varlets is injured?" asked Magda.

"The footing was treacherous and he fell into the river," replied Mirit.

Scoffing, Adelaid surveyed Nigel. "You should have left him to his fate. One varlet is as good as another."

"Lives of men are cheap here," said Nigel to Chad, but not low enough to avoid being heard.

"Silence!" Adelaid's sword leveled at Nigel's face.

Mirit used her blade to knock the sword down and stepped between Nigel and Adelaid. In height, the Sigvard stood a few inches taller and outweighed her by at least twenty pounds.

"Peace, Adelaid! Put up your sword," ordered Magda.

Adelaid's temper wasn't easily cooled. "She allows her varlet to speak impertinently."

"Exactly! My varlet. How I treat him and what I allow him to do or not do is my decision!"

Magda stood at Adelaid's shoulder. By the fire's light they were equal in height and weight, only Adelaid had blonde hair, but both possessed cold, fiercesome blue eyes. "I have offered them hospitality, so put up your sword and act accordingly."

Adelaid's eyes narrowed at Mirit before storming off.

Magda surveyed the lighter and lissome Mirit. "You may be a Sigvard, but your ways are not our ways. I advise you to be cautious. Especially around Adelaid, she is not as tolerant as others."

"Providing such caution is given to our Sigvard," said Wren.

"Adelaid is well aware of the code of hospitality, Great One. She will not offend your Sigvard again. Now, follow me. Elfrida, Orly, see to Rae," Magda said and they left the campsite.

The crude, sturdy wilderness outpost of stone and wood had weathered to a dark dull gray. Two watchtowers stood diagonal from each other on the southwest and northeast corners of the outpost. The walls rose ten feet with a main gate constructed from thick oak planks fastened together by iron bars.

Passing through the gate, they entered a courtyard where they were met by a woman dressed in a metal cuirass wore over a leather jerkin. A red cloak attached to the shoulders of the cuirass and upon her head she wore a metal helmet from under which fell a long thick braid of yellow hair. Metal leggings were strapped over her boots. She stood six feet tall, her fair features reddened by the winter chill. Hazel eyes regarded the newcomers. A group of ten Sigvard gathered behind her.

Magda saluted the woman by clasping crossed arms to her chest, fists closed, bowing her head. "Grissel. These are strangers we were told about— "

Grissel pushed passed her to Elfrida and Orly dragging a hastily fashioned litter upon which lay Rae, a shaft lodged deep in her left breast.

"Who?!" she demanded.

"When your Sigvard attacked, I returned fire," said Wren.

Grissel glared at Wren, though tempered in voice. "You killed her?"

"In self-defense."

"It is true, Grissel. They mistook Rae's warning shot for an attack," said Magda.

"Did you not warn them first?"

"I … an oversight."

Grissel's vicious backhand sent Magda staggering. "Fool! Rae died for nothing. We can only hope the Valkerish will accept her soul in Aster when we make *Vorish*. Prepare the body," she said to Elfrida and Orly. Regaining her composure, Grissel spoke to Auriel and Wren. "When we heard of unknown Valkerish in the forest I sent Magda to investigate. Harm was never intended, if you come in peace. Who are you?"

"I am Auriel. This is Wren, my bother Avatar, and our Sigvard, Mirit. We come from the place of beginning."

Curious murmurs came from the Sigvard and Grissel put up a hand for silence. "No one has come from there in over a thousand years. The last to do so were the Tavar, and now they threaten the balance of power within the Valkerish."

"That is why we have come," said Wren.

Grissel studied Wren, cautious yet curious. "If that is true, you are welcome. The unbalance has split the Sigvard. More of our sisters now serve the Tavar. Only a handful of us remain loyal to the High Priestess and the Valkerish."

"Nigel," said Chad in concern when Nigel fainted, his weight making Chad stumble.

"The varlet is ill?" asked Grissel.

"Ja," said Avatar, taking the unconscious Nigel from Chad.

Grissel features flashed in ire at Avatar's speech.

Auriel intervened. "My brother dares to speak because this varlet is well-known and liked among our kind. His illness is the result of falling into the frozen river. My brother knows herbs and is tending him, only our journey has not allowed for proper care. It would cause great distress if he dies."

"Then he shall receive the best of care. Magda."

Magda saluted and went to take Nigel from Avatar, but the Guardian refused to yield his charge. Intense silver eyes made her balk. "Come," she snapped at him.

Mirit tried to keep concern from her face when they left.

"If you'll come with me, Great Ones, I'll see your needs are met. We can talk more in the morning. Your other varlets can make use of the stables," said Grissel.

Auriel, Wren and Mirit followed Grissel into the main house.

The room at the back of the outpost was not a guest room as told by the rough, sparse furnishing.

"Put him on the bed," said Magda.

"This will not do. There is no hearth or stove to keep him warm."

She stiffened in annoyance. "You may be brother to the Valkerish, but your speech is offensive."

"It will be of greater offense if he dies!" Avatar's silver eyes direct on Magda. A Guardian exerted authority with a look of command few mortals could withstand. Confusion and contrition crossed her face and she nodded.

The next room they entered was upstairs along the back hall. The furnishings were better and it had a small stove.

"This will do. Please, move the blankets so I can lay him down," said Avatar, adding politeness for her benefit. She did so. "Thank you. In a few moments I will require wood for the stove, a basin, pitcher of water, towels, jug of wine and a cup."

Magda curtly nodded and left.

Avatar removed Nigel's gear and outer garments. He felt the raging fever and heard several mumblings of delirium. After tucking Nigel under the covers, he withdrew the herbs from his knapsack for preparation.

"No!" shouted Nigel, and began thrashing about, his eyes closed.

Avatar tried to calm him. "Easy, *daor cairdean*, easy. You are safe and I am here." Nigel's body relaxed but breathing labored, brows furrowed and eyes closed. He continued to mumble a few words under his breath, but audibly spoke *"Avatar"* then a few unintelligible words followed by Mirit's name. "Mirit and I are safe. So is Chad."

There came a knock, but Avatar didn't want to leave Nigel to open the door. "Enter!"

Magda returned, followed by two varlets, one older man near sixty and a boy of twelve. The man carried an armful of wood, the boy a basin with a pitcher in it and towels over his arms. She carried the cup and jug.

"Start the fire. Put those on the table," she told the man and boy. When they finished, she waved them out. Nigel's jerking caught her attention. "The fever has taken hold?"

"Ja. I will need you to hold him while I mix a remedy to calm him and lower the fever."

Magda's frowned to the contrary and didn't move to comply.

"Then fetch our Sigvard!" he snapped when Nigel jerked again and he dared not release him.

Magda slammed the door behind her.

Avatar muttered in the Ancient, "Lord, give me patience before I throttle these women."

Barely two minutes passed when Mirit hurried in. "How is he?"

"Delirious. I require assistance, but the Sigvard was unwilling."

Mirit sat on the bed to deal with Nigel allowing Avatar to make the preparation. Nigel was pale and haggard and covered in sweat. He squirmed, groaned and mumbled.

"Easy," she said taking his face in her hands. His whole body jerked at her touch. "Nigel, it's Mirit."

He said her name in reply, eyes still closed, but his body kept twitching.

"I've not seen delirium this bad."

"As a child, whenever ill or greatly agitated in mind and spirit, he experienced nightmares. Reliving horrible memories, like the accident. This one involves you." Avatar finished the preparation and returned to the bed.

"The sacrifice."

"Ay." He held Nigel's head in a manner so he could drink the remedy. Even in a semi-conscious state, Nigel fought and choked on the remedy but emptied the cup. He gently laid Nigel's head back on the pillow. "He should be asleep shortly."

She brushed the matted hair from Nigel's forehead. "Will he—" She stopped at Avatar's hand on her shoulder and saw him smile.

"He will survive. I do not sense this is a fever unto death." He became thoughtful. "Still, the earlier remedies should have worked. The fact they did not—"

"What?" she asked when he hesitated.

"I'm not sure. The reason may become clear in time. Until then we must wait, have faith and trust in the *Ealmih*."

She relaxed at his discrete reference to Jor'el with the Ancient term *Almighty*.

Chapter 6

S HORTLY AFTER DAWN, Wren and Auriel stood on the northwest tower watching the Sigvard gather in a small clearing not far from the outpost where a pyre had been constructed. Rae's body lay upon the pyre dressed in full plate armor over a leather tunic, sword at her side and wearing a metal helmet.

"It seems barbaric to burn the body," chided Wren.

"According to Elfrida it is a way to honor the warrior by preventing the enemy from humiliating the fallen."

"Rather extreme."

"Apparently some graves have been desecrated and this is the only way to keep that from happening. Everything dear to the warrior is burned with them."

Chad joined them. "So that is Vorish?"

"Ja," said Wren in disapproval.

Auriel turned her back to Vorish to chastise Wren. "Just because you object doesn't mean it is wrong. Besides, we disappear when vanquished. If I were a mortal slain in battle I would not want the enemy to use my corpse to celebrate victory."

Wren didn't reply to Auriel, instead asked Chad, "What of Nigel?"

"The old man wouldn't let me in the house. Said he has orders from Magda. I should have gone with him last night."

She flashed a friendly smile and patted his shoulder. "You have a good heart, Chad."

Fire engulfed the pyre and Chad wrinkled his nose in disgust.

"Come. We don't need to see or smell this barbaric act." Wren steered him from the tower.

Adelaid noticed Wren and Chad's departure but Auriel remained. "These foreign Valkerish are stranger creatures."

Magda stood beside Adelaid. "Ja."

"You two speak during Vorish? Why?" demanded Grissel.

"Forgive us. We mean no disrespect. Our guests are unusual." Magda motioned to the tower.

"That's putting it mildly," groused Adelaid.

Grissel put a hand up to stop any further speech. "Sisters," she said to the others. "Make your show of honor then return to the outpost." She motioned Magda and Adelaid away from the pyre. "Speak plainly."

"The varlets are full of impertinence and they do nothing to correct them," chided Adelaid.

"I sense more. The brother is unnerving in the eyes and his voice fills me with fear. The only others who made me feel this way were the *mas-Tavar*." Magda spoke the name low and harsh.

Grissel's stiffened in dreaded anticipated. "A bad omen."

Adelaid became concerned by the reaction. "You don't think they are here to overthrow the Valkerish and destroy we who remain loyal?"

"I'm not certain. We may have to go to Manheim and speak to Ludmilla."

"They want to go to Manheim. Perhaps to complete their coup."

"They claim to be from the place of beginning," refuted Magda.

"Which could be a trick to deceive us!"

"The only way to find out is to take them to Ludmilla. If any one can discern their hearts it is the high priestess," said Grissel.

"They will refuse to travel until the varlet is recovered," said Magda.

"Then that is when we will leave. Spread the word. I will test these Valkerish at breakfast."

An hour later, Grissel was in the Great Hall speaking again to Magda and Adelaid when Wren and Auriel arrived. Alaric, Leif and Chad followed the Guardians. Grissel acted cordial.

"I hope the accommodations are to your liking, Great Ones."

"They served well enough," said Auriel.

"Your brother and Sigvard won't be joining us for breakfast?"

"Avatar tends to his charge and Mirit sleeps after a night of watchfulness."

Grissel tried to hid her distaste, but some crept into her voice. "She cares so much for a varlet?"

"As I said, he is well-known and well-liked."

"Please, Great Ones." She motioned to a table filled with food. Once seated, four varlets, two boys and two older men, served them. "We have varlets who serve us."

"Old men and boys," said Wren, nodding her thanks to Chad for filling her cup with cider.

"The age doesn't matter. From birth they are taught to serve. That is why they are bred."

"Bred?" echoed Wren, incredulous.

At the hostile reaction, Chad paused in filling Auriel's cup. Auriel nudged him to continue when Adelaid glared at him.

"Ja. Don't you breed your varlets?" Adelaid's voice challenged the Guardians and Chad.

"No. Ours enter service willingly," said Auriel.

Adelaid glanced to Magda and both laughed. "Willingly? Since when does a varlet do anything willing?"

"They come to bed willingly." Magda winked at Chad. He blushed.

Wren tore off a piece of bread to cover her growing irritation.

85

Auriel spoke, "If you breed varlets, then what do you do for farmers and craftsmen?"

"Their path is determined at birth. Same as the girls," said Grissel.

Wren could only keep her temper for so long. "No one has free choice?"

Auriel laid a restraining hand on Wren's arm. "What she means is we allow our varlets and Sigvards to make their own decision. That way their service is from the heart."

"Which is why the *heart* of your Sigvard cares for this varlet," accused Adelaid.

The intensity of anger in Wren's brilliant green eyes made Adelaid recoil.

Grissel intervened. "Great One, please understand. Such concern for a varlet is unusual to us. Only a few times has *lufu* happened. Using a varlet to breed is one thing, choosing one for a mate is forbidden. Seeing your Sigvard has done so causes objections among our sisters."

Wren's hot glare turned to Grissel. "We did not mean to cause disruption. We are simply making our way to Manheim to greet our sister Valkerish. The accident was unfortunate. However, our ways are not up for debate or judgment by you or anyone else."

"Then the sooner we are on our way the better," said Grissel.

"We?"

"We plan to accompany you to Manheim and present you to High Priestess Ludmilla. When your varlet is well enough to travel, of course."

Auriel and Wren exchanged cautious, conferring glances. "Very well," said Auriel.

"Now, let us speak no more of our differences as we break bread together," said Grissel.

Avatar answered a knock at the door. Chad entered carrying a tray of food and drink. Avatar placed a finger to his lips then pointing to Mirit, who slept curled up in a chair beside the bed, a blanket over her.

Chad put the tray down on a side table. "How is he?" he whispered.

"The fever is gone. In few days he should be fine."

"Good."

"Do I smell food?" asked Nigel, his eyes slowly opening.

"Breakfast. If you feel up to eating," replied Chad.

"If he doesn't I do." Mirit yawned and stretched. "Glad you're awake." She felt Nigel's forehead and smiled. "Fever's gone."

"I feel weak as a babe and have a headache."

"From the delirium," said Avatar.

Sheepish in regard, Nigel said, "I hope I wasn't too bad."

Avatar flashed a teasing grin. "I sent for Mirit to help control you."

Nigel turned to her. "Do I even want to know what I did or said?"

"Later." She smiled and kissed his forehead.

"I wouldn't do that anymore, Mirit," said Chad in the Ancient to get their attention.

"Do what?" she returned in the Ancient.

"Show affection or preference to Nigel. It is causing trouble with the Sigvard. At breakfast, Grissel spoke to Wren and Auriel about your unusual concern. They only use *varlets* for breeding, choosing one for a mate is forbidden."

"Mate?" she repeated, briefly startled. Nigel smiled, making her shy.

"Ay. Interest is prompting Grissel to have the Sigvard accompany us to Manheim when Nigel is fit to travel."

"I need to speak to Wren and Auriel," said Avatar.

"I'll go with you. I was told to bring the tray and promptly return." They left.

Mirit grew awkward. "Are you hungry? I'll get—" She stirred to rise, when he stopped her.

"Why do you avoid the subject? Does thought of marrying me repulse you?" he asked with a hint of pain

"No!"

"Then what? I told you my heart, but for months you remain silent."

She swallowed back her emotion to speak. "I have wrestled with my feelings since you told me. Yet wanted to be certain they were genuine and not the result of gratitude."

She avoided looking at him so he couldn't read her eyes but her voice and posture made him wary. "And?"

She looked at him, her eyes moist, heightening the turquoise hue. "Watching you fall into the river was frightening, but when you weren't breathing and Avatar blew air into your mouth, the reality I might lose you terrified me! I knew then it isn't gratitude. I love you, Nigel."

He laughed in joyful relief, kissing her hand. "How I've longed to hear you say that."

She relaxed, yet looked regretful. "I'm sorry it took so long, but I needed time for my mind and heart to become settled."

"You know I understand. I didn't hold any bitterness or anger when I returned home, but I hadn't been around my family for years and being thrust back into the role of eldest son and brother was uncomfortable at first. They all had expectations I didn't believe I could fulfill."

"You have, and more," she insisted. "Coming to Tunlund for Titus not only took courage, but love and commitment."

He smiled warm and tender. "Our relationship is stronger and I thank Jor'el. And I am thankful for you."

"You weren't always."

"No. Still, it is amazing to see what can happen when one lets go of anger and disappointment."

"I'm not angry. Although I get frustrated when I have lapses in memory. Some things I recall vividly, some things are vague, disjointed, and still others I don't recall at all."

He squeezed her hand. "Eldric said he never saw such an extent of restoration, and he's the premier Guardian physician. Jor'el blessed you by giving back almost all of what you lost. Don't minimize it."

She grinned. "I'm not. I am eternally grateful. Only I'm still learning how to cope when those lapses happen."

At a knock on the door, they exchanged glances of cautious concern since they spoke openly about their affection. Before Mirit reached the door, it opened and Avatar entered.

The Guardian wryly smiled. "I thought my knocking would give you both time to recover from whatever you were discussing."

She chuckled and slapped his arm. "What did Wren and Auriel say?"

Avatar replied in the Ancient, "They confirm Grissel is escorting us to High Priestess Ludmilla. We best play our roles more carefully. That starts by you leaving while I feed Nigel."

"I can feed myself."

Mirit placed a slice of cheese and a piece of sausage on a small loaf of flat bread. "I haven't eaten either."

Downstairs, Mirit met Wren and Auriel at the main door to the courtyard. "Morning, Great Ones," she mumbled, finishing her food.

Already in a sour mood, Wren scowled at the address.

"We heard the varlet is much improved," said Auriel.

"Ja. The fever is gone, but it will be a day or two before he is strong enough to travel."

"Should give us time to observe our sisters," said Auriel, drawing immediate dispute from Wren.

"Sisterhood is formed and proven over time, not during a single meal."

"Which is why I said *observe* to determine if they are true sisters. In the warrior sense." She pointed to a training exercise taking place between the stables and east wing. "For strategic purposes."

Wren grinned in sly approval.

Elfrida lead the exercise in mock combat of four other Sigvard. She was a large, strong woman with a voice to match, barking out orders.

"Your blades are lightweight and too flexible to do much damage," said Mirit.

Insulted, Elfrida confronted Mirit. She stood a head taller and thirty pounds heavier so she glared down her nose at Mirit. "These are practice weapons for the younger less experienced of our sisters. Once they master it, they move up in rank."

"Interesting. But if they grow accustomed to the weight and movement with such weapons, how will they know how to handle a real sword should they be engaged before graduating?"

Elfrida pulled her sword from the sheath strapped to her back. "Mine appears to be a real sword compared your puny stick. Could you handle me?"

"I ask a question and you offer a challenge?"

"You refuse?" scoffed Elfrida. "So much for courage."

"So much for brains if you think brawn is the only thing that can save you."

"I said observe, not insult," chided Auriel.

"You are as cowardly as your Sigvard."

Auriel's vibrant jade eyes flashed at Elfrida. "Beware, mortal. I can kill you where you stand."

"Elfrida!" Magda hurried over. "You insult our guests."

"Forgive me. My temper got the best of me," said Elfrida in reluctant apology.

"It is not from me you must ask forgiveness." Magda motioned to Auriel.

Elfrida's resistance proved momentary as she gazed into Auriel's eyes. She got down on one knee. "Forgive me, Great One. My mouth often speaks before my head can reason."

With fixed features, Auriel looked down at Elfrida. "Then Mirit is correct. You rely more on your size and strength. Forgiveness is granted. However, a lesson is needed." She turned to Mirit, the command still in her eyes. "Teach her a lesson."

Mirit fought to keep the surprise from her face and sent quick look to Wren. The Guardian huntress did not appear pleased yet remained silent. "As you say, Great One," she said to Auriel.

Mirit and Elfrida took their places, and a crowd gathered.

Wren seized Auriel's arm and hastily said, "I hope you know what you're doing."

"I do." Auriel spied Chad, Alaric and Leif at the entrance to the stables. She smiled at Chad, but the squire did not relax.

Mirit just removed her cloak and drew her sword when Elfrida attacked. Mirit barely parried, Elfrida's sheer force and weight drove her backwards and into a stable post. They came together at the hilt, the strain showed on Mirit's face when Elfrida pressed her full weight against her. She stomped on Elfrida's foot to distract her and gain some leverage, but Elfrida slammed her against the post then shoved her sideways to the ground. Mirit had to get control of the situation or suffer the worst of it.

Elfrida made a downward hack. On one knee, Mirit used both hands to hold the sword level and block the attack. In a quick fluid movement, she shoved Elfrida's blade to one side, her own hands braced on the ground where she balanced herself and did a swift sweeping kick and took Elfrida's feet out from under her.

For being large, Elfrida moved swift to rise and attack. She put all her anger and might into each blow, forcing Mirit to use both hands to parry. Elfrida used all her strength and determination to get at Mirit and ignored footing and balance. Mirit sidestepped an attack, making Elfrida stumble. Avoiding an awkward defensive swipe, Mirit came up from behind and struck Elfrida between the shoulder blades with the hilt, sending her to her knees.

"That could have been a dagger," said Mirit.

Angry, Elfrida threw dirt at Mirit, temporarily blinding her and rose to attack. Mirit saw enough to parry and rolled up Elfrida's sword arm to come from behind. She kicked the back of Elfrida's right knee, causing it to buckle. Elfrida maintained her balance and only stumbled. An enraged shout followed as she whirled about making a swipe capable of slicing Mirit in two if she hadn't dove under the blade and rolled away. Mirit sprung to her feet and assumed the Jor'ellian defensive stance, right sword arm raised above her head, left arm straight out before her for balance.

There was a brief pause in which Elfrida surveyed the unusual stance. The moment Elfrida moved to attack, Mirit joined both hands to arc the sword above her head and met the charge. The force of her blade knocked Elfrida to one side, exposing her back. Using the flat of the blade, Mirit smacked Elfrida hard and sent her sprawling to the ground stunned and winded. Mirit labored to breathe and she braced her feet to remain standing. Elfrida was a powerful opponent.

Chad rushed over to support Mirit. "Are you all right?"

She nodded, still recovering her breath.

Several of the Sigvard helped Elfrida, who grimaced in pain.

Hot with anger, Adelaid confronted Mirit. "You tried to kill her!"

Auriel pulled Adelaid from Mirit's face. "No! A lesson needed to be learned. Not just Elfrida, but all of you! A quick mind can be as dangerous as a strong blade. You see the size difference between them, but Mirit won. She outthought Elfrida, who let her strength guide her rather than use her mind to anticipate a smaller more agile opponent."

Mirit sheathed her sword and sat on a nearby bench. Chad placed her cloak about her shoulders. Despite being warm from the bout, the morning was cold. Alaric fetched a bucket with a ladle and offered her water, which she drank.

Grissel rushed over. "What is going on?"

"A friendly bout," said Auriel.

"No! She tried to kill Elfrida, same as this one did Rae." Adelaid gestured at Mirit and Wren.

"I acted in self-defense, while Mirit defended an insult to her Valkerish!"

"Is this true?" demanded Grissel.

Adelaid hesitated to reply, but did so after Magda poked her in the ribs. "Ja. Elfrida called this Great One a coward," she said of Auriel.

Grissel's jowls tightened in rage. "Then Elfrida got the smarting she deserved for insolence, didn't she?" She spoke to the others. "As will any one of you for insulting our guests!" She turned to Auriel and Wren but spoke in a calmer voice. "For the duration of your stay, perhaps it would be best to refrain from such bouts."

"We shall do better. We shall confine ourselves to the main house," said Wren.

Grissel was taken back. "Great One, I would not even suggest such a thing."

"I said before we did not mean to cause disruption. Since that has happened, we shall take it upon ourselves to remove the disruption."

Wren signaled Mirit, Chad, Alaric and Leif to follow. Inside, Auriel caught up to her fellow Guardian.

"I don't think that was wise."

"Your test caused the trouble I'm trying to rectify." Wren headed upstairs to Nigel's room.

Nigel sat up propped against pillows with Avatar beside the bed. Mirit plopped in the chair on the opposite side of the bed; a disgruntled huff escaping and she rotated her shoulders.

"You look flush and dirty. What were you doing?" asked Nigel.

"Fighting," she grumbled.

"What?"

"A lesson," said Auriel.

"To you, but not to Elfrida. She fought hard. Wild, but hard."

"Someone explain," said Nigel, firmly.

By the end of Wren's commentary, his annoyed glance shifted between Auriel and Mirit.

"It wasn't my idea, but how could I refuse?" said Mirit, defensively.

"I admit it didn't turn out as I hoped, but it wasn't fruitless. We learned they are driven by emotion and not logic or skill," said Auriel.

"Elfrida at least," groused Mirit.

"And Adelaid, and Magda. Both of whom become combative over trifles."

"She has a point," began Chad. "The Sigvard are passionate and accept no speech from a varlet. I've been cuffed a couple of times for just acknowledging an order."

"We tried to warn all of you," said Alaric.

Nigel nodded. "You did. Unfortunately, warnings are sometimes difficult to fully appreciate if you don't have an understanding of the situation. We can only hope and pray our lack of understanding hasn't compromised our mission."

"There is still wine in the jug and bread left over from breakfast," said Avatar.

"You said it is not uncommon to pray, correct?" Nigel said to Alaric.

"Ja."

"Then you and Leif keep watch in the hall while we do so."

Once the door closed, Avatar poured the wine into the largest cup. Nigel changed his position to sit crossed legged under the covers. Wren fetched an unlit candle from the table and placed it on the bed in front of Nigel. Auriel placed the bread beside the candle. Chad took the matches and flint from Avatar's knapsack and also placed them beside the candle. They formed a semi-circle around the bed. Mirit stood beside the head of the bed opposite Avatar, who held the cup. Chad stood next to Mirit, then Auriel and Wren.

Nigel spoke in the Ancient. "Great Jor'el, creator of the universe we come before you with bread and wine to pay homage, beseeching you for strength and wisdom." He stuck a match. "May this, your light, give us insight into this enemy who threatens us." He lit the candle.

"*Tangiel,*" the others said.

Nigel took the cup from Avatar. "May this wine give strength to our hearts and spirits to complete our task." He drank and handed the flask to Mirit, who repeated what he said before drinking and giving it to Chad who did the same, as did, Auriel, Wren and lastly, Avatar. Once Avatar finished drinking, he set the cup on the floor beside him.

Nigel took the bread. "May this bread give strength to our frail bodies in conjunction with the wine to strengthen our hearts." He broke off a piece and ate. The rest did the same in turn. When he received the bread, he placed it next to the candle. "To your will we commend our prayers, our lives, and our mission. *Tangiel.*"

"*Tangiel*," the others repeated.

With all put back, Auriel asked Nigel, "When will you be fit to travel?"

"Tomorrow."

"So soon?" Mirit felt his forehead. "We left Erik's too soon, let's not do it again."

"I feel better than when we left Erik's."

"Your fever wasn't gone then."

"It is now. And I have spent an entire day in bed, unlike last time."

"It would be too conspicuous for us to remain here too long," said Avatar.

"Ay. But no more fights or testing," said Nigel in feigned scolding of Mirit, who rolled her eyes.

Auriel smiled. "Wren, Mirit and I will simply mingle about the house."

"Don't you mean snoop?" asked Wren.

"Of course she does. It goes along with her version of a *lesson*," said Mirit, flashing a smirk to Nigel before leaving with the Guardians.

Downstairs they found Grissel and Magda.

"Ah, Grissel, good news. The varlet is well enough to be on our way first thing tomorrow morning," said Auriel.

"Really?"

"My brother has a healer's touch."

"With the weather so cold and harsh, do you not fear a relapse?"

Wren regarded Grissel with skepticism. "I thought you didn't care for varlets? Why this sudden concern for his welfare?"

Grissel flashed an awkward smile. "Simply trying to be a good host and accommodate your concern, Great One."

"Is this genuine concern or that you and the Sigvard will not be ready to leave by morning?"

"We shall be ready, Great One."

"Whether you are or not doesn't matter. We did not ask for your company." Grissel subdued, Wren smiled and changed the subject. "What do you do for amusement?"

"Pardon?" asked Grissel surprised by the abrupt switch in topics.

"Amusement. Fun. Do you have a library for reading? What about sport?"

"Other than mock combat," added Mirit, dryly.

"Ja, we play cards and read," said Grissel, still baffled.

"Although not as we once did. The times are too precarious for such frivolity," said Magda, disdain creeping into her voice.

"Did you learn nothing from earlier? Or do the Valkerish need to give you personal instruction?" inquired Auriel.

"No, Great One."

"Then, as host, entertain us."

"Great One, Magda and I were discussing our departure. Let me entertain you while she sees to our sisters' readiness and the feast."

Mirit grew rigid at hearing the word *feast*. "What feast?"

"We always feast before departing the outpost since we never know if it will be our last meal or the last time we see a sister in this life."

Although the explanation did little to ease Mirit's concern, Auriel said, "Very well. Proceed."

Magda saluted and left while Grissel provided entertainment. For the remainder of the morning and early afternoon, she introduced Auriel, Wren and Mirit to various Sigvard amusements. Despite her earlier uneasiness concerning the feast, Mirit knew how to play *hasenpfeffer* and *dry bones* from her trading days in Tunlund. Anything requiring hand and eye coordination, Wren immediately mastered. Auriel stirred the competitive spirit of the Sigvard by betting on her fellow Valkerish or Mirit in their respective games. When finished exploited their host, Grissel escorted them to the library. From there, she excused herself to see to the evening feast.

The room only contained two-dozen books, not enough to be considered a true library, but enough to get a sense of Soren society. Wren and Mirit thumbed through the books.

"They're not very literate people," said Wren.

Mirit frowned in studying the book she held. "We may share a common language but there are too many unfamiliar terms for me to clearly understand."

Wren flipped through another book. "Most of the text is about warfare or tales extolling the virtues of individual Valkerish."

"How many Valkerish?"

Wren read a few pages. "Eight. Five females and three males. One male was a healer, another familiar with agriculture, and the third, believed to control the weather."

Mirit replaced her book on the shelf. "What about the females?"

Wren flipped several more pages for the information. "Freja appears to be the leader and is referred to as the Protector of Soren. One gives the law and instruction about religion and government. Another is associated with the sea; a fourth is mentioned along with the seasons while the fifth," she paused in thoughtful consideration, "sounds very much like what I can do."

"Control animals?" Auriel read over Wren's arm.

She tilted the book to accommodate Auriel. "Actually, all the descriptions are too familiar, if you understand my meaning."

"You mean Guar—" began Mirit, but stopped when Auriel laid a hand on her shoulder.

"Too soon to speculate. Besides it goes against what is believed."

"The wolves were controlled by some kind of power," said Wren.

"How? Based upon what we do know, they don't have a central belief system, so where would this power come from if not … your kind?" asked Mirit.

Wren put her book back on the shelf. "I believe we'll learn more in Manheim than from these books."

"What about the feast? Did you read anything connected with it? I remember how uncomfortable Nigel and Chad were in Tunlund."

"Perhaps Alaric and Leif can tell us about it," said Auriel.

Going upstairs they found Alaric and Leif again outside Nigel's room.

"Join us," said Auriel to the brothers, and entered the chamber.

Nigel stood by the window gazing out at the countryside. Chad put another log in the stove and Avatar packed his knapsack.

"I was wondering aloud about you three. Any news?" asked Nigel.

"They're coarse gamblers, as passionate and reckless in their games as in arms," said Auriel.

"Goes along with not being very literate. The few books they possess are about the Valkerish. Nothing of science, medicine, or engineering," said Mirit.

"Not by choice," began Alaric. "The Valkerish are selective concerning to whom knowledge given, and limited to the type of learning needed for their respective livelihoods."

"The priestesses have a large library in Manheim. As farmers, we are taught what is needed for agriculture and not much else. They say there is no need," said Leif.

"Where you born on a farm or was it chosen for you?" asked Wren.

"Both," replied Alaric. "Being first born, I would take our father's place in the fields. Leif always had a way with animals and wanted to study about caring for sick animals. Alas, the local priestess forbade it since we already have a man who care for them in our region."

"One way to keep the populace in line, deny them access to knowledge by which they could better themselves," said Avatar.

"Do you have a book about your history or beliefs?" asked Mirit.

"Not personally," began Alaric. "When we attend the local temple for holy days, the priestess recites the history of that day and the virtues of the Valkerish it honors."

"Do these holy days include feasts?"

"Ja. Some more elaborate than others."

"What happens at these feasts?"

"Why are you interested in feasts?" asked Nigel.

Mirit's response and gaze were direct. "They are having a feast tonight. Grissel said they do so before every departure from the outpost since it may be a Sigvard's last meal."

Nigel's jowls flexed, his eyes narrow on Alaric and Leif. "Do you make sacrifice during your feasts?"

"No," said Alaric.

"You mentioned human sacrifice!"

"The Tavar!" he insisted, growing uneasy. "The Valkerish never required sacrifice."

"They do ask a place remain vacant with a full plate of food and drink, incase they decide to bless us with their presence," said Leif.

"Has that ever happened?" asked Chad.

"Ja. Once. When our father was young. The planting feast was held on our family's farm. He said a tall, beautiful woman appeared. She called herself Wilda, and so pleased by the hospitality, she blessed grandfather and he had his best harvest ever. Father married mother and built a second house on our lands. He named our sister after Wilda."

"Sounds like the Valkerish are benevolent," said Chad.

"Ja. That is why we fear the Tavar."

"Then there should be no sacrifice this evening since Grissel claims they serve the Valkerish and not the Tavar," said Mirit.

"This should be interesting," said Nigel.

"You feel well enough to attend?"

"I'm up, aren't I? I don't feel fatigued or dizzy."

"You cannot attend unless you serve," said Alaric.

"Then I'll serve."

Mirit lightly bit her lip to stop laughing but spoke to his baffled reaction. "You don't know how. At the inn you filled my cup from the right and not the left."

"You remember how a servant is supposed to fill your cup, but not much else about your childhood?"

Chad grinned and said, "I told her what you did wrong."

"Then you can tell me what to do right before tonight."

Sigvard filled the great hall. Aromas of various types of food mingled with the smell of a fire in the large hearth and burning torches for light. Three places of honor were reserved for Auriel, Mirit and Wren.

"Welcome," said Grissel. She stood and motioned to the vacant seats. "Your brother may join the sisters at the other table."

Auriel sat on Grissel's right and next to Adelaid. Wren and Mirit sat on Grissel's left with Magda next to Mirit. Avatar did as bade. Chad, Nigel, Alaric and Leif were ushered away by the other varlets.

Grissel remained standing as they took their places. "It is good to see your varlet is well enough to join us."

"It is good to see he is well enough to do anything," said Mirit.

Grissel flashed a tolerant smile then spoke aloud. "Sisters! Tonight we feast before making pilgrimage to Manheim to join our guests in paying tribute to High Priestess. Let us thank the Valkerish for this bounty and their blessing of choosing us to serve them. Since we are honored to have two from the place of beginning, let us enjoy this feast in their names." She took her cup and raised it in salute. "To Auriel, the Valkerish of Justice, who dealt justly with Elfrida for her insolence. To Wren, the Valkerish of Wisdom, who choses discretion over force."

The Sigvard stood and raise their cups. "To Auriel and Wren!"

Mirit remained seated trying to mask her uncertainty. However, at Grissel's prompting glance she began to rise, but Wren stopped her.

"Your kind tribute is overwhelming and more than we ask of our Sigvard. Please," Wren said to all, "be seated and enjoy."

Grissel signaled the Sigvard to sit. "What tribute do you require of your Sigvard?"

"Nothing."

"You ask no sacrifice, no show of loyalty of any kind?" asked Magda.

Mirit stiffened, her eyes narrowed in challenge. "Have you ever seen an animal sacrifice and heard the squeals of terror as it is being slaughtered?"

Magda shifted a bit uneasily in her seat. "No."

"Then how can you claim it is an act of loyalty?"

"Have you seen it?" asked Adelaid, coming to Magda's defense.

Mirit's face grew fixed, and an angry edge to her voice. "Ja. It is barbaric and serves no purpose." She felt a hand on the back of her left shoulder. Nigel leaned over to fill her tankard. She briefly met his gaze and saw his cautious warning. The Sigvard didn't notice the exchange or at least made no comment, rather continued on the topic of sacrifice.

"We have to kill to eat," said Adelaid, drawing Mirit back to the conversation.

"Killing to survive is one thing. Killing an innocent beast to satisfy another's bloodlust is an entirely different matter. It is solely for ego and dominance that such a requirement is made."

"Our Valkerish do not require sacrifice," said Grissel.

"Then why test me by such questions?"

"Your attitudes are different towards varlets and warfare. We wanted to know in what other ways you differ before we reach Manheim."

"You could simply ask rather than provoke," scolded Wren.

"From now on we shall remember that, Great One," said Grissel, a look of warning to Adelaid and Magda.

Fortunately, the rest of the night passed in relative civility. They even treated Avatar with a limited amount of respect. Still, he chose to speak only when addressed, preferring to listen and observe. Part of his observation was Nigel, who appeared to be doing well for his first night of activity. The true test of his endurance would happen on the journey.

Chapter 7

SIGVARDS ASSEMBLED IN THE COURTYARD. In total, twenty waited, but only four saddled horses. Grissel inspected the harnesses and supplies packed in the saddlebags. The others arrived.

"Great Ones, I told you we would be ready."

"Who is to ride?" asked Auriel.

"Both of you and your Sigvard. Along with myself as your guide."

"Some of the snow was so deep we had to wear shoes. Will the horses pass?" asked Mirit.

"We know a less snowy route from here to Manheim."

"Will it take longer?" asked Wren.

"No, Great One."

Wren's face showed her discomfort at the title. "Very well. Let us be off." She leapt into the saddle without touching the stirrup.

"Show off," said Mirit in a low snicker.

Avatar held the bridle of Mirit's horse. "She'll even help the horse with speed so as not to follow anyone," he said in private jest to her.

"You brother is impertinent toward superiors?" chided Grissel

"I'll see he keeps his tongue from now on," said Auriel.

Mirit spoke in Avatar's defense. "I spoke to him, Great One."

"Then both of you need to hold your tongues," replied Auriel without pause or break in character. "Lead on," she commanded Grissel.

Nigel joined Avatar to help curtail the warrior's anger when Mirit left. "*Fois,*" he spoke the Ancient for *peace.*

"Follow in single file," began Magda in harsh command to Nigel and the others. "It is important to stay in the horses' tracks if you want to make it through the snow!"

Without another word, they fell in behind Magda.

Once out of the wood, following the horse tracks proved more crucial in deeper snow. The weather remained mild with shafts of sun peaking through the trees. Conversation kept to a minimum due to the mode of single file travel. To talk, often required yelling.

Nigel walked directly behind Avatar, with Chad following him. He didn't feel weak like he did when leaving the settlement, and he attributed that to Avatar's diligence and praying over the remedies. Once again he owed the loyal Guardian his life. Not that Avatar kept count.

Oh, he does to tease me. But never holds me accountable. For that I should thank him. Simply saying 'thanks' after so many times ... His gaze shifted to Auriel some distance ahead. *She accepted the farmer's gratitude in a manner I've never seen a Guardian do and without objection to having a day named for her. Then the feast. Wren was uncomfortable but she wasn't—No. Avatar says she knows better.*

Avatar glanced back. "How are you doing? Any fatigue or headache?"

"No. Well, at least no headache," he admitted at seeing skepticism. "Fatigue is mild and no fever," he added in his usual banter, but when Avatar shook his head in wry response, he added, "Avatar. Thank you."

The Guardian smiled and faced forward.

"He deserves more than thanks. They all do," said Chad.

Nigel looked askew to Chad. "I know, but what do you mean?"

He shrugged. "I guess I mean a token of appreciation. We give gifts to each other on special occasions, why not to them?"

Piqued, Nigel scolded in low voice. "Because the notion borders on blasphemy."

"I don't mean an offering."

Nigel looked past Chad to Alaric and Leif, some twenty feet behind. The Sigvard trailed after the brothers. "Beware of such talk, Chad. You must keep your wits. These Valkerish are still unknown to us."

"They seem kind from what we're told."

"*Seem*, Chad, *seem*. Bear that in mind until we know for certain."

"If you say so."

Up ahead, Mirit turned in the saddle. Nigel spoke to Chad, making the latter frown.

Magda walked behind Mirit's horse. "Is the varlet worth such affection?"

Curious, Mirit studied Magda a moment before answering. "Have you not felt affection for a man?"

She heaved an awkward shrug. "Men are only trouble."

"You don't sound convinced of that."

"It is not a subject we speak of."

"Why?"

Grissel rode far enough in the lead not to overhear; still Magda spoke with caution. "We just don't. Sigvards are among the chosen few and taught from when we are weaned to be strong and independent. Trained in arms and service to the Valkerish. Men are a distraction."

Mirit chuckled. "They can be a distraction. They can also be supportive, kind and generous."

Magda glanced to Nigel, her expression skeptical. "He is all that?"

"And much more."

She shook her head. "Your ways are strange."

"I can say the same about you." When Mirit turned forward, Grissel stopped at the edge of the trees and waited. Once she, Auriel and Wren joined Grissel, the Sigvard leader spoke.

"We have reached the edge of Sigwald. It is best to rest before proceeding into the open. The way will be difficult until we reach the meadow." She dismounted.

"How far is that?" asked Wren.

"A few hours. Magda, tell the others to rest and take nourishment."

Magda saluted and departed.

"Is there a settlement or a place to pass the night in the meadow?" asked Auriel.

"Ja. We have an outpost every day's journey between here and Manheim. Sigvard rarely mingle among the common folk. When they see us, it usual means we have come to levy justice. Limiting contact until then adds to our authority." Grissel removed the provision from her saddlebag and handed the food to Mirit, Auriel, and Wren.

"Don't you mean intimidation?" Mirit sat by her horse to eat.

Although Grissel wasn't pleased, Adelaid spoke. "Do not the populace tremble at your arrival? Or is your employment similar to your lack of tribute, shallow and trivial? Duty blinded by love for a varlet."

Mirit bolted to her feet.

Auriel stepped between them to stop confrontation. "Enough! Both of you will hold your tongue for the remainder of the journey."

Mirit's balked at the rebuke and looked to Wren with concern.

"I have spoken. You do not need Wren's permission to obey me."

Gazing into Auriel's eyes, Mirit felt compelled to agree. "As you wish, Great One."

Adelaid gripped the hilt of her sword when Auriel looked directly at her. "As the Valkerish commands."

"Return to your post."

Adelaid saluted and left.

"You may continue eating," she said to Mirit then drew Grissel away to continue speaking.

Wren's displeasure softened to an encouraging grin and motioned for Mirit to sit and eat. Nigel, Chad and Avatar gathered across the way and appeared ignorant of the disruption. Nigel's reclined against a tree facing in her direction but spoke to Chad, then chuckled and faced forward. In catching his eye, she visually attempted to convey concern, to which he made a questioning tilt of his head. Under the circumstance, she couldn't just go over and speak to him so she cautiously turned her head to look at Auriel, who engaged in conversation with Grissel, the latter gesturing to the darkening sky. He followed her glance with some curiosity. Unfortunately, their visual exchange became interrupted when Grissel announced they would be leaving in five minutes if they were to make the outpost before the storm struck. Any discussion had to wait.

Twenty minutes later, they climbed to a plateau where the snow reached the horses knees. It became imperative for those on foot to stay in the horse tracks. Add to that a storm began with winds howling. The snow fell heavier, swirling and threatening to become a blizzard.

Grissel turned in the saddle to survey the group. "Magda! Pick up the pace! But watch your step! I'm going to start the descent sooner!"

Magda waved an acknowledgement and relayed the instructions.

"How steep is the descent?" asked Auriel.

"Not too steep, but slippery in this weather."

Heading due south, Grissel started her descent from the plateau to the meadow. Rather than hunkering down to minimize their profile to the storm, Grissel, Auriel, Wren and Mirit leaned back in the saddle to help their horses from slipping. No use keeping the hood or cloak closed against the howling wind, so Mirit didn't try, concentrating on steering her horse. The animal slipped several times but managed to right itself before completely falling.

Guardians were not bothered by the weather like mortals. All the same, Auriel and Wren found the storm annoying in dealing with constantly slipping horses. Wren's mount fell forward, tossing her over its head. The horse managed to right itself and skidded down the rest of the way downhill but Wren didn't stop tumbling till she reached the bottom. She batted aside the cloak to stand. Upon rising, her left foot gave way and she fell to her knees.

"Wren!" Avatar slid down on the snow to her.

"I'm all right. Just a twisted ankle. It got caught in the stirrup when the beast threw me. I'll manage." She stood and reached for the horse, but missed due to stumbling. He caught the reins, tossed them over the horse's head and hoisted her into the saddle.

Auriel pulled her horse to a stop. "Are you all right?"

Avatar flashed a teasing grin. "I'd say more wounded pride in falling off a horse than pain from a twisted ankle."

"You can't even stop when someone's hurt, can you?" Auriel jerked her horse to move and join Grissel.

"Leave her be," warned Wren.

"You said that before, but twice she's scolded me. What is wrong?"

"I also said I would tell you when I know. For now we must play our parts, no matter how rough it maybe." She turned from him at hearing Grissel speak.

"The way is level from here and the snow not so deep. In two hours we should reach the outpost."

Not so deep was relative considering the snow reached halfway up the horses' legs. During this part of the journey Mirit and Grissel hunched down to keep the cloaks closed. Mirit removed her helmet, pulled up the hood and put the helmet over it to keep the hood in place. At least now her ears would stop hurting from the cold. She wanted to rub them warm, but that was wrong. If frostbitten, she could damage the skin. She was grateful for the sealskin boots and gloves with fur lining.

What am I saying? What about Nigel and Chad? They have to walk?

In the swirling white snow she could barely distinguish people. In fact, she couldn't see past two distinctive shapes fighting their way against the wind.

"We could lose people!" she called forward.

"Stop!" shouted Grissel. She took the rope from her saddlebag. "Keep the horses close. Mirit, tie this to your saddlebow then hand the rope to Magda. Magda will hand it back with instructions to keep hold of the rope and keep pace!"

Mirit did so, then Magda followed suit, telling Avatar, who told Nigel, then Chad, all the way back to Elfrida.

"I have it!" Elfrida's shout was dimly heard over the storm.

107

Mirit kept close watch of the rope. At the first sign of slack she would stop her horse and call ahead to Grissel. Concerned for Nigel, she kept looking back, hoping to see him and Chad, but only made out gray shapes behind Magda and Avatar. *Please, Jor'el keep him safe and whole.* So far the rope had not gone slack.

The cold and howling wind made the journey seem endless. The Sorens and Sigvard were hardy people while Mirit wished to get warm as soon as possible. Even in Tunlund winter was not so harsh. She smelled fire. Good. The sooner they were out of the blizzard the better.

From the veil of swirling white came the hazy image of a long house and several smaller out buildings including a rough-hewn barn and corral. Grissel called to the house and three Sigvard emerged.

Once at the house, Mirit dismounted and waited beside her horse. Avatar arrived first and appeared whole and hardy. Then again nothing seemed to affect him. Finally Nigel and Chad arrived, both looked weary, but in one piece. Leif and Alaric joined them.

"Inside!" said Grissel once everyone was accounted for.

The warmth of the fire felt good. Mirit, Nigel, Chad and several Sigvard sniffled. Cold tended to make the nose run. Mirit's hands were warm enough from the gloves to feel Nigel's forehead.

"I'm cold, not feverish," he said.

"I just wanted to make sure."

"Grissel," said the outpost commander. "What brings you here? Who are these Great Ones?"

"They have come for the place of beginning. We are taking them to Manheim. We will only be staying the night."

"Providing the storm is gone by morning," said Wren.

"Just so, Great One. Food and drink, commander"

"Come, varlets," she said to Alaric, Leif, Chad and Nigel.

Bread and hot cider were immediately served but it would take almost an hour for the main meal of sausage, potatoes, and onions to be ready. Not many spoke since they were more concerned about drying their wet clothes and eating.

The long house was divided into three rooms downstairs, two at either end with the main hall in the middle. Above the two side rooms were lofts for sleeping. A large hearth heated the main hall, with small stoves in each of the flanking rooms.

"Great Ones, you can use the west room. It is the largest," said Grissel.

"Very good. After eating we shall retire. The varlet looks pale, but did well," said Auriel. Nigel ate in the corner with Leif, Chad, and Alaric.

Indeed Nigel did better than expected, but Mirit took exception to Auriel's attitude. For all his role-playing, Nigel was still a prince and Auriel seemed to be forgetting that. *She seems to be forgetting a lot of things.* She caught the Guardian's eyes, only not so rough and commanding. Even so, she turned aside to finish her cider.

Wren noticed the exchange. "I think I'll go lie down. Mirit, lend me your shoulder."

"You are fatigued, Great One?" asked Magda.

"No, but I need to nurse my ankle. The quicker I'm off my feet, the better."

"I thought Valkerish can heal themselves?" said Adelaid stiffly.

"We can. Come morning, I will be fit. It would take a week for your ankle to heal."

Mirit let Wren lean on her as they left the table to enter the west room. Auriel and the others joined them. The room was furnished with one large bed, two bunk beds, hooks on the wall and two chests. In all the room could accommodate six, if two shared the bed.

"Chad, shut the door," said Wren as she sat on the foot chest.

"I thought you said you were all right?" asked Avatar.

"I am. The sprain is minor. I didn't need Mirit's help, I simply wanted to avoid more confrontation." She spoke the last part of the sentence to Auriel.

"I didn't mean to be gruff earlier, but like you, I wanted to avoid confrontation. I'm sorry."

"Apology accepted," said Mirit.

Auriel nodded. "Now rest." She went to tend to the stove and increase the heat.

"Is that what you meant earlier? A problem with Auriel?" Nigel asked Mirit in a low, conferring voice.

"She is taking her role to heart."

Auriel turned from checking the stove, so Nigel said aloud to Mirit, "You take the bed." He took the snowshoes off his back and placed them against the wall next to the bed.

Mirit understood his change in speech. "You're the one who's ill."

He shrugged. "Fine. You take one side, I'll take the other." He sat on the right side of the bed to remove his boots and didn't see her flush.

Avatar smiled at Mirit's embarrassment. "I'll be in the middle."

Nigel chuckled. "You're too big."

Avatar sat at the end of the bed.

"Fair enough." Nigel smiled, removed his cloak and sword and got under the covers.

Mirit removed her boots, cloak, sword, and helmet before climbing into bed. Nigel laid with his back to her. Although he teased her, he would never compromise her or break his Jor'ellian vow. *Not until marriage.* She privately smiled. Now that she spoke her heart, marriage didn't seem so frightening. She closed her eyes and fell asleep.

Mirit woke to hearing a rooster. She yawned and stretched but surprised when her feet touched someone. Avatar. She forgot he was there. She felt a stirring beside her and saw Nigel smiling at her.

"I hope you slept well. I know I did," he said.

"I slept very well, thank you."

He laughed, tossing aside the covers to sit up and pull on his boots. A pillow smacked the back of his head.

"I was tired."

Avatar chuckled and went to check his knapsack for supplies.

Auriel looked out the window. The morning sun glistening off new snow but no signs of clouds anywhere on the horizon. "Looks clear. We should be able to leave when everyone is ready." She left.

Grissel and the Sigvard assembled in the main room and bowed to Auriel when she emerged from the room.

"I hope all is well this morning, Great One?"

"It is. How far to Manheim?"

"Hard to say. The storm left several more inches of snow."

"Snow doesn't change the distance from one place to another. And the weather is clear."

"Manheim is two days from here, so if the weather holds, and we leave shortly, we could reach the next outpost by tonight."

"Excellent. A quick breakfast and we'll be off."

"What of Wren?" asked Adelaid.

"I'm fine." Wren emerged from the room and stomped her left foot.

"Your varlet didn't suffer a relapse?" asked Grissel.

"See for yourself," said Wren when Nigel, Mirit, and Chad joined them. Avatar, Alaric and Leif followed carrying knapsacks.

Grissel looked Nigel up and down. "His recovery is very impressive."

"I told you my brother has a healer's touch," said Auriel.

The order of travel followed the same pattern as the previous day. The weather may have been better, but the increase of snow made travel slower across the meadow. Two miles into the journey, they entered a thick patch of wood, mostly evergreens, where the snow was half the depth of the meadow, and in the shadier places, almost nonexistent.

Unlike the flat terrain of Sigwald, this forest was filled with ravines and inclines. A large stream wound its way through the trees forcing them to cross it multiple times. With a large amount of melting snow, the water ran at a good steady current.

During the crossings, Mirit closely watched Nigel make his way down the slick muddy inclines. The last thing they needed was for him to fall into cold water again. Despite the swift current, the stream only reached the top of Nigel's boots. Once he grabbed Avatar to keep from falling. Alaric slipped on the mud during the second crossing and landed on his rear in the water.

At the third crossing Grissel stopped on the bank. Here, the stream fed into a large pool before continuing over a twenty-foot rocky waterfall into a basin.

"How deep is it?" asked Wren.

"Perhaps waist deep. The water is running fast since I can't see the rocks in the center."

"Can we cross some place else?"

"No. The speed off the waterfall feeds the current and not much further down it joins the river. This is the final place to cross. The horses can make it, but we'll take a rope across for those on foot to use for balance." Grissel took the rope from her saddlebow and gave one end to Magda, who tied it to the tree closest to the pool.

"Nigel." Mirit waved him over to mount behind her.

"You will carry the varlet across?" asked Adelaid.

"He became ill because of falling into such frigid water. I don't want that to happen again."

"I can make it across, mistress," he said, eyes direct on Mirit.

She didn't flinch and firmly said, "No, you will mount, *varlet*." He curbed his natural annoyance at being spoken to in such a manner and reached for her hand, placing his other hand on the back of the saddle and stepped in the stirrup she cleared for him to mount behind her.

Auriel and Wren pushed their horses into the water in front of Grissel. Mirit kicked her horse to enter the water when motioned by Grissel. The Sigvard leader followed, letting out the rope as she went.

"Adelaid doesn't approve of your kindness to a varlet," said Nigel in the Ancient.

Mirit replied in the Ancient, "I don't care what she or any of the Sigvard think. I don't want to take the chance of you getting ill again."

"Just one of the things I love about you, you don't bow to convention."

"Really? That's funny, considering after we're wed I'll be a princess, then what about convention?"

He smiled. "Wed. Now, there's a pleasant thought."

Conversation stopped upon reaching the other side of the pool. Grissel swiftly drew her horse to a halt and dismounted to tie the rope to a tree. She said nothing as Nigel dismounted, her expression of disdain enough. Auriel also appeared displeased and Mirit switched back to normal speech.

"I didn't want to take a chance of him getting wet and falling ill again."

With his back to Grissel, Nigel glared at Auriel. Despite their role-playing he was a prince of Allon and commander of the mission. The Guardian carefully nodded, her expression turning agreeable.

"One at a time, send them across! Varlets first!" called Grissel.

Magda waved for Chad, Alaric and Leif. "You first, then the lad and you last," she said to Alaric, Chad and Leif respectively. "Hold on tight to the rope."

When Alaric reached the halfway point, Magda made Chad start his crossing. Alaric reached the other side safely, and Chad in the center of the pond, Leif was ordered to go.

"You next," said Magda to Avatar. "Adelaid, have the sisters line up for crossing. You and I will be last."

Avatar started crossing when Chad reached the other side and Leif in the center. Leif slipped but caught the rope and cautiously continued to the other side. One of the younger Sigvard followed Avatar. She became wary upon reaching the spot where Leif slipped, but not careful enough. She slipped and fell completely underwater, releasing the rope

"Karin!" called Magda.

She headed toward the falls. Avatar raced back into the water, but slipped and fell short of her. He lunged and snatched her, but they were too close to the falls, and went over.

"Avatar!" Nigel raced along the shoreline to the edge of the falls. Chad ran behind him.

Mirit dismounted beside them. "Where is he?"

Nigel shook his head, anxiously watching. Auriel, Wren and the others joined them at the water's edge.

"There!" Chad pointed. Avatar emerged but not the Sigvard.

"Where is Karin?" called Grissel to Avatar.

"I can't see her!"

"I do!" Auriel disappeared in a flash of light, startling Grissel and the other Sigvard. She reappeared at the end of the basin where the stream continued. Karin lay face down in the water caught between a log and the rocky shore. She lifted Karin in her arms and disappeared again, reappearing beside the others on shore.

Grissel roused herself from shock to ask, "Is she dead?"

"Not for long." Auriel spoke the Ancient then blew air into Karin's mouth. Three times she spoke and three times she blew air into Karin's mouth. She gasped and coughed. Auriel rolled her on her side so the water would come out of her mouth and not go back into her lungs.

"She lives!" said Grissel in amazement. All the Sigvard watched in awe when Auriel helped a dazed Karin to sit up.

Grissel fell to her knees, the other Sigvard following her example. "Great One! Never have I seen—You raised our sister from the dead! How can we thank you?"

Karin knelt before Auriel and took the Guardian's hand. "Command of me what you will, I pledge myself to your service, Great One."

Avatar climbed out of the water to hear Karin. He stiffened at the pledge of devotion, silver eyes staring at Auriel.

Auriel balked under his glare. "We shall speak of it at another time. For now, you must get warm. Build a fire for her," she instructed Grissel.

"Help them," said Wren to Alaric and Leif.

When Grissel, the Sigvard and brothers left to comply, Avatar grabbed Auriel's arm to keep her from following. His voice in low and harsh, as he spoke in the Ancient. "What was that about? She couldn't have been dead. None of us have the power of life and death."

Auriel's jowls became rigid with anger. "She wasn't breathing."

"Not breathing is one thing, being dead is something else. You deceived them."

She jerked away. "I did what was necessary, same as you with Nigel. If they are to take us to the Valkerish they must believe we are Valkerish."

Again, he stopped her from leaving. "Be sure you don't believe it."

Her eyes narrowed in irate suspicion. "Meaning what, *brother?*"

"Take care, Auriel. Too much is at stake, and by their reaction they have not seen such power."

"Remember, the Valkerish may be mortal," said Wren in warning.

Auriel made a hasty excuse. "It was a normal reaction to seeing a mortal in danger not calculated. Now, I'd like to see how she is doing."

Avatar let her go and she left. He continued speaking in the Ancient. "Some Guardians take duty too seriously when charged with a mission."

"Like you in Tunlund?" chided Chad. "You appear in a flash and rescue us from a fire, then a few days ago saved Nigel from the wolf and drowning. Auriel did the same for Karin. I see little difference." He left.

"Chad," called Nigel, yet careful not to draw attention.

"No, Nigel. He is young and cannot discern subtleties. To the young everything is black and white. You once thought the same," said Avatar.

"My lack of discernment led to horrible consequences."

"You can't make him avoid your mistakes. He must make his own choices."

Mirit shook her head. "The problem isn't Chad, it's Auriel. Whereas he's young, she should know better, especially being a Guardian."

"Sad to say, we Guardians aren't perfect," groused Avatar.

"No, but we shouldn't use duty to vent age-old grudges," said Wren.

"Meaning?"

"I don't know. You tell me why she's angry with you. She claims you abused her in the past."

"What?" he exclaimed in surprise, drawing attention.

"Is there a problem?" asked Grissel, rising from her seat at the fire.

"No," said Nigel. Grissel resumed her seat and focus on Karin so he switched back to the Ancient. "Think of what you did to *abuse* her. I'm going to try to speak to Chad."

Avatar delayed Wren. "Is she still angry after all these centuries because Kell disciplined her for striking me? I didn't report her. In fact, I felt responsible for what caused her anger and willing to let it pass."

She shrugged in uncertainty. "Hard to tell with her volatile nature."

"Stop being evasive!"

"I'm not. I just don't know yet. She has always been touchy and defensive, which is what made her hit you back then."

"If it is something that can jeopardize our mission—"

"I'll tell you. My ankle is one thing, but you don't need another fat lip." She moved toward the fire with him following.

At the fire, Auriel asked Avatar to mix a remedy for Karin. Since her tone was benign, he complied. Once Karin felt recovered enough to travel, they continued.

Several times during the journey Nigel longed for a moment to speak privately to Chad, not only about Auriel, but the mission. Unlike Tunlund, they had a set time to complete their task, but being joined by the Sigvard complicated the situation and hindered their movement, communication and planning.

Shortly after dark, they reached the outpost situated in a small clearing in the forest. The construction was similar to the other outpost. Nigel felt tired, almost too tired to eat, but he knew that was foolish. He took his bowl of potato-pea soup, a hunk of bread and a tankard of warm cider and sat with Alaric and Leif in the varlet's corner. Chad waited on Auriel. He said something to her and she replied. Nigel couldn't hear clearly though Auriel smiled and looked cheerful. Chad even bowed to her when calling her 'Great One'.

Are they both taking their roles too seriously? He defended her actions and said they deserve more than thanks—gifts. He felt sourness in his stomach. Across the way Avatar spoke privately to Wren. By their glances at Auriel and Chad, they sensed something was wrong. *But what? Jor'el, grant us time to speak and discern what is happening.*

That night, they were given the larger of the two flanking rooms for sleeping. Preoccupied, Nigel pulled off his boots and got into bed. Again Avatar sat at the end of the bed. This time, Nigel faced Mirit, so she turned to him.

"What's wrong?" she whispered.

He placed a finger to his lips as the others settled down for the night. Chad, Leif and Alaric slept on three of the four bunk beds. Although Guardians didn't require sleep, they did refresh themselves in a meditative state. Avatar did his meditation at the foot of the bed and could be instantly alert if needed. Wren convinced Auriel she would take the watch and allow Auriel the entire night to rest since Wren needed the previous night to heal her ankle and Auriel remained watchful.

At Avatar's signal the others were asleep or in meditation, Nigel whispered to Mirit in the Ancient. "Have you spoken to Chad?"

"No. His comments to Avatar troubling you?"

"Among other things, but I've not been able to speak to him. He seems more agreeable to Auriel than to my counsel."

She took his hand. "I'm sorry I can't ease your mind. I know how fond you are of him. I will try to speak to him tomorrow."

He rolled over on his back; a low, heartfelt sigh as he closed his eyes.

Chapter 8

THE NEXT DAY, Nigel appeared tired. Mirit felt his forehead, but no sign of fever, and he didn't say much, which was typical when troubled. Even before witnessing Nigel's nightmares brought on by deep-seated worry or agitation, the time spent together showed his tendency toward brooding silence. Concern for Chad must have kept him awake most of the night but she didn't notice his disturbance. Or else he curbed manifesting it to avoid waking her.

She sat beside him on his side of the bed watching him pull on his boots after feeling his forehead. "Are you rested enough to travel?"

He nodded.

"And your appetite?"

He didn't answer, adjusting the boots on his feet. He stood to buckle on his sword then gathered his cloak and snowshoes.

His reticence made her hesitate in either speaking or moving. Although not directed at her or due to her behavior, it pricked her. She looked up at feeling a hand on her shoulder. He still didn't speak but a small smile crossed his lips. She returned his smile and gathered her things before leaving the room together.

The rest of the group gathered at breakfast with the Sigvard. Chad went about his morning duties seemingly unaware of, or at worse, disinterested in Nigel's depressed state. Mirit hoped it was role-playing and not real apathy. She hardly imagined that, considering their close relationship, but Chad acted unusual this trip, and not like the stalwart companion and loyal friend in Tunlund.

After breakfast, she caught Chad's attention and waved him outside. "I need your help with my horse."

"What about Nigel? He's your varlet," said Chad, lightly.

"I want to talk to you about Nigel," she said in the Ancient. She handed him a horse brush.

Her change in speech gave him a moment's pause before replying in the Ancient. "Is he ill again?"

"No. He's worried about you."

"Me? Why?" He brushed the horse.

She put the bridle on the horse. "That should be obvious by the way you dressed down Avatar yesterday."

He rolled his eyes and continued to brush the horse.

She didn't let his teenage display of annoyance stop her. "You said something to upset him. He won't say what, only expressed concern."

"He took it the wrong way. He's been around *them* all his life. He can't see their worth or benevolence because of familiarity."

She snatched his arm, to stop his brushing. "Avatar petitioned for Nigel's healing. If anyone knows their worth, he does."

"So why can Avatar act in his capacity, but not Auriel? Because he is blinded by prejudice."

She stared incredulously at him. "I don't believe I'm hearing this from you."

"Nigel called it blasphemy," he scoffed.

"Mind your tongue! You are speaking of your lord and master."

He winced at the rebuke. "I thought my friend also, but I assumed wrongly. I won't do so again, my lady." He bowed, put down the brush and fetched the saddle.

She wanted to pursue the conversation, but the others arrived at the barn. She hoped to ease Nigel's mind, not add to his concern. When he spotted her, she carefully shook her head.

The journey began the same way, with the horses leading the way and the rest following on foot. From the outpost, they traveled another three miles in the forest; only the trees grew thinner in size and more spaced out allowing the snow to accumulate. From a small plateau, rugged snowcapped mountains appeared on the horizon.

Grissel stopped her horse to allow Auriel, Wren and Mirit to join her. "The largest peak is Astrid, home of the Valkerish. In the foothills is Manheim with the temple at the base of Astrid."

"How much further?" asked Auriel.

"Ten miles."

"Ten miles?" echoed Mirit, gaping at the mountain.

Grissel smiled. "Ja. Astrid is an impressive sight. Come."

Mirit turned in the saddle and spoke to Avatar. "Did you hear? Ten miles to Manheim at the base of the mountain."

Avatar didn't reply as Nigel moved alongside him.

"Well, this is what we came for," said Nigel.

"Let's hope it's worth the trip," said the Guardian.

Mirit looked past them to Chad, who stayed with Alaric and Leif. She sent an apologetic smile to Nigel before kicking her horse to follow the others.

Avatar moved on, but Nigel pretended to check his boots so Chad could catch up to him. Avatar walked ten feet ahead of them, Magda another ten or so feet in front of Avatar. With little chance of Magda overhearing, Nigel didn't switch languages.

"I know Mirit spoke to you this morning. I hope you're not angry with her. She spoke to you on my behalf."

"I know, master," he added the title in a low voice.

Nigel frowned at the formality, and took Chad's arm to pick up the pace and put distance between Alaric and Leif. This time, he spoke in the Ancient. "In station only. In heart I am your friend."

"I believed the same, but Lady Mirit reminded me of my station."

"Why?"

"She misunderstood me, the same as you have."

Nigel scowled in frustration. "We must find a way for all of us to speak privately. These snippets of conversations are causing confusion and conflict where there should be none."

"I didn't mean to cause you concern."

He grinned and clasped the back of Chad's neck. "I bear some blame. I forget you're only seventeen and expect you to understand beyond your years."

"I'm not naïve and ignorant."

"No, of course not. But you still have maturing to do, both in years and worldly knowledge." He smiled. "I remember when I was sixteen and on holiday on the East Coast. I boldly told my father of my maturity and tired of book learning alongside my little sisters. I had skill in all knightly arms, was strong and quick in mock battle. The time had come to put my manly maturity to the test."

Chad looked sideways in mildly disbelief. "What did he say?"

"He agreed, and said he would arrange a shortened form of the Contest to test my skill after we return to Waldron." Nigel's smile faded to sullenness his hand dropping from Chad's shoulder. "I never took the test. The Morvenian visit delayed it, while the ambush changed everything. You know my story; how shame kept me from telling them I was alive. I acted cruelly. Don't grow up too fast, Chad. A false sense of understanding and maturity can lead to horrible consequences."

"You think I've done that?"

"In your heart, I believe you mean well. But your understanding is incomplete, which is what made you confront Avatar. He is over eighteen hundred years old, with more knowledge and experience than we will ever have. You must listen, watch and learn. And when the time comes, you will know how to act."

Chad nodded, a brooding expression on his face.

Nigel said enough and they walked in silence. A few times he caught Avatar and Mirit looking back; perhaps to check on their progress or see what transpired between them. Whatever the reason, he determined to find a way for all of them to speak and very soon.

The climb became more noticeable as they neared the foothills. The road grew steep and winding in some places then flattened out to a broad avenue. After a steep climb, Grissel stopped. By the position of the sun, it was well after noon. Manheim was still three miles away.

"Elfrida!" she called and the Sigvard appeared. "Go ahead and alert High Priestess Ludmilla to our arrival."

"Won't she need a horse for the journey?" asked Auriel.

"She can take mine. I don't mind walking the rest of the way," said Mirit, who dismounted.

Elfrida suspiciously eyed Mirit but said nothing. Since being defeated, she did not speak to Mirit and always sneered when faced with her. She mounted, kicked the horse into a gallop for Manheim.

"If not careful, she'll kill the beast with one wrong step," said Wren.

"Elfrida knows what she's doing. Now rest and take nourishment."

Nigel, Mirit, Chad and Avatar gathered in a circle away from the Sigvard. Nigel drank from his flask. Avatar pulled bread and cheese from his knapsack. Chad produced a small roll of sausage from his pack.

"Where did you get that?" asked Mirit

"Karin."

"Really? I don't find the Sigvard generous toward varlets."

"Auriel then."

"What?" asked Nigel.

"Karin gave the sausage to Auriel in a token of appreciation, and Auriel gave it to me." Chad used his dagger and cut off a piece of sausage for Mirit. He did the same for Nigel. When he offered a slice to Avatar, the Guardian shook his head in refusal. "Why? Because it's a gift of gratitude?"

"No, because I'm not hungry. Have you seen me eat since we left the first outpost?"

"No."

"And I won't until all this is over."

"Soren food not to your liking?"

Avatar steadily regarded the contentious youth. "No, the thought of entering a temple to an unknown god is not to my liking."

Chad became vexed at the response and turned away. He felt a hand on his shoulder. Nigel leaned closer to speak.

"Remember why *they* exist and what I said earlier."

The conversation ceased when Adelaid approached, glaring at Mirit. "You prefer the company of varlets to your own kind?"

"Considering the difference between us, I don't really know that you are my *kind*."

Adelaid assumed a challenging posture, hands resting on her sword and replied, "Meaning?"

Mirit handed her remaining bread to Nigel and stood to reply but kept her voice placid. "Meaning I see no reasoning or compassion, rather reckless and thoughtless bullying."

Nigel lowly groaned in exasperation.

"Your varlet disapproves of your bold words. Does he dictate your actions as well as command your heart?"

"I don't —" began Nigel in despute when Mirit waved him silent.

She accosted Adelaid. "That is the thoughtlessness I mean! You provoke for no reason with baseless accusation."

"Enough!" snapped Auriel. She arrived with Wren and Grissel. "I commanded the two of you to silence for the remainder of the journey."

"Ja, Great One," said Adelaid.

Auriel's look at Mirit was fierce. "I hoped better from you, *Sigvard*."

Mirit flushed and pressed her lips together to keep her temper.

Nigel and Avatar stood at the rebuke; only Avatar was behind Mirit and in Auriel's direct line of sight. His movement and reproving expression caught attention. She stepped back, drawing Adelaid from Mirit to withdraw. At Avatar's nod, Wren left to join Grissel and Auriel.

"You shouldn't fall for her obvious ploys," said Nigel.

"I can handle Adelaid," said Mirit a bit harsher than intended and she sighed in frustration, but turned at Avatar. "Auriel *is* the problem."

"Tonight we must speak."

"With or without her?"

"Without, I'm afraid."

"Why? Because she stopped Mirit and Adelaid from coming to blows?" chided Chad.

Avatar stared at Chad. "No. Something stirs her to confront. The same as it does you."

The teen shook his head. "Nothing stirs me. I just don't understand your objection to her doing the same as you. It seems wrong."

"I'm not accepting undue gratitude and taking it seriously."

"Maybe you should."

"Chad!" scolded Nigel.

"Forgive me, *master*, but prejudice blinds you." He stormed off to join Alaric and Leif.

Perplexed, Nigel stared after Chad. Avatar's regard of Chad showed fixed resolution.

"Time to leave!" called Grissel.

As everyone assembled to move, Magda took hold of Mirit's sleeve. "If you wish to obey the Valkerish, walk with me."

"I'm surprised you want to be seen with me, the foreign upstart of a Sigvard."

"Perhaps it's not you I'm interested in helping. Adelaid isn't strong like Elfrida or quick like you."

"Then why does she provoke me?"

"To prove herself, why else? If she can succeed where Elfrida failed, she will have earned respect."

Mirit looked along her shoulder at Magda. "You earn respect by beating up on each other?"

"How else is the strongest to lead?"

"By brains and example. Didn't you understand that when I defeated Elfrida?"

"I do, but others do not. Nor do they want to. Have you never fought to prove yourself?"

Mirit sighed, a pricked frown appearing.

"You have! Yet scorn us."

"I once lived by the sword, until I learned a better way to live, by faith and trust."

"In your Valkerish?"

She chuckled. "They're part of it, but not the entirety."

"What part?"

"The visible part. Faith is invisible. The supernatural, a higher power that moves all."

"Including the Valkerish?"

Feeling she spoke too much already, Mirit pondered her next answer. Not that Jor'el deserved less than her full testimony and service, but was it wise at the moment? *Jor'el, grant me wisdom.* With a sense of new calm in her spirit, she replied. "It depends upon what we learn of your Valkerish. Which is why we came from the place of beginning, remember?"

Magda pursed her lips in consideration. "So this higher power would have you test them?"

"In a manner of speaking. Are they true Valkerish, or imposters?"

"They are real," said Magda with great offense. "Once I had the privilege of seeing Wilda at Sigrid, our annual feast celebrating the calling of the Sigvard. She appeared and blessed the gathering."

"Did she do anything? Make food, or wine, or anything unusual?"

Magda shook her head. "No, but one moment she was there and the next she was gone."

"Did you witness her come or go? Like Auriel with Karin?"

"Not personally, but I've heard many tales of Valkerish power. So they are real and your higher power has sent you for nothing."

Mirit frowned at her miscue. *Jor'el, please!* She silently prayed before being prompted to speak aloud. "Your prophecy says that before the end there will come Valkerish from the place of beginning. Why?"

Magda thought for a moment before replying. "To be tested and found true or false. If true, then they would be exalted to the heaven, if false, destroyed." By the end of her own answer, she stared at Mirit with understanding.

"Magda, you can either help us, or hinder us. The choice is yours. Although I would encourage you not to be like Elfrida and Adelaid, and be receptive to reason."

"They are my sisters. Sworn to serve the Valkerish and each other."

"For now. I believe in the near future each will be forced to follow their individual conscience. That is when faith and trust will be tested."

Magda chewed on her lip for a moment before asking, "Have you faced this test?"

Mirit expression grew sober in remembrance. "Ja, and I will not deceive you, it is a difficult choice. It cost my life."

"Your life of the sword."

"No, my life," she said, looking directly at Magda.

The Sigvard shivered at the implication and asked in a hushed voice, "Like Karin?"

"She almost drowned. I was killed in a ritual sacrifice."

Magda first became frightened then curious. "The Tavar do such things! How did you survive?"

"Faith and trust restored me."

"The higher power?"

"Ja. Since then I have tasks to fulfill. This journey is one of them."

Magda shook her head in befuddlement. "I'm not certain I understand."

Mirit watched the conflict with regret. "Perhaps I said more than I should, though what I tell you is the truth." She laid hold of Magda's arm. "For your own sake, say nothing of what we have discussed. Time and our mission will give you the answers you need for complete understanding. Be patient until then."

"I'll try."

It began to snow. "Wonderful," groused Mirit. "I hope we make it by nightfall.

"We will. You'll be able to see the city from around the bend."

Manheim sprawled out along the base of the mountain, with a wall for protection, and using the mountain as the back. Being built of gray stone and the roofs white with snow, the city looked like an extension of the mountain.

"The largest structure is the temple." Magda pointed to it.

Mirit turned from viewing Manheim to her companions. Intense scrutiny filled Avatar's glare at the city. Nigel's interest shifted from the city to Avatar, measuring both the city and the Guardian's reaction. Chad appeared indifferent. Avatar diverted his gaze from the temple and caught her eye. She smiled and he nodded, his expression softening. What an amazing and dear being. Despite his personal disquietude, he would not let it affect others. She had not known him as long as Nigel or Chad, but spending seven months in Tunlund taught her much about Guardians. They were dedicated and selfless in caring for their mortal charges. Most of what she learned from Avatar was confirmed in other Guardians like Kell, Armus, Mahon and Wren.

Auriel she thought, her eyes changing focus to Auriel, who remained with Grissel. On this venture she noticed a contradiction. *Then again, Avatar said some Guardians take themselves too seriously in performing their duty.*

For the last mile, the road to Manheim was clear of snow. At the main gate, two mounted Sigvards waited; one high-ranking as told by her golden breastplate and dark blue cloak, the other also wearing an impressive silver breastplate and dark blue cloak.

Grissel drew rein and saluted the golden Sigvard. "Hail, Ulrika."

"Hail, Grissel." Ulrika, the older woman of forty, had piercing green eyes and commanding features; her golden hair fashioned like a braided crown upon her head.

"I present Auriel and Wren, Valkerish from the place of beginning."

Ulrika saluted. "Welcome, Great Ones. This is an unexpected honor. I am the supreme commander of the Sigvard and this is Perti, my second-in-command."

"Great Ones." Perti saluted. She was few years younger than Ulrika with strawberry blonde hair and deep brown eyes.

"Has the high priestess been informed of our arrival?" asked Auriel.

"Indeed, Great One. However, she begs your indulgence. It is late and she wishes to make a proper reception for the morning. Tonight you will feast with the Sigvard High Command at Falken."

"Very well. Lead on."

The citizens of Manheim watched the procession from the main gate to Falken. The reactions varied from awe, to fear, to skepticism. Some bowed, some saluted, others scurried away, while still others scowled and closed the shutters on the night.

En route to Falken, they passed the temple; an impressive structure compared to the rest of Soren's common and humble dwellings. It stood tall and wide, with layered slate roofs coming to an apex. Stone carving capped the apexes and eaves. Upon the pinnacle stood a figure of a female warrior with her sword held high. The archways were intricate reliefs of geometric shapes.

Wren stirred uneasy in the saddle and fought to keep her features from betraying anger or disrespect at sight of the temple. In her eighteen hundreds of years of existence, this was her first venture outside of Allon. Facing Dagar and the Shadow Warriors on Allonian soil was one thing, but confronting unknown foreign deities on foreign soil was another matter. Of her fellow Guardians, Auriel surveyed the massive structure taking in every detail while Avatar walked with shoulders squared, hand on the hilt of his sword, and eyes straight ahead. What a difference between the two warriors; one casual, the other rigid and ready for action. Considering Auriel's behavior causing discord, Wren took Avatar's example and turned forward in the saddle, her eyes focused anywhere else but on the temple.

The building next to the temple appeared similar in construction to the outpost, being long, built of stone with two stories and battlements on the roof. The archways on the first floor and galley way of second floor were also of geometric carvings. Smoke rose from several chimneys along the back wall. At each archway along the first floor, Sigvard stood guard holding long spears. They came to attention and placed spears in front of their faces as a salute.

"Welcome to Falken, Great Ones," said Ulrika.

Once on foot, Auriel and Wren towered above Ulrika by a foot to eighteen inches, impressing the Sigvard guarding the main entrance. The guards became doubly concerned at seeing Avatar's brooding countenance. Nigel, Chad, Alaric and Leif were whisked away to join the other varlets in preparing and serving the feast.

During the feast, the Sigvard saluted and toasted Wren and Auriel after the stories told by Karin and her sisters concerning their coming and saving of Karin's life. They even permitted Avatar to sit among the Sigvard of Grissel's command. Mirit sat at the end of high table in respect for her station as Sigvard of the new Valkerish.

After the feast, they were taken to different parts of Falken for sleeping. Auriel, Wren and Mirit were given Ulrika's personal apartment, while Avatar the best guest chamber, and the others slept in the servant's hall. There would be no meeting that night. Well, at least, they made it safely to Manheim.

Chapter 9

Nigel made certain he, Chad, Alaric and Leif were up before sunrise so they could get to their companions without hindrance. They kept to their varlet roles by fetching all the necessities for morning toiletry.

"Morning, Great Ones." Nigel spoke for the benefit of the Sigvard guarding the room entrance. A towel draped over one arm and hand, which he held against his body. He held the door open for Chad, Alaric and Leif to enter carrying a basin, and two pitchers.

"Good. I could use a splash of cold water to wake up," said Mirit.

A smile appeared after closing the door. "Didn't sleep well alone?"

She smirked and jerked the towel off his arm, exposing a loaf of bread and cup.

"The pitcher Alaric is holding contains wine. Substance for what we must face this morning."

"I don't think it would be wise for Alaric and I to leave as we did before," said Leif. He poured water from the pitcher he carried into the basin for Mirit to wash her face.

"You can watch, but I'm afraid you can't participate," said Avatar.

"Because the Almighty would not approve?"

"Remember what was told us of the reaction to Gilda's blasphemy," said Alaric to Leif. "We will watch with all respect."

Nigel set the candle and bread on a small table. He then took the pitcher to fill the cup and placed it beside the candle and bread. He used the matches provided in the room for regular use. Once ready, Mirit stood to his right, Avatar to his left, with Auriel, Wren and Chad took their places around the table.

Alaric and Leif waited to one side. They didn't understand since Nigel spoke in the Ancient. He lit the candle then drank from the cup. The cup passed around the circle, with each taking a drink. When Nigel received the cup back, he placed it down then broke off a piece of bread to eat. The process repeated with each individual in the circle. When finished with the bread, the group joined hands and bowed their heads. Nigel spoke what must have been a prayer, ending with all saying *Tangiel* in unison.

Alaric smiled. "The Almighty will bless us this day, ja?"

"He will give us strength and wisdom to face what we must."

"Speaking of face. Are you going to shave?" Mirit scratched Nigel's whiskers.

"I don't know. A good beard would keep my face warm in this weather."

"I prefer you clean-shaven."

"He's right, miss. Most Soren men have a winter's beard, except for Alaric. He has trouble growing whiskers."

Annoyed, Alaric slapped his brother's arm.

Chad answered a knock at the door. Ulrika and Grissel entered and saluted Auriel and Wren.

"Great Ones. I heard your varlets were waiting upon you," began Ulrika. "Breakfast is ready. We usually eat at sunrise. Afterward we are commanded to the Temple."

"Commanded?" asked Auriel with offense.

Ulrika quickly corrected herself. "I meant *we*, the Sigvard, are commanded to escort you to the High Priestess. Great Ones."

Fortunately with time pressing, conversation kept to a minimum during breakfast. In the courtyard, Sigvard held the bridles of seven finely saddled horses. Standard bearers stood behind the horses with at least fifty Sigvard in ranks behind the bearers.

"This is much show for going next door," said Wren.

"It is to honor you that we assemble, Great One. Even your brother is to ride," Ulrika added to Auriel.

Once everyone mounted, Nigel, Chad, Leif and Alaric moved between the horses and standard bearers.

Perti took exception to the action. "Your varlets are bold creatures! How dare they take position in the procession?"

"Our varlets will accompany us," said Wren.

"That is unheard of."

"Peace," said Ulrika to Perti. "Great Ones, Grissel told me of our differences. I'm uncertain how the High Priestess will accept this breach of protocol."

"May I suggest a compromise?" asked Avatar, respectful of Wren, who nodded. He asked Ulrika, "Are spectators allowed?"

"Ja, but only selected individuals from the city."

"I propose the varlets continue in the procession, then join the spectators and not accompany us to the meeting with High Priestess."

She seemed pleased. "Your reasoning is sound. However, the varlets must be the last to enter and slip in among the crowd."

"Agreed."

Taking position at the head of the procession, Ulrika signaled the trumpeters on the battlements. The blaring call of the Sigvard drowned the nearby crowing of a rooster and noise of early morning traffic. The crowd watched the short procession in subdued silence.

"They must have risen before sunrise to be here," said Mirit to Avatar, as they rode side-by-side.

"Or been roused from their sleep to make this show."

"You're as cynical as Nigel."

"We prefer pragmatic."

At the temple gates, Nigel, Chad, Leif and Alaric left the procession and made their way through the selected citizens to take up position at the bottom of the four large stone steps leading to the temple porch.

On the porch, half a dozen priestesses waited. They wore ankle length gowns of pale yellow with fitted bodices accented by a multi-color belt. Upon their heads, a single gold circlet held a veil in place. The veil cascaded down their back to the ankles, and was attached to the belt at their sides, creating a cape-like effect. Four of the priestesses wore green veils, while the other two wore white. Ringlets of various shades of yellow to light brown hair framed their faces from under the circlet. The priestesses ranged in age from age sixteen to fifty with the eldest woman standing ahead of the others.

Alaric seized Leif's arm. "Bergeta!"

"What?" asked Nigel.

"My daughter. The second on the left with the white veil."

Nigel and Chad followed Alaric's careful indication. A fresh-faced, rosy-cheeked girl of sixteen stood gazing at the procession.

"She's beautiful," said Chad in admiration.

"She looks like her mother." Alaric moved to get a better view.

Bergeta's eyes went wide at seeing Alaric move so Chad pulled him back into place. In doing so, Chad caught Bergeta's gaze and flashed a gallant smile. She turned away at hearing the elder priestess greet Ulrika.

At the bottom of the steps, Ulrika, Grissel, Perti, Auriel, Wren, Avatar and Mirit dismounted. Ulrika bowed and returned the greeting. "Hail, Iryn."

"Welcome, Great Ones." Iryn inclined her head in a partial bow and a cross-arm salute. The other priestesses mimicked her. "High Priestess Ludmilla awaits your pleasure."

Auriel and Wren climbed the steps after the priestesses. Avatar followed with Mirit, Ulrika, Perti and Grissel behind them and the procession of Sigvard in the rear.

Nigel and Chad held Alaric and Leif back. "Remember, we are to blend with the spectators," said Nigel.

Wren spoke to Ulrika, who nodded and motioned to Perti. The second-in-command withdrew from the procession and waited for her sisters to pass before beckoning for the varlets.

"Hold your tongues and be grateful for this opportunity." She escorted them inside and raised a hand for them to stop. "Stay here." She rejoined Ulrika.

"Charming," said Chad under his breath.

"Like a badger," groused Nigel, glaring at Perti's back.

"I meant her." Chad carefully motioned to Bergeta, who took her place among the other priestesses on the near side of the altar.

"Keep your mind on why we're here."

"She *is* why we are here."

Nigel didn't argue since Alaric's petition for help for his daughter brought about the mission. He took stock of the temple. It was humble compared to the magnificent splendor of Allon's Temple of Providence, but for Soren, it showed superior craftsmanship in stone and metalwork. Carvings of various scenes decorated the walls, while large intricate torches were spaced every five feet. Three glassless windows dominated the back wall allowing air and natural light into the temple. In the center of the polished stone floor rose a triangular altar. On each side of the altar were carved different runes and symbols. A large golden tri-branched candlestick with a center cup sat upon the altar. From the center cup incense burned while the three candles remained unlit. The incense filled the temple with a pleasant mix of soothing aromas.

A woman near sixty years of age waited at the bottom of the altar. Her dress was the same pale yellow only with a scarlet belt. Lush gray hair was braided and arranged on her head like a crown, jewels inserted at various intervals to complete the crowning affect. From the center of her hair a scarlet veil cascaded down her back forming the same cape-like appearance. Around her neck she wore a crest divided into three parts, each containing a symbol represented on the altar.

"High Priestess Ludmilla, I present the Great Ones from the place of beginning," said Iryn.

"Great Ones, this is an honor." Ludmilla paid her respects to Auriel and Wren. Her eyes darted to Avatar, concern on her face at seeing his stoic expression and piercing silver eyes.

When the priestess tensed, Auriel said, "My brother."

"Indeed. You will forgive my impertinence, Great One, but with the recent imbalance his presence is disturbing."

"You have nothing to fear from him."

Ludmilla inclined her head in submission, but another look to Avatar betrayed her skepticism. "Since you have come from the place of beginning, we will call upon the Valkerish to welcome you."

"They would do that?" asked Mirit, drawing a frown of irritation from Ludmilla. "Since we are here according to prophecy," she added.

"Why would they not welcome their sisters from afar?"

Mirit shrugged, flushing at her miscue.

Ludmilla spoke to the crowd, "We shall call upon the Valkerish." She held out her hand and a priestess from the left came and gave her a lit candle. Ludmilla mounted the platform. The other priestesses assumed their places along the three sides of the altar with Iryn at the apex opposite the High Priestess.

Ludmilla raised the lit candle in direction of the three windows and spoke: "Freja, High Valkerish of Soren, our protector and guide, hear the voice of your servants and answer! Grace us with your presence!"

"Freja, hear our voice and answer! Grace us with your presence!" repeated the priestesses and Ludmilla lit one of the branches of the golden tripod candlestick.

For a second time Ludmilla raised the candle and spoke, "Wilda, Valkerish of All Living Things, who gives us meat and bread, hear the voice of your servants and answer! Grace us with your presence!"

The priestesses repeated what she said, and she lit another candle.

A third time she raised the candle and spoke: "Karah, Valkerish of Truth and Honor, who teaches us and gives us law, hear the voice of your servants and answer. Grace us with your presence."

The priestesses repeated the phrase and Ludmilla lit the final candle.

Avatar's fingers flexed over the hilt of his sword in anticipation. Wren shifted her weight to reach her crossbow if needed. Mirit moved her hands into position for a fast draw of her sword. Only Auriel remained motionless, eyes focused on Ludmilla.

At a loud clap of thunder, the spectators jumped or gasped in surprise. Even Mirit flinched, stepping sideways into Avatar's sword arm. He steadied her, eyes alert for the source of the thunder.

"Why do you summon us?" a voice echoed in the room.

The reaction among the crowd to the voice was measurable. Even the younger priestesses with the white veils looked nervously about for a body to go with the voice, but there was none.

The older priestesses and Ludmilla remained calm. The high priestess answered. "Two sister Valkerish have come from the place of beginning and wish to meet you. See for yourselves as they stand before your altar."

For a brief moment there was silence. Mirit and the Guardians stood in watchful anticipation. A loud caw echoed in the temple before a crow flew through the center window and landed on the altar. Wren doubled over in great pain and staggered backwards. Avatar caught her, protective in his hold. Auriel took up a defensive stance in front of Wren, her sword still in its sheath but ready to draw. Mirit joined Auriel to form a shield between Wren and the crow causing her distress.

"Who are you?" Auriel demanded of the crow.

"I could ask you the same since you seek us," it answered.

"We come from the place of beginning and wish to meet face-to-face to see if you truly are Valkerish."

The crow angrily cawed, flapping its wings. "You dare question us? What is your name?"

"Auriel, Valkerish of Justice."

The crow's head moved to view Auriel from various angles then flew out of the temple, its loud caw echoing in the chamber.

Ludmilla gasped in surprise. "What have you done?"

"Nothing, but state my name."

Ludmilla stood before the altar, her hands lifted. "Great Ones—"

"Have them come to Astrid immediately!" commanded the voice.

Ludmilla paled in fear. "Go! Before the Valkerish become angry," she snapped at the Guardians. "The rest of you, return to your homes and pray we can avoid the wrath of the Valkerish!" She rushed from the platform, the priestesses following.

"Wren?" asked Avatar.

Her face relaxed and she stood on her own. "I'm better."

"What happened?"

"No time for questions. You heard Ludmilla, leave!" Ulrika signaled the Sigvard to escort the Guardians and Mirit.

Avatar maintained a supporting hold of Wren since the color was slow to return to her face. He, Mirit and Auriel turned to leave when they heard a shout, "Bergeta!"

Alaric bolted toward the back of the temple in the direction of the departing priestesses. Chad, Nigel and Leif pursued. There was nothing they could do since the Sigvard insisted upon their departure.

Bergeta turned at hearing her name. "Papa?"

Chad intercepted Alaric before he could grab her. "You're going to cause trouble."

Alaric struggled. "Let go! She's my daughter."

"No, Papa! You must go," she urged.

"What?"

She batted imploring blue eyes at Chad. "Take him home."

He kindly smiled. "I will, miss."

An older priestess with a green veil pulled Bergeta away.

"Brother, you can't cause trouble," said Leif. He aided Chad in restraining Alaric.

Three Sigvard stepped in-between them and the departing priestesses. "To your mistress, varlets."

On the porch, Ulrika grabbed Mirit. "Only the Valkerish, you stay."

The Guardians stopped their descent. "Why?" demanded Avatar.

"Precaution."

"Go. I'll tend to things here," said Mirit. By his expression, Avatar didn't like the idea. Then again, he didn't like anything forcing him from his duty. He yielded when Wren tugged on his arm.

"Collect your varlets and confine yourselves to Falken," Ulrika told Mirit before mounting and leaving.

Mirit mumbled an Ancient prayer for their protection. Shortly, Nigel, Chad, Alaric and Leif exited the temple. She hurried to speak, eyes of warning on them, "Come, varlets, we are to wait at Falken."

They fell in step when she went mounted then hurried to keep pace. Inside the main entrance to the compound, Sigvard from Grissel's command lingered in the courtyard. Immediately upon dismounting, Adelaid and Elfrida prevented Mirit from moving. When she tried to go around, they blocked her path.

Adelaid sneered. "We knew you were trouble. Your Valkerish are going to Astrid, leaving only varlets for aid. How brave are you now?"

Mirit glared in warning. "You don't want to do this."

"Oh, we do," said Elfrida, and drew her sword.

Other Sigvard seized Chad, Nigel, Alaric and Leif to prevent any help. There was no way to avoid the confrontation. Still, Mirit knew Nigel and Chad would not let it go too far before helping, no matter the odds against the Sigvard.

"Two against one is hardly brave on your part."

Remembering the last encounter, Mirit knew what to expect, at least from Elfrida. When she reached to take off her cloak for ease of movement, Elfrida attacked. This time Mirit used her cloak to wrap around Elfrida's blade and kicked her aside, jerking the cloak off the sword. Elfrida fell. Adelaid came at Mirit, but the move was anticipated, so she parried using her sword then flashed the cloak in Adelaid's face to put some distance between them.

Elfrida rose to join the attack. Elfrida was strong and Adelaid determined. Individually Mirit could handle each, but together they made an unpredictable pair. She had to find a way to even the odds. Against two opponents having two weapons was preferable, but since she didn't have a dagger the cloak would serve. She parried one while keeping the other at bay by using the cloak. This worked until Elfrida grabbed the cloak and ripped it from her, causing Mirit to stumble. She avoided Adelaid's swipe but found herself face-to-face with Elfrida, who sent her staggering sideways with a vicious backhand across the face.

Mirit caught herself on a pillar to keep from falling yet dropped her sword. Her jaw ached, lip throbbed and she tasted blood in her mouth. Elfrida's attack forced her to duck behind the pillar. Adelaid thrust from the other side and Mirit dove under the blade and rolled away. She came to her knees beside her cloak, but her sword lay too far away.

Elfrida came at her. Mirit threw a handful of dirt at Elfrida, forcing her to turn away. Mirit sprung up, tossed the cloak over Elfrida's head, and pulled it tight, blinding Elfrida. Hearing a war cry from Adelaid, she used the blinded Elfrida for a shield. A loud gasp of surprise and pain came when Adelaid's sword passed through the cloak into Elfrida, who began to collapse so Mirit released her.

In horror, Adelaid knelt and removed the cloak to discover a serious wound in the left side of Elfrida's chest. Enraged beyond reason, Adelaid launched at Mirit, took her to the ground and wrapped her hands about Mirit's throat.

"Adelaid!" Magda rushed over to stop Adelaid from strangling Mirit.

Nigel waylaid the Sigvard holding him to be free and join Magda in separating Adelaid from Mirit. His added strength broke Adelaid's hold and he tossed her aside. Mirit gasped for air and he held her steady while she recovered her breath.

On the ground, Adelaid snarled up at Magda. "Why did you save her? You saw what she made me do!" She noticed other Sigvard carrying Elfrida from the courtyard.

"You wounded Elfrida?"

"She used her as a shield against me!"

Mirit breathed a bit easier now, sitting and leaning against Nigel. "I had to. They attacked me for no reason."

Adelaid cried out in rage and bolted to her feet intent on attacking Mirit. She stopped when Magda's sword pointed at her. "Out of my way!"

Magda remained between Adelaid and Mirit. "Grissel warned you about insulting our guests. You not only defied her orders but also seriously wounded Elfrida. You will be confined to quarters to await punishment. Karin, Rudel, Lavinia, see she is guarded well."

Adelaid reluctantly went with the Sigvard, a snarl at Mirit in passing.

Mirit stood. "I'm sorry about Elfrida, but I had to defend myself."

"I know. I saw it all. I wanted Adelaid to admit what she did. For this, they will both be severely punished, if Elfrida survives. In the meantime, stay out of trouble until your Valkerish return from Astrid."

"That will be easier said than done under the circumstances." Mirit glanced about the courtyard at the other Sigvard. Many were drawn by the commotion and looked none too friendly. Even the guards at the posts showed signs of anger.

Magda noticed the same. "It is best if you stay at the temple."

"How will it be any better?"

"The priestesses aren't bent on killing you. Come. I'll take you myself."

Mirit walked beside Magda. Nigel, Chad, Alaric and Leif followed them back to the temple. Once at the bottom of the temple steps, Magda made them wait as she went to speak to Ludmilla.

"Are you all right?" asked Nigel.

"Ay. Let's hope all goes well with the Valkerish."

"Indeed. Only three days remain before we must leave."

"What about Bergeta?" asked Alaric low and urgent.

"We'll try to speak to her, but she is not our main concern."

"She may be able to help us understand the priestess," insisted Chad.

Nigel looked askew to Chad and tried to contain his annoyance. "I said we'll try."

"Here comes, Magda," warned Mirit. "That was quick."

"Ludmilla couldn't say much when I invoked *sauf*. She agreed, at least until Ulrika and Grissel return."

"And our Valkerish."

Magda shrugged. "Depends on how they are received. For now, I'm to take you to the novices. The priestesses won't deal with you until they know where you stand with the Valkerish."

She led them to the rear of the compound to Novice Hall. A young woman of twenty years old greeted them outside the building.

"Magda. The high priestess placed them in my charge."

Magda turned to Mirit. "I will inform you when there is news."

"Thank you." Mirit made the Sigvard's salute.

Magda returned the gesture, a small smile appearing before departing.

"I am Ingrid, the eldest novice. Follow me," she said with formality.

The interior was starkly drab and void of decoration or excess furniture. The main hall stretched about fifty feet in length and served as the gathering and eating area with three tables and benches for sitting. A large hearth dominated the far wall with an added stove about ten feet from the entrance. Off to either side were tens doors to individual rooms for a total of twenty rooms. Novices ranged in age from twelve to twenty, and went about performing various tasks. Several sat near the fire sewing, others were at the table nearest the hearth studying; still others scrubbed the floor. To one side of the hearth was a table used for meal preparation. Bergeta and a thirteen-year old novice manned the table. When the group entered, they picked up trays and approached. Bergeta tried to keep her expression under control at seeing her father.

"Food and warm drink," said Ingrid.

Mirit and Nigel sat. Alaric and Leif remained standing, Alaric staring at his daughter.

Chad took the tray from Bergeta. "Allow me, miss."

"It is Bergeta's duty," chided Ingrid.

"Mine also," said Chad. He set the tray on the table and served Mirit and Nigel bread, cheese and mulled wine.

"Is he not a varlet?" asked Ingrid about Nigel.

"He is recovering from illness and injury." Mirit indicated the healing scar on Nigel's forehead. "I asked he be excused from duty for a week and the Valkerish agreed."

"As you say, Sigvard."

"Excuse us, as Gertrid and I will prepare the rooms," said Bergeta.

Ingrid nodded and they withdrew. "The high priestess requests you remain either in the Novice Hall or the courtyard. You are not to enter the temple or leave the compound. Doing so would violate *sauf*. If there is anything you require, have one of the younger novice's inform me." She left.

"She is different," said Alaric.

"Ja," agreed Leif.

"At least being here, you have a chance to talk to her," said Mirit.

Alaric sat and spoke in haste. "No, to take her home."

"That may not be so easy. Our situation is unpredictable right now," began Nigel. "Speak to your daughter, and then we will consider what to do next. But," he stressed, leaning across the table, "we can do nothing until the others return."

"If they return."

"They will return."

Bergeta entered a room across the hall and Alaric moved to follow her, Leif in pursuit.

"I'll make sure they don't cause trouble," said Chad.

"No, you want a better look at her," Nigel muttered in his drink.

"Has he expressed interest?" asked Mirit.

He scowled in frustration and nodded. "Not exactly good timing."

"Was your timing any better?"

He smirked and shook his head. "No. But I'm not a seventeen-year-old boy who doesn't yet know his mind."

Inside the room, Alaric embraced Bergeta. She accepted his affection with a slight frown. "Oh, Papa, why did you come here?"

"What do you mean, why? They took you from me!"

She shook her head, but hesitated when Leif and Chad entered. She grew annoyed. "Papa, you must leave."

"Not without you."

Her anger found Chad. "I asked you to take him home."

He shrugged in awkwardness. "I've not had the opportunity."

"Forget the lad. What have they done that you shun me?"

"Nothing! And you wouldn't understand. You never did."

Alaric studied his daughter's staunch features and braced posture. "They have done something! You would never defy me."

"Oh, Papa!" She went to leave only Alaric seized her.

"You will explain yourself."

Leif shut the door.

With nervous vexation she asked, "What are you going to do to me?"

"I am your father. You owe me an explanation."

She pursed her lips, her gaze passing from Leif and Chad back to Alaric. "Very well," she said, once more trying to be free of his hold. This time he let her go. "I wasn't forced, I went willingly."

"They snatched you in the middle of the night."

"No! I told them when to come because you wouldn't let me go."

Alaric was stunned by the declaration, so Leif voiced surprise. "You faked your own kidnapping? How could you do that to your father?"

Bergeta sneered at her uncle. "You're as bad as him. If someone disagrees with either of you, they must be wrong, deceived or coerced. We'll I'm not any of those. I want to serve the Valkerish, whether you approve or not."

Alaric's features went from shock to disbelief and finally anger. "I left Soren to get help to free you from the Valkerish. To save you from the danger to come."

"Quietly, Alaric," warned Chad.

"She is my daughter!"

Chad took a step closer, his voice low and harsh. "Someone could overhear and you would lose this opportunity to speak to her like a father should, calm and with reason, not bullying."

Alaric turned red-faced.

"The lad's right, brother. You may not get this opportunity again. Perhaps it is best you hear what she has to say."

Alaric turned to Bergeta. "Speak!" he said harshly then added, "Please," in a more subdued tone when Chad squared his shoulders and rested a hand on the hilt of his sword.

Chad's expression softened toward Bergeta and he nodded. She spoke to Alaric. "I believe in the Valkerish, in their goodness. I know you think me naïve about the Tavar, but I am not. In order to defeat the Tavar, the Valkerish need loyal supporters. I have not the strength to be a Sigvard, though I would fight to the death if asked. Being a priestess is the only I way I can show my loyalty."

The explanation confused him. "Since when have you been so loyal?"

"Since I saw her last year. She was so beautiful and kind."

"Who?"

"Wilda. She came in response to my prayers of revenge for mother's death. She said if I pledged my life to serve her she would help. I agreed."

With Alaric stunned to the core Chad asked, "How did she die?"

"In sacrifice to the Tavar."

"We recognized Ivor because he is Olga's brother," said Leif.

Sudden understanding registered on Chad's face. "Ivor said his sister was among those first sacrificed."

"Ja, Alaric's wife and Bergeta's mother."

She shied from Chad's sympathetic gaze, returning to her father. "I had to come, Papa. It is the only way to do what must be done."

"No! I won't lose you too."

The door opened and Nigel and Mirit quickly entered and shut the door. "What is going on? We could hear raised voices," scolded Nigel.

"Nothing!" Bergeta pushed passed him to leave.

Chad stopped Alaric from pursuing her. "She made her choice."

Alaric had all he could take. "Don't press me, boy."

Unfazed by the threat, Chad spoke to Leif. "See he cools his temper before there is real trouble."

Alaric shook off Leif and stormed out, but his brother at his heels.

"What happened?" asked Nigel.

"Bergeta faked her own kidnapping when Alaric stopped her from becoming a priestess after an encounter with Wilda."

"She's seen the Valkerish?" asked Mirit.

Chad nodded. "There's more. Ivor's sister, the one sacrificed, was Alaric's wife and Bergeta's mother. That's how they recognized him."

Nigel folded his arms across his chest. "I wonder what else they haven't told us?"

Mirit shrugged. "No telling. But there is nothing we can do until the others return."

"I believe Bergeta will tell me," said Chad.

"Oh? What makes you believe that?" asked Nigel.

Mirit snickered at Nigel. "You saw the way he protected her from Alaric. How could she refuse her protector?"

"The same way you did. Douse him with a bucket of water."

Chad rolled his eyes and left.

Chapter 10

ULRIKA, PERTI AND GRISSEL PRESSED THEIR HORSES on the journey from Manheim to the base of Astrid. Auriel, Wren and Avatar went along with the urgency. Being surrounded by over thirty Sigvard wasn't the time to exhibit Guardian powers and place their mission in jeopardy.

Ulrika's horse protested the sudden stop, tossing its head and neighing. Perti's horse barely stopped when she leapt from the saddle. She grabbed the reins of Avatar's horse. Two other Sigvard did the same to Auriel and Wren's horses. The Guardians dismounted.

"The trail leads up the mountain. We are forbidden from going any further, so we will wait for your return or your judgment," said Ulrika.

Astrid rose approximately three thousand feet; the climb steep and winding. Portions were clear of snow, while others portions covered. Auriel headed for the trail, but Wren paused beside Ulrika's horse. The green probing eyes focused on the Sigvard commander.

"You will make certain our Sigvard and varlets are treated properly whether we return or not."

Ulrika flinched under the intense stare. When she tried to avert her eyes, she met Avatar's intense silver gaze. His eyes proved more unnerving than Wren. "Ja, Great One."

Wren followed Auriel, Avatar behind her. The trail grew narrow, steep and winding, but not difficult for the Guardians. Forced to make the climb in single file, they remained visible to the Sigvard during the first thousand feet. Approximately two hundred feet further ahead, a bend would take them out of view.

Avatar looked down at the Sigvard making camp. Auriel moved about ten feet ahead of Wren, who walked in front of him. "We should be able to dimension travel once out of sight."

"Why? Is the mighty Avatar tired of climbing?" chided Auriel.

"No. I don't want to waste time with the others waiting in Manheim. These particular Sorens aren't glad to see us. I don't trust the priestess."

"Why because she's a female?"

"What does that have to do with anything?"

Wren slipped on loose rock and fell face first. She pushed herself onto her hands and knees, wiping the dirt from her mouth. "Maybe we should travel now."

Avatar chuckled and helped her up. "First you fall off a horse, now you slip on rocks, what next?"

"Oh, shut up! Must you criticize everyone?" scolded Auriel.

His temper flared. "Not criticizing, teasing. Wren knows that. Besides, when I have criticized you?"

Auriel didn't answer, her anger prompting her to make the climb quicker.

Wren shrugged ignorance to his inquiring gaze. Annoyed, he hurried around the bend to a small ledge suitable for resting before the trail continued and snatched Auriel's arm.

"I asked you a question. Be good enough to answer."

"I'm as good a warrior as you."

The answer baffled him and briefly stemmed his irritation. "I know your capabilities, but that doesn't answer my question. When have I criticized you? Or done anything to make you so angry at me?"

"You have my answer."

"Does this have anything to do with the past?"

Rather than answer, she jerked away to continue the trek.

"Leave her be. There are more important matters," said Wren.

This time he wouldn't be put off. "She grows more angry towards me and I want to know why."

She frowned and sighed. "I believe it's more to do with Jedrek's death. So, please, back off. I'll speak to her." She followed Auriel

Avatar grimaced at her mention of Jedrek, a fellow warrior killed during the kidnapping of young Prince Titus a year ago. Jedrek mentored Auriel and they were very close friends, which made the explanation plausible. The incident between him and Auriel that resulted in her striking him, happened centuries ago just prior to the Great Battle; too long to hold a grudge without it being manifest before now. His pondering lasted only a moment, when a powerful blow to the back of his head sent him crashing face first into side of the mountain.

Wren turned at hearing a thwack and painful thud. Avatar lay huddled on his left side, his face toward the wall. "Avatar?" She knelt beside him and examined the back of his head, which was bloody.

Auriel arrived. "What happened?"

"I don't know. I heard something and found him like this."

Bright light filled the ledge. Although partly blinded by the light, Wren stood, her crossbow cocked and loaded. Auriel drew her sword and tried to see into the light. When the brilliance faded, Auriel found a naked sword before her eyes, and held by a large, powerful female warrior with golden hair and violet eyes.

"Put down your weapons."

Wren didn't comply and a voice said in her ear, "Do as she says."

Instantly she turned, crossbow first but froze in surprise, not at seeing a crossbow aim at her, rather the individual. "Willow?"

Willow appeared similar in size and outfit to Wren, only with flaxen hair and light moss green eyes. She flinched, her crossbow partly lowering in a display of discomposure. "Wren."

"So this is Vidar's protégé?" said a third female. She stood half a head taller than Wren with brown hair and pale gold eyes; and most definitely a warrior as told by her clothes and the sword strapped to her back. She surveyed Wren up and down. "Not very impressive." She snatched Wren's crossbow away before passing to Auriel, whom she looked at eye-to-eye. "I didn't know there were any female warriors left. I don't recognize you. What is your name?"

"Auriel."

"Lioness of Jor'el, interesting." She left Auriel and glared down at Avatar. She used her foot to turn him onto his back. He groaned but didn't wake. His forehead and face scraped and bruised along with a bloody, broken nose. "Look who we have here. Not so quick with your sword now."

"Who are you?" asked Auriel.

"Your sister-in-arms," she said with a mock bow.

"You're no sister Guardian of mine," chided Wren. A quick unexpected backhand sent her sideways and split her lower lip.

"I'm a warrior, not a lowly archer!" The pale gold eyes flared with intense warning.

Wren's return stare showed no intimidation at the assault.

She continued in an arrogant tone. "I was once called Farren, equal in strength to Armus, although not given equal position. I'm sure you've heard of Armus, Kell's lackey?"

Neither Auriel nor Wren replied for the answer was obvious.

"I renounced that name and all that goes with it. Here I am Freja, the mighty protector of Soren."

"And given all the respect and authority you never had in Allon," said Auriel, drawing a scathing look from Wren and a caustic smile from Farren.

"Ay. The respect we all deserve. Willow, as Wren once knew her, is now Wilda, Valkerish of All Living Things. Keara is now Karah, known for truth and honor." She spoke of the one holding her sword at Auriel.

"That explains the wolves and crow," said Auriel.

Wren looked long and hard at Willow and didn't attempt to hide the hurtful scowl. "That doesn't explain the Tavar."

Farren accosted Wren. "Those creatures are not like us."

"Not Guardians?"

"No. Female. They are like him," she said, pointing to Avatar. "They are dark and evil."

"And what you do is good?"

Farren struck Wren again, only hard enough to spin her around and send her falling on top of Avatar's chest. His eyes snapped open at impact.

"Stay as you were," she whispered, blocking Farren's view.

"You're hurt," he said, barely moving his lips.

She wiped her mouth, which bled more from the second blow. A hand grabbed her, and she mouthed '*stay*' and he closed his eyes.

Farren jerked Wren to her feet. "Mind your tongue, archer!"

"You say they are dark and evil but not female or Guardians," said Auriel, diverting Farren's attention from Wren.

"I said they were not female. I didn't say they weren't Guardians."

"They are not like any Guardians I've ever seen," complained Keara.

"Ay. We forfeited our stations, but these have lost themselves," said Willow.

"Shadow Warriors," said Wren, a quick disturbed glance to Auriel.

"What are Shadow Warriors?" asked Farren.

"Guardians changed by Dagar and his Dark Way after he led a rebellion against Jor'el," said Auriel.

"Dagar rebelled?" said Farren in astonishment.

"Ay."

"It would explain why they are so powerful," said Keara.

Farren nodded, her brow wrinkled in thought. "We must retire to consider this new information, and what to do with our guests. For now, take them to Astrid, I'll tend to *him.*"

Willow took hold of Wren, while Keara did the same to Auriel. In a flash they were gone.

Farren bent down to pull him to Avatar feet. He seized her, and for a moment they wrestled with him ending on top, pinning her arms above her head. His eyes went wide in surprised recognition. "You?!"

Angry, she kneed him in the kidney and he rolled to one side in pain. She scrambled to her feet and drew her sword. He rose to one knee, his sword in hand to block her attack and shoved her back to stand. He swayed from the head wound and could not breath through his nose.

Farren wickedly smiled. "Seeing me is last thing you will ever do." She attacked.

Using all his strength, he sent her flying backwards fifteen to the edge of the cliff. Immediately, he vanished, reappearing in the brush one hundred yards from the Sigvard camp where he fainted.

❦

In the hall of Astrid, Wren jerked away from Willow and lashed out. "How could you turn your back on Jor'el? On Vidar?"

"You couldn't begin to understand. You are blind toward Vidar and the Allonian mortals."

"What do you mean?"

"I understand," said Auriel.

Farren entered. "Do you?" she asked.

"Ay. It is a blindness to duty defying logic or reason, and if left unchecked can even harm the mortals more by action than if we did nothing."

Farren grinned in approval but Wren voiced disturbance.

"You can't be serious?"

"Very much so. You don't have to look far for an example. Remember how Avatar became devastated because he couldn't protect

Nigel from the accident? It took an act of Jor'el to restore him. If he kept his wits that wouldn't have happened."

"You hold a grudge against him!"

Auriel calmly continued. "There are other examples: Armus with Tristine, Kell with Shannan. Avatar was the first who came to mind."

Wren noticed Farren watched their argument with pleasure and became aware she was alone. "Wait! Where is Avatar?"

"Gone," said Farren, non-chalant.

"Gone?" echoed Wren in fearful apprehension. "You killed him?"

"Let's just say he's gone and leave it at that."

Wren turned aside, fighting back angry tears.

"I don't see what is to get upset about. He makes one less male to deal with."

Wren shot a withering glare at Farren, still struggling with emotions.

"Come now, you can't be attached. Or don't you agree with our sister here that we deserve respect?" She spoke in reference to Auriel.

Auriel's expression remained passive, almost bordering on disinterest. When she averted her gaze, Wren lashed out, "She killed Avatar! Doesn't that mean anything to you?"

"Put her in a cell," said Farren to Willow and Keara.

Wren bolted in an attempt to escape, but Farren commanded, "*Dorcha sinteag!*"

Spurean manacles ensnared Wren's wrists. She cried out in agony and fell to her knees.

Auriel grew wide-eyed in surprise. "How did you do that?"

"A little trick I learned from the Tavar. I think she'll be more manageable now."

Wren gritted back the pain, unable to resist when Willow and Keara pulled her to her feet. More pain shot through her since movement activated the spurean manacles. She shouted at Auriel while being dragged away. "If you agree with them, you forfeit your station!"

Farren stepped in front of Auriel to block the view of Wren's departure. "Let us speak plainly, warrior to warrior."

Auriel curtly nodded, to which Farren motioned toward a table. They sat opposite each other

"You said you understand, perhaps you share our feelings."

"Let's just say, you are not the only ones who experienced scorn and been taken for granted and leave it at that."

Farren smiled. "Good enough, for now. You spoke harshly of Avatar. I remember his creation. Being an Original, I held a high position among the elite Guardian warriors alongside Kell and Armus, but when *he* arrived, he became their protégé. I was demoted to Trio Leader of the West Coast. When I protested, Kell said it wasn't a demotion, rather a reassignment for the good of Allon."

"So you killed him for revenge?"

"Do you regret his death?"

"Not in the way you think. To die is battle is one thing. To be struck down blindly is another."

Farren pursed her lips in consideration. "Perhaps. However, with what you call Shadow Warriors plaguing us for centuries, I acted in self-defense. He was a male, and I could not trust him to fight fairly or with honor."

"Avatar would have fought honorably."

"Oh? So you do regret his death."

She shook her head. "He was arrogant, brash, critical and blindly loyal to mortals. And one time, his actions caused many of my comrades to fall in battle. Still, he was a mighty and honorable warrior."

"High praise, indeed."

"I didn't mean it as praise, merely an objective assessment."

"It is good when one can see an enemy's strengths along with his weaknesses."

Auriel balked. "I didn't consider Avatar my enemy."

"No? You said he cost the lives of many of your comrades."

"Dagar, Shadow Warriors and the Dark Way actually caused their demise, though we followed his plan to confront them."

"Competitive rival then," said Farren with a sarcastic smirk. "What can you tell me about these Shadow Warriors? About Dagar's rebellion?"

Auriel shrugged. "Being an Original, you knew Dagar better than I."

"What I recall doesn't make sense to learning of his rebellion."

"Does killing Avatar make sense for Kell reassigning you?"

"I didn't lead a rebellion."

"You left Allon."

"Enough!" snapped Farren, her good humor fading. "Answer the question. Unless you wish you to join Wren."

Auriel stiffened. "You don't need to make threats. This is supposed to be a conversation between warriors." Farren inclined her head in agreement, so she answered the question. "Not being of the elite, it was said severe discontent drove Dagar to renounce Jor'el. Instead of being reassigned, Jor'el dispatched Kell to remove him from his position."

"That is extreme."

"Dagar brought it on himself. He became emboldened by his arrogance and power. He maimed several vassals sent with warnings. He maimed one so badly, Jor'el set his spirit free."

Farren's brow grew level. "So Jor'el made an example of Dagar."

"Ay. Only the action enraged Dagar and he hatched a plot of revenge. He fathered two sons by a mortal female. Together they led an insurrection of Guardians and mortals. Somehow the Guardians who followed him were altered. I don't know the particulars, but fought the results. Actually Armus denounced them as *shadow warriors* for following Dagar, only the name stuck. The rebellion was so bad, Jor'el banished all Guardians from Allon until the fulfillment of Prophecy."

Farren listened with great interest. "Since you come from Allon, Prophecy has been fulfilled."

"Ay. A little over thirty years ago the Son of Tristan destroyed Dagar and reclaimed the throne. At present the Great King reigns."

"The Great King?" echoed Farren in momentary surprise.

"The king in prophecy, our king," said Auriel with purpose. "He is of mixed heritage, Guardian and mortal."

Farren chewed on her lips, brows furrowed. "So he sent you to destroy us?"

"No, for reconnaissance. The discovery of the Tavars' plan to destroy the Valkerish and invade Allon, compelled Tyrone to sent us to scout for information about an unknown enemy."

"Tyrone? Is that his name?"

Auriel nodded.

"I had no knowledge of their desire beyond defeating us."

"How could you not?"

"We are hardly on speaking terms." She stood and began to pace.

Auriel watched the contemplation. "What will you do now that you know?"

Farren gave a short scoffing laugh. "Do? About Allon? We can barely keep Soren from falling apart."

"We could help."

Her laughter increased. "Didn't you hear what Wren said?" She leaned upon the table to look directly at Auriel. "Choose to side with us and forfeit your station. By Jor'el's own word we are outcasts."

"Kell said mortals were banished and nothing about Guardians."

Farren's features grew somber. "He didn't know."

The answer surprised Auriel. "How could Kell not know?"

Farren sat again, regret emerging. "Because we left of our own accord. Jor'el banished the mortals and their descendents, but we were attached to the mortals." She sighed in remorse. "I was in love with one. Because of that *love* I pledged to protect the people of Soren."

"You left Allon because you fell in love with a mortal?"

Farren's response came slow and deliberate. "Kerwin led the rebellion. He foolishly challenged Jor'el with nothing but his own resources. Kell, Armus, Avatar, Vidar, a company of others, and myself went to Radnor to put it down. Mortals are no match for us, but they were stubborn. The more they fought, the more Kell and the others were forced to react."

"You too."

155

Farren shook her head. "I cleverly avoided the worse of the fighting. I couldn't go against Kerwin. After three days, ten thousand mortals lay dead and not a single Guardian lost, despite suffering wounds. It left a bitter sting of blood and death on Allon that lead to their banishment. You're a warrior, but I don't recall seeing you there. You are old enough to remember, aren't you?"

"I'm fourteen hundred and some odd years. It was before my time."

Farren nodded before continuing. "Although I understood the need to put down the rebellion, I was deeply disturbed by the severity and concerned for Kerwin. Such much so, I secretly followed my heart and him to Soren. Together we established a new kingdom and religion utilizing Guardian powers."

"What of Willow and Keara?"

"My Trio mates. They freely chose to join me."

Auriel tugged at lower lip, considering her next question. "I understand your dismay about Radnor. What I don't understand is you claim to have loved a mortal male, yet now hate all males, why?"

Bitter anger formed on Farren's face. "A few years later I discovered he used me, used us and our powers for his own ends. He didn't care about me like I did him. When he found a female mortal for his mate, I became relegated to a position of lackey; only called upon when needed."

"Did this happen before or after your pledge?"

"Before."

"Then why make the pledge?"

Farren stirred a bit uncomfortable. "When she died during the birth of their fourth child, and only girl, Kerwin was so overcome by grief he couldn't stand to look at the child and came to Manheim offering her to me in place of the child we could never have together. He truly loved his mate. Seeing the pain her death caused, I took pity and made the pledge. Only I would never be foolhardy again. I raised the child as a warrior and used her to create the Sigvard, loyal mortal *female* warriors. Through them, the Valkerish have ruled with a firm hand while dispensing truth and wisdom through the priestesses. Never again to be used by a male."

The conversation stopped when Willow and Keara returned.

"Wren is secured, but holding her is risky. If Vidar finds out he will come for her," said Willow.

"We'll take that chance. Take Auriel to her cell."

"No," said Auriel, standing in anticipation of being seized. "I said I would help."

Farren fixed eyes on Auriel. "Why forfeit your station for us? Because of Radnor?"

"You spoke of losing your position. For me, when Jedrek died, I lost the only Guardian who ever respected me. The Allonians are so accustomed to us, they think nothing of who we are or what we are capable of."

Farren's thoughtful look past to Willow and Keara. "We are a Trio."

"I do not want a position of authority. It is enough to be appreciated. I will follow your orders, Freja." Auriel made the Sigvard salute.

For a moment she considered, then asked, "What say you, sisters?"

"How can we refuse if she is willing to give up everything?" said Keara.

"Agreed," said Willow.

"So be it. Welcome, Auriel, Valkerish of Justice," said Farren.

The prison cells of Astrid's dungeon were enclosed by bars on the upper half of the door serving as the only opening to the cell from the hallway. Each cell had a window, but to escape by it meant death since the dungeon perched on the cliff side of Mount Astrid. The interior of each cell contained a carved out stone bed.

Wren tried to get comfortable on the cold, hard stone, but movement caused pain. How Farren got the manacles on her was impressive and disturbing. *I only know of a few who have authority to control the elements that render us helpless. Then again, if she is older, which makes her an Original and she knows things Avatar and I do not.*

"Oh, Avatar," she moaned. He couldn't be dead. Not like that. Not struck down from behind. She closed her eyes and took in a deep breath.

She slowly exhaled and stretched out her senses, searching for any indication of Avatar. She felt the pain of the manacles and pushed pass it, but the more she pushed, the greater the pain. It radiated from her wrists, up her arms and finally burning in her head and she blacked out.

She slowly exhaled and stretched out her senses, searching for any indication of Avatar. She felt the pain of the manacles and pushed pass it, but the more she pushed, the greater the pain. It radiated from her wrists, up her arms and finally burning in her head and she blacked out.

Avatar snapped awake. His heart raced in surprise and he took several deep breaths through his mouth to calm himself. With a nose broken, breathing normally proved difficult. Someone woke him and he sensed trouble. He lay on the ground behind large thick bushes at the edge of a forest, his sword by his side. He ignored the pain in his head and sat up but immediately felt dizzy. Not good. He winced at touching the wound on the back of his head. Blood appeared on his hand.

He began remembering what happened; Wren fell on top of him and warned him. "Wren. That's who woke me," he spoke under his breath. He glanced around but couldn't see anyone. "Wren?" he carefully called, but no response. He recalled snippets of the conversation he heard. The most startling was hearing her declaration of Shadow Warriors.

"Oooh." He held his head, avoiding touching his nose and wound. "Bad concussion. Can't fight like this. I did fight. Farren!" he sneered.

He became aware of loud speech and laughter coming from the other side of the bushes. He gingerly moved to see the cause. The Sigvard encamped at the trailhead about a quarter mile away. He couldn't remain and risk being discovered. Dimension travel would drain the strength he needed to heal. He had to find a place close by to rest and recover.

He tried to stand, but became dizzy and fell to his knees. *Worse than I thought.* He crawled to the safety of trees to avoid being seen. Using his sword for balance he stood. He gripped the hilt to remain on his feet when the dizziness returned, this time making him nauseous. He swallowed back the sickness then used his sword like a cane to take several uneven steps. He fell to one knee.

"Give me strength, Jor'el," he prayed in the Ancient. Once more he pushed himself up on his sword and moved deeper into the woods.

After several hundred yards, he stepped wrong and slipped down an incline. He didn't stop sliding until he crashed into a large log at the bottom of the ravine. For a moment he remained on the ground recovering his breath. He took stock of his surroundings. The log lay at the stream bank, which was good since he needed water for healing.

Gingerly sitting up against the log, he noticed what appeared to be a cave or at least a hollowed out portion of a ravine ten yards down and across the stream. This time he used the log to balance himself to stand. His sword lay half submerged in the water. He sloshed into the stream, fetched his sword, and crossed to investigate the cave. It was large enough to accommodate his frame and hide from view.

He returned to the stream, dropped to his knees and spoke the Ancient before drinking water from cupped hands. He washed his face and head. From his pouch, he pulled out a small vial containing herbs crushed into a fine powder. He tapped the powder into the palm of his left hand. Again speaking in the Ancient, he sprinkled water on the herbs and stirred it with his fingers. Placing some of the paste on his fingers he reached around his head to dab it on his wound. It was difficult, but he managed. Some of the paste he wiped it on his nose. He moved back to the hollow and made himself comfortable. He cradled his sword in a position of support and readiness, he closed his eyes and spoke in the Ancient, "Jor'el, heal your servant for what must be done," and slept.

Chapter 11

NIGEL WAS ANTSY. He found it difficult to wait while confined to the temple of a foreign deity. Mirit tried to help occupy his mind with various topics of discussion. She met with moderate success. However, Ingrid kept watch of their every movement. She tried to be unobtrusive, staying at a respectful distance but they knew better.

They sat on a bench next to the livestock pen to observe the novices and priestesses go about their daily chores. He played with stalks of hay as they continued to converse in the Ancient.

"So you're comfortable being here like this?" he asked.

"No. I'm just more accustomed to being among people of different beliefs. Didn't you learn anything in Tunlund?"

"That was different. We were there to help them establish to Fortresses."

"Not at first."

He chomped down on a blade of hay between his teeth. Chad crossed the compound to intercept Bergeta. "Chad seems comfortable and that concerns me. His fancy could get in the way."

"Like yours did with me?"

He looked askew, a mix of hurt and annoyance in his blue eyes.

"I'm sorry. I wasn't being mean, simply pointing out the similarities. Sometimes your expectations interfere with what you see."

He turned back to watching Chad and Bergeta.

She took his hand. "It may not be bad. He could be using his charm to our advantage in getting information."

He looked at her hand in his. "I hope you're right."

Bergeta lowered the bucket into the well and caught sight of Ingrid nearby. "You can't keep following me with Ingrid watching."

"She's watching me not you. At least she knows where I am."

She giggled. The bucket hit water so she pushed the rope from side to side to fill it then went to turn the crank to lift the bucket. He stopped her, his hand on top of hers.

"Allow me," he said with a gallant smile.

"Following me is one thing, doing my chores is another."

"Fine. I'll crank up the bucket and you pour the water."

He turned the handle. She watched the bucket rise, grabbed the rope and pulled it aside to fill one of the two bucket she carried. She playfully nudged him away from the crank and lowered the bucket.

"We can work together. I don't think Ingrid can object to that."

He smiled and swayed the bucket at the bottom of the well. Finished, she nodded for him to start cranking but became sullen at seeing Alaric. "You may convince Ingrid, but not my father."

"He's concerned. At least your father is alive to be concerned for you. I'm an orphan."

Big blue eyes full of sympathy gazed at him. "How old were you when your parents died?"

"My mother died during my birth, my father when I was five. He had been ill for a long time. Since then, I made my own way in the world." He stopped cranking when the bucket reached the top.

She filled the second bucket and set the well bucket on its hook beside the crank. She looked at him in admiration. "For a varlet you're articulate, intelligent, strong, and very handsome."

He smiled, wide and proud.

"Truly, I can't recall a man with such red hair and pretty green eyes. Your hair shines like a sunset and your eyes sparkle like emeralds."

"I can say the same about you. Your lovely gold hair, pretty face and beautiful blue eyes." He stroked her hair.

She bit her lip, eyes darting to Ingrid. She laid hold of his arm and leaned closer. "Come to my room tonight. We can speak privately." She picked up the buckets and left, pausing to speak a hasty word to Ingrid before continuing on her way.

For Chad, the invitation proved startling and intriguing. Startling, because he had never been asked to a woman's room before and intriguing, at wondering what she had to tell him she couldn't speak openly. Ingrid tossed him a suspicious frown. He smiled at her and joined Nigel and Mirit. He hopped up on the livestock fence.

"I told you she would speak to me."

"What did she say?" asked Nigel in the Ancient.

Chad's smile took on a roguish edge. "I'll find out tonight. She told me to come to her room to speak privately."

"Her room?"

"Not like that," he said with offense. "She is a novice, intent on being a priestess. It's probably the only time and place we can speak privately."

Nigel appeared skeptical, chomping hard on the hay.

Mirit intervened. "Providing we are still here. What will do you if the others return before tonight?"

"Why should that stop me from meeting her? If they return, then they succeeded and we won't be confined to the temple. In fact, it should increase our standing among the Sorens."

"He has a point," she said to Nigel.

He nodded. "Just remember your vow."

"I'm not a Jor'ellian, only a squire."

"All the same, keep your wits."

Chad scowled, jumped off the fence and left.

"I realize you mean well, but he's not a child," she said.

"I know. Only his obstinate and combative behavior of late doesn't give me much hope he can keep his wits."

She took his arm so he would face her. "Your words undermine his attempts to gain your complete trust and confidence. Think about what you just said. We spent two nights in the same bed and you kept your wits. But you can't trust him to meet this girl and do the same?"

He took the hay from between his teeth and tossed it aside. "I'm treating him no differently than my father did me at his age."

"Maybe now that you realize it, you can change. Uh-oh. Speaking of keeping wits."

Alaric charged like a bull toward Chad. Leif followed like a hapless puppy.

He seized Chad. "What do you think you're doing, boy?"

"Nothing. Just talking to her. Something you might try doing."

"Alaric!" Nigel grabbed him from behind, pinning his arms by his side. He had a four-inch height advantage, but Alaric was strong.

"Let him go. I can handle this," said Chad.

"Not out here."

"Nigel," said Mirit in warning when Iryn arrived.

He released Alaric.

"Is there a problem with your varlets, Sigvard?" asked Iryn, her disdain clearly evident.

"A misunderstanding."

"I suggest you resolve it elsewhere and not disrupt the daily routine."

"As you wish, priestess." Mirit made the Sigvard salute. She motioned for the men to follow her back to the Novice Hall.

The hall was vacant, but Mirit took no chances and led them to the nearest corner. She proceeded to scold Alaric. "We appreciate the fact Bergeta is your daughter and you disapprove of her being here, but Chad spoke to her to try and gain information to help us. Your temper could place our mission in jeopardy, and possibly lose the only chance of swaying your daughter by further alienating her. Is that what you want?"

Alaric was properly shamed. "No, miss."

"Leif, help him keep his head and find Bergeta to speak to her."

"Ja, miss. Now will you listen to me?" he asked Alaric as they left.

"One problem averted," said Nigel.

"Now for the other," she began in the Ancient, folding her arms, eyes coming to rest on Chad. "What is your problem?"

"Me?"

"Ay, and don't deny it. You've been angry and obstinate, taking offense at everything anybody does or says."

He shrugged, taken back by the rebuff. "I don't know."

"That's not an answer," said Nigel.

"Don't be so cocky," she scolded Nigel. "You've been overbearing." She put up her hand when Nigel went to protest and Chad stiffened. "Difference in stations aside, you're supposed to be friends. At least that is what I've believed all these months. Or am I mistaken?"

Chastened, Chad shifted his weight and glanced down to his feet.

"You're not mistaken," said Nigel. He placed a hand on Chad's shoulder. "You befriended me as a cripple, and I, you as a orphan, not as prince and subject."

"But it's who we are. Perhaps there is some lack of understanding."

"How so?"

Chad pursed his lips in consideration before answering. "You are kind, generous and have taught me much. A better master cannot be found, and I shall always be grateful. However, you are your own man, while I am not."

The reply stymied Nigel. "I never asked you to lose yourself."

"No, but in all these years, you have not asked me *if* I want to be a Jor'ellian, rather assume I do because I serve you."

"I never heard you say you didn't want to."

"How can I refuse? You are not simply my friend and master, but the prince."

Nigel became offended yet spoke with restraint. "I never used my station to coerce you."

Chad grew frustrated. "It's not what you have or haven't done, it's who you are. And the reason I have not spoken my mind."

"Quiet," warned Mirit. Two younger novices entered and made their way toward the hearth.

Chad chewed on his lip and Nigel scratched at his whiskers.

"Chad," began Mirit once the novices were a safe distance away. "Nigel can't help who he is any more than you can. Still, he cares about you. Has he ever been inapproachable?"

"Not completely."

Mirit stopped Nigel from speaking by seizing his arm. She further questioned Chad. "Really? Or is your perception preventing you from speaking candidly to him?"

Chad didn't reply, considering the question.

She pressed her point. "You corrected my perception in Misow, remember? You were confident Nigel would come for us no matter what. I didn't believe it because I only saw the hurt I caused him. Happily you were right."

He avoided eye contact with either of them. "Maybe. Only it doesn't change reality for me as it did for you. You are of nobility, I am not."

Nigel voice was thick. "What do you want, Chad? To quit my service and be your own man?"

Chad couldn't respond. Instead, he bowed and left.

The action made Nigel flinch and grouse, "I pushed him too far."

"No. But *I* owe you an apology. You were right. He doesn't yet know his mind. Until he does we must keep our wits in dealing with him."

In the compound, Iryn approached Ingrid after the others left. "Have you learned anything?"

"Not much, I'm afraid. They are cordial whenever I approach, but when they are alone they speak another language. Perhaps it is the native tongue of the place of beginning."

"The prophecy about their coming is disturbing. I want to know more."

Ingrid was confused. "I thought prophecy spoke of them helping the Valkerish. How can that be disturbing?"

Iryn looked sharp in rebuke. "Help to destroy them, or help them to defeat the Tavar is the question to be answered. They are clever."

"The one called Chad is interested in Bergeta. She told me."

A smile appeared on Iran's lips. "Has Bergeta chosen her *gemate*?"

"I don't know if she's even aware of that part yet. She's only been here a month and Danka is her instructor, not I."

"Send her to my quarters."

Ingrid saluted Iryn and the older priestess left.

Iryn's quarters were located on the far side of temple. Compared to the cells of novices it was large and nicely furnished. Upon entering, an arm pulled her in and slammed the door shut.

In fright, she stared at the very tall, handsome, dark-haired man clad in a fine black suit and cloak both trimmed in crimson. He placed his hands on his hips, which drew back the cloak revealing the impressive sword at his side. He was an imposing figure wearing a black patch over his right eye, the other eye unnerving in its cold pearly brilliance.

"You disappointment me, Iryn. When were you going to tell me of these strangers?"

She swallowed back her fear to speak. "As soon as I knew their identity, my lord Skule."

"Really? They approach the Valkerish as we speak. How could you allow this?"

"Not my choice, lord! Ludmilla—"

"Ludmilla," he scowled. "She is a thorn in our plans. It will be my pleasure to eliminate her when the time comes." He folded his arms across his chest, his good eye steady on Iryn. "What can you tell me about the strangers?"

She began her answer, watchful of his reaction. "They claim to come from the place of beginning. During the welcoming temple ceremony,

Ludmilla called upon the Valkerish. The exchange was brief when the Valkerish summoned them to Astrid."

Skule's brow furrowed with curious annoyance during the explanation. "They did not identify themselves during the ceremony?"

"One did. She called her self Auriel, Valkerish of Justice."

He tugged at his lower lip, thoughtful. "The others said nothing?"

"The other female doubled over in pain when the Valkerish appeared. He held her—"

"He?"

"Ja, the third is male and fearsome in appearance. Perhaps even a bit larger than you, my lord. With intimidating silver eyes."

He shook his head in dispute. "I heard of a fourth with them."

"A Sigvard. But she is not the only one. Four varlets also. They are here under *sauf* while the Valkerish are at Astrid."

"Interesting. Have the varlets said anything?"

"Not yet, lord. I am endeavoring to draw one of them out. He has taken a fancy to a new novice."

"Excellent. Have her work fast. I want information by morning."

At a knock on the door Skule vanished in a flash of white light, leaving Iryn staring in bewilderment at the spot he occupied. The knock persisted, but she did not recover from her stupor until a voice called and identified herself. She gathered her emotions to answer the door.

"Come in, Bergeta."

"Priestess, are you well? You look pale."

Iryn smiled and closed the door. "I'm fine. I called you to discuss your future with us. Are you settling in well? Finding all you need?"

"Ja. Danka is most helpful and the other novices kind."

"Has Danka been thorough in her instruction?"

"Ja. The other day we went to Mistress Hetta to see her stock."

Iryn widely smiled. "Excellent. How did you find the experience?"

Bergeta blushed. "Exciting, but intimidating."

"Did any catch your eye?"

Her blush deepened. "I'm still considering."

Iryn nodded. "You are wise, child. It should not be a decision made in haste. However, I heard report that one of the foreign varlets has acted unseemly," she said, paying attention to Bergeta's reaction.

"No! Chad is kind and—" the girl stopped, suddenly embarrassed.

"And what?"

"I … I don't know if it is appropriate to speak of him. He is not among the chosen stock of the temple."

Iryn grinned at the naiveté. "He is a varlet serving a Valkerish. That makes him better than Mistress Hetta's stock, more worthy."

Bergeta beamed with pleasure. "I'm to meet him tonight. Oh, I mean to talk. He wanted to speak to me in private."

Iryn laughed. "No need to be shy, my dear. We all must choose our *gemate*."

"Then you approve of him?"

"Ja. Go to the closet and take the wine and cake."

"Thank you, priestess," said Bergeta with excitement. She saluted Iryn and left.

⁂

Chad spent the rest of the day avoiding Nigel and Mirit. He had much to consider and wanted a quiet place to think. The most secluded place he found was a tool shed along the back wall. He faced many challenges over the last year and tried to discern his own feelings.

The mission to rescue Prince Titus brought him into direct conflict with evil for the first time since the attempted coup of King Ellis, Nigel's father. At age eight, he didn't completely understand what was happening the day he met Nigel, a wandering cripple. By then he traveled the roads alone for a year and grew tired of being hungry and desperate. The abuse he suffered at the hands of the farmer sent him looking for a better life. At sight of a crippled beggar being mishandled and further injured, he recognized someone less fortunate and offered to help. From that day Nigel took him in, feed him, clothed him, taught him and gave him the better life. He went from an abused orphan to the squire of a prince.

How can I be discontent with that? Still, questions gnawed at his brain.

During the rescue mission to Tunlund, the situation remained clear, good verse evil. Helmer actually proved to be a Guardian vassal. He kidnapped Titus to display his power against Jor'el but it proved his undoing when Tyrone invaded Tunlund and defeated him. The situation became less clear for Chad when they returned to Tunlund to help Vicar Uriah establish the worship of Jor'el.

The Tunlundians were a complex people with many versions of worship to various gods. Until then he viewed good and evil in stark terms, so when shades of gray emerged, he had difficulty seeing the moral choices. Nigel tried to counsel him by using Verse and reducing the complexities to simple concepts. But on the seven-month tour of Tunlund, he saw Nigel in a different light than as friend and master, or even the prince. Nigel acted strict, almost to the point of inflexible when dealing with the Tunlundians. True, he adhered to his knightly training and discipline, but knowing how to fight was a matter of life and death, while belief in the divine a matter of the heart and conscience. Thus he came to believe Nigel's weakness was being unable to separate the two, and a weakness that troubled him because he completely disagreed.

If not for Mirit, he considered feigning illness and requesting to be sent home to Allon. She lived among the Tunlundians for many years and proved more tolerant to their objections and questions. She countered Nigel's brashness. Perhaps with her help, Nigel would recognize his weakness. After all, she could speak freely since they were in love and he listened to what she said. Unfortunately, she didn't realize it was no longer what he witnessed in Tunlund, but now also in Soren. Bad enough Nigel challenged the faith of the Tunlundians, why make light of the Guardians? Avatar remained fiercely loyal to Nigel, almost dying in Tunlund, and what appreciation was shown?

In response to the thought, Nigel's word echoed in Chad's brain. *"I appreciate Avatar more than I can say. In fact, I love him like a member of my family, but I don't worship him."*

"No, you favor him above other Guardians, and by that contradict yourself and are blinded to your own prejudice," he muttered.

Again Nigel's voice came to mind, only with a very disturbing question, and the question making him avoid Nigel. *"What do you want, Chad? To quit my service and be your own man?"*

A hand on his shoulder made him jump. He smiled in relief at Bergeta.

"You missed supper," she said.

"I'm not hungry."

She brushed his hair behind his ears. "Are you troubled about meeting me tonight?"

"No."

"Good. I feared you might reconsider."

"Why should I?"

"Your friends seem distant. Like they don't approve of us."

"Don't let their attitude disturb you. They don't appreciate anyone who is different."

She smiled, her eyes sparkling. "I'm glad you're not like them."

The words hung in his ears and he forced himself to listen when she continued to speak.

"The novices will be retiring in an hour. Wait about a half hour more to make certain all are asleep so we can talk undisturbed. My room is the first one of the left as you enter the hall."

"I'll be there."

She widely smiled, a light blush to her cheeks. She left.

Her words repeated in his brain. *"I'm glad you're not like them."* Part of him wondered what she meant, another part was pleased she noticed a difference. Whereas he fretted away the day in avoidance of Nigel, he looked forward to see Bergeta again.

The hour and a half passed slowly for Chad. Upon opening the door to Novice Hall, everything appeared quiet. Except for the dying fire in the hearth at the end of the hall, it was empty. As he approached Bergeta's door he wondered if he should knock. *No, she is expecting me.*

Trying the knob he found the door unlocked. He entered and quietly shut the door. She sat on the bed in a nightgown, her hair loose and cascading over her shoulders. The candlelight danced on her gold hair.

"Am I late?" he asked, a touch awkward.

"No." She rose, took his hand and led him to the bed to sit.

"I thought we were going to talk?"

"We are. First, let's have some wine and cake." She indicated a bottle and small cake on the nightstand. "Since you missed supper."

"I am hungry."

She poured the wine into two cups and gave Chad a cup. She made a small salute with the cup and drank.

He mimicked her. "This is good. What kind of wine is it?"

"Elderberry. Less intoxicating. Cake?"

He took the piece she offered and ate. Bergeta also ate a piece of the cake. "This is good too," he said with a mouthful.

"There is another piece."

He took the other piece. She refilled his cup and he washed down the cake. When he finished eating, she took the cup and placed it on the nightstand.

"Are you pleased?"

"With the wine and cake, ja."

"No, with me. Am I pleasant to look at?" she asked in a tone of uncertainty that made him smile.

"You are very beautiful. Especially with your hair down and in the candlelight."

She kissed him on the lips, placing her arms about his neck and moving closer.

He stiffened and backed away. "I don't know about this. After all you are a priestess, or rather, on the way to becoming a priestess."

She giggled. "Naturally. And you are a varlet." She kissed him again, pressing against him.

He had never been this close to a woman before or tasted a passionate kiss. Still, something wasn't right. She moved from kissing his lips to his neck, stroking his hair. "I think we may want to talk about this," he said under her advance.

She hurtfully pouted, eyes misty. "I displease you."

"No. You're beautiful and desirable."

She wept. "You mock me when I want to do is please you."

Seeing her tears, he lifted her head in his hand. He returned her kiss with passion and intent.

Chapter 12

ULRIKA HEARD A RUMBLE NEXT TO HER EAR and her eyes opened in time to see a flash of light. The sky was still dark so it wasn't sunrise. Someone watched her. Farren. Ulrika scrambled to her knees and bowed her head. "My lady!"

"Ulrika. I have a task for you. The male, Avatar, is on the loose. You are to capture him using these. *Dorcha sinteag,*" said Farren. Spurean manacles appeared on the ground in front of Ulrika. "Also, the Sigvard accompanying them is to be imprisoned and await my pleasure."

Ulrika picked up the manacle. "What about the varlets?"

"Foreign varlets?"

"Two are foreign, two are local."

"Imprison the foreigners and whip the locals as punishment."

"Only a whipping?"

Farren raised a scolding eyebrow. "You would punish the simple, who are pawns for their betters? You disappoint me, Ulrika."

"Your pardon, my lady."

Farren nodded. "When you have captured Avatar, bring him to Astrid."

"As you command, my lady."

Farren disappeared.

Ulrika stood and shouted, "Up! We ride to Falken."

Perti stretched and rubbed the sleep from her eyes. "Why the urgency?"

"The foreigners have angered the Valkerish. We are to imprison their company and capture the male." She showed Perti the manacles.

"Why Falken? We brought them here, so he could be nearby."

"Take care of the enemy you know about, then seek the one who is missing. Besides, he may have returned to Manheim to fetch them."

<hr />

Avatar stirred at hearing a voice say, "Arise and eat, Avatar." His eyes sprang open and he listened again. Nothing, but the words were distinctive and commanding. "Jor'el."

His nose didn't hurt so he took a deep breath through his nostrils. He touched the back of his head expecting to feel a wound or see blood on his fingers, nothing. He smiled at the physical healing. Jor'el said to eat since a good meal would aid his energy after injury. Sword in hand, he moved to the opening. The sky showed the gray of early dawn.

"Wren says dawn is the best time to hunt." To his surprise a rabbit hopped in front of the opening. He snatched it. "Thank you, Jor'el."

By dawn, he finished cooking and eating the rabbit, buried the carcass and smothered the fire. The first thing to do was take stock of the Sigvard camp. Perhaps he could learn news of Auriel and Wren.

Quiet and cautious, he arrived at edge of the forest near the campsite. The Sigvard were gone! Not good. What of Wren and Auriel? He sensed Wren and trouble but not Auriel. For a moment he studied Astrid and the trail. He estimated a mile from where he was waylaid to the top. He didn't fear being sensed, but to investigate what became of Wren and Auriel he had two choices: dimension travel and risk meeting trouble when he reappeared, or attempt to hide his essence and race the path to the top. The problem with the latter choice is the technique wasn't always effective; especially considering Farren was an Original and with the ability to sense things others could not.

"Kell once said my tracking skills outdid Dagar, maybe I can elude Farren." He drew his sword. He held the blade in front of his face and bowed his head so his forehead touched the blade. He spoke in the Ancient. "Jor'el, aid my effort. From spirit and sight hide this form, till the task is done, in the name of heaven on high."

He bolted from his concealment and raced up the path at incredible speed, taking no heed to the perils of loose rocks or patches of ice. He wasn't even breathing hard when he reached the main entrance of Astrid, nor did he pause in opening the door, but only far enough to slip through and close the door behind him.

So far so good, but he couldn't stop to determine if anyone sensed him and risk losing the element of surprise. The room through the opposite archway appeared to be the great hall. There were two more archways on either side leading to hallways. He crossed to the opposite archway and peeked inside. Sure enough, it was the great hall. At either end of the room, stairs led up to the second floor. Upon hearing muffled voices and footsteps, he darted to the left steps and hid under the stairwell. His grip tightened on the hilt of his sword when they entered the hall. He didn't want to fight before finding out about his companions, while remaining in one place too long could leave a sense to be discovered. Surprise registered on his face at hearing Auriel speak.

"It would be unwise to harm Nigel. Hueil tried that with his son and Tyrone invaded Tunlund."

"I told Ulrika to imprison him and others, not to harm them. Besides, I didn't identify him as the prince of Allon," said Farren.

"Good thing you killed Avatar, otherwise there would be trouble."

This told him that they wouldn't even be looking for his essence.

"What about Wren?" asked another voice familiar to Avatar.

He risked peeking out to confirm Willow's identity and ducked back, jowls tight in anger. *Calm down or they will sense you,* he scolded himself.

"She's been rendered ineffective, what more do you want?"

Ineffective? He did feel danger, meaning Wren injured or worse.

"You think Avatar capable of causing trouble? What about Vidar when he learns we have her?" argued Auriel.

Relief. *Wren is alive.*

"Not our main concern," said Farren. "The immediate is preparing for the Tavar. Once they learn what has happened, they will know we are discovered and seek to destroy us."

"Perhaps I can persuade her to join us or at least make a suggestion."

Farren laughed. "I don't think so."

"Worth a try."

"Just be glad she is inhibited by the manacles. Willow, return to your watch, I'm going to keep an eye on things in Manheim. However," her tone changing to warning. "I want Wren here when I get back."

"Have no fear. If she's gone, then she got through me to be free," said Auriel.

At a flash of light and hearing fading footsteps, he peeked out to see Farren and Willow gone and Auriel heading toward the other stairs. Discovery or not, she betrayed them! In quick strides, he crossed the room and snared her from behind. One hand covered her mouth and held her against his body. His sword raised in front of her face.

"Give me one reason I shouldn't finish you!"

Her eyes went wide at hearing his harsh voice in her ear.

"You thought Farren killed me. Funny how she didn't tell you the truth when you spoke about Nigel." She tried to fight free only to stop when he exerted pressure on her neck making her wince and groan in pain. "You may be a warrior, but I am stronger. Now, take me to Wren. But be warned, one false move or deception and I will dispatch you."

More pressure on her neck and she groaned in pain but managed a muffled agreement.

Suddenly, he tilted his head at hearing a crossbow cock and twang of release coming from behind. He tossed Auriel aside and dodged the arrow whizzing past his face and into the wall. Willow loaded another arrow. He disappeared in a flash just as she fired her second shot, which also lodged in the wall.

"Farren lied!" shouted Auriel. "Make sure Wren is secure." She seized Willow and added, "Don't tell her Avatar is alive." She shoved Willow away, drew her sword and raced to the main entrance. He wasn't there, so she went to the overlook. From this vantage point most of the surrounding countryside could be seen. He raced into the woods, then a flash of light indicating dimension travel. Angry, she ran back inside.

Wren lay on the stone bed weary in body and drained in spirit. Several times she tried to meditate and search for any sense of Avatar, only to black out. She knew the spurean manacles inhibited her power and senses, but she couldn't give up. Other Guardians suffered far worse when prisoners of Dagar and survived, Vidar being one of them. Thinking of her friend and mentor helped her to try again.

She closed her eyes and stretched her senses past the pain in her wrists that would eventually overtake her. This time she didn't push too far and felt something close. Her eyes snapped open. "Avatar."

Hurried footsteps echoed in the hall, and she forced herself to sit up in anticipation. A head appear at the bars. Willow. Disappointed, Wren sagged against the wall, but steeled herself when Willow entered.

"You look secure enough. What are you up to?"

"Nothing."

"You lie."

Despite the pain, Wren raised her arms. "I can't do anything."

Willow remained skeptical. "Vidar is clever. He taught you some trick to get around those."

Wren snorted in annoyance but didn't answer.

"I could kill you." Willow held up Wren's crossbow. "And with your own weapon. I always admired this bow. Far superior to mine. I hope you don't mind I took it? Then again, you're in no position to object."

Conflicting emotions played across Wren's face. "Vidar and I thought you were vanquished during the mortal uprising. Only you've been here pretending to be a deity. What happened to you, Willow?"

Auriel arrived. "Is everything under control?"

"Ay." She turned to leave with Auriel.

"Willow! Please, tell me what changed you," said Wren in desperation.

Auriel spoke instead. "You still don't understand?"

"I understand you grieve for Jedrek and vent your spleen on Avatar because of the Great Battle and accuse him of things he didn't do."

"This isn't about Jedrek or Avatar, it about us!" Auriel struck her chest in a motioning gesture. "We're just as good, if not better, than our male counterparts, but they refuse to see it."

"That's not true," insisted Wren, then spoke to Willow. "Vidar mentored you, showed you how to move silently in the forest, speak to nature, to shoot, he taught you everything! He taught us both, side-by-side. Is this how you repay him, by turning against Jor'el and your duty?"

Willow lashed out. "It was Vidar's *duty* to instruct us, but he favored you in friendship! I mastered every skill, but your accomplishments pleased him."

Wren shook her head in bewilderment. "I don't know what you're talking about. He boasted of you. If anything I had to live up to your potential."

Willow furrowed her brows in confusion. "You're just saying that."

"No! You were his prize pupil, not me! Kell even acknowledged your skill and prowess when Vidar and I mourned your loss."

Willow's whole countenance changed from fierce to thoughtful.

"Don't believe her," said Farren. She and Keara entered unnoticed.

"I thought you went to Manheim?" said Auriel.

"I became alerted to trouble." Farren addressed Willow. "She's trying to deceive you. Vidar has always been arrogant and self-righteous, same as the others. Kell worst of all."

"No!" rebuffed Wren. "When Vidar was captured by Dagar, I thought I lost both of you. He escaped and helped to defeat Dagar, yet not before suffering for centuries in these." She thrust the spurean manacles in Willow's face, ignoring the pain of movement.

Farren pulled Willow from Wren and had Keara take her from the cell. She turned her full attention to Wren, her eyes narrow and probing. "Have you never been insulted, mocked, or teased by the males?"

Wren didn't want to answer and fought against her weakened state to withstand Farren's compelling glance.

"She has. If she says otherwise, she is lying. Avatar, even Vidar tease her," said Auriel.

"Teasing isn't mockery or insults," said Wren in weak protest.

"Tell that to Ewert or Zadok. How about Gresham? Or better yet, Armus."

Wren hung her head, a weary sigh escaping. Her whole body felt weak and drained.

"What? You don't disagree?" asked Farren.

"She can't, because it's true."

Wren slumped against the wall, exhausted by both the manacles and the conversation. "All of us do it to each other. It's not simply males against females."

"Does that make it right? Does it excuse them?"

Wren closed her eyes and swallowed back her emotions to answer in a hollow voice. "No."

With a pleased smile, Farren said, "There may be hope for her."

"If she can get past her attachment to certain males."

"You believe she has feelings for Vidar or Avatar?"

"Both."

"No. It's not like that," whimpered Wren. She fought to remain awake, but upon hearing the door close, she slipped from the wall into unconsciousness.

The pale light of dawn shone through the only Novice Hall window, a large circular glass one above the main entrance. Mirit emerged from her room. Nigel sat at a table with his head down. Whether he slept or prayed she couldn't tell. Drawing near she heard the rhythmic breathing of sleep. He must have been sitting there most of the night. Quietly, she sat next to him, watching for a moment.

"You're such a dear heart for worrying so," she whispered and stroked his cheek.

He stirred at her touch and opened his eyes. "Mirit."

"Good morning to you too, sleepy head."

He sat up, stiff and stretched. "Sorry. A table is not the most comfortable place for sleeping."

She stood to massage his neck and shoulders. "How long have you been here? I remember seeing you retire."

He didn't reply immediately, enjoying the massage. "I waited for Chad to return from his *meeting* only I fell asleep."

She sat beside him. "You are perhaps the most caring man I know, even when there is no reason. But with caring, you must learn there is a time to let go."

He kissed her hand. "I know. I waited up to tell him that if he wants to quit my service and be his own man, he does so with my blessing. No hard feelings, just wishing him the best."

She smiled. "You can learn."

"I maybe thickheaded, but I'd like to think I'm not hopeless."

"No." She leaned her head against his shoulder. "I once felt hopeless, but you showed me otherwise." Seeing a door open, she sat up.

Across the hall, Chad emerged from the far room, his back to them as he kissed Bergeta.

Nigel stiffened and muttered, "What has he done?"

"Don't." She seized him with both hands to prevent him from rising.

Chad saw them. With a curt bow of his head, left Novice Hall.

Mirit held fast when Nigel again stirred to rise. "Would you destroy him with your words?"

"What?"

"You said he could leave with your blessing. Will you risk cursing him with your condemnation?"

His whole body slumped, his arms on the table and head falling into his hands. "Where did I go wrong with him, Mirit?"

"You didn't! You taught him all you could, but you can't control his choices—"

"There they are!"

A squad of Sigvard rushed upon them. Not being armed, they offered no resistance. However, Mirit rose to confront them. "What is the meaning of this?" The answer came as a sword leveled at her face.

Alaric and Leif emerged from a room, sleepy eyed, yet became alert when Sigvard grabbed them.

"Come with us," commanded the squad leader.

Bergeta ran from her room. "Where's Chad?" she asked, but ignored.

In the compound Nigel, Mirit, Alaric and Leif were brought before a fierce looking Ulrika. Chad was already there and held by two Sigvard.

"What's the meaning of this?" demanded Mirit.

Ulrika slapped Mirit, hard. "Treacherous wench! You don't deserve the title Sigvard."

Mirit spat out blood form a split lip. It was second time being struck on the same side of her face and the assault reopened the earlier cut.

"Take them to the dungeon at Falken."

"No! Wait!" cried Bergeta, moving to Chad. "He is my *gemate*."

"What is going on?" Ludmilla and Iryn rushed to arrive.

"Priestess. We have orders from the Valkerish to imprison the Sigvard and foreign varlets. These two," Ulrika pointed to Alaric and Leif, "are to be whipped."

"Then they have rejected their sisters," said Ludmilla with dread.

"High Priestess, please hear me," pleaded Bergeta. "This varlet is my *gemate*. Do not let them take him!"

"It is true," said Iryn. "She told me yesterday of her choice. Since he is varlet to Valkerish, I gave permission to take the wine and cake."

"You were with her last night?" Ludmilla questioned Chad.

Chad didn't immediately answer for seeing Nigel's stoic features, but his eyes showed hurt and disappointment. Silent or vocal, the truth was already known so he replied, "I was."

"He stays."

"You can't disobey the Valkerish," chided Ulrika.

"He is her *gemate!* A state established by the Valkerish. Take these others and go. The boy stays."

The Sigvard roughly released Chad and Bergeta caught him to keep him from stumbling. He tried to jerk away to when Nigel and Mirit were escorted from the compound.

"No! I just saved you," she said, pulling hard on his arm. "If you leave I will also be imprisoned." She stroked his face to get his attention. "You are now *gemate*. I can protect you, but if you chase after them we are both lost."

"I don't understand. What is *gemate?*"

"Don't you know? You drank the wine, ate the cake and came to my bed. We are now mated for life."

He paled at the implication. "You mean—married?"

"Ja. It is part of being a priestess to choose a mate for service and breeding." She took his hand and placed it on her stomach. "I know I am fertile and could bear a child soon."

He pulled his hand away, growing paler in fear and dread.

She became upset at his reaction. "I don't understand. I chose you because I favored you. After last night, I love you."

"Love? You don't know me."

"I want to."

Overwhelmed by frustration and angst, he took her face in his hands. "Dear Bergeta, how can I make you understand? Last night was wonderful and you are beautiful, but it was a mistake. I'm not who you think I am."

"Maybe, but what is done cannot be undone without us both suffering great consequences."

"There have already been consequences you are not aware of, and I don't know if I can ever set right." He looked in agonizing regret toward the temple gate.

Angry and upset, she lashed out. "I gave myself to you and protected you from the High Priestess and the Sigvard. I favor you above all others including my father, who will be whipped for helping you and your friends!" She wept bitter tears.

When he went to comfort her, she pulled away.

"You must choose. The life you once had, which you claim is damaged beyond repair, or a new life with me, one who willingly chose you."

The truth of her words hit him hard and filled him with hopeless dread. She turned to leave and he snatched her arm. "Today I lost friends because I disappointed them. When you get to know me, will also you be too disappointed to love me as you say you do now?"

Through a teary smile she said, "No. I will not be a fair weather friend or mate."

He pulled her to him and held on tight, trying not to weep.

Avatar reappeared just outside Manheim. Travelers came and went from the city. He spied a lone older man in a large heavy cloak walking with a cane. He intercepted the man and drew him into the trees. He spoke in the Ancient and the old man fell asleep. Avatar removed the cloak and gently laid him on the ground. The cloak barely hid his bulk, but the hood concealed his face. Before leaving, he placed his hand on the old man's head.

"You will sleep until I return."

Stooped over, Avatar pretended to limp and use the cane as he entered Manheim. No one paid him any attention so he made his way to the temple. He paused before entering. The disguise helped, but playing the invalid could draw unwanted attention and hinder his task in finding the others. However, dimension travel was not a good choice either. What mortals could not sense other Guardians could and with Shadow Warriors on the loose he needed to be cautious.

He made his way from the main gate toward Falken, taking mental note of alleyways and passages en route. Spying a promising passageway he reckoned led to the back of the temple compound, he diverted his course. He discovered the smaller rear gate closed, but unlocked. He opened it enough to peek inside. The gate opened to a passageway behind the temple where they kept the refuse. Entering, he turned his back to shut the gate when someone accosted him.

"What are you doing here?" asked a middle-age priestess.

His silver gaze direct, he said, "Nothing, and you see no one."

For a moment she stared at him. Without another word she turned and made her way to the main compound.

He waited before proceeding in the same direction, only paused at the corner to view the compound. Novices and priestess went about their daily chores. Novice Hall lay across from the back alley. Chad entered the hall in the company of a girl. Not waiting for a more opportune time, Avatar dashed after them. Before either Chad or Bergeta realized what was happening, Avatar pulled them into the nearest room, which by coincidence was Bergeta's room. Chad moved to make defense when the hood was thrown back.

"Avatar!"

Bergeta clung to him, gaping in fear.

Avatar took brief notice of her before questioning Chad. "Where are Nigel and Mirit?"

He balked, avoiding eye contact. "They, Alaric and Leif, were arrested by the Sigvard and taken to Falken."

"I hoped to return in time. Why are you still here?"

Again, Chad averted his eyes to look sympathetically at the girl.

"This is Bergeta, Alaric's daughter and my *gemate*. Or rather I'm her *gemate*. Her mate."

Avatar's gaze turned harsh. "I know what it means. How and when?"

Chad grew flustered. "Last night I came to speak to Bergeta, that was all. One thing led to another, and well," he sighed in painful regret," we were together all night."

"Does Nigel know?" his voice tight in asking.

Chad nodded.

The Guardian scowled, disappointment and anger crossing his face.

"I'm sorry!" clamored Chad. "I never meant for it happen. Nor did I know the wine and cake were part of a marriage ceremony."

"I did not deceive you! Being a varlet I thought you understood. You willingly responded."

"I did," he admitted in reluctance.

For Avatar, Chad's manner told him of more disturbing truths yet to admit. "What does this have to do with Nigel and Mirit and why you are not with them?"

Chad shook his head in confusion. "The Sigvard claimed orders from the Valkerish to imprison the foreigners. Bergeta," he said holding her hand, "saved me by declaring I am her mate, which in the eyes of the Valkerish is sacred. Ludmilla told Ulrika she couldn't take me."

Avatar's studied the young people. There was a definite attraction, but lousy timing given the circumstances. Chad's recent discontentment transgressed into thoughtless action. He pressed his lips in regard of the youth. "Nothing can be done to rectify last night, but together we can save the others."

"I can't!"

"What do you mean you can't?"

"To help will place Bergeta in danger. She risked her life to save me. I can't abandon her."

"You will forsake Nigel and Mirit for the girl?" When Chad shied way, Avatar knew the answer. He gripped the hilt of his sword to stem the rise of his own hurt and anger. "In your heart, you already turned your back on them. And Jor'el."

Chad winced in pain, looking further away. "I don't know about Jor'el! It's all confusing."

"Who is Jor'el?" asked Bergeta.

Avatar became incredulous. "You have not told her about the Almighty who created both mortals and Guardians, yet you wed?"

"Avatar, I—"

"No! You made your choice. Now you must live with the consequences." He turned to leave when Chad seized his arm.

"I'm sorry! I didn't mean to disappoint any of you."

The Guardian looked from the hand on his arm to Chad's face. Indeed, he saw genuine regret, but the deed was done. "You are not the first mortal to disappointment me, and I doubt you will be the last. Yet, you are one of the more surprising ones. But most disturbing, is how easily you did this to Nigel."

Chad blinked back tears. "I swear, I didn't mean it!"

Avatar would hear no more, and left the hall and temple compound by the back gate. Once in the alley, he paused to gather his emotions. It was not good for a Guardian to become too attached to their charges, though sometimes difficult to remember. Of all the mortals he has known, he felt most attached to Nigel. What a painful blow this must to him. In his musings, Avatar admitted a soft spot for the unpretentious orphan who willing gave aid years ago.

Why, Chad? Have you learned nothing after all these years? Jor'el, have mercy and bring the boy to his senses.

Avatar made his way back to where he left the old man. After placing the cloak on the man, he touched the man's forehead and spoke in the Ancient. "Awake and remember nothing." He drifted back into the woods before the man awoke.

Finding a secluded spot, Avatar sat cross-legged and took several deep breaths to calm his mind and heart before closing his eyes to begin his mediation. The last twenty-four hours were a whirlwind of events and emotions. Aside from discovering Auriel and Chad's individual betrayal, Nigel and Mirit became prisoners, he suffered wounds and learned the

Valkerish were Guardians and Shadows Warriors were the Tavar. Now he understood why they wanted to invade Allon.

On a personal level, Auriel's betrayal stung far worse than Chad's recklessness. Whereas Chad could claim being a confused mortal teenager with hope for future redemption, Auriel was a seasoned Guardian warrior, who freely forfeited her station and became an enemy of Jor'el. In reflecting on her choice, he recalled how she taunted him and provoked him since leaving. Now the final act of betrayal placed everyone's life in danger. His anger swelled against her.

"I should have snapped your neck when I had the chance. No, Wren. If I killed Auriel they would have taken revenge on her."

He closed his eyes and he stretched out his spirit, searching for Wren's essence. Suddenly a sense touched his mind and spirit, causing his eyes to snap open. For a moment he considered the new sensation. He closed his eyes again, allowing his spirit to seek the sense. It became stronger and familiar, making him smile. This time when his opened his eyes, he stood and disappeared in a flash of light.

Chapter 13

EACH STEP FROM THE TEMPLE TO FALKEN, the weight of Nigel's discouragement increased. Everything was unraveling but he had to keep his wits and not be overcome by despondency about Chad and the possible fates of Avatar, Wren and Auriel. Only by keeping a sharp mind and his emotions in check could he figure a way out.

Once inside the courtyard of Falken, Ulrika stopped the group. "Strip them and prepare the lash," she said of Alaric and Leif then she spoke to Mirit. "Let this be a lesson in how real Sigvard serve their mistresses. With strength and honor."

"If abusing the weaker is a sign of Sigvard honor, then I am glad not to be among your sisters."

Ulrika went to strike, but Mirit caught her hand inches from her face. She tightened her grip around Ulrika's wrist and let her nails dig into Ulrika's skin.

Ulrika flinched and pulled away. "Thirty lashes each!"

Nigel stiffened at the pronouncement and took hold of Mirit's arm. She may have been ready for Ulrika's predictable response, but it couldn't go any further. He barely shook his head in warning and saw she understood. Along with the understanding was a hint of pain, not for herself. The small bruises on her face from being struck multiple times showed that, rather for Alaric and Leif.

The cracking of a whip caught their attention. Now stripped to the waist, the brothers were tied to posts near the stables. Two Sigvard held the whips. The beating would be simultaneous. Nigel couldn't recall ever seeing multiple whippings before. Not that he wanted to witness this one. They came to Soren in response to a plea for help, now Alaric and Leif would pay for that help.

Some help. We're prisoners. Avatar, Auriel and Wren are who knows where. Or what's become of them? While Chad— His jowls tightened and his brow leveled against the personal pain. Sounds of whips striking flesh and muffled cries made him push the disturbing thoughts away. He could not show weakness, not now. *Jor'el, have mercy on them. They came to us for help and we failed them.* But each lash drove home his thought of failure.

After twenty lashes, Alaric sagged. Leif faired only slightly better. By lash twenty-five, Alaric hung limp against the post, but the whipping continued. Mirit lowly gasped and fiercely bit her lip to keep silent. Nigel's eyes narrowed in anger on Ulrika, who watched with stoic indifference. At lash twenty-eight, Leif collapsed into semi-consciousness.

"Enough!" snapped Ulrika upon the thirtieth lash. "Throw them all in the dungeon."

Grissel and a half-dozen Sigvard escorted Nigel and Mirit. Four others carried and dragged Alaric and Leif. They descended the stairs to the dungeon, a circular room with six iron-barred cells and a central guard station for easy managing of prisoners. Torches provided enough light for the two Sigvard guards to keep an eye on all the prisoners.

"Those two in that cell," she instructed the guards concerning Alaric and Leif. "Open these two for the others." She pointed at adjoining cells.

"Shouldn't they be kept further apart?" asked a guard.

"Why? Are you threatened by their presence?"

The guard gave no further dispute and opened the bars. Both Nigel and Mirit were shoved into the cells. Nigel moved to sit in the back of the cell against the wall. Mirit stood at the gate, watching Grissel and the others leave. For a brief moment Magda lingered, returning Mirit's steady regard. Without a word, she left and the guards returned to their meal.

Mirit moved to the rear of her cell and sat near Nigel. She lowly spoke in the Ancient. "I hoped I convinced Magda about Jor'el, although not by name."

"I thought I had done more than convince Chad," he droned.

"What happened is not your fault."

"Tell that to Alaric and Leif." He drew his knees up and lowered his head to rest his forehead on his knees not wanting to hear any more excuses.

Ulrika and Perti were in the hall of Falken when Grissel and Magda entered. "Are they secure?" asked Ulrika.

"Ja," said Grissel. "What do you plan to do with them?"

"Await further orders from the Valkerish."

"It would be best if we killed them," sneered Perti.

"Why?" asked Magda

"You ask that after what happened to Elfrida and Adelaid?"

"Mirit defended herself and used unfamiliar moves," replied Magda, more heated than appropriate as told by their expressions.

"You defend a foreign Sigvard against your sisters?" rebuffed Ulrika.

"No, stating facts of what I saw."

"You agree with these facts, Grissel?"

"Mirit is very skilled and twice defeated Elfrida, who is my strongest fighter. Adelaid is reckless and hot tempered—"

"I trained Adelaid before sending her to you," chided Perti.

"Which is why you should be cautious since Mirit defeated her also," said Magda.

Perti threw up her hands and confronted Ulrika. "Will you continue to listen to this nonsense?"

"Mind your tongue, Perti! You know I consider all sides of an issue before deciding. However, in this case the choice of action is not mine to make. So take heed. Nothing will be done to the prisoners until I have heard from either the Valkerish or Ludmilla."

Perti gripped the hilt of her sword and made a stiff, if reluctant, nod.

Ulrika turned to Grissel. "Speaking of Elfrida, how is she today?"

"Not well. Her recovery is still in doubt. Adelaid frets—"

"And spouts curses against Mirit," said Magda, drawing a look of ire from Perti and a warning glare from Grissel, who continued to speak.

"Adelaid frets and swears it is not her fault. Until I know for certain about Elfrida, I must keep Adelaid confined to quarters."

"Despite what she or others think of Mirit, Adelaid's sword inflicted the wound, and for that, she must take responsibility," said Ulrika.

Perti frowned and nodded.

"Now, we must tend to our duties. Since you are more familiar with this Avatar, take your Sigvard along with these and find him quickly." Ulrika gave Grissel the spurean manacles.

Grissel saluted and they left. Once outside the hall she scolded Magda. "You must mind you tongue about Mirit. She is an enemy."

"I'm not so certain."

She pulled Magda into a corner. "What do you mean?"

"We were at Astrid, and we don't know what happened with the Valkerish. So how could Mirit who was here at Falken? The only blame she bears is faithful service, just like us. Did you see the Valkerish give the orders to Ulrika?"

"No, but that means nothing. We often receive orders without knowing the origin."

"The same can be said for Mirit."

Grissel sighed in resignation. "I see your point. However, her fate lies with the Valkerish."

Magda shook her head. "With the Tavar growing stronger and her Valkerish coming for the place of beginning, prophecy is being fulfilled. Punishing Mirit won't change that."

"True. However, we have a task, and maybe capturing Avatar will help Mirit." Without further discussion, Grissel and Magda gathered their Sigvard and rode from Falken. For this task, all would be mounted.

Mirit knew Nigel cared for Chad like a brother and took his responsibilities and duties very seriously. Those hurt feelings compounded by failure of the mission made him retreat just like in Misow when he discovered her involvement with kidnapping Titus. He initially lashed out before retreating. For all of his good qualities, he tended to withdraw when emotionally hurt. She knew his habit developed out of self-defense when a wandering cripple because Avatar told her. In fact, the more she thought, the more she realized Nigel only spoke of that time in general terms not specifics. His relationship to Tyrone dated back to those days, but he never said how they met. She only knew details of how he met Chad, because Chad told her. She also became familiar with Nigel's healing because Avatar told her.

In Tunlund, she began to see a contrast. Being forced to face her past and speak about it to complete strangers, she came to grips with what happened. The more she spoke, the less it troubled her and the more she felt confident in dealing with others.

Nigel doesn't suffer from lack of confidence; at least not in public situations. Personal relationships are different as he cares so much.

He sat in the same position with his forehead resting on his knees, arms wrapped around as if shielding his face. There was too much at stake to allow the heavy, brooding silence to continue. She spoke in the Ancient. "I understand you are hurt and disappointed but why shut me out and refuse to speak?"

He neither replied nor moved in response.

"I suppose it sounds like a silly question, since I rebuffed you when you told me your heart. Oh, Nigel! We can't do this to each other anymore."

He remained still and quiet.

She sighed and said with a catch in her voice, "We're stubborn people. It didn't need to take seven months for me to tell you I love you. I could have told you in your chamber at Waldron when I thought you were leaving without saying good-bye. I didn't speak then because I was so used to guarding my heart and protecting myself that I developed a sharp tongue rather than speaking softly and candidly. Since knowing you, I've been trying to break my habit."

Emotions choked her words and she covered her face with her hands. A hand reached to take her hand. Their eyes met, but still he didn't speak. At least this was a first step toward breaking his habit of retreating.

"With Jor'el's help, we'll find a way out this," she said.

He squeezed her hand.

Inside the high priestess' apartment, an annoyed Iryn watched Ludmilla gaze out the window with her arms folded inside her sleeves. The view from the second story chamber toward Astrid was impressive and soothing in spring and fall. But at this moment, the view could not change her pensive and pale features.

"How long do you plan to wait before acting?" asked Iryn.

"I don't know. These are tenuous times. I hoped their coming would bring help and hope for the Valkerish. Alas, it has not and I'm not certain what to do, or if I should do anything."

"You are the high priestess. You can act to protect the people."

Ludmilla turned from the window. "From whom? The Tavar or the foreigners? I don't know who poses the more serious threat."

A large brilliant flash of light engulfed the room, blinding them.

"Perhaps we can help you decide," said a female voice.

Although the light faded, the mortals' eyesight was slow to return. When their vision cleared, three tall, large, powerful males and one familiar female, Farren stood before them. The two other males were dressed like Skule in black and crimson.

"Great One!" stammered an awestruck Ludmilla.

"You seem confused and frightened, High Priestess. Why is that?" began Farren in a cool, dispassionate voice. "Oh, could it be my companions? Allow me to introduce you to the Tavar. Skule, Dark Lord of the Tavar and his associates, Breck and Lokien."

Breck was stocky, square-jawed, and thick-necked with shoulder length brown hair and angry blue eyes. Lokien was slender and handsome with curly blonde hair and pale gold eyes. Skule appeared far more intimidating with a black patch over one eye and the other a cold, penetrating opalescence.

Ludmilla could not speak for fear.

"Great One. My lord," said Iryn in all reverence to Farren and Skule. "I'm trying to convince the high priestess to kill the foreign Sigvard and varlet for aiding the enemy."

"Their aid has proven useful," said Skule.

"You do not want them executed?"

"Eventually, but for the time being, they are more useful where they are. However, our time has come."

Iryn tried to keep the smile from her face.

"What do you mean?" asked Ludmilla, finding her voice.

Deliberate in step and intent, Skule approached Ludmilla. "I mean, the time of the Valkerish is past, and the reign of the Tavar will be supreme in Soren." He raised a hand in front of Ludmilla's face and clenched his fist.

Ludmilla became short of breath. Terror grew on her face as he choked the breath from her body. She collapsed to the floor gasping, eyes glazing over, until she ceased moving.

Iryn stared at the Ludmilla and swallowed back her own fear.

Skule smiled and flexed his fingers. "That felt good."

Breck and Lokien laughed but Farren showed no emotion.

"Now, High Priestess Iryn," began Skule, making Iryn turn to him. "Inform the people about the untimely death of Ludmilla."

"What shall I tell them she died of?"

"Tell them she became so distraught over the incident with the foreign Valkerish her heart failed under the burden of guilt."

"Guilt?"

"Ja. She took them at their word rather than make inquiry before presenting them to the Valkerish, thus causing this chaos."

"As you command, my lord." Iryn bowed to them and left.

"What now?" asked Breck.

"Patience. Our plan is in motion, it won't be much longer."

"It can't take full form until we deal with Avatar."

"Ay. We must be rid of him and Wren before they can warn Kell of our plans," said Lokien.

"Avatar won't leave Wren behind. She will serve as bait," said Skule.

Breck frowned, a disapproving glance to Farren. "She left her in Auriel's charge and I'm not sure I trust her just yet, if at all."

"Let me worry about Auriel." Farren grew concerned. "Something is wrong at Astrid!" she snapped, which made Skule fiercely scowl.

"Lokien, stay here and make certain Iryn dances to our tune," ordered Skule before he, Farren and Breck disappeared.

Auriel walked the rampart of Astrid, deep in thought of what she had done. Her long-standing personal grudge against Avatar may have been a catalyst, howbeit, one she held singularly. He seemed oblivious to it. *Typical. All males, mortals and Guardians, seemed to have the same weakness when it comes to perception. Except for Kell and Tyrone.*

Thought of Tyrone made her stop. He was her king, King of the Guardians, just like she told Farren. Her defection may have dire consequences for him and Allon. She shook the vexing thought from her head. "I can't think about it. What's done is done."

A powerful force knocked her sideways into the wall, where she barely stopped from falling over the side. She shook her head clear but saw no one. Something waylaid her and she dreaded the meaning. She raced from the rampart to the great hall. Willow and Keara lay sprawled on the floor, slow to regain their senses. She helped Willow sit up. Light filled the room. Farren, Skule, and Breck appeared together.

"What happened?" demanded Skule.

Willow and Keara gaped, both too stunned at seeing him to speak.

"Shadow Warriors!" Auriel reached for her sword but Farren stopped her. Auriel's eyes narrowed in suspicious anger. "You're allied with them, that is why you lied about Avatar."

"That's unimportant at the moment. What of Wren?"

"I don't know. One moment I was standing watch, then next, knocked off my feet."

Willow and Keara shrugged and shook their heads. Farren hurried from the hall, Skule and Breck at her heels.

"You both better make yourselves scarce if wish to survive this day," said Auriel hurriedly.

"Abandon Farren?" asked Keara.

"She abandoned you by allying with them!"

"Farren has reasons. We've been together too long and forfeited too much."

"Fools! If you oppose them, they will kill—" Auriel stopped at a howl of anger coming from the back of the hall. "Wren is gone."

They heard Farren and Skule's arguing grow louder and closer.

"Stay if you wish to die!" Auriel vanished.

Breck drew his sword when he, Skule and Farren rushed into the hall. "Where is Auriel?"

"We don't know," stammered Willow.

"I told you I didn't trust her," said an irate Breck to Skule. "Now our plans are threatened and she's responsible!" His sword plunged through Farren's body.

Willow and Keara watched in horror as Farren collapsed.

Skule sent a vicious backhand across Breck face, staggering the formidable Warrior. "Fool! Why did you do that? We need her!"

Farren groaned in agony and Skule knelt beside her. He laid one hand on her forehead and the other over her wound. She flinched. His good eye sparkled in cold brilliance as he said, *"Le cumhachd de dorchadas bi fallain agus fritheil mi. By the power of darkness be healthy and serve me."*

For a moment Farren appeared uncertain of what to do or say, her wound glowing. Finally she replied in the Ancient: "Ay, my lord and master." At that moment, she became healed.

Skule passed his hand over her from head to toe, and her clothes were transformed to the black and crimson of the Tavar, of a Shadow Warrior.

Willow backed away in utter terror, only to be stopped by Breck. He also seized Keara. "What about these two?"

"Depends on our newest recruit." Skule helped Farren stand.

Bewildered, Farren stared at her transformed clothes and healed wound. She shook her head. "How did you do that?"

"In time you will learn what we know, now that you too are a Shadow Warrior."

Farren stared at him. "Auriel said Shadow Warriors were a result of Dagar's rebellion."

Skule laughed, loud and mocking. "Did you believe everything Auriel told you? In fact, where is she now?"

"She left, and told us to do the same if we wanted to survive," said Willow.

Skule turned his attention to Keara and Willow. "Yet, you stayed. Why?"

"We've been together for centuries. First as a Trio and then here."

"Loyalty. A good trait. Now, you have new allies. Ones who are stronger."

"We fought each other for centuries," said Keara in dispute.

"Ay. Now we unite against a common enemy. For the good of Soren, which is why Farren sought us out, to make a truce."

"What?" said Keara in disbelief.

"It was inevitable," said Farren. "Either be destroyed forever or form an alliance. I did it for our survival. For the survival of Soren."

Keara was beside herself with anger. "You placed us right back under authority without consulting us? Has what we accomplished here been for nothing?"

"No," said Skule. "Only a step in reaching the ultimate goal. Not only to subjugate an entire country, but to utilize its power and resources to conquer another. The prize being the invading and conquering of our place of origin, the place of beginning."

Willow vigorously shook her head. "No! We will be destroyed if we set foot in Allon again."

"Not if you join us. You saw the power I command. Observe Farren. Doesn't she look more powerful, more intimidating and fierce?" He moved closer to Willow and smiled. "You too can have power and no longer shrink in fear from me or … your old mentor."

"Vidar?"

"Ay, Vidar." He steadily regarded her, a taunting smile appearing. "What do you say? Would you like to face Vidar and show him up?"

"You claim to resent Vidar as much as I resent Avatar. Now I feel I can kill him. No deception, no blind blow from behind, rather in face-to-face combat," said Farren.

"I'd like to see that."

"Same as I to watch you show up Vidar. If not kill him."

Willow grinned. "Ay."

Skule placed a hand on Willow's head and looked in her eyes. "By the power of darkness, be transformed and serve me."

Willow shivered when she gazed in to Skule's single eye and replied; "Ay, my lord and master." His hand passed down the length of her body and her clothes changed. When the transformation was complete, she smiled. "I do feel more powerful."

Farren turned to Keara. "It is your choice, sister. Willow and I would miss you if you chose not to join us."

"You would let them kill me?"

"No," said Skule, his face void of expression. "She would kill you." Keara paled and Skule laughed in mockery. "Just kidding. Where would you go and what would you do?"

Keara turned from Skule to Willow and Farren. "I have no choice." She turned back to Skule, took his hand and placed it on her forehead. Once more he spoke his command and Keara was transformed.

Chapter 14

BACK IN BERGETA'S CHAMBER in Novice Hall, Chad watched her weep at the news of Ludmilla's death. He tried to console her.

"You speak words of comfort, but your heart is not in those words," she said.

"No, I mean what I say. Only this is all too suspicious for me."

"Why?"

He considered his answer. She deserved an explanation, but he needed to be discreet. "Dear Bergeta, I'm beginning to see how innocent and naïve you are." She tried to pull away from him, but he wouldn't let her. "I'm not being insulting, but think about what has happened since we arrived. My Valkerish are whisked away to Astrid where they reportedly run afoul of your Valkerish. As a result Nigel and Mirit are imprisoned, Alaric and Leif are ordered whipped, but Avatar returns in disguise, which means he escaped Astrid, and now Ludmilla dies of guilt. Taken together, is all too suspicious. There must be more here."

"I don't know," she said in exasperation. "But I am vexed by what Avatar said about Jor'el and Guardians. Who are Guardians? And he called Jor'el the Almighty."

Due to guilt, he tried to avoid the issue. His actions were not only a betrayal of Nigel, but also a sin against Jor'el law of moral purity. But avoidance was no longer possible. "Jor'el is the eternal god of my people. He created all living things. Guardians, well, Avatar is a Guardian. So are Wren and Auriel. They are powerful, immortal beings Jor'el created to serve him and mortals."

She shook her head in confusion. "Guardians sound no different than the Valkerish."

"I honestly don't know. That is why we came to Soren, to learn the identity of the Valkerish and why they threaten my people."

"The Valkerish never threatened anyone! They are peaceful beings. The Tavar are evil."

"Again, I don't know. Nor will I while Nigel and Mirit are prisoners and Avatar doing what I should be." Painful anger crept into his voice.

"The only way for you to do something is to abandon me! You promised not to do that."

He took her hands, but the conflict evident on this face. "I won't abandon you, but I have reconsidered remaining idle. The problem is reconciling the two."

"What can you without causing more trouble?"

"Nigel said when the time came to act, I would know. Alas, I failed him in my most simple task: to keep his equipment safe and in good order. They were unarmed when captured."

"I don't understand. You're both varlets to Mirit, your Sigvard."

"No. I told you I am not who I appear, neither are Nigel and Mirit." Her confusion made him lean closer to whisper. "We took on these roles for our mission to learn about the Valkerish. Nigel is a prince and a knight and I am *his* squire. Mirit is his lady and a very formidable fighter."

She began to understand. "That is why he looked so hurt and disappointed. He feels you betrayed him."

"Ja," he murmured in a voice barely above a tormented whisper.

She consoled him. "I'm sorry for your pain. But, he may not accept your help."

He screwed his eyes shut in an effort to stop a wave of tears. "There is nothing I can say or do to correct my mistake or change his mind. All I can do is act according to my heart and conscience."

"Then all I am to you is a mistake?" she spoke with biting accusation.

"No! You are lovely, charming, and I believe I began to have feelings for you at first sight. But how we came to be together is a mistake according to what I believe. It would have been better if we took time to become acquainted." He clenched her hands, looking directly into her eyes. "I will keep my promise, but please do not hold my regret against me. If anything, help me to do what is right for both of us."

She smiled, howbeit sheepish. "I have something which may ease your regret. I apologize for not give it to you sooner, but I needed to be certain of your heart toward me, toward us." She rose from sitting beside him on the bed to kneel and reach under the bed. "One of the younger novices brought it to me for safe keeping since you are my gemate." She pulled out a sheathed sword.

"Nigel's sword!" Chad stood and seized it.

"I'm glad you're not angry for my delay."

He buckled the sword about his waist. He flashed a relieved smile. "Thank you. It will not leave my side until I can find a way to give it back to him." He drew her to him and kissed her.

A ruckus from outside interrupted them and the door to Bergeta's chamber thrust open. A pale, breathless Ingrid appeared in the threshold. "Iryn commands all to temple! Hurry!"

Auriel dimmed her appearance in a remote corner of the temple courtyard. Chad and a girl crossed from Novice Hall toward the temple. The girl was immaterial, while Chad served Nigel, and ultimately Tyrone. If he knew of her defection there could be trouble, if not ...

"Chad," she called in low, hoarse voice. She caught his attention only he turned and spoke to the girl.

"Go. I'll be along shortly."

"Why?"

"Trust me" He kissed her cheek and sent her on her way. He waited a moment to be sure she was gone before joining Auriel in the shadows. "Is Avatar or Wren with you?"

"No. We became separated." His question told her he didn't know.

"What happened at Astrid?"

She shook her head with some impatience. "Too much to explain. You appear whole. Who is the girl?"

"Alaric's daughter. She saved me from being imprisoned along with Nigel and Mirit."

"Where are they?"

"Falken. At least that is where Ulrika said they were taking them since it is believed you failed with their Valkerish."

She stood rigid and alert. "They're coming!"

"Who?"

She ignored his question and pulled him toward the back gate. Perhaps one last service could be rendered. "We must act fast."

"I can't leave!"

"Why not?"

He frowned in reluctant annoyance. "Too much to explain. Save Nigel and Mirit. I'll keep an eye on things here." He unbuckled the sword from about his waist. "Give this to Nigel. He'll need it."

"He'll use it to fetch you."

Heavy sorrow filled his face and his voice quivered. "Not this time."

He shied under her scrutiny. "The girl swayed you against him."

"No. The choice and fault are mine alone. No one else is to blame for my betrayal."

His words resounded in her heart for she did the same to her fellow Guardians. For a moment she stared at Nigel's sword. Chad kept it as his last act of service for his master, just like this was a last act of service to her former life. "I'll see he gets it," she said, abruptly turning and leaving by the back gate.

She buckled the sword about her waist and made her way down the alley. Since her own sword was strapped to her back, it wouldn't interfere if she needed to make defense. Upon reaching the street, she paused to watch people flock to the temple. Uncertain of what Farren and Skule were planning, she had to get Nigel and Mirit to safety. Saving them would not atone for forfeiting her station; nothing could. However, leaving them in the hands of Shadow Warriors was unthinkable. She fingered the hilt of Nigel's sword.

Perhaps with this a Jor'ellian would stand a chance of survival.

She mumbled a phrase in the Ancient and dashed to Falken, passing through the crowd unnoticed. Even the Sigvard standing guard at the entrance to Falken did not see her. She paused in a dark corner of the courtyard to get her bearings. Like any good warrior, she took in every detail of Falken during their first visit. She located the stairs leading to the dungeon. Using speed not normal for a mortal, she raced down the stairs and caught the guards by surprise. They never knew what hit them, both rendered unconscious before they were aware of an intruder.

Mirit bolted to his feet. "Auriel."

Nigel approached the cell door.

"Stand back." Auriel drew her sword and sliced off the lock on Nigel's cell then did the same to Mirit's cell. "We must be quick. They're gathering at the temple."

"What about Alaric and Leif?" asked Mirit.

"No, miss. We're in no condition. Save yourselves," moaned Alaric.

Auriel unbuckled Nigel's sword. "Chad sends this to you."

Nigel's jowls tightened and he briefly stared at his sword still in her hand. He snatched it, and fastening the buckle about his waist. He drew the blade and waved Auriel to take the point. He and Mirit followed.

They paused at the top of the stairs and Auriel whispered, "I managed to block my presence to enter, but with three of us it would require too much effort to go undetected."

"A distraction?" asked Mirit.

"Ay. Once outside, the streets should be clear since everyone is commanded to the temple. *Buair!*" Auriel clapped her hands. The Sigvard at the gate looked left then began running in that direction.

She, Nigel and Mirit raced from the stairs, through the gate and out into the street, darting behind a cart to pause and plan their next move.

"The street is clear—" Auriel shivered and paled. "Farren is here. You must leave Manheim now!"

"Not without Chad," said Nigel.

"He won't leave and you know it."

"Then I'll make him leave!"

"No, Nigel," said Mirit. "It must be of Chad's own free will or he will come to resent you."

He again stared at his sword, his face tight. Without another word, he ran toward the city's main gate, Mirit and Auriel at his heels.

Auriel stopped just outside the gate and pointed out the road. "Make your way quickly to the coast. I'll handle the Shadow Warriors and give you as much time as I can."

"Shadow Warriors?" echoed Nigel in surprised disturbance.

"The Tavar are Shadow Warriors and the Valkerish, Guardians."

"Avatar and Wren?"

"I don't know. We became separated, but I don't sense demise, and you *know* Avatar will find you." Her head snapped back toward the city, agitated and expectant. "Go!"

Mirit pulled on Nigel's arm, urging him in their flight. She looked sympathetically to Auriel. "Jor'el be with you."

Auriel flinched at the statement spoken in all sincerity and ignorance of her choice. "And … with you, my lady," she stuttered before turning on her heels to go back into the city.

Her spirit winced with each step as Mirit's blessing echoed in her ears. At first she didn't regret her action, truly feeling discontent and resentful about her treatment by fellow Guardians. However, Farren lying about Avatar and discovering the Tavar are Shadow Warriors brought a new reality to the situation. Her own destruction was inevitable. Whether by the hand of a former comrade, or by the Shadow Warriors, she could not escape it. Thus she would choose her fate.

She moved down the alley toward the rear of the temple when a force from behind sent her sprawling. She scrambled to her feet and whirled about sword in hand to face whatever waylaid her.

Avatar readied his sword. "It's not your neck I'll snap."

She swallowed back her concern. Now was not the time she wanted to face him, not for fear of facing him but lousy timing. "You'd make a mistake by killing me."

He launched his attack.

The force of his blow made her sword spark and she retreated. "They are no longer prisoners!" She needed both hands to parry the force of his attack yet still stumbled aside. Being of the Guardian High Trio, he was the stronger warrior, and passion increased the ferociousness of his blows. She dodged his blade and fell to her knees in the process. "I said Nigel and Mirit are free!"

"Why should I believe you?"

"Because I freed them and set them on the road from Manheim a few moments ago!"

"Liar!" He hacked down, forcing her to hold her sword like a quarterstaff to stop his blow. Unfortunately, this left her vulnerable and he took advantage of her miscue.

She cried out in pain when his sword sliced through her left side. She dropped her sword and collapsed in a painful heap at his feet. She held up her right arm in surrender and said, "I swear it is true! I gave Nigel his sword. Chad gave it to me to give to him, but he chose the girl. Mirit even offered me Jor'el's blessing."

His eyes narrowed in suspicion. "Why would you free them after betraying us?"

"Farren lied about killing you to get information because she made a pact with the Tavar, who are Shadow Warriors. They're planning something. I don't know what. I freed Nigel and Mirit rather than leave them to the Warriors. I was a fool, and I'm sorry!"

His betrayed conflicting emotions. "It doesn't change what you did."

"I know. And I will be destroyed for it."

He backed away, his sword arm lowering to his side. "If we meet again—" He couldn't finish, the anger in his face and voice making it unnecessary.

"I understand. I don't believe we will meet again."

A sense of cold evil filled the alley, making Avatar flinch in anticipation of a confrontation and Auriel murmur in pain.

"They're here!" she said through gritted teeth. "Go! Once they learn Nigel and Mirit are gone they will seek to kill them."

Avatar ran from the alley. Auriel used her sword to stand and staggered toward the back gate of the temple. He dealt her a very serious and painful wound, but not life threatening. Thinking back on the fight, she wondered why he didn't kill her.

He had me right where any warrior wants the enemy, vulnerable and helpless. Her step faltered when the truth struck her at hearing his words, "If we meet again . . ." *You pulled the fatal blow! Even betrayed you can't bring yourself to take revenge on another Guardian. You spared me to save your conscience!*

She was uncertain how to accept the truth yet grateful to be alive and continue her course of action; only his self-righteous arrogance always infuriated her. She tried to shake the frustrating thought from her mind. *I have a path to follow he cannot understand. Upon that path I must focus my strength and mind.*

The pain in her side increased and she stumbled, falling against the back gate, but used her weight to open the latch. She entered and heard voices coming from the temple through the three glassless windows. She gingerly sat beside the gate to listen.

Inside the temple, Chad weaved his way through the crowd to stand behind Bergeta. He placed a finger to his lip to signal her silent.

Iryn stood on the bottom step in front of the altar. The Sigvard lined the perimeter for security. Ulrika joined Iryn.

Iryn addressed the crowd. "This day is one of great sorrow and grief in the passing of our beloved high priestess. Although it is good for us to come together to console each other that is not why I summoned everyone. I fear Ludmilla's death is only the beginning of difficult days ahead for all Soren. The Valkerish desire to speak personally to you, to tell you and to reassure you." Iryn turned to the altar. "Freja, High Valkerish of Soren, our protector and guide, hear the voice of your servants and answer. Grace us with your presence."

With a clap of thunder and bright flash of light, Farren appeared. In her striking black and crimson suit she was an imposing figure.

Chad muttered in dread; "A Shadow Warrior!"

"What?" asked Bergeta.

He seized her shoulders and made her face forward. "Listen and be still," he whispered in warning, his eyes focused on Farren.

"People of Soren, loyal servants and subjects, we of the Valkerish mourn the passing of our favored high priestess, especially at this critical hour. As you recall, Valkerish who claim to come from the place of beginning stood in the temple just the other day requesting an audience that we graciously granted." She paused for effect, her features and voice become harsh. "They deceived us! They did not come in peace but to destroy us and conquer Soren for themselves!"

The stunned and angry reaction from the crowd was measurable and Farren raised her arms for calm and silence.

"Have no fear, good people. Your Valkerish put down their threat for now. But a challenge remains. Those who sent these false Valkerish must be dealt with. As such, we have taken a desperate course of action, but one that will ensure the survival of Soren. Behold, our allies!"

The room rumbled and blinding light forced some to turn away to shield their eyes. When the light faded, five figures stood on the platform; three males, two females, and all dressed in black and crimson. Some women screamed and others fainted.

Chad's breath caught in his throat. Bergeta grabbed hold of him, terrified.

"Take heart, good people. You are in no danger. Though we were once enemies, the Tavar have join forces to protect Soren," declared Farren.

208

"It is true!" Skule's loud voice echoed in temple and caused a deep hush to fall on the crowd. "To the Valkerish we have pledged to work together for the good and protection of Soren. Petty individual squabbles pale against total domination by a foreign power."

"To seal our pledge the foreigners will be publicly executed." Farren turned to Ulrika. "Bring the prisoners!"

"Do you think—" began Bergeta, but Chad covered her mouth.

He glared at Skule as his anger grew with each word spoken. He knew the situation was nearly hopeless for him, but if Auriel or Avatar succeeded, Nigel and Mirit would be free and making their way back to Allon to warn the king.

"Once the foreigners are executed we shall take the fight to enemy, strike them at their home, and wipeout their very existence!"

"No!" shouted Chad. He left Bergeta to push his way through the crowd. "They lie! They are not who they claim."

"You dare defy me? Who are you?"

"He is one of the foreign varlets, my lord," said Iryn.

The Sigvard seized Chad, who did not resist capture.

"Why wasn't he imprisoned with the others?" asked Farren, a critical eye finding Perti since Ulrika left to fetch the prisoners.

"He is *gemate* to one of the novices. I thought it wise to use his infatuation with the girl to our advantage and instructed her to take him," said Iryn.

"No!" said Bergeta, stunned.

Farren motioned for Bergeta to be brought forth and the Sigvard complied. She couldn't resist, looking fearful and confused.

Skule stepped off the platform and surveyed Bergeta. "She is a pretty mortal. I see your wisdom in using her to trap him."

She shook her head at Chad. "I didn't do it for them, I did it for you. I love you."

Chad screwed his eyes shut to contain his anger and pain. When he looked again, she wept. What he knew of her charm and naiveté, he could not imagine she purposely deceived him. "I believe you."

Skule laughed. "How quaint, but your belief doesn't matter, boy. Soon you'll be dead and she will be free to choose another."

"No!" Bergeta sobbed, pleading eyes on Willow. "Because of you I became a novice, please spare him."

Willow fought indecision at the plea, but before she replied, Ulrika rushed in, angry and flush and announced, "They have escaped!"

"What? You failed!" chided Farren.

"No, Great One," said Ulrika, falling to one knee. "Remember your other charge to me at Astrid concerning Avatar."

Farren sneered at the reminder.

"Our friend seems to be busy," chided Lokien.

"Find the foreigners and destroy them!" said Skule.

Lokien laid hold of Keara's arm and together they disappeared.

Outside, Auriel heard everything. "Hurry, Avatar!" she said to the air.

A moment later, Breck appeared. She didn't move, her wound preventing her.

"Well, what have we here? A wounded warrior? My, how the mighty have fallen."

She glared at him.

The insolent expression incited him and he seized her. "I can crush your throat with one hand. Not a glorious way for a warrior to die."

"Threaten and bellow all you want, but when I cease to exist, I will take all of you with me."

He laughed in mockery. "You are bold to say such a thing in your condition." When she tried to turn away, he seized her face his smile growing wicked. "I have a better idea. Come meet your new lord and master." They disappeared.

Auriel fell to her knees when they reappeared inside the temple, but Breck kept hold on the back of her collar.

Chad strained against the Sigvard's hold at seeing her wounded.

"Your doing?" asked Skule.

"No. I found her this way. I thought you might want to persuade her to join us."

Skule slyly grinned. "This may prove a good object lesson. To show the people we are invincible by converting one of the enemy." He motioned to Breck and Willow. "Hold her."

They pulled Auriel to her feet, holding her arms so she couldn't move. Farren walked behind Auriel to hold her head still.

Skule slyly grinned. "This won't hurt. In fact, you will thank me." He placed one hand firmly on her forehead and the other hand on her wound, making her wince in pain. Skule spoke in the Ancient loud enough for all to hear. *"Le cumhachd de dorchadas bi fallain agus fritheil mi."*

Each word he spoke made Auriel's snarl at him deepen. However, her wound grew warm, a sign of healing. He held his hand there until she knew her it was healed. But in the eyes the true battle occurred and she acknowledged him. "My lord and master."

"Witness the reality of your statement." He ran his hand from her head to tow, transforming her clothes into black and crimson.

Curiosity filled her face at the healing and wearing the uniform of a former enemy.

Chad watched in horror, as before his eyes, a Guardian of Jor'el became a Shadow Warrior.

"Behold! The conquered enemy is now under our control," said Skule to the amazed crowd. "So will all be when we defeat them."

People cheered and someone called out to execute the foreigner. Skule nodded his approval of the suggestion and waved to the Sigvard holding Chad.

"Wait! He may be of use," said Auriel.

"She is only buying time," chided Farren.

"No. He knows the enemy and is squire to the Prince of Allon."

"What makes you think he'll cooperate?" asked Skule.

"Because I can persuade him." Auriel approached Chad, her jade eyes level and direct. "We forfeited our former service for the same reason. There is nothing left for us back there, but we can start new here."

"I'd rather die than betray him further or bring danger to Allon!"

"It is not you who will die." Her eyes darted to Bergeta.

His mouth dropped open at the threat. "You wouldn't?"

Auriel shrugged. "Refusal is the only way to find out."

He swallowed his fear and disbelief. At Bergeta's distress, he nodded then lowered his head in shame.

Auriel turned to Skule. "See, he can be useful."

"You don't play fair."

Farren addressed the crowd. "Today all of you witnessed the combined power of the Valkerish and Tavar. Go to you homes and make ready to heed our call and defeat our enemy."

Ulrika signaled the Sigvard to clear the temple.

"Willow, take care of the girl. The boy is yours," Skule said to Auriel, but there was no mistaking the glare of warning in the single cold eye.

Auriel inclined her head in a submissive bow. The transformation was now complete.

Chapter 15

NIGEL AND MIRIT RAN AS FAST AS THEY COULD over the mile of the snow-cleared main road. But after an additional half-mile of increasing snow depth, they stopped to catch their breath. Mirit bent over, hands on her knees, gasping for air. Nigel took several deep breaths of recovery and wiped the sweat from his forehead. He looked back at Manheim.

"We can't rest too long. They'll be coming after us soon."

She nodded, still catching her breath.

"Let's keep moving."

She rolled her eyes in exhaustion, took a deep breath and straightened to begin moving. Before taking her first step, something slammed her against the tree, knocking her unconscious. Nigel drew his sword and shielded his eyes at a flash of light.

Keara and Lokien appeared, and with their swords drawn.

"How did you miss him?" Lokien scolded Keara.

"I wasn't aiming at him. He's your quarry."

"I'm nobody's quarry," said Nigel then spoke in the Ancient, "By Jor'el's will I fight His enemies," and assumed his fighting stance.

"A Jor'ellian!" sneered Lokien.

"A what?" asked Keara.

"He's your quarry now." He shoved Keara toward Nigel.

She regained her balance in time to block Nigel's defensive swing. He stepped aside to prepare for another attack, keeping both Keara and Lokien in view. It would be foolish, no deadly, to turn his back. Keara attacked. Although powerful, Nigel was comfortable fighting a Guardian. Often he and Avatar sparred in mock battles. Since he couldn't match a Guardian's strength, he learned from those matches where and how to parry and to use his smaller size and agility to his advantage.

Keara snarled at his repeated success in keeping her at bay. She launched her fifth attack and he ducked under her blade, rolling on the ground to come up behind her. He managed to rise up to one knee when she whirled about. She lifted the sword above her head to hack down at him, a move he anticipated. He jumped up, thrust sword his deep into the left side of her chest. Her eyes went wide in surprise. He jerked his sword out. She collapsed and disappeared before reaching the ground.

Lokien stared in amazed anger at Keara's demise at the hand of a mortal! "Prepare to die, Jor'ellian!"

Nigel spent a good deal of strength and energy running from Manheim and fighting Keara. He wasn't certain he could stand another battle against a Shadow Warrior. He snatched a glance to see Mirit still unconscious so he'd get no help from her. *"Thoir mi an luiths, Jor'el!"*

"Strength? You want strength, Jor'ellian? Try this." Lokien shoved Nigel aside with his sword then waved his left hand and sent him flying backwards across the road and into a tree. Nigel lay at the base of a tree huddled in pain from impact. "Is that enough strength? Or do you need to more? Keara was a new Shadow Warrior, but I was honed by Dagar."

It proved painful to breathe and Nigel wondered if he also hit his head since his ears rang. Still, he bit back the pain and braced himself against the tree to stand, determination on his face in confronting Lokien. "My father defeated Dagar. I am Prince Nigel, son of King Ellis, the Son of Tristan."

"Then prepare to pay for your father's sin!"

Lokien's attack brought Nigel to his knees where he managed to deflect the Warrior's sword and roll away before Lokien could retaliate. Nigel used his sword to push himself to his feet. His entire body hurt and he grew weak from exertion, even a bit dizzy.

"You may be a Jor'ellian, but you are mortal and grow weary and weak. It is only a matter of time before I kill you."

"Not if I kill you first. For Jor'el and Allon!" he shouted and thrust at Lokien. When Lokien parried, he pulled back and swung with all his strength at Lokien's body. His sword cut deep into the Warrior's left side.

The momentum of Nigel's attack carried him past Lokien. In pain and fatigue, he pulled to an unsteady halt and turned in anticipation of retaliation. He thought he only landed a glancing blow and surprised to see Lokien collapsed in a heap. Suddenly overcome, Nigel sank to the ground, a haze of white light swirling around his head then all went dark.

<hr />

Nigel's eyes blinked, then opened, trying to focus his disoriented mind. He noticed light, only not white rather a soft yellow hue. Upon further investigation, he discovered he was inside a room with warm wood paneling. The feel of something soft beneath him, told him he lay on a bed that slightly swayed.

"How are you feeling?" asked a familiar male voice.

Nigel raised himself on his elbows and smiled at Avatar. Wren sat on a bench and looked unusually pale and tired. "Wren. You look awful."

She wearily grinned. "I'll be fine, Highness. Spurean sickness can take a day or two to wear off depending upon time of exposure."

His gaze shifted to Mirit, who slept on the bed beside Wren.

"She'll be fine. Although she'll have a bad headache when she wakes," said Avatar.

"Where am I? And how did I get here?"

"We brought you here," said another male from across the room.

"Kell?" Nigel sat up in surprise.

He smiled. "Finding you and Mirit was easier than rescuing Wren."

Nigel's question stopped when the cabin door opened and Vidar entered. The famed Guardian hunter was as old as Kell, with light brown hair and bright copper eyes. His appearances were as rare as Kell and just as ominous, for with it, he dispensed holy justice. He wore the uniform of his former Guardian leadership station and function, a forest green jerkin, brown cowl, green breeches and brown leather boots.

"Highness, you're awake."

"Vidar? I don't understand. What are you and Kell doing in Soren?"

"We came at request of the king," said Kell, his voice circumspect along with a cautious glance at Vidar then back to Nigel, "to escort you home. We are no longer in Soren."

"What? Where are we?"

"On the ship bound for Allon."

Irate, Nigel accosted Avatar. "Where is Chad?"

Avatar pursed his lips, hesitant to answer.

He scowled with fierce anger and stood. "Turn this ship around!"

Kell snatched Nigel's arm when he moved passed him toward the cabin door. "Avatar spoke to Chad, and the boy confirmed his choice."

Avatar nodded, his features filled with sobriety. "Chad says he's sorry and never meant to hurt or disappoint you."

Nigel pulled away from Kell and left the cabin.

The day was bright and crisp with a steady breeze. Gulliver manned the helm. Priscilla stood in the crow's nest guiding the wind. Mahon watched from the bow and Ewert and Bailey sat on deck. The warriors greeted him, but he didn't respond and made his way to the stern.

For several moments he watched the vanishing coastline. In his heart, he knew what Avatar said was true, but he didn't want to give up on Chad. Now, hope faded with the coastline. Soon it could be gone. He leaned on the rail, his head bowed and eyes screwed shut.

"Jor'el, protect him and keep him safe until we meet again."

Later in the captain's quarters, Nigel and Mirit sat to eat. Both were bathed and changed from their Soren disguises to their normal clothes.

216

Nigel's somber mood had not improved and he picked at his food. Kell, Avatar, Wren and Vidar waited in attendance.

"Brooding won't help Chad,'" said Avatar.

Nigel tossed the bread on his plate. "Not just Chad. We failed. In doing so we not only lost him and Auriel, but placed the Sorens in a worse position than if we remained neutral."

"Highness, your mission was to uncover the threat to Allon. You succeeded. Now the king can be fully prepared," said Kell.

Nigel sharply regarded Kell. "Can you tell me it was worth the cost?"

Pricked, he frowned. "If losing them will save Allon, then ay."

Nigel slumped back in his chair and sighed. "If only we learned how many Shadow Warriors we'll be facing."

"You dispatched one," said Vidar.

"He said Keara was new to being a Shadow Warrior."

Wren's brow furrowed with confused curiosity. "Keara wasn't a Shadow Warrior but among the Trio claiming to be the Valkerish. Along with Farren and Willow."

Vidar's countenance grew dark with a measure of regret. "It's difficult to believe Willow capable of such treachery."

Wren avoided his gaze, her voice uneasy. "She blames me for her downfall, same as Farren blames Avatar. They are bitter and resentful."

The others became concerned at her disquietude. Vidar touched her shoulder and asked, "Did something happen you haven't told us?"

"No. Their taunting and threats were difficult to hear."

"I'm sorry I wasn't able to rescue you sooner," said Avatar.

She flashed a thin, humorless smile. "No need to apologize. It could have been worse."

"Chad and Auriel aside, by Jor'el's mercy you escaped alive," said Kell.

Vidar chuckled and said to Kell, "To think, *we* wondered why Tyrone requested my presence and then instructed us to rendezvous with them."

Avatar grinned. "Tyrone seems to be one step ahead of everyone, including Jor'el's Captain and His Defender of Justice."

Nigel tried to keep from choking on his drink for laughing. "If so, then he can explain how a Guardian becomes a Shadow Warrior almost overnight because she certainly looked like a Shadow Warrior."

"That can't happen," refuted Kell. "Dagar had to break a Guardian's will before they bent to his control, which sometimes took centuries."

"Ay. He was merciless," said Vidar in remembrance.

"Dagar also had access to power only few of us who remain from the beginning can claim. Did you witness this so-called transformation?" inquired Kell.

"No, I made the judgment based on her appearance."

"And what Auriel told us about them," added Mirit.

"We can alter our appearance. What makes a Shadow Warrior is the evil Dagar infused in them. It shows in their faces and in their eyes, not only in their manner of dress."

Nigel snorted a sarcastic laugh. "I didn't get a chance to notice her eyes." Then a thought struck him. "He shoved her toward me and she fought more clumsy than I expected. He, on the other hand, was very powerful. I felt it when he sent me flying." He rotated his neck. "I'll be sore for a week."

"Be grateful nothing is broken," said Mirit.

"Ay, yet surprised when he fell. I didn't think I landed a good blow."

"Not you. The power of our arrival downed him," said Avatar, pointing to himself, Kell, and Vidar.

"The white light!" said Nigel in recognition. "I thought I fainted from exhaustion, but it was dimension travel."

"Partly. You were exhausted and didn't wake up until six hours later."

"Six hours?"

"Be fair. You gave him something for the pain and to make him sleep," said Wren.

Avatar shrugged, a casual smile appearing. "I didn't want to hear him complain about how he could have handled the situation if I hadn't shown up."

Mirit muffled her amusement at Nigel's askew glance. "Don't look at me. I was out cold."

"There is no shame in needing help," said Kell with a small smile. "Besides, you accomplished what few Jor'ellians have by defeating a Guardian in combat. Ellis didn't. He slew Latham, while I sent Dagar back to his former state."

Nigel was thunderstruck by the statement. "I exceeded my father? I thought he was the greatest knight, Jor'el's chosen."

"Ellis was chosen to be *king* and reclaim Allon, not a Jor'ellian Knight. Where few men wear the crown, few also have the honor and privilege to be the King's Champion."

"I realize that. Only I never expected to exceed my father in anything. Not that I was trying. I am content with my station and role."

Kell smiled at the modesty. "Ambition may win a crown, but it is faith and dedication that defeats the enemy."

"Enough! You're making my head swell."

Mirit smiled, wide and teasing. "I think it is amusing to see you blushing and off balance."

Gulliver entered with Ewert and Bailey. "The old wind-bag hasn't lost her touch. At this rate we should reach Leith in two days."

Wren lashed out. "Mind your tongue! Just because Priscilla's a female doesn't give you the right to degrade her abilities by your sarcasm."

Gulliver's initial surprise turned to annoyance but before he could reply, Kell spoke to Wren. "Peace! Now is not the time."

"When?"

"When I convene a meeting of the Trio Leaders to address the issue. What happened with Auriel causes me great concern, and I will not let it go unresolved, but do not turn this into a personal matter."

Agitated, she crossed to the porthole, turning her back to the others.

"Wren, I'm only asking you to be patient. I feel personally responsible for Farren, and won't let this issue go unresolved."

"As I do for Willow," said Vidar.

She took a deep breath and spoke over her shoulder. "I don't hold any single Guardian to blame. It's more a general attitude."

"Which isn't restricted to Guardian males," added Mirit.

Nigel's eyes flashed in warning at Mirit. "Not all males, Guardians or mortals, share that attitude. Whereas you and Wren don't want us to generally criticize females, don't make all of us out to be tyrants."

"I meant it *is* a learned behavior. In Tunlund the females are taught to debase themselves for the sake of the males, while the males take full advantage. Fortunately, Lukas didn't agree to the practice and encouraged my rejection of it."

"In Soren, the females rule."

"In hopes of correcting an injustice," she said, but added at his frown, "Which doesn't make it right, but does give an explanation."

Avatar's expression showed his difficulty to comprehend. "This issue is personally hard to understand. I never thought my teasing to be directed at a particular individual or gender."

Wren turned. "Your teasing is not mean-spirited like others." She made a curt motion to Gulliver.

"By the heavenlies, lass, I bear no ill-will toward Priscilla. She's just irritating at times. Kell knows that better than I."

Kell scowled at the statement, while Avatar and Vidar tried to hide their smiles. It was well known how Priscilla's flighty and carefree nature proved constant source of vexation for the serious-minded Kell, and served for great amusement among the Guardians.

She wouldn't back down and pressed Gulliver. "You came in calling her an old wind-bag. What irritation did she do to deserve such scorn?"

He went to reply, then stopped, befuddled.

"She did nothing, did she?" chided Wren. She turned to the others, her hand gesturing at Gulliver. "This is the exact attitude Mirit and I mean. Thoughtless, inconsiderate, comments while Priscilla is in the crow's nest doing what she was created to do. And he isn't even the worst of the complainers," she added to Ewert, who squared his shoulders, insulted.

"Hold your tongue. She has a point," said Bailey, making Ewert sneer, but he said nothing.

Wren nodded, pleased, and said of Ewert and Gulliver, "If these two can learn, perhaps there is hope for the rest of you."

"Wren!" said Kell firmly.

She returned to the porthole, her back to them. A hand gripped her shoulder and she looked sideways see Vidar. "I'm sorry."

"No need to apologize. I agree with you. Only be patient. Kell will see the matter is addressed." He leaned closer. "I'm proud of you for not giving into Farren and Willow."

She took in a deep affected breath. "I couldn't imagine betraying Jor'el. Not because I'd forfeit my station, but because I've seen his goodness to those who remain loyal and faithful." She turned to face him. "I would have been content if I ceased to exist while a prisoner."

He kindly smiled. "I know. So does Jor'el."

She cocked a grin. "I'll try to be patient and hold my tongue."

While Vidar spoke privately to Wren, Kell left the wardroom and headed to the quarterdeck. He passed Mahon manning the helm on his way aft. He sat on a bulkhead looking out to sea. This was not an outcome he expected and it deeply troubled him. Auriel faithfully served in her capacity, but discontent? Why had he not seen it? True, she grew moody since Jedrek's death, but he sensed nothing unusual in that. After all, they served together for a thousand years and grief was natural.

Avatar joined Kell. "You think about Auriel."

"Hard not to."

"Ay. We fought and she begged for mercy—" he couldn't finish.

"You take too much upon yourself, old friend."

Avatar heaved a hapless shrug. "Who else is to blame? Gresham's force was nearly wiped out due to my failed battle plan. She had every right to strike me for the demise of her comrades."

"I wasn't your fault, then or now!" chided Kell. "Auriel held the grudge and nursed it until she made her choice. You didn't make it for

221

her. Just like Nigel didn't force Chad to stay with the girl. But," he added with a heavy sigh, "if anyone bears blame, I do. As captain, I am responsible for all Guardians, and never realized the problem ran so deep as to drive Auriel, Farren, Willow and Keara to make such decisions. I thought my punishment got through to her since she appeared to change, while I believed good-natured teasing and competition healthy among the ranks. Where I don't tolerate disrespect, such banter seemed harmless."

"Now who is taking too much upon himself?"

"I suppose there is enough blame to go around. Yet, *they* made the choice. To avoid such in the future, we must change our ways."

Avatar cocked a challenging grin. "Meaning you'll be more tolerant of Priscilla teasing you?"

Kell chuckled. "That maybe taking things too far. Don't tell her I said so."

"I don't have to. She's standing right behind you."

Kell's smile vanished and he turned; only Priscilla wasn't there. Avatar laughed. "You will be my primary example to the others of what not to do." His brief good humor faded. "This goes beyond Auriel's choice and Priscilla's flippancy. Wren's change in attitude troubles me."

"I thought she would physically attack Gulliver. Granted his salty manner can be irritating, but her outburst was surprising."

Vidar came from behind to stand in front of them and casually leaned back against the rail. "You two don't need to worry about Wren. She withstood Farren and Willow."

"I hope you're right," droned Avatar.

"I am as certain of her mettle as Kell was of you when you went to Tunlund and faced down Hueil."

He looked with mild surprise at Kell. "Really?"

"Ay. You're strength and courage will not accept failure, doubly so when Nigel is involved."

"Since taking over my position, Wren has dedicated herself to the welfare of the royal family," said Vidar.

"I never doubted her dedication to duty," refuted Avatar.

"Why question her mettle? Because she's female and weaker?"

"What? No! I never mean that when I tease her."

"Maybe not consciously, but why apologize for not rescuing her sooner? Did you think she couldn't handle what was thrown at her?"

"No. I didn't want her to suffer. I felt responsible for her capture."

"How? You were knocked unconscious," said Wren, surprising them by her arrival. "I wondered where all of you had gone. I knew I upset everyone and I came to apologize."

Frustrated, Vidar threw up his hands, passion making him stand off the rail. "Everyone is apologizing when there is no need. Avatar because he feels responsible for everything going wrong in Soren, you," he said to Wren, "because you spoke truth, Nigel because of supposed failure with Chad, and Kell because he never saw Auriel's discontent. Have any of you stopped to consider another purpose of this mission was to uncover all these things so they can be dealt with?"

Kell looked askew to Vidar. "That is some tongue lashing."

He folded his arm and again assumed a casual posture against the rail, but copper eyes challenging. "So what are going to do about it, *Captain*?"

Kell stood, making him head and shoulders taller than Vidar, who continued to lean on the rail. With a deadpan expression capable of making any Guardian repine, he said, "Aside from suppressing the desire to throw you overboard, devise a plan to present to Tyrone based upon intelligence and find a way to change our attitude toward one another." He turned on his heels and left the quarterdeck.

Unnerved, Wren turned from watching Kell leave to Vidar. "He wouldn't do that, throw you overboard?"

"In a heartbeat."

"Your speech saved him from getting wet," said Avatar.

She shook her head, flashing a nervous smile. "You're both kidding."

"I provoked Kell by scolding him and challenging his authority. He's our captain. Which means, he could do more than threaten to throw me overboard. Don't you understand? Although some take teasing and good-natured ribbing too far, our lighter side keeps us from taking ourselves and our position too seriously and doing each other harm."

Uttering a frustrated sigh, she sat beside Avatar. "I believed that also, but after listening to Farren, Willow and Auriel's bitter complaints I see they have a point. Yet to go from that to abandoning their station is hard to understand much less accept. Especially Willow." Her brows furrowed. "At one point I thought I got through to her then Farren arrived and had Keara take her from the room. I didn't see her again."

"Farren can be very forceful," began Avatar. "I've tried to think of how I caused her harm, but all I recall is when she exhausted Kell's patience and I mediated. Maybe she felt I was interfering and held a grudge. I don't know. Other than the incident before the Great Battle, I can't think of anything else over the centuries to incite Auriel."

"I can't think of anything with Willow," said Vidar.

Wren refuted both of them, Avatar first. "The near demise of Gresham's forces was a result of Dagar employing the Dark Way and creatures of infrinn, not anything you did. The same happened to us in the Southern Forest—and *you* weren't involved. That aside, I can't imagine either one of you intentionally harming another Guardian."

"Thanks for the vote of confidence, but their actions show otherwise," he groused.

She punched him in the upper arm. "I said not intentional. You can't help the way another takes your comments."

He chuckled, pretending to rub his injury and spoke to Vidar. "I think she's back to normal now."

Vidar smiled and pushed himself off the rail. "I hope it didn't hurt."

"Nothing I can't handle." They began to leave the quarterdeck.

Irate, Wren stared after them. Mahon laughed and she bolted in pursuit of them. "You did this on purpose. It was all an act."

Avatar paused at the top of the steps to the main deck next to the helm. "You scolding Gulliver was out of character. Whereas punching me is a typical response."

"And part of the lighter side that keeps our relationships on an even keel," added Vidar.

Mahon laughed louder, making Wren irate. She jerked the helm from Mahon's hands and turned hard to port, sending the ship sharply in one direction. The sudden move sent Avatar and Vidar tumbling down the steps to the main deck. Mahon caught the rail to stay on his feet. She released the helm and he lunged to grab the wheel and keep it from spinning in the opposite direction.

"Mahon! You big, dumb lummox!" bellowed Gulliver from below. He appeared on deck, complaining, "Can't trust a warrior to anything requiring brains!" while avoiding Avatar and Vidar's attempt to stand. A smiling Wren passed Gulliver on his way to the quarterdeck.

Chapter 16

Breck, Skule, Farren, Willow, Lokien and Auriel met at Astrid. Lokien sat at the table for Auriel to tend his wound from his battle with Nigel. Farren and Willow were grim-faced.

"Since we no longer need to keep our presence a secret, why are we still meeting here rather than at the temple?" asked Breck.

"Security. Besides, it keeps the impression of godhood," said Skule.

"Not if they learn about Keara's demise," snapped Willow.

"Who's going to tell them?" chided Lokien. "They never heard of a Jor'ellian."

Willow accosted Auriel. "Why didn't you tell us about this Jor'ellian?"

"Everything happened so fast, I didn't have a chance. I was lucky to escape Avatar alive."

"Or make the ruse believable enough to fool us," accused Breck.

"Enough!" said Skule. "She is one of us now. As such, she will assume Keara's role."

"Not in our Trio!" rebuffed Willow.

"No, in our plan."

"Doing what?" asked Auriel with guarded skepticism.

"Help Lokien secure the landing site. Farren and I will lead the main strike force with Willow and Breck in support."

"Where do you plan on landing? Leith is too well guarded and Panos Point too busy and open."

"Ten miles north of Leith is a perfect cove that is shielded from land observation. From there it is about three miles inland to a broad open field fit for battle."

"Outside Bradney?"

"Ah, you've of heard of it," said Skule with pleasure.

"Ay, from Vidar. He said Queen Shannan hoped to draw out Sullivan to Bradney when she returned with troops from Tunlund and Gorham in support of King Ellis. Unfortunately, it never happened and she was killed during the coup."

"Where she failed, we will succeed and draw out Tyrone to his destruction."

"Don't be so cocky. Remember he is of Guardian heritage. He won't fall like other mortals."

"No, his fall will be harsher and more triumphant since we take down one of our own."

"What about Kell and Armus?" asked Farren.

"And Vidar," added Willow.

Skule gave a dismissive wave. "You are now capable of facing them, so stop fretting. What about the boy? Will he do as told?"

"He is coming around to seeing things our way," said Auriel.

He shook his head in disapproval. "Not good enough. He must be willing to serve or die."

"The girl is collateral. To save her, he will act."

"Make sure he does, or I will kill them both," sneered Breck.

She ignored him and continued with Skule. "When do we leave?"

"I instructed Ulrika to dispatch riders to all the Sigvard outposts ordering them and their varlets to assemble in Bergen by the end of the week. That gives us a force of six thousand, four thousand Sigvard with two thousand varlets."

"Since I only have a few days, I need to make certain Chad is well trained by then. Alone," she stressed to Breck and left.

In Astrid's dungeon Chad and Bergeta were kept in separate cells. He sat on the floor by the door listening to her soft sobbing and tried to speak words of encouragement. Under the circumstance, it was little consolation. In fact, he more spoke to himself than Bergeta. Hearing footsteps in the hall, he stood and waited in wary anticipation. A key turned the lock of his cell. Auriel entered.

"We need to talk," she said after closing the door.

"What do we have to talk about?" he scoffed and sat on the bed.

"Don't play the innocent game with me, Chad. Our individual choices brought us here."

"What do you want?"

"Your cooperation."

He glared sharply up at her. "To invade Allon? I don't think so."

She easily pulled him to his feet. "They will kill the girl if you don't cooperate."

"I thought you would kill her."

Her voice grew low and harsh. "Boy, I'm trying to keep you alive! She is immaterial."

"Not to me."

She scowled. "I may be able to save her, but everything depends upon *your* cooperation."

He studied her, guarded and suspicious. "Is this a Shadow Warrior trick? Pretend to help me for your own gains?"

She stared back, jade eyes intense, making him slightly repine. "You are too young to fully understand the subtleties of what is happening."

"I understand we betrayed those who trusted and depended upon us for selfish reasons."

She shoved him against the wall, but retained hold of him. Leaning closer, she spoke in a husky whisper. "You're a foolish boy. The invasion will happen. The question is what are you willing to do to prevent it?

Think about what I've said, Chad. Then when you are ready to face reality like a man, we'll talk." She released him and left.

For a moment he stood bewildered by the encounter. She came threatening Bergeta to gain his cooperation for the invasion of Allon then said he should consider how to prevent it? *This must be a trick. She seeks to confuse me so I will lower my guard and agree to help. How will I save Bergeta by agreeing, and how can I aid Nigel if I help them to invade Allon? To invade means to find a place for landing an army. Once there—* "Allon. Once I'm in Allon." He moved to the door "Auriel!"

"Ay." She stood against the wall beside the door.

"I'm ready to talk."

She waved him back from the door and entered. "I'm glad you are as quick and intelligent as Nigel said."

"At least I lived up to some of his expectations."

"Fulfill the rest and he may forgive you."

He shook his head, a look of hopelessness in his eyes. "No. You didn't see the hurt and disappointment on his face when it happened."

"No, I saw his reaction when receiving his sword and hearing you kept it for him. He wanted to go back for you, but couldn't."

His whole body sagged in grief at the implication; so much so, he had to sit on the stone bed before his knees gave way. "I don't deserve it."

"Grace and forgiveness aren't deserved. But I didn't come here to talk about that."

"No, you want my cooperation. How?"

"Trust me and do as I tell you."

"Just like that? No further explanation?"

She crossed her arms, glaring at him. "If you want to live through this, if you want *her* to live, then think like a man and understand what I'm offering you."

Pricked, he bolted to his feet. "That's the second time you said *think like a man*. What do you mean? I am a man."

"You're a boy, Chad! You have only to see the mess you've made by your lack of wisdom and foresight." She seized his collar drawing his face close enough to whisper. "Use the enemy to your advantage. When you have him in your sights, strike when he least expects and without mercy."

He stared at her, the jade eyes compelling and bright. He saw no evil in those eyes, not like he did in Hueil or Skule, their evil too obvious to hide. She may look the part of a Shadow Warrior, but she offered him a chance to save himself and Bergeta, and perhaps redeem himself to Nigel. "I believe I understand and will do as you say."

"Good." She released him. "At the end of the week, we leave for Allon. Keep your tongue and wits."

Auriel reached the stairs leading up from the dungeon where Breck waited. In some ways he reminded her of Armus, both large and powerfully built with similar hair color. In the eyes and mannerism the similarities ended. Breck's eyes were a cold blue compared to Armus' vivid and light chestnut brown. In character, Breck behaved abrasive and menacing while Armus confident and cocky, yet surprisingly gentle and tender toward mortals.

"Did you convince the boy?" he demanded.

"He has agreed to help." She tried to walk past him to go upstairs.

He stopped her. "Help us or help you use him against us?"

She jerked away. "Why don't you believe Skule that I'm now a Shadow Warrior?"

He glared at her. "You know why."

She forced herself to withstand his icy stare. "No, I don't."

"Maybe not. All the same, I don't trust you."

She shrugged. "Makes no difference to me. I didn't join my sisters for you to trust me. In fact, I don't trust you, so we reached a point of agreement, mutual distrust."

He snarled, his eyes narrow. "Be glad you're paired with Lokien, or else you might not reach Allon in one piece."

"Don't make threats you can't succeed in fulfilling." She once again began to go upstairs, but he seized her, his dagger at her throat.

"One false move, one hint of betrayal and I'll send you to oblivion."

"Breck!" snapped Lokien.

"I was just telling your new partner to watch her back." He released Auriel and marched upstairs.

"You all right?"

"Ay. He is always so friendly?"

"I don't think Breck ever trusted anyone. He only tolerates me because I'm faster and smarter than he is while Skule is more powerful."

"More powerful? Breck could crush any one of us using one hand."

Lokien pointed to his head. "There are different types of power." He glanced down the corridor. "What about the boy?"

"I persuaded him that it would be in his best interest to help us."

He slyly smiled. "Come. There is a centuries old map of Allon I want you to look at and tell me if it is still valid."

He led her to a room in the west wing of Astrid, a library of sorts with some books, maps and parchments. The bookshelves, tables and chairs were not very elaborate, but functional.

"On the table."

She leaned over to study the map. "Where did you get this?"

"Farren fetched it before she left the Region of Sanctuary. What do you think?"

She indicated a compass with symbols around it. "This map was done by a sea Guardian called Dugian. Perhaps by order of Kell or even Jor'el. It is very old and only a few settlements and cities marked. This is the cove and Bradney over here."

"Very good. We thought to take the northern route to avoid the normal shipping lanes leading to Leith." He indicated on the map.

"Might work. Although some fishing villages are now located along the shore. To avoid being seen by the villagers will mean narrowing the choice of approaches to these two." She used a finger to indicate the direction of travel.

"Now that is something we didn't know. How far out do the fisherman travel?"

She shrugged, her lips pursed in thought. "Being winter, if they do go out, maybe only a couple of miles. But, I'm not knowledgeable about currents and tides."

"That was our guess also."

"Skule said the army would number six thousand. Are there enough ships to transport so many?"

"Ay. Skule has thought of everything."

"So I assume he has the pilots and crew for each ship."

He widely smiled. "Oh, ay! He has a captain."

She found his answer intriguing. "What do you mean?"

He tugged at his lip for moment of thought. "Well, you are now a part of this, so I suppose it won't hurt to tell you."

"You sound like Breck, and don't trust me."

Skule entered with Farren, Breck and a sandy-haired female Guardian whose bright sea-green eyes were penetrating in their regard of Auriel.

"You were right about the map being made by Dugian," he said.

"You identified everything correctly," said the new Guardian.

Auriel's gaze narrowed at Skule. "This was a test?"

"Ay, and you passed. This is Dugian."

"How many Guardians do you have?"

He casually shrugged. "Not enough to counter Kell's force in battle, but more than he will be expecting."

"Still, you'll be defeated unless you can gain an advantage."

He sarcastically grinned "Any suggestions?"

When Auriel hesitated, Farren said, "Maybe Breck is right about her."

"She confirmed the map," said Lokien.

Skule's good eye never felt Auriel. "She knows what is at stake."

Her focus shifted to Farren. "You made the manacle appear on Wren's wrists, but I figured out how you did it. You either have spurean chain or stygian metal since you can't create something from nothing. You than likely obtained it from them," she motioned to the Warriors, "since the metals weren't forged into weapons until after Radnor."

Skule laughed with pleasure, much to Farren's chagrin.

"Ay," chided Farren in agreement.

Auriel turned to Skule. "When Tyrone invaded Tunlund to rescue his son, Hueil had mortals forge the metal into arrows to use against us. It worked, until being disarmed by Vidar, Avatar and others. We could use those for an unexpected advantage."

"Anything else?"

"Depending upon the amount of metal, you could also forge some swords and attach them to regular hilts."

He still smiled. "You can now hear the full plan. To do so, we will go to Borkien."

She grew suspicious. "Where and what is Borkien?"

"The place of the Tavar. You don't think we share Astrid?" he said, chuckling. "Farren, Willow, stay here and make certain the Sigvard comply and do as Auriel suggests with the metal. We'll meet at the coast in four days." He held out his hand to Auriel. "Come. I'll lead the way.

In a brilliant flash of light Auriel, Skule, Lokien, Breck and Dugian traveled to Borkien. They reappeared outside so Auriel could take in the view. Compared to Astrid, Borkien was a stark, brooding fortress nestled between the twin peaks of a pinnacle some eight miles away from Astrid.

"Impressive, isn't it?" asked Skule.

"The view at least."

The interior of Borkien continued the same severe and foreboding atmosphere as the exterior with little furnishings; the gray stonewalls bare of decoration and dimly lit by torches.

"Cozy. Did you pattern this after Dagar's netherworld?"

"With all the comforts of home."

"Including stygian cages," said Breck.

Auriel became concerned. "Is this where you're keeping the others?"

"A few of the less agreeable ones," said Skule.

Uneasiness grew in the pit of her being as she followed Skule into the bowels of Borkien. She recalled Dagar's nether dimension when assigned to Mahon's team to make a sweep of the place for any wayward Shadow Warriors after Dagar's defeat. It was a cavernous domain, cold and damp. The *reconditioning chamber* where Guardians suffered tortured for centuries measured one hundred feet in diameter by fifty feet high with various implements of 'instruction' and cages surrounding a central floor of different levels. Stone stairways and narrow walkways circumvented the chamber and went between levels. In all the cages, Guardians of different castes and genders were kept, all in various stages of suffering. Now at Borkien, Auriel entered a dungeon roughly one-third the size of the reconditioning chamber, but the details remained the same.

Two large powerful females warriors approached Skule. "My lord," said one. "This is an unexpected pleasure."

Skule thinly smiled. "I'm showing our newest recruit our facilities. Auriel, two of my loyal guards, Rane and Mab."

Mab had dark hair and cool pale green eyes and in contrast to Rane's fair hair and warm amber eyes. "Your name sounds familiar to me, why?" said Mab.

Auriel knew their names; former Trio Mates of Gresham, who joined Dagar before she became his militia commander and before Jedrek … "We've never met," was her evasive answer.

"Who trained you?"

"Armus but eventually I ended up assigned to another."

"Jedrek, I think Farren said you mentioned," said Lokien.

Auriel flinched when Lokien spoke Jedrek's name. Skule tried to hide a pleased smile when a private look passed between him, Breck and Lokien. Dugian remained impassive.

Mab sneered in mockery. "I know Jedrek. That may be how I recognize your name."

"Jedrek is no more," said Auriel, wary of Mab's reaction.

"Really? I thought he survived the Great Battle?"

"He did. He fell last year protecting his mortal charge."

"Pity. I looked forward to meeting him again."

"Meet to kill him, you mean," said Rane.

Auriel narrowed her eyes at Mab. "You hold a grudge against him because he replaced you after deserting Gresham."

"Oh?" said Mab, impressed at the intelligence, but quickly faded. "Whatever my past, you wouldn't be here if you didn't hold a grudge against another Guardian, and deep enough to turn. Who? Armus, perhaps?"

Auriel lips compressed, unwilling to answer.

"Avatar," said Breck.

"Avatar?" Mab laughed. "She thinks she can best Avatar. Oh, marvelous. We'd like to see that."

"Well, before you can amuse yourselves, our time has come," began Skule. "How many did you convince to join us?"

"All except one. He's still stubborn."

"Perhaps our newest recruit can persuade him," said Lokien.

Skule snorted a laugh. "You can be cruel, Lokien."

"Part of having a mischievous nature."

"Who is this stubborn Guardian?" asked Auriel, wary.

"If you knew Jedrek well, you will know him."

Auriel clenched her fists in an effort to stem the rising sense of apprehension as Skule led her through the dungeon to a separate cell. Inside, laid a fair-haired male Guardian with his back to the gate.

Skule hit the cell bars with a rock. "Wake up! You have a visitor."

His body jerked in surprise at the rude awakening. It took effort for him to sit up and turn.

Auriel gasped in astonishment at first sight of him. His fair-hair and icy light blue eyes dulled by pain and fatigue didn't prevent her from recognizing him immediately. Except for the color of his eyes, he bore a striking resemblance to his twin Jedrek. "Virgil."

It took a moment for Virgil to recognize her. "Auriel?"

"I said you would know him."

She stared at Virgil, mist in her eyes. "We thought you vanquished during the Great Battle."

He wearily shook his head. "Although it would have been better."

"I captured him," said Mab with pride. "I hoped to use him against Jedrek. Unfortunately, from you said, that's not possible."

"What?" asked Virgil, his gaze heavy on Auriel.

She turned aside. "He fell last year in the line of duty."

He screwed his eyes shut. "I knew I sensed something wrong."

"Pity there can't be a family reunion, but here is Auriel, Jedrek's protégé. So cheer up!" said Skule in mock amusement.

Virgil regarded Auriel with curious suspicion. "Why are you here?"

She hesitated to respond so Skule spoke: "She is our newest recruit."

Virgil scowled in disbelief. "You tricked her. Maybe even faked Jedrek's death to make her betray him."

Again she avoided his eyes. "Jedrek's death is real, just like being here by my own choice."

Virgil winced in fighting to contain his anguish and grief.

"A touching reunion, but our time is come. What say you now, Virgil? Your twin is dead and his protégé among our ranks. Allon is within our reach to conquer. Will you help us?"

His jowls flexed. "What do you want?"

"The same we always have—your added strength and sword. Four male warriors joined with ten female warriors, four thousand Sigvard and two thousand varlets is an impressive force."

"Besides, what is left? After so long in captivity, do you think Kell will let you rejoin the ranks of the Guardians?" asked Lokien.

"Being in this cell so long I don't know if I have strength to lift a sword, much less fight," complained Virgil.

"Easily remedied," said Skule.

Virgil closed his eyes, and with a deep resigned sigh, nodded.

Skule grinned. "Mab, see to his refreshing. We leave in two days. Dugian, prepare the ships."

Auriel stepped back for Mab to open the gate and fetch Virgil. He may have moved uncertain on his feet, but nothing uncertain in the menacing look at Auriel when passed her in leaving the cell.

Rane flashed a mocking grin. "Don't turn your back on him." She followed Mab.

"Lokien, take Auriel and review the plans for landing," said Skule.

Auriel left with Lokien.

"I don't trust either of them," said Breck, eyes narrow.

"You think I do? There is an old mortal saying 'Keep your friends close and your enemies closer'. One wrong move and you can kill them."

Chapter 17

SINCE SENDING NIGEL AND OTHERS TO SOREN, Tyrone interviewed Ivor and Gilda several times. Ivor willingly cooperated, but being a servant he couldn't provide much intelligence. Gilda remained stubborn and belligerent, wearing on his patience. Still, a deep disturbing uneasiness increased with each unsuccessful interview concerning the Sorens and their threat of invasion. It is what prompted him to dispatch Kell and Vidar. Nigel would take exception to being retrieved from his mission, but he had to discover why the situation so unsettled him. He accepted the fact it was natural to be agitated, concerned and stirred to action by Titus' kidnapping. However, this time, what could happen was almost unthinkable.

Unfortunately, his worried preoccupation became noticeable. He ate little; slept only when absolutely necessary; spent hours in physical training, planning sessions, speaking to Master Hampton or praying. Time spent with Tristine and the children became limited to family meals. Even then, he was often distracted or called away.

In the castle training facility he engaged Armus in mock combat. Tyrone's size of six feet eight inches and added strength of being half-Guardian, made sparring bouts with most mortal soldiers nearly impossible, thus he fought Armus, Avatar, Mahon or any other Guardian warrior. On their part, no Guardian pulled their blows and gave Tyrone the full measure of their strength. Drenched in sweat and breathing hard, he and Armus separated.

"Sire, three hours is sufficient for today."

Tyrone used a towel to wipe the sweat from his face before pouring water into a cup. "Battle lasts longer than a few hours." He drank.

Armus caught sight of Tristine in the threshold. Tyrone's back was to the door so he approached Tyrone to speak privately. "Some grow concerned by your troubled mind and spirit, wondering about the soundness of conflicting mortal and Guardian aspects."

Tyrone's glance was sharp. "My mind is sound. Only a sense of uneasiness has vexed my heart and spirit since Kell appeared. No amount of prayer or exercise has alleviated it. In fact the sense grows stronger with each day they are gone."

"Have you spoken to Tristine?"

He shook his head and took another drink before replying. "I'm not sure what to tell her. Nothing's clear. Or rather, what I feel must done is unthinkable and hard to comprehend."

"You can't continue to shut her out." Armus motioned Tyrone's attention to the threshold.

Tyrone softly smiled. "Ay." He handed Armus the cup and approached her. "Care accompany me to our chamber? I need a bath."

"That's the first time you've asked me to join you in anything these past few weeks."

"An invitation long over due." He steered her from the hall. "I realized I've been preoccupied and bit neglectful of late. I am sorry."

"I understand what preoccupies you, for they are always on my mind. What I don't understand is your unwillingness to talk with me."

He indicated for her to be quiet as they crossed the courtyard. Servants, soldiers, priests and Guardians went about their daily activity. In fact, the silence continued into the royal chamber.

"Tyrone," she began.

He placed a finger on her lips. "I promise we'll talk but I really want to get clean."

She grabbed his arm to prevent his leaving. "No more delays. I've been waiting for weeks. Is it what you fear Nigel might discover in Soren that troubles you?"

He took her hands, regret and frustration on his face. "I wish I could tell you, but until I speak to Nigel I dare not. Perhaps with the information he brings back I can put the pieces together. Please be patient with me a little longer. Now, let me get clean." He kissed her forehead and went to the privy.

Tyrone barely finished dressing and toweling his hair dry after the bath when Armus came with news of the group's return. He snatched Tristine's hand and hastened to the study, where they welcomed Nigel, Mirit, Wren, Avatar, Kell and Vidar.

"You look tired," she said to Nigel.

He heaved a non-committal shrug. "I spent weeks traveling and just returned."

"Don't be fooled by his bravado, the journey proved difficult," said Mirit. "We were fortunate the king sent Kell and Vidar."

"I feared something was wrong. I'm sorry my fears proved true."

"Nigel?" asked Tristine, seeing his downcast expression.

"Personally worse than I expected or ever anticipated. We lost Chad and Auriel."

"Oh, Nigel, no! How?"

"Not in death, rather personal choice."

Disturbed, Tyrone studied Nigel. "Chad chose to leave you?"

He nodded, sobriety and pain on his face.

"Auriel forfeited her station to join the Valkerish, who are Guardians, and the Tavar are Shadow Warriors," said Avatar, fighting to keep harshness from his voice.

Armus could not hide his surprise but Tyrone reacted like one hit by an unexpected blow and he nearly fell in his attempt to sit in a chair.

Concerned, Tristine knelt beside him. "Tyrone?"

He didn't reply, his face unusually pale and stricken.

"Is something wrong with him?" asked Nigel.

She shook her head and heaved a partial shrug. "He's been troubled since you left, which is why he asked Jor'el for Vidar's help and sent him and Kell to fetch you. Only he won't tell me why."

Tyrone squeezed her hand but spoke to Nigel. "I need to know everything. Leave out no detail, however insignificant you think it is. Only then will I be able to understand and explain."

For the next two hours, Nigel, Mirit, Wren and Avatar told their stories. Kell and Vidar added their involvement in the various rescues.

Tristine regarded Nigel with admiration. "I thought the tales of a Jor'ellian defeating a Guardian were only legend. Father would have been very proud."

He flashed a tired smile. "I'm not certain how to feel. It happened suddenly. Mirit was out cold so I didn't have a choice. I knew I would not survive against another Shadow Warrior and glad for the rescue."

Tyrone now stood in front of the fire, staring at the flames. "Auriel freed you both despite her choice while Chad kept your sword. On the surface, it appears to conflict with their choices, but maybe not." He turned to Kell. "Why did you insist on Auriel going?"

"Part of Jor'el's instruction prior to sending me from the heavenlies. I don't know the reason, but I will before this is over."

"Perhaps it's as I said, to uncover these problems. Surely Jor'el knew Auriel's heart and this mission would force her to face her discontentment and make a decision," said Vidar.

"The wrong decision," groused Wren.

"Why help after she turned her back on everything? Seems contrary to what you said about the others. Once they made their decision and thought nothing about killing Guardians or mortals," said Tyrone.

Wren shrugged her ignorance without answering.

"I'm certain Chad acted out of great remorse," said Tristine.

"Ay, he did," affirmed Avatar.

"We should have forced him to come back!" snapped Nigel, beginning to pace in agitation.

"Why? Only to regret leaving Bergeta?" said Mirit.

"He barely knows her yet turns his back on everything. Makes no sense."

Tyrone shook his head. "Your argument doesn't work. I only knew Tristine for two days, yet left everything to help her because I fell in love."

Nigel waved it aside. "That's different. You two were meant to be together according to Prophecy. Remember, I directed her to you."

Mirit took hold of his arm to stop his pacing. "What about us? There is no prophecy concerning our relationship."

He frowned and sighed with sobriety. "No. If only I could have spoken to him before we left, maybe things would be different. Now, I may never learn what happens to him."

"You can't blame yourself. You befriended him, taught him, and made him your squire. You did everything to help him," said Tristine.

"We tried to tell him so, only he won't listen," said Mirit.

"I can't turn my feelings off because you both tell me to!"

"Easy, brother. We're expressing concern, not condemning how you feel," said Tyrone.

"Tell them!" Nigel waved at Mirit and Tristine then crossed to the other side of the room.

Hurt, Tristine bit her lip but Mirit rebuffed him. "Fine. Wallow in self-pity."

He whirled about. "Self-pity?"

She confronted him. "Ay. You think whatever you say or do effects every situation and no one else has a choice."

"That's not true."

"Oh, but it is. You thought you could talk me into falling in love with you, but you didn't. I did so in my own time. Now you say if you had been able to speak to Chad the situation would be different, but Avatar said Chad told him otherwise. You can't accept it."

Nigel turned red-faced, his eyes flashing at the others. He began to move away when she seized him, her voice pleading but low so only he could hear. "There is too much at stake to withdraw. For your own heart's sake, for our love's sake, and for Allon, you must let Chad go."

"You ask a lot."

She touched his cheek. "Because I love you and understand you better than you will admit. You must be provoked to change your mood when no immediate solution is apparent or else you brood."

"Avatar told you that."

"No. I learned from your behavior in Tunlund."

"Nigel," began Tyrone, his voice sympathetic, "whereas losing Chad is difficult for you, Auriel was also lost, affecting others just as deeply."

"Ay," agreed Armus. "Losing one in battle or as a result of duty is different than by betrayal. What made her do it?" he demanded of Avatar, making the warrior stiffen at the rebuff.

Kell gripped Armus' shoulder to draw him away. "Avatar is not to blame. Auriel let her discontentment rule and chose wrongly. Discontent she's held since the Great Battle."

Armus' expression showed he understood and grew sympathetic. "Avatar," he went to apologize, but Avatar turned aside.

"What's the problem?" asked Tyrone in a tone of wanting an answer.

"She blames me for the death of many comrades in a skirmish before the Great Battle," said Avatar in a thick voice, his features set.

"It wasn't your fault," refuted Kell.

"It was my plan!"

"Which I approved and Gresham executed!"

Armus intervened at seeing Tyrone's displeasure of the argument between his fellow Guardians. "Gresham led his forces to a breach in the nether dimension in an attempt to stop Dagar from gaining access to the creatures of *infrinn*. Unfortunately, they arrived too late. Dagar used the creatures and the Dark Way to defeat Gresham, and also defeat Vidar and I in the Southern Forest. Thus setting the stage for the final conflict at the Temple."

"Was Auriel among Gresham's forces?" asked Tyrone.

"His militia commander."

"At her young age, I didn't believe she was ready for such responsibility, only Gresham and Jedrek convinced me. She was Jedrek's apprentice," said Kell, his voice calmer.

"How old was she then?"

"Nine hundred, and among the last group of Guardians created. Such assignments are given to the older, more experienced Guardians. At the time Avatar was fourteen hundred and proven in battle and his plan well thought out when I gave approval."

Nigel's appeared befuddled. "She held a grudge for over four hundred years?"

"Apparently," droned Avatar. "I believed all was settled when she split my lip."

"What?" asked Nigel in surprise.

"She landed a good one," said Wren, motioning to her lower lip and chin. "Split right down into the chin. Took a week to heal."

Kell explained, "I punished her for striking a superior officer and believed she tempered her attitude as a result. I would not have reinstated her and given her more responsibilities over the centuries, including Trio Leader, if I thought otherwise."

In a congenial tone, Tyrone spoke to Avatar. "After so long you are not to blame."

"Perhaps, yet she accused me of provoking her since then. Only I can't think of another incident."

"Not directly," began Wren. "She got angry whenever you teased me, citing your cutting manner and sarcasm."

"Wonderful! Makes me feel much better knowing my whole personality is a catalyst."

She recoiled at his rebuff.

"Sire, I will speak to the Trio leaders concerning the problem. Perhaps, we can deal with it before the worst happens," said Kell.

"Wren, do you know of other females who expressed such sentiments?" asked Tyrone.

She grew hesitant. His question was not a command yet his gray eyes direct in their regard. "Not to the extent of Auriel and the others. At least I don't believe so."

"Who?" asked Kell.

The conflict was evident on her face and in her voice. "Must you know, Captain? Isn't it enough we sometimes feel slighted?"

"I never slighted you," insisted Avatar, only to be ignored.

"I can't fix a problem if I don't know the extent."

"Wren. None of you have anything to fear," said Tyrone.

"The subject is a sensitive one, Sire." She then spoke to Kell. "Priscilla expressed annoyance about Gulliver and Ewert. Mona mentioned Gresham. Callie, Janis, Nixie, even I have complained on occasion, but like I said before, it's a general attitude, so most of the time we shrug off the comments or retaliate in our own way."

"Ay, you get physical," said Avatar with a snicker.

"Priscilla blows in and out like a foul wind," added Vidar.

Wren hands went to her hips in confronting Vidar. "What do you expect? She can't match your skill. Kell is our captain. Armus is a hulking brute and Avatar sharp witted. So she flies around causing what little chaos she can to avoid conflict with any of you."

Armus looked surprise. "She does her flighty wind-bag routine because she's afraid we'll harm her?"

"In part, ay."

"Why *in part?*"

She sheepishly frowned. "It's her nature to be flighty."

"So we're not completely responsible."

"No, but she acts in self-defense. Most of the female who aren't warriors fear those who are."

"We would never harm them!"

"I know, but it's the perception of strength."

"Wren, there is little that can be done about someone's perception," said Tyrone.

"I know, Sire, so do most of the females. Thus we shrug it off or retaliate." She turned to Avatar. "And why I said you can't help the way another takes your comments. When the individual takes things to heart and dwells on them, discontentment can happen."

Kell scowled in vexation. "This is not a problem easily remedied."

Tyrone pursed his lips and tilted his head in thought. "No, yet if understanding comes from talking about the matter, then perhaps one who harbors discontentment can be turned. And be quick. We don't know how long until the invasion and we must be prepared without any surprises coming from our ranks."

"Ay, Sire. I'll call an immediate meeting and inform the Trio Leaders of Auriel and the Shadow Warriors—"

Tyrone paled in fear and sat.

"Sire?"

He waved Kell off. "To your meeting, Captain. Armus." He hurried from the study with the Guardian lieutenant at his heels.

"Time we approach Jor'el," said Kell to Vidar once Tyrone left. They vanished before questions or objections could be voiced.

"Tristine, what troubles Tyrone?" asked Nigel.

She shrugged, her expression worried. "He kept putting me off until you returned and said only then can he put the pieces together."

"Perhaps he's made a connection," said Avatar, drawing a look of ire from Tristine.

"Do you know?"

"No, Majesty. However, he became upset each time Shadow Warriors were mentioned."

"Since he used me as an excuse, I intend to find out," said Nigel.

"I'm going with you," declared Tristine.

"No, wait here—"

"I've been waiting for weeks! The only time I see my husband is when I wake up."

The statement disturbed Nigel. "Very well. Only let me approach him first. He may speak freely if you're not immediately noticed."

"We'll give you the chance." Mirit took Tristine's arm in a show of support.

After the mortals left, Avatar and Wren remained. A moment of awkward silence passed before he spoke. "Wren, about my earlier outburst, I'm sorry. I would never do anything to hurt you. And my teasing, is simply teasing and not a slight."

"I know. I defended your *sarcastic personality*," she said with small, wry smile that quickly faded. "She may consider your personality a catalyst, but never stated her motivation beyond a lack of appreciation. Willow claimed jealousy of me and my relationship to Vidar." She grew impassioned. "She was always better than me! If anything I had to prove myself. Kell even acknowledged her superior skill." Bewildered, she shook her head. "I always thought Vidar befriended me because I needed more help. How could she think I was the more favored one?"

"Perhaps the same way Farren believes I usurped her when I became Kell's apprentice and nothing to do with us, rather the other individual involved."

"You mean feeling shunned by Kell and Vidar?"

"Ay. Farren and I never had a vicious or tense encounter like I did with Auriel, yet she holds me responsible for replacing her and being demoted. Willow admitted jealousy while you say she was the better. Rather than taking out their feelings on two of the premier Guardians, we became their scapegoats."

"Makes sense. I was also accused of being *attached* to certain males."

A gregarious smile appeared. "Which males?"

"Doesn't matter," she said in dismissal at her miscue.

"Vidar, certainly," he continued in his humor. "Mahon? No, too tolerant and not capable of fending off your shots. Ah! Gulliver!"

"Oh, stop it!" she protested, despite laughing. "The point is: you're right about Willow and Farren."

His smile remained.

"I'll see you at Arundine," she said and vanished.

Armus fell in step behind Tyrone. The last eight years he served as Guardian advisor. Prior to his new assignment, he watched over Tristine from birth, serving as her friend, mentor, and general sidekick; an assignment he very much enjoyed and took to heart. During his search for a runaway Tristine, he met Tyrone and discovered his half–Guardian heritage, a fact unknown to Tyrone at the time. Circumstances meant only one thing: Tyrone was the Great King, the king to unite Guardians and mortals.

Since then, their relationship grew and he tutored Tyrone in the Ancient, instructed him in Guardian hierarchy and culture, became his partner in mock combat and counted among Tyrone's closest friends. It was a unique position for any Guardian. Seeing Tyrone's reactions to the mention of Shadow Warriors made him keenly aware he had to act and not accept excuses any longer. However, out of respect he held his tongue until they reached the Chapel.

Once inside, Armus waved everyone out. The three priests and two servants complied. When the chapel door shut, he began his inquiry, his light chestnut eyes direct.

"Tyrone," he said, purposely using his name rather than title, "you must tell me what is wrong and not put me off any longer."

He sighed with resignation and nodded. "Of anyone, you would understand." He sat on the front pew, Armus sitting beside him. "What is required is not of me, but of Tristine. In truth, I am to do nothing with confronting the enemy. I am to let my beloved wife defend Allon without a proper army against an unknown enemy!"

Stunned, Armus blinked, uncertain of what to say.

"Your reaction is the same as mine when Jor'el first gave me instruction: shock, disbelief. Now we learn the enemy is composed of Shadow Warriors."

Armus recovered his voice. "Have you told Kell?"

"No. I can barely find the words to tell you." Agitated, he bolted up to pace. "Although Tristine is not to act alone. Mirit is involved. Together they are to face the enemy with only one hundred Guardians in support. How do I tell Nigel? It's bad enough his sister must face Shadow Warriors. The possibility of Mirit being killed a second time will not be easy for him to accept."

Nigel stepped into the rim of altar light. "So that's it."

Tyrone winced at discovery. "What are you doing here?"

"What do you think? Twice you appeared on the verge of fainting then Tristine said you wouldn't talk her. Now I know why."

He gripped Nigel's arm. "I assure you, brother, day and night I plead with Jor'el not to let it be, but each time he confirms his will and the fact we are to do nothing."

"I can understand why you haven't told Tristine."

"I don't," said Tristine. Her face fixed yet a hint of pain in her eyes. Mirit stood with her.

Nigel heaved a hapless shrug at Tyrone's annoyance.

"Tristine, Tyrone was speaking to me when Nigel arrived and overheard," said Armus.

"I should have been the first he told."

"I didn't know how to tell you."

"Am I not queen? My father was the Son of Tristan, whose name I bear. How else would you tell me, but directly?"

"You are also my wife, the mother of my children!" he shot back. "I'm sorry." He took her hands and kissed the knuckles. "I love you and I couldn't bear losing you."

"I feel the same, yet had to let you go to Tunlund; to trust your judgment and have faith Jor'el would bring you, Titus and Nigel home. Now, you must do the same with me."

"It is difficult to accept the danger both as husband and king."

Nigel snorted in annoyance. "At least you both share a life together. Mirit and I have yet to start when I hear she is a part in this."

"I always had a part. Remember, this began when Alaric and Leif came seeking my help."

"It doesn't make it any easier to accept *this* part."

"Of course not, but all along I sensed something more was required of me than going to Soren, something dealing with Allon and the invasion. Now it makes sense. To the Sorens I am a warrior and only natural I face them in battle."

"With me taking the lead since I am queen. Every time Alaric and Leif went to speak they looked to Mirit and I for permission. Don't you see? Even then Jor'el gave us wisdom in how to face them."

A bright flash of light stopped a response. Kell and Vidar appeared.

"Sire, Jor'el says Auriel is a warning. Discontentment must be rooted out and their place among us reinforced and strengthened before a new division happens, one that could be worse than Dagar. Thus the force must be only females Guardians," said Kell.

"To show the Sorens and others that Allon stands united, mortals and Guardians, females and males," added Vidar.

"How, with no males present?" asked Nigel.

"We will be present, but not participants. Jor'el will make his presence known. We have only to obey and trust Him," said Kell.

"Did you know any of this before, Captain?" chided Tyrone.

"No, Sire. I would have told you if I did."

"Kell, you have a habit of not telling everything you know."

"Sorry, Sire. It is sometimes difficult to discern what to say and what not say in my capacity when dealing with mortals."

"And fellow Guardians," groused Armus.

Kell ignored the comment and continued. "With the fate of mortal and Guardian unity hanging in the balance, I assure you, Sire, I withheld nothing. Queen Tristine and Lady Mirit are to lead the force when the enemy invades and we are to stand and watch."

"When?" asked Tristine.

"Perhaps a matter of days. I'll speak to the Trio Leaders at midnight, and will have the female warriors ready at your command, Majesty."

"No, Captain, Wren will. This is to be a female undertaking and we must assume full responsibility."

"So be it. Any further instructions, Majesty?"

"Not at the moment. If we think of something, we'll let you know."

"If that's all, I could use some rest. I don't know which hurts more, my head from fatigue or my spirit from this," groused Nigel.

"You mean your head and *ego*," said Mirit.

Nigel chafed at the barb. "I'm a prince of Allon, Jor'ellian knight, and King's Champion, trained to fight not sit and watch. Only through rest and prayer can I reconcile myself to the situation."

Tyrone took Nigel by the shoulders to steer him from the chapel. "Then let us do so and swiftly. Our women need our full support."

On the way to the study, Tyrone dispatched a servant to fetch bread and wine. He and Nigel entered and found Titus sitting at the desk.

Egan rushed in, frowning in frustrated disapproval at Titus. He was a quiet and unassuming Guardian warrior whose very light blue eyes were in marked contrast to his black hair. He assumed Jedrek's role of Guardian to Prince Titus after he returned from Tunlund.

"I gather he slipped past you again."

"I'm sorry, Sire."

Tyrone waved him off. "I realize you're doing your best, Egan." He turned to Titus. "I thought your mother sent you to bed?"

The boy grew sheepish. "Ay. But I know something is wrong, maybe even war. I'm not a child anymore, I've seen war."

Nigel tried not to laugh and coughed to cover himself at Tyrone's ire.

"Seeing war and engaging in battle are different," said Tyrone.

"So there will be war. That's why Uncle Nigel went to Soren. And why you've been so worried."

"He has your perception," said Nigel.

Tyrone steadily regarded his son. After a brief moment, he took Titus by the hand and led him to a sofa to sit. "Ay, war will happen soon. A dangerous enemy seeks to invade Allon."

"You won't let it happen. You and Uncle Nigel will stop them," declared Titus. "With Jor'el's help of course," he added.

"The situation is too complex and sensitive to explain, so you must have faith in Jor'el and trust our judgment."

"I do. I just wish Mother would stop treating me like a child and tell me what you have." Titus pouted and folded his arms.

"I will not tolerate disrespect toward your mother! She didn't tell you because I didn't tell her until this evening. She acted in your best interest, protecting you until she understood the situation."

"I'm sorry."

Tyrone nodded, his expression softening and he chose his words carefully. "The battle to come will be a test for Guardians and mortals, and your mother and Lady Mirit will play key roles."

Titus gaped in disbelief. "Mother will fight? Does she know how? Mirit does, but Mother?"

Nigel snorted a laugh. "She is more capable that you think. I helped to instruct her when we were children."

"Oh. Then she'll do well. What can I do?"

"As prince royal, your duty is to help your brothers and sister, which is why I will send for Angus to advise you." Tyrone saw Titus didn't like the answer. "Hear me, son," he began in a firm, no-nonsense voice. "With your mother, Uncle Nigel, and myself away from Waldron, your responsibility is here for the sake of your siblings and the people of Allon. Do you understand?"

"I think so. Although I'd rather be with all of you."

"Even as king I must do things I don't always want to do for the good of others. Mikaela is an infant and needs protection while Fraser and Eli may be easily frightened since they have not seen war. As the eldest, you must protect, comfort and encourage them."

Titus' expression grew considerate. "I suppose so."

Nigel sat on the arm of the sofa beside Titus. "Speaking as one elder brother to another, there were times I was given charge of my sisters and I didn't always like it." He smiled in remembrance. "Those times I took myself too seriously and they became annoyed. But strengthened our relationship, especially with your mother. Don't discount duty to your siblings, for later in life it can serve you all well."

"All right. I'll be as good a brother as you."

"I hope better. I'm still trying to make up for the years I missed."

"Now go to bed," said Tyrone then to Egan. "Keep him there."

"I'll try, Sire, but he has his mother's skill for escaping."

Nigel fought a smile in asking, "Have you been speaking to Armus?"

Titus flushed. "I asked him to tell me what Mother was like."

Tyrone ignored Nigel's muffled laughter. "So he tells you the stories and you take advantage." He picked up Titus, handed him to Egan and waved for them to leave. "I'm going to have a long talk with Armus," he grumbled when the door closed.

"Don't be too hard on him. She often beguiled him and left him as hapless as Egan. Remember, he was looking for her when he found you."

Tyrone grinned despite his annoyance. "Still, Titus didn't give Jedrek so much trouble. I think Kell was mistaken in his choice of replacement."

Nigel nodded in agreement. "Avatar told me how Ellan tested his patience when he replaced Morrell after they believed me killed. Titus is testing Egan. You know he was fond of Jedrek. Change isn't easy."

A servant entered carrying a tray containing bread and wine.

"I hope Titus listens and stays put when we leave." Tyrone observed the bread and wine. "This night we must come to terms with the situation. In the morning, I'll send Armus for Angus and dispatch word to the entire Council. We must stand united behind our women."

"We shall." Nigel arranged the candle, bread, and wine for their meditation and prayer.

Chapter 18

I N THE FOREST OF MIDESSEX, in the heart of Allon stood Arundine, Council Hall of the Guardians, a small domed shrine of white marble, similar to the Temple of Providence. The interior of Arundine was larger than anticipated by the exterior. Twelve pillars held up the dome while between each stood a marble chair. Under the dome on the marble floor was a map of Allon, naming each province in front of its respective chair.

A few minutes before midnight, the Trio Leaders began to arrive. Wren and Avatar greeted them on the portico. Priscilla, Guardian of Fair Winds from the East Coast whose flowing sea foam and dark green gown made a lasting impression on mortal sailors. Mona, Guardian of Legends of the North Plains was a gifted vassal who could change personas to suit any given situation. Nixie was an older female warrior from the Meadowlands who replaced Zinna after she fell in the battle of Tunlund.

Barnum of the Highlands was brawny warrior with a grizzled beard and good-natured sneer. Gresham and Alrick appeared together. Gresham of Midessex displayed his intelligence by supplementing his russet and tan vassal uniform with modest ornamentations, including a jeweled hilted dagger. Alrick was a redheaded older Guardian of the Delta, whose appearance belied the mind and heart of a cunning warrior. Chase was a mild-tempered sea Guardian placed in command of the West Coast. Derwin of the Lowlands had a temperament opposite Chase, fiery and outspoken. Derwin and Zadok got along well. Zadok was the most likely Guardian to place in charge of most treasured province the Region of Sanctuary. He was a surly warrior, fully of retorts and complaints, but with the stubbornness of a mule and sword of iron. Callie of the Northern Forest, a quiet unassuming female warrior, rounded out the Guardian leadership.

"Is Armus here?" asked Zadok.

"Not yet," replied Avatar.

"I suppose Kell once again kept the reason for this meeting a secret?"

"No."

"Well?"

"Well, what?"

"You're as bad as Armus!" Zadok marched off.

Wren jabbed her elbow into Avatar's side. "You are as bad as Armus. You both purposely provoke him."

"No one needs to provoke Zadok."

In a flash of light, Kell, Armus, Vidar and a female warrior with strawberry blonde and periwinkle blue eyes appeared on the portico.

"Is everyone here?" asked Kell.

"Ay," said Avatar.

Inside, Wren took her seat in the Southern Forest chair and the others continued to the platform.

Grave in expression, Kell surveyed the Trio Leaders. "Times like this I wish the duties of captain fell to another. One among us is missing."

"Auriel," said Mona, motioning to the empty South Plains chair.

"Did the mission to Soren fail?" asked Derwin.

"Not entirely," said Kell and nodded to Avatar to speak.

"We learned the Valkerish are Guardian females who deserted, and the Tavar are Shadow Warriors."

"Who are the females?" asked Nixie.

"Farren, Willow and Keara."

Zadok snorted in mock annoyance. Mona grew pale at hearing the names. Priscilla, Alrick and Chase showed either surprise or anger.

Barnum turned to Wren and asked, "Willow?"

She nodded, unable to reply, but visible signs of her temper rising.

"That is only half the problem," began Kell, his voice firm and deliberate. "Auriel's seat is empty because she chose to join the females and forfeit her station."

"Impossible!" exclaimed Zadok.

The others also voiced various degrees of disbelief.

Pricked by the reactions, Wren bolted up. "It's true! I was imprisoned by them because I didn't agree that all males are insensitive louts like Zadok."

Zadok pushed himself out of his chair to advance on Wren, but Avatar hastened from the platform to stand between them.

The same time Zadok and Avatar moved Kell snapped, "Wren!"

"Let her speak, Captain!" said Avatar but his intense focus remained on Zadok. "It may not be the way you want, but it's the truth. And the reason for this meeting."

Kell's ire flared, but Armus' agreement stopped his rebuff.

"He is right, Captain."

Kell's jowls flexed to contain his temper. "Very well, Lieutenant."

"What do you mean because you didn't agree?" asked Priscilla.

Wren took a deep breath to curb her passion in responding. "They believe all males are callous and not to be trusted. Farren claimed being slighted by Kell in favor of Avatar. Willow felt the same of Vidar because of me. Auriel said only Jedrek respected her as a warrior, no other male." She gazed at each female while speaking. "A sentiment we all expressed at one time or another."

"Not to the point of forfeiting our station," insisted Mona.

"No, and not always outwardly manifesting our feelings. Everyone's reaction shows the depth of Auriel's discontent was unknown. Once revealed, she vented her spleen on Avatar and mocked me. Because of her betrayal we were fortunate to escape Soren."

"Except Chad," said Avatar.

"What happened to him?" asked Gresham.

For the first time Avatar took his eyes off Zadok to answer. "Like Auriel, he held discontentment in his heart that neither Prince Nigel nor myself suspected. Unlike Auriel, he regrets the pain he caused, but will abide by his choice since aligning himself with a Soren girl. Nigel was greatly distressed by the loss."

"For the boy, but not Auriel," complained Zadok.

Avatar seized Zadok. "Speak badly of Nigel again and I will thrash you!"

Kell moved so fast Avatar barely finished speaking when he and Zadok were jerked apart. This time Kell didn't curb, his temper. "Zadok, You will hold your peace! For too long I have tolerated your surly tongue, but no more. If you value your position as Trio Leader and servant of Jor'el you will tame your tongue from now on."

The warrior repined at Kell's hot rebuke, and golden eyes flashing with authority. "Ay, Captain."

Kell's head snapped around to Avatar. "Threaten another Guardian in my presence and you will feel *my* sword after your demotion!"

Avatar flinched as if woken from a bad dream, clapped his sword and inclined his head in a submissive bow.

Kell shoved Avatar to return to the platform. He addressed the Trio Leaders. "All of you take heed. This bickering, surliness, insults and mocking each other will stop before conflict tears us apart! Auriel's betrayal is a warning. No Guardian, male or female, warrior, vassal, hunter, archer, or whatever position is better than another. Did we survive Dagar's uprising and Musetta's attempted coup only to wound each other by thoughtless words? We are on the brink of invasion from those who rebelled and must stand united!"

He walked the length of Arundine, making eye contact with each Leader. Alrick and Chase shook their heads to the question. Gresham and Derwin stiffened in a display of pride. Zadok chewed on his lower lip to hold his tongue. Priscilla lowered her head, making Kell pause and take notice of her timid reaction. Mona, Nixie and Callie became thoughtful. Wren remained standing and the only one of the Leaders to meet Kell's gaze.

Finally Barnum broke the heavy silence following the impassioned speech. "What do you want us to do, Captain?"

Kell replied in a more controlled voice. "Spread the word of what I said and tend to anyone, especially females, who feel threatened, ridiculed, mocked, neglected or anything leading to discontentment and trouble. It is only a matter of days before the invasion."

Whether by verbal answer or by nod they all agreed.

"What is the king doing to prepare?" asked Chase.

"Nothing. By Jor'el's design, the challenge falls to Queen Tristine and Lady Mirit. They are to face the enemy with one hundred female Guardian warriors while the king, Prince Nigel, myself and the rest of the male Guardians from Waldron will be visible but not interfere."

"What? " "How?" "That can't be!" came various reactions.

"One hundred of us against how many of the enemy?" asked Nixie.

"We don't know. But Jor'el intends to make His presence known."

"This is incredible," snorted Zadok.

"For once I agree with you," said Avatar.

Kell's sternness returned. "It is Jor'el's will and we are His servants! We must tend to our ranks while preparing for invasion. As such, Caryn will assume Leadership of the South Plains," he said indicating the female warrior who accompanied him and the others. "Now be quick about this business. I need—" he stopped. "Rather, Wren will be in command."

"She is not a warrior," said Alrick.

"The Sorens consider her a Valkerish, and it is the queen's command."

Wren spoke, "Nixie, Callie, Caryn, you and the others you select are to meet me at Waldron immediately."

They saluted.

"Return to your duties," said Kell in dismissal. As the Trio Leaders filed out, he intercepted Priscilla at the threshold. "We need to talk."

For a moment she appeared apprehensive, yet quickly assumed her flighty smile. "Very well."

He drew her back inside. Her shying away during his speech and the unmistakable look of concern when he said he wanted to speak to her confirmed what Wren said earlier. "I am not sure how to say this, or if you'll accept it. I realize I haven't always been gentle or even sensitive in dealing with you. I'm sorry. All I can say is I will try to do better."

She was taken back by his confession. "Well, this is unexpected. I thought you just summoned us for a scolding."

He frowned and sighed. "I suppose it seemed that way, but no. News of Auriel and the others deeply troubles me. I don't want to lose any more Guardians to thoughtlessness, especially you."

"Me? I'm just a flighty wind-bag."

He shook his head with a hapless expression. "You're not going make this easy, are you?"

"Why should I?"

"Because we've been through too much together to allow thoughtless and stupid words to come between us."

For a moment she regarded the earnest expression and sincerity in his golden eyes. "You really mean that."

"Ay. There aren't many of us who remain from the beginning. After each loss I come to appreciate that fact more. We may not agree often and are different in nature and character, but I do care what happens to you. If you don't believe anything else about me, please believe that."

"Is the care as captain or as Kell?"

He heaved a shrug. "Both. I am who I was created to be. Can you make the wind blow in all four directions simultaneously?"

"Swirl and go in circles, but not all four directions at once." She flashed a mischievous smile. "I'll accept your apology on one condition."

"Condition?" he asked, wary.

"That I can occasionally ruffle your feathers. It gives the others such pleasure to see you confounded and we shouldn't spoil their fun. Besides, you look so cute when flustered."

He chuckled in relief. "If it will smooth over our differences, I agree to your condition."

"Good." She smiled and waved both hands. "Bye." She vanished.

Armus and Vidar approached Kell. Avatar remained, but held back.

"What was that about?" asked Armus.

"Trying to soothe over all wounds."

"And Priscilla agreed?" he asked with a high skepticism.

Kell scowled at the sarcasm. "Contrary to popular opinion, she's not unreasonable."

Armus chuckled. "No. You two are so opposite you naturally clash." He clapped Kell on the shoulder. "I'm glad to hear you finally came to your senses about Priscilla."

"*I* finally came to my senses? What about you?"

"Don't change the subject. You're the one she flusters, not me. Besides, I have my own fences to mend with Mona and Wren."

"Wren?" asked Vidar and Kell in chorus.

He heaved a shrug, his face sheepish. "I wasn't kind to her when you were in Tunlund. I nagged her about tracking the traitor and Titus' kidnappers. I let my concern for Tristine guide my words and actions."

"Go! Speak to her before returning to Waldron." Kell waved for Armus to leave, and he did. "I'm beginning to think there are more broken fences than can be mended in a few days."

Vidar flashed a kind smiled. "Take heart. At least we've started to address the problem." He left.

Avatar lingered, but circumspect in his approach, that was until Kell noticed him.

"Captain," he began with contrition. "I'm sorry, both for refuting you in public and threatening Zadok. It's a touchy subject. However, if you deem me unworthy, I will step down as your aide rather than force you into the unenviable position of publicly demoting me." He started to withdraw his blade but Kell stopped him.

"No. You are not unworthy, nor are you the only one who lost his temper. Truth be told, I knew it must be brought to light and confronted, I just didn't know how to deal with it. You and Wren forced me. That is why I lost my temper because of my inept handling of the meeting not your rebuke. However," his tone changed to serious, "threatening Zadok crossed the line."

"By the heavenlies, Kell, I swear it will never happen again! Whereas, I admit parental concern for Nigel, duty to Jor'el, Allon and my comrades is my first priority."

Kell curbed a smile. "You are not condemned for your attachment. Those who serve as Overseers can't help but deeply care for their mortals charges. It served well in Nigel's healing and unmasking Hueil."

"And what made me lash out at Zadok."

"Some would say Zadok deserved it." Wren moved from the threshold to join them, putting up a hand to forestall Kell's response. "I'm not here to start an argument, Captain. I came to relay a message from one who wants to remain anonymous."

"What?"

"The real reason Farren left Allon."

"Was I right, a scapegoat?" asked Avatar, jerking a thumb at Kell.

"In a way. You became the focus of her discontentment since she couldn't vent her spleen on the *Captain* because of Radnor."

"Radnor?" echoed Avatar in disturbance.

Kell stiffened, golden eyes narrow. "We had no choice, Wren."

"I remember," she said in sympathy. "But reasons don't matter to a female Guardian in love with the mortal male who led the rebellion."

For a brief, stunned moment Kell and Avatar stared at her before Kell finally spoke. "Love? Who told you this?"

"I will not say. Only rest assured, it is the truth from one who knew Farren well."

Avatar shook his head, stupefied. "How did she go from loving a male to hating all males?"

"She didn't say."

"She? Your source or Farren?" asked Kell.

Wren balked at the miscue and evaded Kell's question to answer Avatar, "Shadow Warriors, I suspect. Farren said they were males."

Kell touched Wren's shoulder to get her attention. "Tell the individual, the information is helpful." He gave her a gentle nudge toward the door.

Avatar spoke after Wren departed. "How is it helpful? I again became Farren's scapegoat since she couldn't vent on Shadow Warriors."

"Helpful in the fact *she*–Mona–felt safe enough to send me a message. It is an encouraging step toward mending the rift."

"Mona?"

"She and Farren served together for two hundred years before Farren became my aide, filling the fifty year gap between Altari's reassignment and your creation. But she was never a member of the High Trio like Altari, whose position you assumed. Farren, Willow and Keara made a good Trio. When they disappeared shortly after Radnor—"

"You dispatched me to learn what became of them. And like Dagar and Hueil, I learned." Avatar looked askew to Kell. "Next time you need to find a wayward Guardian can you please send someone else?"

Kell laughed. "Only when you stop succeeding. Come. Time to return to Waldron."

Chapter 19

Tyrone dispatched vassal Guardians from Waldron to eleven members of the Council of Twelve ordering them to make haste to Waldron. He personally sent Armus to fetch Angus. After making the dispatches, Nigel, Avatar and Mathias entered the study.

"Mathias. I just sent a messenger to you. When did you arrive?"

"After midnight, Sire. I knew time was near for the prince and Mirit to return. Forgive my impatience, but I couldn't wait for a dispatch."

Tyrone smiled. "I understand. Only my dispatch wasn't concerning their return. How are the patrols going?"

"So far no signs of increased naval activity."

"That will change." He motioned Mathias to a chair. "You may want to sit to hear this."

"Is Mirit not well?"

"No, she is fit and whole," said Nigel with a reassuring smile. "The news from Soren is the issue."

Choosing words carefully since Mathias was Mirit's father, they told him about the discovery of Guardians and Shadow Warriors in Soren, and the role Tristine and Mirit would play in facing the enemy. Still, Mathias had difficulty accepting the plan.

"Impossible!"

"For mortals, maybe, but this is Jor'el's will."

A brief knock on the door was followed by Tristine and Mirit's entrance. Kell and Elgin accompanied the women.

"Papa," said Mirit, and greeted Mathias with a hug. Upon separating, she noticed his despondency. "What's wrong?"

"We told him about the situation," said Nigel.

"Ah," she said with understanding, her smile gentle at Mathias. "I won't be alone."

"You will be without the king and prince, or troops in support."

"Mathias, would you be willing to help?" asked Tristine. The twinkle in her eye made Mathias, Nigel and Tyrone suspicious.

"Of course. But the king said we can't help."

"Once the enemy has *landed*."

"What are you talking about?" asked Tyrone.

"You and Nigel are not the only ones seeking wisdom and assurance. Mirit and I spent most of the night in prayer. Although Kell confirmed Jor'el's plan once the enemy is landed, the fleet can be employed to dwindle the enemy's forces at sea."

Mathias flashed a predatory grin. "Say the word, Majesty, and my ships will crush them."

"The word is given, Mathias."

Kell said, "Gulliver, Chase and six other sea Guardians wait in the courtyard to accompany you to Leith. Elgin will serve as messenger when you have encountered the enemy."

Tristine continued her instructions. "You are to patrol north, and at first sign of the enemy, send Elgin, then attack."

"How? He's not a sea Guardian capable of locating land. Nor can we dimension travel between land and sea, only fixed points," said Avatar.

"On this occasion, Jor'el has granted Elgin a special ability of honing on my essence while out at sea," said Kell. "Though not a fix point, my spirit is the strongest."

"We will be leaving Waldron shortly," said Tristine.

"Leaving?" asked Tyrone.

"To head for the coast, Sire. It will be quicker to intercept the enemy," said Kell.

"Garwood? I dispatched Armus to fetch Angus. He won't like that."

"No, Garwood is too far north," began Tristine. "Kell suggested Lachlan. It's en route to Leith but we can turn north if needed."

Tyrone flinched at hearing the name of his hometown, the place he endured years of scorn from the locals due to his mixed heritage. He also met Nigel there and eventually, Tristine. The reaction was brief and he asked Kell, "Are you sure?"

"It is the quickest route."

"By your leave, Majesty, I go to hunt the enemy," said Mathias.

Her voice and face grew deadly serious. "Understand this, the Sorens are an affront to Jor'el so by his decree, you are to give no quarter, take no prisoners, and give no aid to any survivors. Those who manage to reach land we will face."

Mathias paled at the order. "The law of the sea compels a captain to rescue—"

"No!" said Kell. "The Sorens are the descendants of those banished forever because of their rebellion. Only a few will be allowed to set foot in Allon again."

Tristine took Mathias' hand to get his full attention. "Mirit and I depend upon you. If Jor'el's orders are not completely followed, she and I could fail."

His face changed to determined. "As I have strength and breath, I shall not fail, Majesty." He kissed her hand.

Mirit embraced him, kissed his check and said: "There'll be a wedding when this is over."

"With your permission, of course, baron," said Nigel.

Mathias laughed and patted Nigel's arm. "Given! I couldn't think of a better man to marry my daughter and call son." He bowed to Tyrone and Tristine. "By your leave." With a confident swagger, he left.

"Strange we didn't sense the same concerning the fleet," said Tyrone.

"No. This is our task and we will see it through no matter the outcome," said Tristine.

Nigel's jowls tensed.

"Are you still not convinced?" asked Mirit.

"No, but it doesn't mean I have to like it. Titus even confronted us when we found him in here last night."

"I sent him to bed," said Tristine in mild offense.

Tyrone chuckled. "He's been inquiring of Armus about what you were like at his age. And taking full advantage of your exploits."

"Egan wore the same hapless express Armus did when you eluded him," said Nigel.

She shook her head, a mix of concern and amusement on her face. "What did you tell him?"

"That as eldest, his duty is here to protect and encourage his siblings. Armus should return any moment with Angus," replied Tyrone.

"Good. Armus should remain at Waldron also. He may anticipate what Egan cannot."

Tyrone slyly smiled. "He anticipated your response and volunteered."

"What about the Council?"

"I already sent for them to join us."

She frowned in dispute. "Allard may try to talk you out of it, while Gareth urge a full assault. Have them meet at the Temple instead."

"I can deal with Allard, and Gareth is much less impulsive since Zebulon retired. Still, why the Temple, we'll be at the battlefield?"

"The possibility of someone acting impulsively increases. At least with you, Nigel and the male Guardians, we may be able to avoid foolish action that could jeopardize us. At the Temple Master Hampton can lead them in prayer on our behalf."

Tyrone went to reach for the bell rope when Armus entered, aiding a pale and disconcerted Angus. "That was quick."

Armus replied in light tone of joviality; "We could have been here sooner, but His Grace needed to regain his senses."

"I never dimension traveled before, and I don't want to again."

Tyrone laughed. "I'm sure Armus explained why."

Angus accepted the glass of wine Nigel gave him to help settle his nerves and took a drink before replying. "Ay. Needless to say, Necie is very worried."

"She's not leaving Garwood to come here, is she?"

"No. We convinced her to remain. Any further developments?"

"In a moment." Tyrone turned to Armus. "Send new dispatches to the Council, except Mathias and Hollis. Instruct them go to the Temple and not come here."

"Any reason for the change?"

"Lady Mirit and I covet their prayers more than their forces on the battlefield. Master Hampton will lead them," answered Tristine.

Armus smiled in approval and left.

Some color returned to Angus' face. "Now, about the developments?"

"Tristine dispatched Mathias to intercept the enemy before landing. The female Guardians are en route here. You heard my orders to the Council. For now that is all that we can do," said Tyrone.

"The last remaining detail is for Mirit and I to arm ourselves," said Tristine. "I'm not certain how. The only time I wore armor was when Nigel let me try on his suit as children."

He smiled. "You were only ten and had to sit because of the weight."

"Then you were thirteen," said an amused Tyrone.

"Ay. It was a practice suit. Father said the metal smith would fit me for a proper suit on my eighteenth birthday, only it never happened."

"You wear the suit of the King's Champion now."

"Ay," said Tristine, pleased with a through. "Nigel's suit will serve as a model for Mirit, only modified for the Queen's Champion."

"So I'll be called the Queen's Champion?"

"Why not? Sounds more impressive than Sigvard."

"Following your line of reason, the Armor of Allon will be modified to fit you," said Tyrone.

She balked at the suggestion. "Oh, I don't know about that."

"Why not? By birth you have more right to wear it than I."

She was still reluctant, almost fearful. "Mother's golden bow perhaps, not Father's armor. It's meant for a king."

"Tristine," began Nigel, "you know the armor and sword were fashioned in the heavenlies to defend Allon. I also recall, you said if this is to be a female undertaking you must take full control."

For a moment she regarded him. "Would Father approve?"

His smile was warm and encouraging. "Ay."

Touched by the reassurance, she simply nodded.

"I'll send for the tailors. Kell, send for the Guardian metalsmith," said Tyrone.

While the others tended to preparations, Nigel slipped away. Through discussions with Tyrone, prayer and mediation, he came to terms with what must be done, but concerning Chad's fate, he had not.

The royal cemetery and crypt were located outside the walls of Waldron nearest to the Chapel. Three people were entombed in the crypt, Queen Shannan, King Ellis and Niles, Shannan's grandfather, who died helping Ellis to become king. Ellis replaced the marker denoting Nigel's death with a clean stone.

The coldness of crypt didn't bother Nigel, as he sat on the bench facing Ellis' tomb. Unlike the others interned in the walls with elaborate markers, Tyrone ordered the crypt's altar hollowed out for Ellis and the top refitted with a life-size stone relief of Ellis in full armor. The Son of Tristan deserved a worthy remembrance. Nigel wasn't certain how long he sat and stared at his father's tomb when Angus joined him.

"I knew you'd be here. You came here frequently after Aunt Shannan died."

"Same as Tristine did after Father died."

"What brings you here now?"

"I finally understand the pain he felt when he thought I was dead." Nigel spoke in a choked voice.

"Chad."

He nodded and motioned to Ellis' tomb. "He didn't have to feel that way. It was my fault he did."

"You made up for it many times over. Often without us asking."

Nigel shook his head, a small smile appearing. "I'm not wallowing in self-pity, rather gaining a new appreciation for what he, Mother and Tristine felt. Necie was too young."

"Necie loves you and missed you."

He smiled and tossed an arm about Angus' shoulders. "You always defended her. But she told me she didn't feel it as deeply, and with regret." Again, he looked at the Ellis' tomb. "Great regret all around."

"Uncle forgave you and didn't harbor any hard feelings after your return, you know that."

Nigel's arm came down and he stood, waving at the altar/tomb. "You didn't hear our first discussions. How deeply hurt he was by my actions. Still, he acknowledged the good from it for Tyrone and Tristine."

"Some good may yet come from Chad's decision."

"It's hard to see past the invasion. Maybe I'm foolish for even trying."

"No. There is hope. Chad kept your sword and told Avatar of his regret." Angus rose to continue, touching Nigel's arm to get his full attention. "Has Tristine told you about the secret hope she and Uncle Ellis shared concerning you during those dark years?"

Nigel grew curious. "No."

Angus grinned. "She often imagined what it would be like if you were alive and things the way they used to be. She even prayed for Jor'el to miraculously reverse time so the accident never happened. She thought she was being silly, but Uncle said he often wished the same."

Nigel's gaze shifted to the tomb. "I wonder why they never said anything?"

"They held a secret hope they thought impossible. Same as you with Chad."

"Not the same. Chad made a choice, mine, an assassination attempt."

Angus shook his head. "It was still within Jor'el's control and good did come from what happened to you. Don't you see? They never gave up hope for you. Don't give up for hope for Chad."

"I hope he listens to you," said Tyrone. He arrived unnoticed.

Nigel waved a finger at Tyrone. "Don't start. I accept what Tristine and Mirit must do."

Tyrone smiled one of his winning smiles that held a hint of mischief. "Good, because, I came to find you and tell you it's time for us to get ready. With Guardian help, all will be complete in a couple of hours."

"That quick?" said Angus in surprise.

"Guess who's not prepared? Come, little brother." Nigel took Angus by the shoulders to steer him from the crypt.

True to estimation, the Guardian metalsmiths and royal tailors crafted a new suit for Mirit and refitted the gold armor for Tristine in two hours. Now came the time for the final fitting.

Tristine dismissed her servants and after the door closed, stared at her reflection in the full-length mirror. Many spoke of the strong resemblance between her and Ellis. Both had golden hair, similar in facial feature, and at six feet she was tall for a woman. Now she wore the armor. The breastplate formed the body of the eagle outstretched, the shoulder guards as wing protecting the arms. The arm and leg armor fashioned to look like feathers, with boots as talons and fitted with smaller straps to accommodate her frame. The helmet had gold and purple plumes and lined to sit firmly on her head with her golden hair in a long braid. New gauntlets were made for her smaller hands. The Sword of Allon strapped about her waist by a new belt. The pommel was shaped in the shortened body of an eagle with the head holding the blade, eyes of imbedded garnet and guard as a craved wing protecting the hands. Staring at the reflection, she saw Ellis' face looking at her.

The door opening drew her from the self-inspection. Armus and Kell entered. Kell wore his full captain's uniform; a gold cuirass emblazoned with the ancient symbol of Jor'el covered his chest. From the shoulder clasps of the cuirass hung a short purple cloak. Instead of a belt, a purple sash held his scabbard. Armus was present during the fitting process, not so Kell, who halted in surprise.

She wryly smiled. "They always said I resembled him."

"Never more so than at this moment."

"I only pray I can do him proud and honor Jor'el."

"You will, little one," said Armus.

Her eyes grew misty. "You haven't called me that in years."

He grinned. "Not an appropriate nickname for a queen."

"Always *little one* to you." She hugged him. "Take care of my children, Guardian of Allon."

"I will, Daughter of Ellis."

"You are as much Shannan's daughter," said Kell. "She too wore white and gold that day, her hair loose and a golden cornet on her brow." He tilted her chin up to look her squarely in the eyes. "I will be with you, just like I was with your parents."

"I know. Now, it's time to go, Captain." She carried the helmet as they left the room.

In the hall, Tyrone, Mirit, Nigel and Angus waited. Mirit's suit appeared almost identical to Nigel. Both wore silver mail under azure tunics with the mail coifs turned down, the rest protecting their neck and shoulders. Both wore thick black leather gloves. A large gold and leather belt held his sword and dagger. Mirit's belt was silver and the sword from the royal armory. She chose to pull back the sides of her hair to prevent it from obscuring her vision.

Tyrone borrowed General Wess' armor. The black breastplate was embossed with the general's red and silver family crest. The black and red undercoat was complete with gloves and knee-high boots. The sword was unusual with an intricate black hilt. With his black hair, the dark ensemble made his gray eyes more imposing and impressive. But all his ability to command with just his eyes did not prepare him for seeing Tristine in armor. He swallowed back a stunned reaction.

"By the heavenlies. You look—" the words stuck in Nigel's throat.

"I'm glad Necie isn't here. She couldn't bear this," said Angus.

Tristine kindly smiled. "She's always been sensitive. I am glad you're here." She squeezed his hand.

"I'd rather be going with you."

"Next to Armus, you remember me best as a child. See Titus behaves himself and not like I did."

He chuckled. "That maybe more of a challenge than facing battle."

She kissed his cheek. "It's time," she said to Tyrone.

"Ay. Let's show them, the Daughter of Ellis will face the enemy."

Once Tristine put on the helmet, they left the family's private quarters. Though the upper galley hallway, down the staircase, through the foyer and out the main entrance, Tristine and Tyrone walked side-by-side with Nigel and Mirit behind them, followed by Angus then Kell, and Armus. Vassal Guardians and mortal servants bowed, speechless.

In the courtyard the female Guardian warriors assembled to one side of the fountain. The few mortals and male Guardian warriors chosen to view the battle stood on the other side of the fountain. Lord Allard of the Meadowlands was among the chosen few. Even at age sixty-three he appeared fit and ready for action. His once full red head of hair was mostly white with the relaxing of age about the mouth and jowls. His green eyes still told of a shrewd mind not dulled by age. He wore a thick heavy buff surcoat of his family colors of green and gold over chainmail and held Nigel's horse by the reins. Master Hampton waited on the portico steps, the book of Verse in his hands.

Wess held the bridles of his and Tyrone's horses. He wore his usual black and red surcoat, only the rest of his armor was plain silver. Wren stood beside Wess holding the reins of Tristine's horse, Dunston.

When the royal couple appeared on the portico, the reaction was measurable. Allard's normal pink fleshy complexion paled at seeing Tristine. Wess drew to his full height, proud and squaring his shoulders. Those Guardians present when Ellis defeated Dagar showed the most impact at seeing Tristine. Avatar and Mahon stood shoulder-to-shoulder and exchanged amazed glances. Ewert and Bailey clapped their swords and bowed. Barnum raised an arched brow and Vidar smiled in affectionate remembrance. Of the female Guardians assembled, only Wren, Nixie and Luann remembered the day. The others were among those freed from Dagar's nether dimension and unable to fight because of their wounds or weak condition.

"Let's hope the enemy sees the same, the Daughter of Ellis, the Son of Tristan," said Kell.

"They were not here when it happened," said Barnum.

"Auriel knows," said Avatar.

"We want all of Allon and the Sorens to know! With Jor'el's blessing we ride to face them." Tyrone nodded to Master Hampton.

The priest lifted his hands holding the book of Verse. When he did so, those wearing helmet or hats removed them and everyone bowed their heads. "Hear us, Jor'el, and attend the voice of our prayer. You have ordained this as the hour our Queen goes forth to meet the enemy. We ask you to protect her and fill her with your knowledge and wisdom. For your Guardian servants we thank you, and ask you grant them strength and might to defend your people. Go with us now and show the enemy the truth of your righteousness and justice. *Tangiel*."

"*Tangiel*," all echoed.

Kell drew his sword and raised it. "For Jor'el and Allon!"

All mimicked him and spoke in unison. "For Jor'el and Allon!"

Taking Tristine's elbow Tyrone escorted her to Dunston. Wren held the stirrup and Tyrone helped her to mount. Once all were ready, Tyrone and Tristine led the force from Waldron.

Chapter 20

O N THE JOURNEY FROM MANHEIM to the coast, then watching the equipment loaded onto twenty ships, Chad remained under Auriel's supervision. A ball and chain fastened around his ankle prevented him from trying to escape. Of course with Auriel close-by, it was already impossible.

He saw Bergeta only a few times and no words passed between them. Pain and anger reflected in her eyes and expression. She claimed to love him, but what did he feel toward her? In comparing his relationship with Bergeta to Nigel and Mirit, or even Tyrone and Tristine, he concluded it wasn't love. True, he found her attractive, sweet, and their time together pleasurable, but not love. His impulsiveness caused such heartache and trouble. He tried to pray for forgiveness and solace of his greatly disturbed spirit, but guilt and sorrow interfered, overwhelming him with a sense of futility. He experienced a small measure of relief learning Nigel and Mirit escaped. Had to be Avatar. Maybe Nigel would believe the Guardian about his remorse. After all, Auriel said Nigel wanted to free him. In the end, his excuse concerning Bergeta was just that, an excuse.

Now he sat on the busy dock at Bergen waiting to board a ship bound for Allon, and not for the purpose of returning home, but to invade and conquer. A few yards away, Auriel spoke to new Guardians, all warriors, seven females and one male. He was surprised at seeing them for they believed the Valkerish and Tavar to be the only Guardians in Soren. He couldn't recall seeing nine female Guardian warriors in one place. At the battle of Tunlund, Zinna and Auriel were the only females.

I don't think Nigel knows about them, hopefully Avatar does. If not, they could be used in a surprise attack. Like I can do anything about it!

His regard of the female passed to the only male, so strikingly familiar the recognition was immediate—Jedrek. As Nigel's squire, he became acquainted with all the Guardians serving the royal family. Titus loved and admired Nigel and whenever he visited Waldron, Titus tried everything to impress him. Didn't take much, since Nigel was very fond of Titus. In fact, they spent a lot of time together. During those times Chad and Jedrek observed or became employed for some scheme or task.

Auriel noticed his regard. She leaned closer to the male and said something he couldn't hear. The male nodded and approached him.

"I've been given charge of you for the journey."

Chad stared at him, the familiarity eerie up close. "What is your name?"

"Virgil."

"Jedrek's twin."

The statement caught Virgil off guard. "How did you know?"

"Auriel hasn't told you who I am?" He spoke the Ancient, further surprising Virgil.

"You're not Soren."

"No—" Chad stopped when Breck approached.

"What are you doing speaking to this foreign varlet?"

"Auriel told me to take charge of him for the journey."

Breck scowled in disapproval, turned on his heels and stormed off to accost Skule. He didn't like Skule's reply, but shortly, brought him back.

"Glad you both finally met," began Skule. "Understand this, Virgil. Anything happens to the boy—say he disappears—the girl dies."

"It will be my pleasure to slit her throat," added Breck.

Virgil grew rigid but remained silent, glaring after Breck when he and Skule left.

"I'm not the only one being forced to undertake this journey," again Chad spoke in the Ancient. Virgil didn't reply. "Jedrek didn't talk much either." To this, Virgil winced and Chad wondered if he should ask the obvious question. "Do you know about Jedrek?"

Virgil nodded, his voice sober. "Auriel told me. She was his protégé."

"I know. Although Jedrek didn't like long conversations, I came to know him pretty well. I am Prince Nigel's squire; his father was the Son of Tristan. Jedrek was Prince Titus' overseer, Nigel's nephew and heir to throne of Allon. How did you come to—?"

Skule's booming voice called for final boarding.

"Enough talk." Virgil took his arm, and Chad didn't resist.

Standing to the rear of the quarterdeck on the fleet's flagship, Magda watched the final boarding. She, Ulrika, Perti and Grissel made up the Sigvard commanders chosen to man the flagship. Most of the Valkerish and Tavar gathered on the helm. Only Skule had yet to arrive.

For a moment Magda's attention was drawn to the gangplank. Willow brought Bergeta on board and took her below to the brig. Behind them came Chad, escorted by an unfamiliar male Tavar. She heard about what happened at the temple from Ulrika and Perti after the unsuccessful hunt for Avatar. Although inwardly pleased to learn of Mirit's escape, seeing Chad caused her a moment's apprehension. He accompanied Mirit to Soren, but through a series of events became involved with Bergeta. Now he was a prisoner being forced to participate in an invasion of his homeland.

"Magda?" Perti interrupted her thought. "What bothers you?"

Her expression changed to benign. "Nothing in particular. Just thinking about what we're doing."

"Ja. Sailing to victory."

"Quiet," said Ulrika, indicating Skule bounding up the quarterdeck steps to the helm.

"This is an historic moment for Soren." He wore a satisfied grin and said, "Set sail."

"Ja, my lord." Dugian began barking out orders and the ship's crew instantly responded to her commands. She looked at the sails. "The wind and tide are with us, my lord. I sense a fair crossing."

Skule gripped Dugian's shoulder. "This is a good beginning."

Twenty ships took positions in the formation, and left Bergen.

Chad felt the swell of movement after Virgil locked him in cell furthest from the exit. Six cells made up the brig along with a guard's table. Willow placed Bergeta in the cell nearest the exit and away from Chad. Before leaving to go topside for the launch, he heard Willow charge Virgil with keeping a sharp eye. Once alone, Chad hoped looks weren't all Virgil and Jedrek shared. Still, he waited until an hour into the journey to speak.

"You realize we sail for Allon."

Virgil sat the guard's table in such a way to watch both Chad and Bergeta. He didn't reply.

"Allon? Is that the place of beginning?" asked Bergeta.

"Ay. My homeland and where the Valkerish, Tavar and Virgil were created."

"Who is Virgil?"

"I am," he said, his icy blue gaze shifting to Bergeta.

Bergeta regarded him. "Are you Tavar or Valkerish?"

"He is a Guardian, like Avatar. I told you about them," said Chad.

"Everything is confusing. If this Jor'el is so powerful why all this trouble and division?"

Chad snorted an ironic chuckle. "It's rather complicated, but mortals haven't made the wisest choices."

"Like claiming I am nothing but a mistake!"

"I am sorry! If I could, I would change events, even if cost my life."

"And my life."

"Not if I can help it."

"You're not a position to do much of anything," said Virgil.

"No, *I'm not*," said Chad, directly.

Virgil turned away without replying.

Chad sighed, his head slumped against the bars. "You forfeited your station like Auriel and the others."

Virgil's expression became clouded and unsure. "I don't know."

Chad's head snapped up at hearing the uncertainty. "How could you not know?"

The Guardian glanced sideways at Chad and replied in a low and hoarse voice. "Mab captured me during the Great Battle. Until a few days ago, I was in spurean chains."

Chad's hand shot out from between the bars trying to reach Virgil, but came short of seizing his sleeve. "You must help me!"

"You are aware of the consequences if either one of us acts." Virgil faced forward.

For a moment Chad regarded the Guardian in confusion and dismay. "You look like Jedrek, but you don't have his courage."

Virgil didn't speak or move, so Chad retreated back into the cell to reconsider his situation. If he could not convince Virgil to help him, what options were left? *I won't know until we reach Allon. Yet Virgil's right, caged like an animal I can't do anything.* He closed his eyes and soon the rhythm of the swaying ship lulled him into a fitful sleep.

⚓

By twilight of the fourth day, Gulliver sensed a disturbance in the water. He glanced at the sails of Mathias' flagship, the *Protectorate*. A good steady wind filled the sails. On this journey, a mortal lookout manned the crow's nest and the bow. Knowing the situation, Gulliver wished Mahon was on board. For all his warrior faults, he had a keen eye.

To port, lay three ships while to starboard four more. In all, eight ships, each captained by a sea Guardian. His gaze passed to the ship directly on his starboard side.

"How goes it, Gulliver?" Mathias mounted the steps to the quarterdeck. His first mate, Master Kasey followed him.

"Still quiet, my lord. Although the sea is beginning to feel rough."

Mathias watched the waves barely lapping in the ship's wake. "The water seems calm."

"Not the waves. A sense of doom; an uneasiness I've not felt in centuries."

"Is it something you can't contend with?"

Gulliver flashed a confident smile. "No. When we encounter the enemy, Jor'el will aid us."

Mathias turned to view the other ships. His attention lingered toward starboard. "In battle I know your skills well. What of Chase and the others? Are they up to your standard?"

"Chase is a Trio Leader, I'm not." He heaved a careless shrug. "Not that I want the position. I enjoy the sea too much to be landlocked. As for the rest, some I trained, some Chase trained."

"Good enough. Once—"

"Ships ahoy! On the horizon!" called the mortal in crow's nest.

Mathias snatched the spyglass from Kasey and looked in the direction indicated. "A half a day or more away."

"Close enough," said Gulliver, who then shouted up to the crow's nest. "Can you see how many?"

It took a moment to respond. "Fifteen! No, wait … twenty," came the reply.

"Twenty?" Using the spyglass, Mathias scanned the horizon. "More than two to one."

"Don't worry. The odds are of no consequence."

"I pray you're right. Tristine says we are the first line of defense. Whatever gets past us, she and Mirit must face."

"Elgin!" Gulliver summoned the vassal Guardian, who quickly appeared. "Report to the queen we have encountered the enemy north, northeast of Leith at the cove outside of Bradney. Will engage no later than dawn tomorrow."

Elgin bowed his head. "Gracious Jor'el, the time has come, lead me to Kell." After a moment, he looked, smiled and disappeared.

"Let's give our forces enough time to reach Bradney," said Mathias.

"Chase and I know a trick or two to keep from being seen too soon. Still, divide the fleet as planned."

Mathias shouted to the signalman. "Signal the *Reliant* to take *Sea Raven* and *Odyssey* to take the enemy's west flank. Then *Sentinel* to take *Allon's Pride* and *Tremain* to the east flank. The *Vigilance* will be with us."

<hr />

"My lord! The enemy fleet!" shouted the lookout on Skule's flagship.

Skule didn't need a spyglass, his Guardian eyes keen enough on their own, even in the dim light of dawn. "How did they get so close without you knowing?" he chided Dugian.

"Gulliver," she sneered.

The answer didn't please him. "Now comes your true test. Can you outmaneuver him since he succeeded in sneaking up on you?"

She glared at him. "You brought me here to do a job. Now shut up and let me do it."

Skule thinly smiled but his good eye filled with malice. "Bring us safely to shore, and I will forget your insolence."

The bravado faded from her face. "Ay, my lord."

The whizzing of cannons caught their attention. One landed in the water beside the ship; another clipped the forward mast.

"They have our range. Prepare the starboard guns!" she shouted.

"You're going to return fire at this range? Why not closer?"

"If you want to reach land, we begin firing now to move in closer. A full frontal assault against Gulliver would be foolish, even suicidal."

Skule leaned threatening close to her face and hissed, "I don't care what you have to do, but the *Defiant* and *Solemn Pledge* are to reach shore. Is that understood?"

"Understood."

He hurried to the wardroom. Ulrika, Perti, Magda, Grissel, the Valkerish and Tavar gathered. "The time has come," he declared.

"We heard the cannons. Gulliver?" asked Lokien.

"Naturally. Who else did you think Kell would send to meet us?"

"How far are we from land?" asked Ulrika.

"A day, maybe less."

Several loud bangs and the ship lurching told them Dugian returned fire. The Sigvard wore worried expressions.

"Ever been in a sea battle?" a sneering Breck asked Ulrika.

"No, my lord," she replied, trying to mask her nervousness.

He leaned down. "It'll get nasty."

Farren jerked Breck back from Ulrika. "No need to frighten them, they're on our side." She turned to the Ulrika. "Pay him no mind."

Breck's dagger was at Farren's throat. "Pay me no mind? Think again."

"Put it away—!" snapped Skule, but the rest of his sentence became interrupted by a cracking sound.

"The forward mast is hit," said Auriel.

"Dugian will get us through."

Frightened, Bergeta clung to the front of the cell. "What is happening?"

"We're under fire," said Virgil.

"Gulliver. Maybe even Chase," said Chad with excitement. They heard a loud crack. "A hit! We're helpless in here," he chided to Virgil.

"You'd be in no better shape on deck."

"A cannon ball comes through and we'll be in horrible shape!"

"If that happens you won't be in those cells. For now stay put."

Bergeta screamed when tossed backward by the lurching of the ship returning fire.

"Stay calm. With Jor'el's help, we'll live through this," said Chad.

"If we live it is because of the Valkerish, not your god! I don't know your god! Great Wilda, save us."

"Virgil!" shouted Chad in pleading anxiety.

The Guardian went topside and discovered the battle fully engaged. The forward mast splintered three quarters of the way up. Four crewmembers lay dead beneath the wreckage and several others badly wounded. He shifted his feet for balance at the firing of another volley. He grabbed onto the rigging and peered out to sea.

"Chad's right. Gulliver and Chase," he said to himself. His grip tightened on the rigging and jowls tensed. At the helm, Dugian barked orders. *The last memory I have of Allon is Guardian against Guardian.* He screwed his eyes shut to maintain his composure.

"Virgil!"

His eyes snapped open. Skule and the others emerged from the wardroom. "Don't worry. The prisoners are secure."

Skule made his way to the helm where Virgil heard him demand a report from Dugian. He only partially listened to the response since he turned back to view the battle. Someone fell into him. Magda. He helped her stand. Horror registered on her face at Sigvard abandoning a nearby fiery ship for the safety of the water.

"You've never seen battle before."

Disconcerted, she shook her head. "I've never been to sea before."

Whizzing grew dangerously close. A cannon ball struck the bow rail. Virgil grabbed Magda and pulled her down before another cannon ball struck the side above the waterline, splashing water up and over where they were standing. She bolted up and looked over the side to the hole. Sounds of injury came from below. He stopped her from leaving the rail.

"Don't go down there. Anyone nearby is probably dead or dying."

"I must!" She pulled away and ran below.

Auriel's grip on his shoulder prevented him from helping Magda. "Get back to the brig. You're their only hope if it's struck."

He stared at her. Once he knew her well, or so he thought. Seeing her again, hearing her confess to joining Skule and learning of Jedrek's death was a serve personal blow. "What made you do it? Were you tortured or imprisoned like me?" He didn't hide the acidity in his face and voice.

Indecision and hesitancy played across on her face. "You wouldn't understand."

"Would Jedrek?"

The explosion of cannon fire rocked the ship and they heard the ripping of sails. She knocked away his hand that kept her from falling and raced to the hold. He ignored the shouts and sounds of injury in returning to the brig.

"What's happening?" demanded Chad.

Virgil regarded the mortal in consideration before replying. "Two Soren ships sunk. Three more heavily damaged and we've been struck above the waterline in the hold."

"And the Allonians?"

"I counted only eight ships. I don't know if that is all we face or some have been sunk by return fire."

Bergeta sobbed uncontrollably.

Chad pleaded in desperation. "Take us from here!"

For a moment Virgil said nothing, his icy blue eyes staring at Chad. "She doesn't believe in Jor'el. I may have been imprisoned since the Great Battle, but I know the Sorens are descendents of those banished and cursed. Nothing good will be waiting for her in Allon."

Chad painfully grimaced. "It's my fault she's here! I can't leave her."

"Then we both have no choice but to remain."

Chad slumped against the bars and whimpered. "I never meant for any of this to happen. Jor'el, forgive me."

Through the morning and well into the afternoon the battle raged. Whatever maneuver Dugian tried, either to evade or attack, Gulliver countered. The guns of Dugian's fleet inflicted some damage upon the Allonians, but not enough to curtail the merciless bombardment. The odds of twenty ships against eight should have swung the battle in the Soren's favor, but it didn't.

Auriel stood on the bow, looked out at the *Protectorate*. "What are your plans for us, Gulliver? What are Jor'el's plans for us?"

You know the penalty for forfeiting your station, she argued with herself. *Hoping for justification from battle is foolish. As is hoping for understanding from my former comrades. So asking for mercy on behalf of others wouldn't be heard. Maybe—*

She made her way to the brig. Virgil stood when she reached the bottom of the stairs. He appeared wary and skeptical. "I came to see if the prisoners survived the battle, and still secure."

Chad sat against the back of his cell and snorted in anger. "We're still here, no thanks to either of you!"

"You're still thinking like a boy, not a man."

"And you're still thinking like a traitor, not a Guardian!"

"We're alive because of the Valkerish," said Bergeta, indicating Auriel and Virgil.

The Guardians exchanged frowning glances at the statement.

Chad confronted them. "She doesn't know the truth like we do."

"The truth didn't prevent our choices," rebuffed Auriel.

"No, but it doesn't mean we can't change."

Her jade eyes narrowed at him. "Easy for a mortal to say, but more difficult to do."

"Help me do it!"

Her jowls tensed and brows furrowed. "I can't!" She left the brig.

"Auriel!"

"You don't understand what it means for a Guardian to forfeit their station," said Virgil.

Chad's confused look grew harsh upon Virgil. "You haven't, yet you refuse to help, why?"

The Guardian balked in frustration. "I said I don't know if I have or not!" He too left the brig.

"Virgil!" Chad angrily tugged at the bars.

"The Valkerish don't know the truth you claim," jeered Bergeta.

"You don't know what you're talking about."

"Then explain again why I'm here when all I did was try to love you."

"It wasn't love."

"According to what, your truth?"

Chad winced at her scorn and sighed in weary dejection. "You have every right to be angry at me, but please don't mock my beliefs."

She stood in the corner of the cell, the sting of bitter rejection on face. "Auriel's right, what you believe didn't stop you from being with me. Although afterwards you claimed it was a mistake. Well, because of that mistake I am a prisoner, my wrists bruised by shackles, herded onto a ship bound for war and locked in a cell with the sounds of death and battle all around me!"

No use arguing any further. He sat against the hull and his head fell into his hands, muffling a prayer of bitter regret and pleas mixed with an occasional sob.

Auriel, Farren and Magda were on the quarterdeck near Dugian. Skule and Breck stood near the stern peering out at the battle.

"Dugian, how long can we can last?" asked Farren.

"As long as needed."

"You know that's not true. It's Gulliver out there. With Jor'el's blessing he'll tear apart this whole fleet before sundown."

"We're going to lose?" asked Magda, disconcerted.

"No," said Skule, he and Breck joining them. "Dugian. Show Magda the power the Valkerish command."

Dugian gave a curt ascending nod. "Take the helm," she told Auriel then ran to the bow. In grim determination she gazed out to the *Protectorate*. "One of us will meet our fate this day, Gulliver." She began speaking in the Ancient. *"Sal ag at, gaoth seid, uile-bheist ionnsaigh!"* Twice more she repeated, "Sea rise, wind blow, leviathan attack!"

On the helm of the *Protectorate*, Gulliver flinched in great pain. The wind increased and the sea swelled. He understood the meaning.

"By Jor'el's strength we do battle!" he declared in the Ancient.

In unison, the Guardian captains' declaration echoed on the wind.

"All hands, spearing hooks and deck guns to bear on my mark!"

The ship violently heaved, forcing Mathias to grab onto the rail for balance. "What is happening?"

An ear-piercing scream echoed all around. A monster rose from the sea. It had the head of a dragon and four tentacles in place of arms.

"By the heavenlies! Jor'el save us!" muttered Mathias in fear.

"Take cover," said Gulliver, but Mathias stood frozen, gaping at the monster unaware of the dangerous flaying tentacles. Not until Gulliver jerked him out of harm's way did Mathias regain his senses.

"My lord! *Vigilance* and *Sea Raven* are coming alongside," said Kasey.

"Signal them to have all port guns and cannons to fire on the up roll on our mark. We'll put a hole into that monster!" Mathias waved Gulliver back to the helm. He waited until Kasey completed the signaling then told Gulliver, "Now!"

The sea Guardian reacted and Kasey raised a red flag. All three ships opened fire on the monster. It jerked and jarred, screaming at the multiple impacts. Two of the tentacles were severed and gaping wounds riddled its body. Gurgling screeches followed the monster back into the swirling water.

On the *Sentinel,* Chase shouted encouragement to his crew, who battled a second monster. "Keep it up, lads!"

Three deck guns fired at the monster's head, one made a direct hit in the jaw, another in the neck. The third nicked the top of its head. Suddenly a shot struck the deck near the first mate, badly wounding him in the leg. Chase looked in the direction the shot came. *Allon's Pride* came to their aid.

"Edison! Signal Jonas to stop firing his deck guns and make a run to distract the creature to give us a clear shot," he told his signalman.

Chase scowled when the frigate *Odyssey* got too close to the monster's tail. One swipe and *Odyssey's* main sail broken in half.

"Edison! Tell *Odyssey* to drop out and *Reliant* cover her withdrawal."

At least one ship could be saved, but his ship was being damaged. Despite being large and well built, he didn't like risking the *Sentinel's* destruction in a battle with a sea monster. He watched *Allon's Pride,* waiting for Jonas to follow his order.

"Come on, lad, remember what I taught you."

A long moment later, he saw Jonas remembered well, and *Allon's Pride* made a maneuver that caught the monster's attention, exposing its back to the *Sentinel.*

"Deck guns, starboard cannons, fire!"

A thunderous roar came when the ten cannons below fired along with the deck guns. The entire back of the monster exploded when fourteen shots hit their mark. A terrifying scream and the monster began falling toward *Allon's Pride.* A fierce volley of ten guns from *Allon's Pride* shattered what remained of the monster and pieces fell into the sea.

Though pleased by the defeat of the second monster, the wind and waves violently lashed the ships. Gulliver looked toward the enemy. Save for a few ripples the sea around the Soren ships was clam.

"Just so we're on even ground, Dugian. *To the enemy do the same, blow and toss in Jor'el's name,*" he commanded in the Ancient.

Immediately the rippling waves became larger and angry, and headed for the Soren ships. Soon, the enemy ships began to rock and the sails flapped in the wind.

"Take it to them, lads. Fire at will!"

The short reprieve the monsters gave the Sorens did not help in repelling the renewed attack. If anything, it stirred the Allonians to new vigor. Gulliver, Chase and the other sea Guardians coordinated a brilliant strategy, cutting the Soren fleet to ribbons. At this rate, the battle could be over by sundown.

Gulliver steered the *Protectorate* through the waning battle at twilight. The ship sustained damage from both the sea monster and battle, with ten crewmen killed and a dozen wounded.

"Another Soren ship is sinking. That makes twelve sunk, three listing and three more heavily damaged," reported Kasey.

"What about our ships?" asked Mathias.

"*Sentinel, Reliant,* and *Sea Raven* report damage but are seaworthy. *Odyssey* is heavy damaged and *Tremain* is listing."

Mathias lifted his spyglass to view the frigate *Tremain.* "Heavy on the keel. Have *Tremain* and *Odyssey* fall out of formation and head for shore to begin repairs and tend the wounded."

"What about the survivors? Should they pick them up on the way?"

"No!" declared Gulliver. "We are to take on no survivors."

Stunned mute, Kasey looked to Mathias for confirmation.

The baron was grim in reply. "Jor'el's direct command. He banished the Soren's ancestors and forbade them from ever returning. Remind the commanders of Jor'el's orders, no survivors are to picked up."

Kasey still couldn't speak.

Gulliver snatched Kasey's arm. "Don't you understand, man? If we pick up a single Soren, Jor'el may turn his back on Queen Tristine and allow the invasion to succeed. Make sure the men know what is at stake."

Kasey paled with understanding. "May Jor'el ease our conscience for what we are about to do," he said before leaving to send the order.

"On deck! Enemy ships withdrawing," said the crow's nest watch.

Mathias looked through his spyglass. "Two making for shore. What do you say?"

Gulliver glanced at the darkening sky. "Night fighting is not good. Two ships could carry a thousand. I suggest we take the *Sentinel, Sea Raven,* and *Allon's Pride* and block their escape once they've landed. The rest can escort the *Tremain* and *Odyssey* back to Leith."

"So be it," said Mathias.

Chapter 21

THE FOLLOWING AFTERNOON, Dugian brought the *Defiant* and *Solemn Pledge* into Bradney Cove. She moved carefully because of the flooding in the hold and the fact Gulliver brought the bulk of the Allonian fleet to form a blockade. The Allonian army could swoop down from land and they would be trapped. However, Skule was determined to bring his forces ashore.

Chad wore manacles and leg irons when Auriel escorted him from the ship and fastened the chain of the leg iron to a tree.

"Safer to keep you in view than leave you alone. And Skule wants Virgil's help for heavy equipment," she said and left.

Chad sat on the ground, leaning his back against the tree. He knew better than to jerk the chain. Guardians were prompt and efficient in their duties. He watched the unloading of supplies and equipment, catching sight of Bergeta in company with Willow. Since lashing out at him, she freely followed Willow. In fact, she wore no manacles or leg irons. She rejected him and now he truly felt abandoned.

Adelaid arrived but he ignored her.

"Comfortable?" she sneered.

He didn't look at her or reply. This annoyed her, and she sent him falling sideways with a vicious backhand, splitting his lip. She seized him by the cowl, pulling him up and grabbing his face.

"Did they tell you Elfrida died because of Mirit?"

"No."

"You're as responsible for this invasion as she and her varlet lover."

"Adelaid!" Magda rushed over. "Get back to work."

She roughly released him and he clumsily fell to one side. She confronted Magda. "You think more of Mirit than Elfrida. Will you protect the boy when the time comes for him to meet his fate?"

"You're out of line, Adelaid."

She pushed passed Magda to leave.

"I'll send Virgil back to watch you," said Magda.

He wiped the blood from his lip and watched her approach Virgil. After a few words, the Guardian made his way back to Chad.

"I can't leave you for a moment."

"I don't see why you would want to. After all, we're in Allon and they are the enemy."

"I view it as helping you and the girl, not them."

Chad looked up at Virgil. "How? By leaving me chained to a tree?"

Virgil squatted to reply, his back to the unloading and his voice confidential. "No, by doing what they want I keep them from killing you both, just like Auriel is doing."

Chad snorted a mocking laugh. "You expect me to believe that?"

Virgil's icy blue eyes stared at him, compelling. "You reached Allon alive, didn't you?"

For a moment he considered the statement. In truth, he wondered if he would survive or at best arrive unharmed. Both happened, and something to be thankful for. During his pondering, he again spied Bergeta. For all her anger at him and his regret for involving her, the last thing he wanted was for her to be physically harmed because of him.

Chad spoke in the Ancient. "You're right. Let's not give them the opportunity but wait for the right time to escape."

Virgil made no reply, rather stood.

By evening, they finished unloading. Ulrika called the Sigvard and varlets into formation for the march inland. The wounded remained with Dugian and the ship's crew, so the total number of the invasion force equaled eleven hundred: six hundred and fifty-four Sigvard, four hundred and twelve varlets and fourteen Guardians. A far cry from the six thousand Skule originally intended, but they were in Allon. Skule instructed Mab to remain with Dugian and help secure the fleet.

"I'll make certain Virgil survives to complete your revenge," said Rane.

"You'll both do what is necessary to secure victory. Personal satisfaction will come later," scolded Skule.

Mab saluted and entered the last boat back to the ship.

"Join the others," he said to Rane, then to Lokien and Auriel, "Do reconnaissance."

"You trust her?" chided Breck.

Skule said nothing rather waved for Lokien and Auriel to leave.

The way inland was an easy trek through thinning woods. Being winter, the trees shed their leaves and the area clear of underbrush. The sea breeze kept the ground from freezing too hard. Lokien and Auriel reached the glen in a matter of minutes. Even at a moderate pace Guardians covered distances quickly and outrun horses if necessary. The terrain appeared relatively flat with a gentle incline from the sea ending in a small plateau one mile from the edge of the wood. A road ran along the top of the plateau.

"That's probably the way they'll come," said Lokien.

She surveyed the glen. "Just to the west, between those scattered trees would be a good place to make camp."

"What about at the edge of the wood? If we don't secure that, they could cut off our escape."

"Skule wants an escape route?" she asked sarcastically.

He grinned. "My mistake. Return and tell him there's no sign of the enemy."

"You trust me to go alone?"

"What are you going to do, tell them we're here? They'll know soon enough."

She wasn't even out of breath when she met Skule and the others a mile from shore. "No sign of them. Lokien is securing the area."

"He trusted you to come back by yourself? For all we know you killed him," said Breck.

"Oh, that would be real smart. Then again, your quick tongue gives your brain little time to think."

Skule stopped Breck from reaching for his dagger. "Save it for the enemy." He told Auriel, "Help Lokien keep it secure."

By the time Skule and the formation reached the glen, Auriel and Lokien completed marking off an area for camp and started several cooking and warming fires for the mortals. Nights in Allon came quickly in winter and the temperature would begin to drop after sunset.

Thirty tents were erected, enough to house all the Sigvard, Valkerish, and Tavar, while the varlets slept outside. Virgil took Chad to one of the smaller tents used by the Guardians.

Once inside, Chad seized the Guardian and whispered, "When?"

"When what?"

"Night is a good time, and the Sigvard are asleep."

Virgil frowned in annoyance. "You don't know what you ask."

His hold stopped Virgil's departure. "I do and so do you."

Virgil leaned down, his expression matching the cynicism in his voice. "You want me to spirit you from here, to where? You betrayed your prince, while I've been assumed dead for centuries. You think Nigel and Kell will simply take us back without hesitation or question?"

The argument stymied Chad. "I hadn't thought about that."

Virgil pursed his lips and shook his head. "No, you believe saying you're sorry will soothe everything, but sometimes it isn't enough."

"I hope to prevent bloodshed by warning them."

"You've survived so far. The rest is in Jor'el's hands."

An earnest hope rose in Chad's eyes when Virgil mentioned *Jor'el* by name. The Guardian ended the conversation by placing a hand on Chad's shoulder to make him sit. "I'll fetch you some food."

Emerging from the tent, Virgil came face-to-face with Breck.

"Touching way to comfort the mortal by invoking *his* name."

"Do you always eavesdrop?" He pushed past Breck to make his way to the cooking fire only Breck pursued him.

"I'm doing more than eavesdropping where you're concerned."

"I'm flattered. Food," he ordered a varlet.

Breck stopped Virgil from accepting the plate of stew. "You shouldn't be flattered. You should be wary."

"There is nothing more you can do to torment me."

"I could destroy you."

"*That* would be a relief." Virgil snatched the plate from the varlet and headed back to the tent.

In the stillness of the late night, Auriel stood at the edge of camp surveying the meadow. This was not the way she expected to return. It felt surreal standing on native soil as an enemy and not a defender. She sensed the end was near. Death in battle did not frighten a warrior. In fact, it was the preferred way to die. Someone appeared beside her. Skule. She ignored him, until he spoke.

"What do you see? The enemy?"

"No sign of them."

"I didn't mean physical."

She chewed on her bottom lip, staring out into the darkness.

"You have not had the time to become detached, to brood, to hate." He watched her profile. "Those emotions bring us here. Hatred for Allon and what it stands for. We once swore to defend, same as you."

She still didn't reply.

He folded his arms across his chest. "The question you're asking is *Why did I do it?*' We all asked that question at first and we all knew the answer. For Farren—love for a mortal and jealousy of Avatar. Willow couldn't handle competition. Being alone terrifies Keara so she followed. Breck, Lokien and myself, had no choice, Dagar saw to that."

"Others withstood Dagar and survived."

"Perhaps. But from the core of our being our choices come, not from what others do. Long ago I accepted the fact Dagar didn't make me do anything I didn't want to. So blaming him and beating myself up over the decision served no purpose. That is a fact you have to accept."

She looked sideways at his one good eye. What he said made sense and the reason she kept arguing with herself.

"Why are you here when at any point you can vanish?" He snapped his fingers. "Dimension travel, but you don't."

"I have my reasons."

"The boy? Take him with you."

Her eyes narrowed on him in suspicion. "The ball and chain is stygian metal."

He made a scoffing laugh. "Are you always so gullible?"

Angered, she fully faced him. "You lied! Just like you did about making us Shadow Warriors. You don't have such power."

His laughter increased. "Very good, but a little late. As I said, Dagar didn't make me do anything I didn't want to do. However, from him, I learned the art of manipulation. Which is why I keep the eye patch, and not because I can't see or be healed, rather part of intimidation. Find another's weakness and vulnerability and exploit it. Something you should understand as warrior. Mortals are easy. Farren, Willow and Keara accepted my *gift* of becoming Shadow Warriors because we succeeded in convincing them they couldn't defeat us."

She turned aside, snarling in annoyance at being duped a second time. The first happened when Farren lied about killing Avatar, now Skule.

He leaned closer, his hand on her shoulder made her turn to face him. His one good eye coolly sparkled. "Take my advice. Acknowledge what brought you here and stop hiding behind the excuse others caused you to be discontent. It's called *pride*. You want to prove to all what a mighty warrior you are. Forfeiting your station and the life of a mortal isn't going to stop you."

She stared at him, the impact of his words stunning.

With a thin smile of pleasure, he left.

Virgil escorted Chad back to the tent from the latrine area and noticed the conversation. He couldn't hear the words yet felt uneasiness in his spirit. News of Auriel's betrayal plagued him while her attitude confused him. She aided Skule and the others yet assigned him to guard Chad. A test of his agreement to help? Why give him the boy and not the girl? Surely she knew he would learn Chad's identity. Or did she do it to vex his troubled spirit? She couldn't have grown that cruel.

The pause was brief when Chad said, "Hard to believe she did this."

Virgil nudged Chad inside the tent.

"Do you know Auriel well?"

"Well enough."

"Enough to convince her to help us?"

"Us? Haven't I gotten through to you yet, boy?"

"Not to escape, to send a warning," Chad spoke with care. "Skule may plan to use her against the king. Assassin perhaps. Tyrone is supposed to be your king, king of Guardians and mortals."

Virgil studied the youth. "You don't give up, do you?"

"No, but obviously you have." Chad sat, snarling in frustration.

Virgil frowned at the accusation and snapped, "Fine. I'll speak to her, but I promise nothing for either of us."

Outside, Auriel now stood alone. A quick look around told him neither Skule nor Breck were close by. In purposeful steps he approached her. "Being here does make one wonder."

She scowled at seeing him. "Why aren't you watching Chad?"

"He can't go anywhere. Besides, it's time we talked. We may not get another opportunity."

"There's nothing to talk about."

"Oh, no? You betray Jedrek and Jor'el so flippantly?"

Incited, she accosted him. "What I've done isn't up for debate, discussion or judgment by you or anyone else. If anything, look to yourself and consider why *you* are here. What is your purpose? If you don't know your own heart, don't confront me about mine!"

Thunderstruck, he couldn't reply and watched her storm back to camp. *She's right. How can I act if I don't know who or what I am?*

"Virgil! Going somewhere?"

The voice close to his ear startled him. Breck. Virgil went rigid, his crystal blue eyes flaring in regard of Breck, who outweighed him by thirty pounds, but in height, he had a slight advantage. "What if I was?"

Breck seemed to recoil a step. "You'd risk the boy's life?"

It may be only a hint of discomfort, but Breck could be made to back down, so Virgil pressed on, forcing more intensity into his icy gaze. "You think I'm foolish? What about the way all of you are provoking Jor'el?"

A throaty uncomfortable growl escaped Breck's tightly pressed lips.

"You can't even say his name. Jor'el."

Breck took an awkward step away and made a curt wave. "Get back to camp or the boy dies!"

Virgil made his point, thus satisfied, he returned to the tent. He steadily regarded Chad. "You're persistence has paid off."

Excited, Chad sprung to his feet. "You convinced her?"

"No. She convinced me."

Chad's brow clouded with uncertainty. "What?"

"Never mind. Just get some rest."

"But I thought—"

Virgil's direct gaze made Chad stop in mid-sentence. "Do as I say."

Chad did as instructed and lay down.

Chapter 22

WREN AND NIXIE CRAWLED ON THEIR BELLIES from the edge of the plateau to the trees. They used caution since Guardians sensed each other within a mile. No need to tip their location to the enemy. Wren stopped and grabbed Nixie's arm in warning. She pointed to the Sigvard sentries. They drifted back and changed direction until clear of the sentries then ran back to their base camp.

The Allonian force waited three miles from the Soren encampment. Wren and Nixie headed straight to the main tent. Mahon and Barnum stood guard and acknowledged their approach. Inside, Tyrone, Tristine, Mirit, Nigel, Allard, Wess, Kell, Avatar and Vidar were receiving reports from Luann, Callie and Caryn. Tristine shed the more cumbersome portions of the armor for the night. The rest remained fully dressed and armed.

"Good, Wren. Did you get a count of troops?" asked Tristine.

"By the number of tents and their capacity, about one thousand."

"I thought more. Five thousand, perhaps," said Wess.

"General, we saw one camp and searched a radius from the landing area to the glen."

"Mathias did it," said Tristine in mild wonder.

"Did you doubt my father?"

"No, his courage and expertise were never in doubt. I just wondered how many would survive and we'd have to face. Jor'el allowed him and Gulliver to lessen the odds considerably."

"Odds are not an issue for Jor'el and you must trust him," said Kell.

"You both misunderstand. I marvel, not doubt or mistrust. Now the enemy is at hand."

"How far out were the sentries from their camp?" asked Wess.

"A mile," replied Nixie.

"Three miles between us. How close do you think we can move at night without being seen?" asked Tristine.

"No more than a mile or risk exposing Guardian presence," said Kell.

"Could we neutralize the sentries?" asked Mirit.

"Possibly. Only it would have to be done with stealth, no Guardian powers can be used or the enemy will be alerted."

"So be it. How many will you need?" Tristine asked Wren.

"The six of us can take care of the sentries, four more as lookouts, with four to secure the road for your arrival. Fourteen."

"Select the ones you need and be quick—"

"Majesty," began Kell. "I suggest we take care of this, leaving you and the females free to move in full force."

"Why? Jor'el appointed us to do this."

"His plan is for you to *face* the enemy."

She frowned in disapproval. "A rather fine distinction to make, Captain. Do you consider females less capable of stealth?"

"No. The whole scheme is to show Allon united, male and female, mortals and Guardians. Mathias and Gulliver took the first step. I believe the final step is your confrontation of enemy. As such, I see no reason why we cannot be employed between the first and last step and still maintain Jor'el's will."

She regarded him from under thoughtful brows. "An interesting analysis, Captain."

"Kell's battle intuition is uncanny," said Tyrone.

"You would use male Guardians in this?"

"Ay. Especially Vidar."

"Wren, see the team make-up is evenly split. Send back word when all is secure."

"Ay, Majesty," said Wren with a smile. She and the females left.

"Mirit, Nigel, prepare the rest to move out quickly and quietly."

"Ay, Majesty," said Mirit, smiling and tugging on Nigel's sleeve.

Tristine looked at Kell, attempting to hide a pleased smile. "Will that satisfy, Captain?

"Ay, Majesty."

In mixed pairs of male and female, Wren gave out the assignments. She and Mahon would take out the eastern sentries while Nixie and Vidar handled the west sentries. Luann and Avatar were assigned to watch the enemy camp. Callie and Barnum watched the forest path from the sea. Lori and Alrick, along with Meredith and Zadok, secured the road.

The eastern Sigvard sentries were not far from the woods. They never heard Wren and Mahon sneak up from behind, seize them, and drag them into the wood. A few words in the Ancient rendered the Sigvard unconscious.

"The camp can be seen from here," said Mahon.

"I'll stuff their cloaks and make it appear they didn't move."

"It might work for a little while, but not upon closer inspection."

"So? By then our force should be in position."

"All right, but be quick. I'll secure them." Mahon handed her the cloaks then began tying and gagging the unconscious Sigvards.

After stuffing the cloaks, Wren carefully put the decoys back in the position they were found. "Done."

"Good. Let's get back to the road."

Nixie scowled at the twenty-foot gap between where she and Vidar hid in the tree line and the west sentries.

"What's the matter? The camp is quiet with no sign of activity," he whispered in her ear.

"Not the camp, the gap. We can't use our powers or make noise."

"Who says?"

She balked when he scrambled away on his hands and knees making animal noises that caught the attention of the sentries.

"Who goes there?" demanded a sentry.

Nixie shrunk back in the shadow of the trees.

"Sounds like an animal," said the second sentry.

"Maybe not," said the first at hearing another sound. The sentries moved cautiously toward the trees.

Behind a large tree, Vidar used a branch to scratch on the ground, drawing the prey to them. When the lead sentry drew close enough, Nixie snatched the Sigvard. The second Sigvard was briefly startled, but before she cried out, Vidar seized her from behind and covered her mouth. The Sigvard fainted at the words spoken in her ear.

For a moment, Vidar and Nixie listened and waited to learn if their activity was discovered. From out of the darkness came a faint sound. Nixie drew her dagger when a hand touched her shoulder. Avatar caught her dagger hand inches from his face.

"I shaved once, I don't ever want to do so again."

She snorted in annoyed relief. "What are you two doing here?"

"We heard a scuffle and came to investigate."

"Nixie didn't want to cross in the open so I lured them to us." Vidar removed the Sigvard's cloak. "Hand me her cloak."

"Why?" asked Nixie, as she complied.

"An old hunter's trick." He stuffed the cloaks with leaves and fallen debris.

"A decoy," said Avatar to her curiosity.

"He'll have to go out there in the open to put them up."

"I'm not crossing into the open, you are." Vidar finished stuffing and folding closed the cloaks.

"Me?"

"Ay. Like this." Vidar demonstrated walking carefully behind the stuff cloak. "Then go down and belly crawl back."

"This is supposed to be a joint effort, remember?" teased Avatar.

Nixie snatched the stuffed cloak from Vidar.

"Easy! You'll ruin my handiwork," he playfully chided then, "Wait. Two went out, two must go back." He handed the other cloak to Avatar. "Joint effort."

Avatar motioned to Nixie. "Ladies first." He followed a few steps behind.

"Over there." Nixie used part of the cloak to point.

"Sitting or standing?"

"Sitting."

"Great," grumbled Avatar. Once the cloak was propped up to sit, it took away part of his cover to shield his retreat. Slowly, he got down on the ground and did a backwards belly crawl. He stopped when his left foot hit something. He tapped his foot along the object. Someone grabbed his leg and pulled him back. He reacted in defense only to have Vidar's hand clamp over his mouth. He realized Vidar pulled him back.

"Let's see if Wren and Mahon were successful." He released Avatar and they made their way to the road.

Zadok's sword was in hand at hearing a noise. Mahon and Meredith stood at his shoulders also armed. Wren held her crossbow ready.

"Shooting me would hurt," said Vidar. He, Nixie, Luann and Avatar emerged from the darkness.

"And the waste of a good bolt," she countered.

"Where are Callie and Barnum?" asked Avatar.

"Still watching the forest path. We wanted everything secure before recalling them," replied Meredith

"Wren, you and Mahon fetch them and meet us back at camp," said Vidar. "Road sentries, remain until we bring up our forces."

301

Tristine stood beside Dunston fussing with the helmet strap. Tyrone just finished helping her back into the armor when word came from Mirit that everyone was assembled. "I don't know which is worse, all the straps and buckles on a suit of armor or lacing up a corset."

He laughed and moved her hand away to buckle her helmet. "It would help if you didn't wear gloves."

"You're mocking me."

"No, but then again, I've never worn a corset."

She chuckled. "Nor do you want to. Despite the weight, you can at least breath in armor."

"Majesty. Sire," said Kell indicating the returning Guardians.

"All is secure, Majesty," said Wren

"Then we move. You and Vidar take the lead." She took Dunstan's reins to walk the horse.

All walked their horses to decrease the sound of armor rattling. They wrapped cloth about the horses' hooves to silence their approach, and moved at a deliberately slow pace. Up ahead, Vidar signaled for a halt. Tristine and Tyrone stopped their horses, and the rest did the same.

Wren returned. "The plateau is two hundred years ahead. From there you can see the enemy's camp."

Tristine noticed the intensity on Kell's face as he stared in the direction of the enemy camp. "Captain, is something wrong?"

"I'm just concerned that our presence hasn't been sensed yet."

"You said this is Jor'el's plan, so why are you surprised?" asked Mirit.

Kell regarded at her, the simplicity of her question gratifying, and he kindly smiled. "Not surprised, merely cautious."

"The question is, do we take up position this early or make a show at first light?" said Tristine.

"If we don't want to lose the high ground we take up position now. It's only an hour until dawn," said Wess.

"A camp usually wakes up at dawn, correct?"

"Ay. Sometimes the cooks are up earlier."

She thought for a moment before issuing orders, first to Wren then the others. "Have the road sentries report the first signs of movement, cooks, sentries, anything. That's when we'll move. Time to unwrap the hooves and mount."

Once astride, Nigel asked, "How do you want to proceed? You, Mirit and the females first with us following?"

"We'll definitely go first, but I'm not sure about the males."

"Leave that to me," said Tyrone.

The black of night began to fade into the gray of early dawn. A heavy frost covered the ground and breath hung in the cold, crisp morning air. Magda and Grissel met Ulrika at the cooking area.

"A brisk morning, but nothing like Manheim," said Ulrika.

"Is that hot chocolate?" asked Grissel.

"Ja."

A commotion sounded at the edge of camp. Several varlets ran towards them pointing to shapes moving across the plateau.

"I don't think we're going to have time for chocolate," said Magda.

"Great One!" said Ulrika when Farren appeared.

"I know. Have your archers arm themselves and report to Wilda."

Ulrika nodded to Grissel, who took off running.

Skule arrived. "Strange your sentries didn't alert us."

"They would not be derelict in their duties. Something must have happened," said Ulrika.

Auriel arrived and carried a stuffed cloak. "Something happened!" She tossed it on the ground and stepped on it to mash out the debris.

"Are the sentries dead?"

"No, but I couldn't wake them," she said, her gaze shifting to Farren and Skule. "They are in an *unnatural* sleep."

"Poisoned?" asked Magda in alarm.

"No, they will live."

"Assemble the troops. Come full light we will see the enemy," ordered Skule. When the mortals left, he seized Auriel's arm. "Why couldn't we sense them?"

"I don't know, but with Kell and Tyrone, anything is possible."

Tristine drew Dunston to a halt at the bottom of the slope. Behind her, Wren and Mirit formed the female Guardians into ranks. For a moment, Tristine was left with her thoughts in plain view of the enemy. She felt overwhelmed, not for fear of battle, rather wondering if she could fulfill all expectations. During the time they awaited word from Gulliver, she spent hours in prayer and meditation. Jor'el made it very clear this responsibility fell to her and the Almighty would be with her, but the 'how' question he never answered. Now the moment arrived.

"Jor'el, let me feel your presence and not succumb to fear. Grant me the strength and wisdom to save Allon," she prayed.

Mirit drew her horse to rein. "Everyone will be in position before full sunlight." She followed Tristine's gaze of the enemy's movement across the field. "Jor'el will aid us."

"Ay."

The first rays of the sun peeked over the trees, when an unexpected flash diverted Auriel's attention from her task of assembling the Sigvard. Dimension travel? When her eyes adjusted from the brief blinding she recognized the cause, sunlight reflecting off golden armor. She froze in uncertainty for the individual was not Tyrone.

"The Son of Tristan?" she muttered.

"What did you say, Great One?" asked Magda.

"Continue to assemble," said Auriel before leaving.

"What's going on?" Chad asked when Virgil returned to the tent.

"They must have arrived during the night."

His face brightened. "When?" He snatched the chain about his ankle.

Virgil shrugged in uncertainty. "If the battle goes well for Tyrone you'll be free."

"If Breck doesn't kill me first."

Virgil knelt and used his bare-hands to break the chain holding the ankle fetter to the supporting post.

"How could you do that? I thought they used stygian metal."

"Skule is good at deceiving everyone. I saw Auriel secure you to the tree upon landing." He broke the fetter between Chad's feet in the same barehanded manner. "She couldn't have touched the chain if it was stygian metal." He snatched Chad's arm and began to leave the tent.

Breck appeared in the threshold. "Where are you going?"

"To secure the boy someplace else. A tent is the first place they will look for him."

"You mean to free him."

"No, I—!" The thrusting of a dagger into his stomach stopped the protest.

"Virgil?" gasped Chad in horrified surprise when the Guardian sank to the ground, badly wounded.

Breck pulled Chad from the tent. He tried to resist, but Breck struck him hard, sending him to the ground. He waved the bloody dagger. "Lay hands on me again, boy, and I'll kill you. But for now, Skule wants you." He jerked Chad to his feet and dragged him to where Skule observed the enemy. Farren and Lokien were also present.

"Here's the whelp." He flung Chad at Skule's feet then sheathed his dagger.

"He gave you trouble?"

"No, but I had the pleasure of dealing with Virgil."

"He knifed Virgil in the stomach," chided Chad.

Skule snarled at Breck. "Idiot! We needed his sword and strength."

"Is he gone?" asked Lokien.

Breck shrugged with indifference. "Not when I left."

"If he survives he'll come after us because of your foolishness!"

"Go back and make sure he's finished," ordered Skule.

Breck no sooner left than Auriel arrived. "Skule! It's not Tyrone."

"Then who is it?"

"Rune forged the armor for the Son of Tristan—"

"You said he is dead."

"His daughter, *Tristine,*" she said the name with purpose.

Breck rushed back. "He's gone."

"Gone as in dead or just disappeared?" demanded Skule.

"I saw no signs he up and walked away."

"Who?" asked Auriel.

"Virgil. Breck knifed him to bring the boy to Skule," said Lokien.

Enraged, Auriel moved to assault Breck when Skule seized her. She strained against the hold to get at Breck. "You killed Virgil?"

"He was going to set the boy free."

"What's done is done. We have more important business. Take care of the boy till I need him," he instructed her.

She jerked away from him and helped Chad to his feet. She drew him a few feet behind the others, her features grim and tight.

"Breck killed your old friend and he'll do the same to me if he gets the chance," said Chad, but she didn't respond. "Virgil said I couldn't understand what it means for a Guardian to forfeit their station, maybe he was right, but I know how it feels to live with guilt and regret for a bad decision. All I want to do is find a way to make up for it."

"That won't change what you did."

"No, but my mistake didn't change who I am."

She regarded at him. "And just who are you?"

"I am Chad, an Allonian orphan, and by Jor'el's kindness, squire to Prince Nigel whose honor I will uphold regardless of today's outcome."

She stared at him a moment before speaking, her voice level but with hint of sympathy. "Mortals are fortunate. When a Guardian betrays their master the change is permanent. I am no longer Auriel, Trio Leader of the South Plains, now I am an enemy of Jor'el. There is no turning back."

"I'm sorry."

"Save your pity for someone who deserves it."

Now, in the full light of morning, Tristine looked to the right and received an affirming wave from Wren that her force was in position. On the left, she received the same signal from Caryn. Facing forward she moved Dunston a few yards ahead, Mirit moving with her.

"People of Soren! I am Tristine, Queen of Allon, Daughter of Ellis, the Son of Tristan! You have landed on Allonian soil in defiance of Jor'el. Heed this last warning, withdraw or feel the full measure of the Almighty's judgment!"

A large male Shadow Warrior with an eye patch stepped forward from the group. "I am Skule! Master of the Tavar, Lord of Soren, former servant of the Dark Lord, Dagar!"

"Dagar is no more! My father defeated him."

"What of Tyrone, the supposed Great King? Does he fear Dagar's reputation that he sends a woman to face me?"

"You should not insult my lord and king if you value your existence."

"Really? I have over a thousand to your one hundred. I not only insult him, I call him coward."

Tristine and Mirit heard the jingle of harness behind them. Neither looked back, knowing it was Tyrone, Nigel, Kell and others taking up position on the plateau. Skule's interest confirmed what they knew.

"What did you say? Or are you frightened into silence in the presence of your king and captain?" challenged Tristine.

Skule whirled about and pushed aside several others before pulling someone forward. "I have a prisoner who might interest you." He forced the boy to his knees.

"Chad," stammered Mirit. She glanced back to seen Nigel lean forward in his saddle, glaring across the field.

Tristine also noticed the reaction, but Skule's voice drew her attention back to him.

"Recognize one of your spies? Pity they failed to prevent our invasion. Then again, he made a bargain without so much as a fuss. Can the same be said of his queen?"

"No, Majesty! I'm not worth it!"

Skule jerked Chad's head back by the hair to silence him.

Her jowls clenched. Despite Nigel's fondness for Chad, and even her own feelings of sympathy, she could not yield, not with the salvation of Allon at stake. She managed to keep emotion from her voice. "You think threatening a boy will make me trade my kingdom for his life?"

"Then you doom him as a sacrifice to me!"

Skule pulled out his dagger. Auriel rushed forward, sword in hand and sent a savage slash to Skule's back. He cried out in pain and anger, turning upon her dagger first.

Auriel shoved Chad back toward camp. "Run!" she commanded. Because of her actions she couldn't dodge Skule's attack. His dagger plunged into the back of her left shoulder. She collapsed to her knees. He leapt upon her but she anticipated him, only the force of his body weight made her lose her sword. They wrestled, and she tried to keep his dagger at bay. He slammed her to the ground, making her cry out in pain, a momentary distraction in which he landed another blow, this time deep into her chest. A flash of grey light, and when it faded Auriel was gone.

"Go! Kill him and the girl," Skule ordered Breck. With a shout and angry, wild gesture, his waved his hand from the Sigvard to the Allonians.

Tristine watched the scene in trepidation and uncertainty at Auriel's demise and Skule's gesture. Then arrows launched from behind the Sigvard warriors. Several female Guardians were struck and vanished.

"Stygian arrows!" she shouted. She detached the shield from the back of Dunston's saddle. "Take the left," she said to Mirit, then rode to the right, shouting. "Form up!"

Mirit started to repeat the order. "Form up—" when her words were cut short by what happened next.

Two arrows struck Dunston, one in the neck, the other in the chest, killing the horse in mid-stride and throwing Tristine to the ground when

Dunston fell. She lay not moving. Mirit kicked her horse and went to help. She leapt from her saddle before the beast stopped, snatched the shield and knelt beside Tristine in time to deflect two more arrows.

"Are you hurt?"

Tristine groaned and slowly pushed herself onto her hands and knees. "I don't think so. Oh, no," she moaned at seeing Dunston dead.

When Tristine fell, Nigel moved his horse and Barnum caught the bridle to stop the advance. Nigel steadied the animal and scowled at the restraint but didn't jerk the horse from Barnum.

Simultaneously, Tyrone reached for his sword but Kell seized him.

"No, Sire! Trust Jor'el." At his resistance, Kell tightened his grip and said, "Tyrone! Listen to me and trust."

Despite the evidence of conflict, Tyrone slammed the sword back in the scabbard.

Wren looked in the direction the arrows came, the forest path leading to the cove. Several female Guardians pursued the retreating Sigvard. She disappeared and reappeared in front of the Guardians at the tree line.

"No! Don't go into the forest. It may be a trap. Protect the queen."

"She's right," said Nixie and commanded the squad to regroup.

Wren heard the twang of an arrow from behind, and whirled about in anticipation. The arrow impaled her under the right collarbone, pinning her to a tree. Searing pain racked her body.

Vidar's crossbow was immediately loaded and aimed. Mahon grabbed it to prevent him from firing.

"You can't help her," said Mahon, his voice filled with emotion.

Vidar ripped the crossbow from Mahon to take aim again. Avatar caught him from behind, pinning his arms, which allowed Mahon to take the crossbow from Vidar.

"No! We'll help her when we can," said Avatar.

"Providing she survives!" Vidar struggled against Avatar's hold.

"Providing any of them survive," chided Mahon.

"We have no choice, and both of you know it! We must stand our ground," said Avatar, but Vidar wasn't easily subdued. "For Jor'el's honor and Allon's survival, Defender of Justice."

Hearing his title, Vidar ceased struggling and nodded. Avatar loosed his hold, but didn't completely release Vidar. Only now his grip was for support, not hindrance.

Although a useless gesture, Chad tried to resist Breck when being dragged him back to the tent. "*Trocaireach Jor'el, cuidich mi!*" he pleaded in the Ancient.

"You want help? Here's help." Breck pulled out his dagger. A sudden blast sent him twenty feet through the air and crashing into a table, breaking it.

Before Chad could comprehend, someone snatched him and he became engulfed in white light. When the light faded, he became dizzy and fell to his knees. Hands held him steady for the moment it took for his head to clear. Finally able to see straight, he realized he was in the trees on the far side of the Sigvard camp. The hands fell away and he heard a deep, painful groan. Virgil collapsed against a tree ashen and in great pain, the entire front of his tunic soaked in blood.

"I thought you were dead."

"Almost," he spoke in hoarse whisper.

With great compassion, Chad regarded Virgil. "What can I do?"

He sluggishly shook his head. "Nothing. I'm beyond help."

Chad's eyes welled with tears. "I'm sorry for what I said."

"No apology. I should have acted sooner. Now, you're free to go."

"No. I'll stay with you until … I'll stay."

Mirit helped Tristine to stand. "Are you well enough to continue?"

"Just sore." She stepped from behind the shield. "Skule! Your rebellion only serves to bring Jor'el's judgment upon Soren!" She drew the Sword of Allon from the scabbard. "For Jor'el's honor and justice, His will be done!" She raised the sword over her head, the blade glowing.

A distant rumble of thunder began when she started to speak and grew deafening by the time she finished.

"Down!" Virgil grabbed Chad to shield him as the glen became consumed by blinding light and an overwhelming sense of power.

For several moments, the light engulfed the field. From across the glen, cries of pain, fear and horror emanated, but nothing could be seen though the brilliant whiteness. Soon the cries ceased and the light faded.

Tristine remained standing, the Sword of Allon raised but her eyes closed. Mirit's buried her face in her hands. Slowly, they opened their eyes and blinked to regain focus.

Tristine lowered the sword and stared in horror. The entire Soren army lay on the ground. Hundred of bodies stretched from one end of the field to the other. A hand on her shoulder startled her and she jumped. Tyrone took the sword from her and she sagged against him with a whimper.

Also stunned speechless, Mirit surveyed the field of bodies. She didn't move or reply when Nigel took her by the shoulders, and spoke his concern for her.

"It is a fearful thing to behold Jor'el's wrath," said Kell with sobriety.

Mirit gasped. "One moves! Magda." She bolted from Nigel to where Magda rose to a sitting position. He followed.

"No!" cried Magda at seeing those around her dead. She jerked back in fear when Mirit and Nigel arrived. "What happened?"

"Jor'el's curse upon the Sorens."

Magda shook her head in confusion. "I am Soren and I'm not dead."

Mirit shrugged in uncertainty. "All I know is those exiled and cursed by Jor'el left Allon and founded Soren almost a thousand years ago."

"Allon? My ancestors came from Rowan and Tunlund."

"You have no Allonian ancestors?" asked Nigel.

"No."

"Could that be the reason some survived?" asked Mirit.

Rather than answer, he looked around to spot his quarry. "Kell!"

The captain was prompt in responding. "Highness?"

"Magda is not of Allonian decent, could Jor'el have spared those not connected to Allon?"

"Possible. When the time comes I will inquire. Right now I must find Skule." Kell left to continue his search.

Vidar and Avatar ran to Wren. She hung on the arrow semi-conscious and pale. Avatar reached for the arrow, but Vidar snatched his hand away.

"What are doing? Pulling it out will do great damage, maybe kill her."

"I'm going to break it."

"It's a stygian arrow. You can't break it!"

"Watch me." He carefully placed his left hand just above her wound, his right hand positioned to grip the arrow. "This is going to hurt."

Her eyes were dulled by pain but she nodded.

"Hold her still." When Vidar had a firm, supportive hold of Wren, Avatar said, "Now!" and gripped the arrow.

Searing pain shot through Wren and she cried out. Vidar tightened his grip to steady her. Avatar gritted his teeth, the strain of the effort showed in his face and the veins in his neck. Vidar became fearful at Avatar's distress then his eyes grew wide in surprise as the arrow bent.

"*Le Jor'el's orduigheah bris!*" growled Avatar. The arrow snapped between his hands. He immediately let the piece fall, collapsing to his knees in pain, his hands and arms hanging useless.

Wren fainted when the arrow broke and slid off the shaft that remained in the tree and into Vidar's arms.

"Avatar?" asked Vidar.

"Take her to Eldric. I'll be all right," his voice weak and sluggish.

"Are you sure?"

"Ay. Go quickly before it's too late." Vidar disappeared with Wren, and Avatar clumsily sat against the tree, exhausted and in pain.

Mahon and Barnum rushed over. "Avatar? Are you hurt?" asked Mahon.

He wearily looked up to the shaft in the tree. "I broke it to free Wren."

Barnum noticed the broken end of the arrow on the ground beside Avatar. "By the heavenlies," he said in awe and indicated it to Mahon.

"We better get him to Eldric." Mahon got on one side of Avatar to lift him while Barnum got on the other.

Virgil saw the Allonians converging on the Soren's camp. "Are you all right?"

"Ay. What happened?" asked Chad stunned and looking at the field.

"Jor'el's judgment."

Chad turned back to ask a question. "Virgil!" he exclaimed seizing the Guardian. "You're healed."

In stupefied wonder, Virgil regarded his current condition. Not only was the wound healed but the Soren tunic replaced by a Guardian warrior's uniform complete with sword and dagger.

"You didn't forfeit your station."

Virgil flashed a smile of relief mixed with curiosity. "It's been so long. I forgot what it feels like. I guess we both escaped judgment this day."

"Judgment," murmured Chad before growing fearful. "Bergeta!"

"I know where she is." He led Chad to a tent at the center of camp.

Chad pulled to an unsteady halt. Bergeta lay motionless on the cot, her head at an awkward angle with bruising on the skin indicating violence. He tentatively reached to feel for life. None. He collapsed to his knees and wept.

Virgil tried to offer comfort but his effort interrupted by the arrival of someone. He whirled about, sword ready in defense, only ... "Kell!" He dropped to his knees; head bowed and placed his sword at Kell's feet.

"Virgil?" asked Kell, very surprised.

"Ay, Captain." He dared not look up.

"He saved my life," said Chad, wiping his eyes.

Kell glanced from the prostrated Virgil to Chad and saw Bergeta. "Is she the girl?"

Chad nodded.

Kell sympathetically regarded them. "Come. You both have much to tell." When Virgil didn't move, he reached down to tug on his shoulder. "There is nothing to fear, Virgil of the Verglas."

Hearing his former title made Virgil look up. The truth reflected in the captain's golden eyes and kind smile.

One hundred Sorens survived, all with no Allonian ancestors. What remained of Skule and the other Guardians were scorched patches of earth. Kell told Tristine he was certain of their destruction. She ordered the mortal prisoners gathered into three large tents and placed under guard. After that, she and Mirit retired. The morning had been difficult, emotionally and physically exhausting. Nixie and Luann attended them, bringing food and drink then standing guard outside. The rest of the securing, she left to Tyrone, Wess and Nigel.

"I understand how you feel," began Mirit. "I knew some of the Sigvard."

"Then I should be comforting you, not the other way around."

"Doesn't minimize your responsibility. You knew Chad and Auriel."

Tristine nodded, fighting back some emotion. "I hope for Nigel's sake Chad—" She stopped when Tyrone, Allard, Wess and Nigel entered. She stood in anticipation, looking at Nigel. "Well?"

"Nothing. We couldn't find him among the Sorens. I only hope and pray Jor'el's judgment didn't find him."

"If Jor'el had mercy on some Sorens, surely he spared Chad."

"We won't know until we find him."

The tent flap opened and Kell appeared. "All is well, Majesty. Mahon and a dozen warriors secured the land access and Gulliver brought the fleet into the cove and seized the Soren ships."

"Kell, have you see Chad?" asked Mirit.

"Ay. He's safe and with Virgil until the situation can be sorted out."

Nigel smiled in relief. "Who is Virgil?"

"Jedrek's twin, who I assumed died in the Great Battle. Apparently Skule's cohorts captured him in hopes of someday enacting revenge against Jedrek."

"He wasn't destroyed like the others?" asked Tristine.

"His help was coerced by threats against Chad and the girl Bergeta. He became seriously wounded trying to protect Chad, yet managed to rescue him and shield him when Jor'el appeared. The others were destroyed, but Virgil restored to warrior status."

"Jor'el showed great mercy along with judgment," said Tyrone.

"For Virgil and Chad, but not the girl."

"Bergeta is dead?" asked Mirit.

Kell made a slow, somber nod.

Vidar arrived with the première Guardian physician.

"Eldric, what news?" asked Tristine

"Ten lost, fifteen seriously wounded, and five with moderate wounds. Majesty, Wren is among those most seriously wounded."

"Wren? Will she survive?" asked Kell.

"I believe so. Some of the others, I not certain about."

"Do what you can and keep us informed."

"Ay, Captain. Majesty." Eldric bowed and left.

"Poor Wren," sighed Tristine.

"It could have been worse if not for Avatar," began Vidar in awe. "She was impaled on a tree by a stygian arrow with only half of it visible. He broke it using his bare hands."

"He what?" asked Kell, shocked.

"Ay! I've never seen a Guardian break a stygian arrow, have you?"

"No."

"Is he all right? Surely it caused him pain," asked Nigel.

"Great pain. Both arms are numb and he collapsed. He's being treated for stygian sickness, but will survive."

"I wonder why Eldric failed to mention him?" chided Nigel.

Vidar shrugged, his expression wary.

"Probably fearing your reaction. Just like scolding Vidar for a report," said Mirit.

He frowned, not accepting her rebuff. "First I want to see Chad then Avatar. Captain."

Kell pushed aside the flap for Nigel and Mirit to leave.

"Do you think we should go also?" Tristine asked Tyrone.

"No. This is between them."

"Sire," began Allard, "since all is secure here, perhaps I should go to the Temple and inform the Council of victory."

"Ay. Vidar, take Lord Allard."

Vidar stood beside Allard, and in a flash of light, they disappeared.

Chad paced the tent, a whirlwind of emotions propelling him. Pain, regret, sorrow, remorse, grief, it all hurt. Feelings of guilt for betraying Nigel weighed heavy on his heart, but Bergeta's death proved nearly unbearable. His face wet with tears and he muttered under his breath.

Virgil compassionately watched. "You're not responsible. She was a Soren of Allonian descent and from her own lips chose the Valkerish over Jor'el."

"She wouldn't have been here if not for me! If she remained in Soren, she'd be alive. For that I am responsible. And you can't ask forgiveness from the dead." Chad sobbed, burying his faced in his hands.

"You can of the living."

His head snapped up at hearing Nigel's voice. Mirit and Kell were with him, but all Chad saw was Nigel's sympathy. "Oh, no, master!" he cried, falling to his knees. "I'm not worthy of your forgiveness."

Nigel reached down to pull Chad to his feet, but he resisted, shying away, thus Nigel knelt. "Chad—"

"No! Bergeta is dead, you and Lady Mirit imprisoned, Auriel gone, all because of me."

He took Chad's face in his hands to look at him. "You take too much on yourself, just like I did when I thought my family would be better off without me. I was wrong then, and so are you now."

"I'm sorry!" Chad wept.

Nigel held him, fighting back his own tears. "I know. And I forgive you." Chad wept louder. "*Shh,*" he soothed. "It'll be all right. I know it doesn't feel like it now, but you'll get through this. You know my mother died unaware I was alive, and I couldn't ask her forgiveness, but I learned to forgive myself, as you will in time."

Kell placed a comforting arm about Mirit's shoulder at hearing her muffled weeping.

For a few moments, Nigel let Chad spend his emotions. "Better?"

Chad shrugged, wiping his eyes and nose on his sleeve.

Nigel guided Chad to his feet. "Come. We need to check on Avatar."

"Is something wrong with him too?" asked Chad with dread.

"He broke a stygian arrow to free Wren."

"Impossible!" said Virgil in surprise.

"So I thought," snickered Kell.

"Don't worry," began Mirit, a growing smile at Chad. "His arms are numb so he can't do anything."

"You mean like throttle me?"

"Or give you a big bear hug." She hugged Chad's neck.

He snorted a half-laugh at her embrace. "Doesn't sound like Avatar."

Avatar sat by Wren's cot, his arms resting on his lap. She lay unconscious with a blanket pulled up to her neck. Her shoulders were bare, except for part of a large bandage. Eldric tried get Avatar to drink but the warrior balked in surprise when Nigel, Mirit and Chad arrived. He jerked his head away from the cup.

"Chad," he said, beginning to rise.

"Stay." Eldric pushed Avatar back into the chair.

His arms feel limp into his lap. "This is ridiculous! I can't even raise my arms to take a drink," he complained.

"Quit whining and finish drinking," ordered Eldric, placing the cup to Avatar's lips. He tipped the cup too far and Avatar choked and turned his head from the cup, coughing to recover.

Mirit laughed. "Can't drink either."

Eldric frowned at the remains in the cup. "Good enough I suppose."

"It'll have to be," said Avatar in a strained voice of recovery.

Nigel suppressed a laugh. "How long before he can use his arms?"

"He should regain full use by this evening."

"What about Wren?"

"She should be fine in a week."

Nigel motioned for Eldric to leave and the physician complied.

"It's good to see you, Chad. I take it since you're with Nigel and Mirit, you've recovered your senses," said Avatar.

"Ay," came the sheepish answered, avoiding direct eye contact.

"He thinks you'll throttle him, once you're able," said Mirit.

The Guardian cocked a grin. "Tempting thought. I often considered it when Nigel was younger. Don't worry, Chad, if I didn't do it him, I certainly wouldn't do it to you." His smile widened, tossing a quick wink to Mirit. "If I could, I'd give you a big bear hug."

Mirit laughed and admitted to Chad, "We talked about how we'd each greet you if you ever returned to us. I was the one who said bear hug, Avatar mentioned throttling."

Chad grew uncomfortable. "I don't know whether to feel better or worse. All of you forgive me without question and I don't deserve it."

"When we sin, none of us deserve forgiveness, but that's where mercy comes in. My family extended it me, how can I not do the same for you?" said Nigel.

"Perhaps I can accept your forgiveness, master, but not your trust. I don't trust myself anymore," said Chad, lowering his head. "Everything I thought I believed has been turned upside down and I'm not sure of anything anymore."

"Give yourself time. Admitting your mistake, accepting forgiveness, and dealing with the consequences are the first steps to recovery."

"What do I do until then?"

"You can take care of Avatar and Wren. He's incapacitated until this evening, and Wren for a week."

"I can do that," Chad eagerly agreed.

Nigel grinned. "We'll come back this evening."

Chad bowed to Nigel and Mirit when they left.

"Poor Chad. Bergeta's death has shaken him," said Mirit.

"Ay. Until he recovers I'll be without my squire."

She mischievously smiled and took hold of his arm. "That could be a good thing, since you'll have a wife who can take care of you."

He smiled in agreement.

319

Chapter 23

AFTER SEVERAL DAYS OF EXTENSIVE INTERVIEWS with the surviving Sorens, Tyrone decided to let them return home in one of the two remaining ships. He ordered the other scuttled in the cove to prevent further landings. Affecting his decision was an urgent dispatch from Angus that Gilda and Ivor had mysteriously died. Angus launched an investigation to uncover the reason. Tyrone sent Barnum to Waldron to explain Jor'el's judgment and suspend the investigation.

Being the highest-ranking Sigvard to survive, Magda agreed to bring a message to High Priest Iryn warning of the consequences of any further hostility against Allon. No missionaries or goodwill ambassadors would be sent to Soren since Jor'el cursed them. Magda did request asylum should Iryn fail to accept the warning and seek revenge upon her. However, for security reasons, Tyrone refused to allow her back on Allonian soil and said, if worse happened, go Tunlund, the home of her ancestors, and by way of a Jor'ellian Fortress she would be provided a new identity and a new home.

Once the Sorens were dealt with, Tyrone sent out a royal proclamation declaring a week of celebration at the Temple in honor of Jor'el's victory. There would be offerings of thanks and praise to Jor'el, feasting, games, with the final day capped by the marriage of Prince Nigel to Lady Mirit.

Among the patches of snow on the plain surrounding the Temple, tents and booths were erected. Each morning and at sunset, a worship service was held in the Temple with activities of celebration taking place throughout the day and evening, sometimes late into the night.

To experience the festival, Titus explored everything, not missing a single sight, smell or taste. Often this meant slipping away from Egan, but what could happen? Among all the nobles, commoners and Guardians, he had nothing to fear. Besides, there was too much to do, not like at Waldron where he eluded Egan simply out of boredom or frustration. Egan wasn't Jedrek. Oh, he was a strong, diligent Guardian warrior, but not the same. Since Kell assigned Egan only a word from Jor'el would change the situation, so Titus hoped to frustrate Egan to the point of asking Kell to be reassigned. So far he succeeded every day of the festival and his parents suspected nothing, or at least they hadn't said anything. With Nigel's wedding that evening, even if he was finally caught, he doubted he would miss such a happy and celebrated event.

Walking toward the east end of the Temple grounds Titus spied a group of Guardians engaged in a lively discussion. Mahon laughed and spoke to a fair-haired male warrior sitting on a crate with his back to Titus. When the warrior turned to Mahon to reply, Titus stopped in his tracks and in sudden excitement, he ran toward the Guardian.

"Jedrek!" he shouted, practically tackling the fair-haired warrior with his enthusiastic hug. "I knew you'd come back."

Virgil appeared uncertain of what to do about the mortal boy hanging on his neck.

"Highness," began Mahon, gently. "He is not Jedrek."

"Of course he is!" insisted Titus, turning from Mahon to Virgil, but found he stared into a pair of unfamiliar crystal clear blue eyes.

Virgil spoke calm and kind. "Mahon's right, Highness, I'm not Jedrek. My name is Virgil."

"But you look like him."

"He was my twin."

Titus studied Virgil. His voice sounded different, but that wasn't what began to bother him. The icy blue eyes were cool and distant, and held a hint of pain. Suddenly frightened, Titus bolted away.

"Highness!" called Mahon.

"I'll find him." Virgil hastened after Titus.

Egan tried his best to cope with the situation but once again his search proved fruitless. He spoke to Armus about not giving Titus pointers from Tristine's past and the lieutenant heeded his concern only it didn't curb Titus' escapades.

Egan sighed in resignation at seeing Tyrone and Armus walking in his direction. The past week he managed to keep Titus' antics from the king, but being discovered without his charge, he couldn't and wouldn't lie. "Sire," he said, trying to mask his frustration.

"Egan. Titus slipped away from you again this week, eh?"

"You know?"

Tyrone smiled, indulgent. "With so many Guardian eyes around here, did you think I wouldn't learn?"

"No, Sire." He sent an irate side-glance to Armus. "I hoped to see the end of his employing the techniques Armus told him."

"Old techniques," said Armus, not offended, in fact, trying not to sound very amused.

"What does it matter when he succeeds?"

Tyrone chuckled. "Do you sense any harm will come to him?"

"No, I don't sense danger." Egan pursed his lips in consideration of what to say next. "I would never shirk my duty, Sire, however, I'm beginning to think it best I be replaced by a Guardian more to His Highness' liking."

Tyrone grew thoughtful. "We'll discuss it after the wed—"

"Egan!" shouted Titus from somewhere nearby.

The warrior turned in the direction of the distress call, and no sooner moved when Titus raced around the corner of a booth and latched onto him, small arms trying to wrap around his hips.

"Highness," called Virgil, rounding the same corner.

Titus buried his head into Egan's hip to avoid looking at Virgil. Egan's hand shielded Titus but curious of Virgil.

"Virgil, what happened?" asked Tyrone, concerned by Titus' fear.

"The prince mistook me for Jedrek. When I told him who I was, he became upset and ran off. I followed to find him and reassure him."

Tyrone squatted and touched Titus' shoulder. "Son, why did you run away from Virgil?"

"He told you. I thought he was Jedrek, but he's not! He's different."

"Ay," said Virgil, a bit confused. "Jedrek and I are different. But that's nothing to be frightened of, Highness. I would never harm you."

"He saved Chad's life," said Tyrone.

Titus' anger turned into a pricked and disappointed frown. "I thought Jor'el heard my prayer and Jedrek returned."

The statement stunned Virgil. "You prayed for Jedrek's return?"

"Ay. Only now I know he will never come back." Titus sobbed, again burying his head in Egan's hip.

In sympathy, Tyrone stroked Titus' head. "I'm sorry, son. It's not easy to lose someone you love." He stood and quietly said to Egan, "Take him back to the tent to rest before the wedding."

"Ay, Sire. Come, little prince." Instead of taking Egan's hand, Titus moved to be picked up and Egan did so. He left carrying Titus.

"Sire, I never meant to upset the prince," said Virgil.

"Actually, I think you've helped him."

"How?"

"Because of his love for Jedrek, he didn't accept Egan as his new Overseer. Seeing you and acknowledging Jedrek will not return appears to have changed his attitude. At the first sign of trouble he ran to Egan, and away from the one who *reminded* him of Jedrek."

"I think I understand," said Virgil, but his expression still troubled.

"You're not sure?" asked Armus.

Virgil shook his head. "It's what he said about praying for Jedrek's return. When Jor'el appeared on the battlefield, I was dying. I used every ounce of energy to save Chad, content to die knowing I did not turn away from my duty. My healing and restoration was unexpected and surprising. Now I know why."

"Titus' prayer," said Tyrone.

"Ay. Even though we shared the same spirit, in many respects Jedrek and I were different. He couldn't come back, but I could."

"The second amazing story I've heard about the battle," said Armus.

"Only the second?" quipped Tyrone.

"In respect to Guardians. Avatar breaking the stygian arrow was the first. I can't say I ever heard of a Guardian being restored because of a mortal's prayer."

"Avatar in Tunlund."

Armus shook his head. "Jor'el directed Vidar's actions."

"Perhaps I should avoid the prince until he can accept the fact of my existence," said Virgil.

"That will hard since I asked Kell to assign you to Waldron."

"Sire," said Virgil in surprise.

Tyrone chuckled. "You've earned it. Now join us. We're on our way to visit the nervous groom."

"Nigel nervous?" questioned Armus, smiling.

Tyrone grinned large and mischievous. "If not, he will be when I'm done. Just like he tried to unnerve me before my wedding.

"No, not that one! Fetch another," snapped Nigel at an older servant, who held a gold and brown doublet. He was in one of the royal tents next to the Temple being fitted for his wedding suit. He stood in front a mirror wearing white breeches, white stockings, and a white silk shirt.

"Highness, this is the sixth doublet you refused. There are no more."

"I wish I could have sent Chad to Waldron, he would know the doublet I want."

"I don't think you know what you want," snickered Avatar.

Nigel sent a rebuking glare to the Guardian then frowned. "You're right. I'm sorry, Harold. Let me see at them again."

Harold laid the six doublets on the bed for Nigel to view.

Tyrone arrived with Armus and Virgil. "How goes it?"

Annoyed, Nigel just grunted.

"That good?"

"He can't even pick out a doublet," said Avatar.

Tyrone laughed. "And you teased me before I married Tristine? At least I could dress myself."

Nigel snatched a white brocade doublet embossed with blue and silver. He gave it to Harold to hold so he could put it on. He didn't fasten the doublet close; rather sat in a chair for Harold to put on his highly polished black boots. "Better?" he asked a greatly amused Tyrone.

"Smile. Mirit doesn't need to see a frowning groom. Unless you've changed your mind?"

"I don't know which is more irritating, not having Chad to tend me or enduring your amusement at my expense."

"My amusement is only half of Tristine. Come, brother," said Tyrone, pulling Nigel to his feet and began fastening the doublet. "This is a joyous day. You're marrying the woman you love."

"I know," said Nigel with a nervous laugh.

Tyrone straightened the collar. "There, perfect." He turned Nigel to the mirror. "You faced death and battle so why fear marriage?"

"I'm not afraid."

"Good. Hold onto that thought because it's still two hours until the wedding."

Nigel gaped at Tyrone in the mirror. "What?"

Tyrone laughed. "I came to keep you company until then."

"We came to keep you company," said another.

They saw Angus' reflection in the mirror. Tyrone laughed, Nigel frowned.

***

Every seat in the Temple was filled, leaving standing room only. Guardians lined the perimeter, all in their dress uniforms. Kell and Vidar stood to the left of the altar platform while Avatar and Armus were on the right. Tyrone, Tristine, Necie and Angus sat on the front pew. Some of Mathias' kin sat on the other side. Master Hampton wore his best robes and waited at the altar. To one side, a choir sang Allon's holy anthem. From the back of the Temple came Prince Titus dressed in royal blue and silver. A few steps behind Titus came Nigel.

"He looks so nervous," whispered Angus.

"You and Tyrone looked worse," chuckled Tristine.

"How would you know? You barely remember our vows due to trembling," whispered Tyrone.

Titus wore a pleased and proud expression as he took his place on the bottom step. Nigel cast a side-glance at Tyrone and Tristine as he assumed his place beside Titus. Both smiled, but in supportive manner not teasing.

The choir sang another hymn and Mirit walked down the aisle holding Mathias arm. Nigel nervousness faded into a beaming smile at the sight of her. She wore the same white and blue gown Tristine lent her the night of their return from Tunlund. He held her gaze until she assumed her place beside him then acknowledged Mathias. The baron bowed and took a seat with his kin.

The rest of the ceremony passed in a haze since Nigel could not take his eyes off Mirit, nor did she look away from him. They spoke their vows at the proper time and when announced man and wife in the sight of Jor'el, Nigel followed the instruction to kiss his bride.

Tyrone rose, and all assembled followed his example in standing. He approached the newly wed couple and waved to someone on the side. Dressed in his squire's uniform Chad stepped forward carrying a large blue velvet pillow upon which sat two silver coronets. Nigel smiled but Chad tried not to break character, and fought to keep a straight face.

"It gives me more pleasure than I can express to perform this part of the ceremony," said Tyrone. Nigel bowed his head to receive a coronet from Tyrone. A maid came to remove Mirit's headdress. Mirit bowed her head to receive a coronet from Tyrone. After the crowning, Tyrone stood between Mirit and Nigel, holding each by the arm. "Allon, hail His Highness, Prince Nigel and *Her* highness, Princess Mirit!"

Three cheers rose from the crowded Temple.

Explore the Kingdom of Allon

www.allonbooks.com

Featuring

- Read excerpts of Allon books
- Original Character Art
- Interactive Map of Allon
- News and Events
- Photo and Video Gallery
- Links to:
    - Facebook - The Kingdom of Allon Page
    - Shawn Lamb's All-On Writing blog
    - Contact Shawn Lamb